W9-BZO-974

DARWINIA

ROBERT CHARLES WILSON

TOR®

A TOM DOHERTY ASSOCIATES BOOK
NEW YORK

This is a work of fiction. All the characters and events portrayed in this book are either products of the author's imagination or are used fictitiously.

DARWINIA

Copyright © 1998 by Robert Charles Wilson

All rights reserved, including the right to reproduce this book, or portions thereof, in any form.

Edited by Patrick and Teresa Nielsen Hayden

A Tor Book
Published by Tom Doherty Associates, LLC
175 Fifth Avenue
New York, NY 10010

www.tor.com

Tor® is a registered trademark of Tom Doherty Associates, LLC.

ISBN: 0-812-56662-9
Library of Congress Catalog Card Number: 98-14538

First edition: June 1998
First mass market edition: July 1999

Printed in the United States of America

0 9 8 7 6 5 4 3 2

To PNH and TNH, for patience and good advice;
Shawna, for believing in my work; and
unindicted coconspirators everywhere
(you know who you are).

PROLOGUE

1912: MARCH

Guilford Law turned fourteen the night the world changed.

It was the watershed of historical time, the night that divided all that followed from everything that went before, but before it was any of that, it was only his birthday. A Saturday in March, cold, under a cloudless sky as deep as a winter pond. He spent the afternoon rolling hoops with his older brother, breathing ribbons of steam into the raw air.

His mother served pork and beans for dinner, Guilford's favorite. The casserole had simmered all day in the oven and filled the kitchen with the sweet incense of ginger and molasses. There had been a birthday present: a bound, blank book in which to draw his pictures. And a new sweater, navy blue, adult.

Guilford had been born in 1898; born, almost, with the century. He was the youngest of three. More than his brother, more than his sister, Guilford belonged to what his parents still called "the new century." It wasn't new to him. He had lived in it almost all his life. He knew how electricity worked. He even understood radio. He was a twentieth-century person, privately scornful of the dusty past, the gaslight and mothball past. On the rare occasions when Guilford had money in his pocket he would buy a copy of *Modern Electrics* and read it until the pages worked loose from the spine.

The family lived in a modest Boston town house. His father was a typesetter in the city. His grandfather, who lived in the upstairs room next to the attic stairs, had fought in the Civil War with the 13th Massachusetts. Guilford's mother cooked, cleaned, budgeted, and grew tomatoes and string beans in the tiny back garden. His brother, everyone said, would one day be a doctor or a lawyer. His sister was thin and quiet and read Robert Chambers novels, of which his father disapproved.

It was past Guilford's bedtime when the sky grew very bright, but he had been allowed to stay up as part of the general mood of indulgence, or simply because he was older now. Guilford didn't understand what was happening when his brother called everyone to the window, and when they all rushed out the kitchen door, even his grandfather, to stand gazing at the night sky, he thought at first this excitement had something to do with his birthday. The idea was wrong, he knew, but so concise. His birthday. The sheets of rainbow light above his house. All of the eastern sky was alight. Maybe something was burning, he thought. Something far off at sea.

"It's like the aurora," his mother said, her voice hushed and uncertain.

It was an aurora that shimmered like a curtain in a slow wind and cast subtle shadows over the white-washed fence and the winter-brown garden. The great wall of light, now green as bottle glass, now blue as the evening sea, made no sound. It was as soundless as Halley's Comet had been, two years ago.

His mother must have been thinking of the Comet, too, because she said the same thing she'd said back then: "It seems like the end of the world. . . ."

Why did she say that? Why did she twist her hands together and shield her eyes? Guilford, secretly delighted, didn't think it was the end of the world. His heart beat like a clock, keeping secret time. Maybe it was the beginning of something. Not a world ending but a new world beginning. Like the turn of a century, he thought.

Guilford didn't fear what was new. The sky didn't frighten him. He believed in science, which (according to the magazines) was unveiling all the mysteries of nature, eroding mankind's ancient ignorance with its patient and persistent questions. Guilford thought he knew what science was. It was nothing more than curiosity . . . tempered by humility, disciplined with patience.

Science meant *looking*—a special kind of looking. Looking especially hard at the things you didn't understand. Looking at the stars, say, and not fearing them, not worshiping them, just asking questions, finding the question that would unlock the door to the next question and the question beyond that.

Unafraid, Guilford sat on the crumbling back steps while the others went inside to huddle in the parlor. For a moment he was happily alone, warm enough in his new sweater, the steam of his breath twining up into the breathless radiance of the sky.

Later—in the months, the years, the century of aftermath—countless analogies would be drawn. The

Flood, Armageddon, the extinction of the dinosaurs. But the event itself, the terrible knowledge of it and the diffusion of that knowledge across what remained of the human world, lacked parallel or precedent.

In 1877 the astronomer Giovanni Schiaparelli had mapped the canals of Mars. For decades afterward his maps were duplicated and refined and accepted as fact, until better lenses proved the canals were an illusion, unless Mars itself had changed since then: hardly unthinkable, in light of what happened to the Earth. Perhaps something had twined through the solar system like a thread borne on a breath of air, something ephemeral but unthinkably immense, touching the cold worlds of the outer solar system; moving through rock, ice, frozen mantle, lifeless geologies. Changing what it touched. Moving toward the Earth.

The sky had been full of signs and omens. In 1907, the Tunguska fireball. In 1910, Halley's Comet. Some, like Guilford Law's mother, thought it was the end of the world. Even then.

The sky that March night was brighter over the northeastern reaches of the Atlantic Ocean than it had been during the Comet's visit. For hours, the horizon flared with blue and violet light. The light, witnesses said, was like a wall. It fell from the zenith. It divided the waters.

It was visible from Khartoum (but in the northern sky) and from Tokyo (faintly, to the west).

From Berlin, Paris, London, all the capitals of Europe, the rippling light enclosed the entire span of the sky. Hundreds of thousands of spectators gathered in the streets, sleepless under the cold efflorescence. Reports flooded into New York until fourteen minutes before midnight.

At 11:46 Eastern Time, the transatlantic cable fell suddenly and inexplicably silent.

It was the era of the fabulous ships: the Great White Fleet, the Cunard and White Star liners; the *Teutonic*, the *Mauretania*, monstrosities of empire.

It was also the dawn of the age of the Marconi wireless. The silence of the Atlantic cable might have been explained by any number of simple catastrophes. The silence of the European land stations was far more ominous.

Radio operators flashed messages and queries across the cold, placid North Atlantic. There was no CQD or the new distress signal, SOS, none of the drama of a foundering ship, but certain vessels were mysteriously unresponsive, including White Star's *Olympic* and Hamburg-American's *Kronprinzzessin Cecilie*—flagship vessels on which, moments before, the wealthy of a dozen nations had crowded frost-rimmed rails to see the phenomenon that cast such a gaudy reflection over the winter-dark and glassy surface of the sea.

The spectacular and unexplained celestial lights vanished abruptly before dawn, scything away from the horizon like a burning blade. The sun rose into turbulent skies over most of the Great Circle route. The sea was restless, winds gusty and at times violent as the day wore on. Beyond roughly 15° west of the Prime Meridian and 40° north of the equator, the silence remained absolute and unbroken.

First to cross the boundary of what the New York wire services had already begun to call "the Wall of Mystery" was the aging White Star liner *Oregon*, out of New York and bound for Queenstown and Liverpool.

Her American captain, Truxton Davies, felt the urgency of the situation although he understood it no better than anyone else. He distrusted the Marconi system. The *Oregon*'s own radio rig was a cumbersome sparker, its range barely a hundred miles. Messages could be garbled; rumors of disaster were often exaggerated. But he had been in San Francisco in 1906, had fled along Market Street barely ahead of the flames, and he knew too well what sort of mischief nature could make, given a chance.

He had slept through the events of the night before. Let the passengers lose sleep gawking at the sky; he preferred the homely comfort of his bunk. Roused before dawn by a nervous radio operator, Davies reviewed the Marconi traffic, then ordered his Chief Engineer to stoke the boilers and his Chief Steward to boil coffee for all hands. His concern was tentative, his attitude still skeptical. Both the *Olympic* and the *Kronprinzzessen Cecilie* had been only hours east of the *Oregon*. If there was an authentic CQD he would have the First Officer rig the ship for rescue; until then . . . well, they would keep alert.

Throughout the morning he continued to monitor the wireless. It was all questions and queries, relayed with cheery but nervous greetings ("GMOM"—*good morning, old man!*) from the gnomish fraternity of nautical radiomen. His sense of disquiet increased. Bleary-eyed passengers, aroused by the suddenly more furious pounding of the engines, pressed him for an explanation. At lunch he told a delegation of First Class worriers that he was making up time lost due to "ice conditions" and asked them to refrain from sending cables for the time being, as the Marconi was being repaired. His stewards relayed this misinformation to Second Class and Steerage. In Davies' experience passengers were like children, poutingly self-important but willing to accept a glib explanation if it would blunt their deep and unmentionable dread of the sea.

The gusty winds and high seas calmed by noon. A tepid sunlight pierced the ragged ceiling of cloud.

That afternoon the forward lookout reported what appeared to be wreckage, perhaps a capsized lifeboat, floating to the northeast. Davies slackened the engines and maneuvered closer. He was on the verge of ordering the boats prepared and cargo nets rigged when his Second Officer lowered his looking glass and said, "Sir, I don't think it's wreckage after all."

They came alongside. It was not wreckage.

What troubled Captain Davies was that he couldn't say *what* it was.

It bobbed in the swell, lazy with death, winter sunlight glistening on its long flanks. Some immense, bloated squid or octopus? Some part of some once-living thing, surely; but it resembled nothing Davies had seen in twenty-seven years at sea.

Rafe Buckley, his young First Officer, gazed at the thing as it bumped *Oregon* at the prow and slowly drifted aft, turning widdershins in the cold, still water. "Sir," he said, "what do you make of it?"

"I'm sure I don't know what to make of it, Mr. Buckley." He wished he hadn't seen it in the first place.

"It looks like—well, a sort of worm."

It was segmented, annular, like a worm. But to call it a worm was to imagine a worm large enough to swallow one of the *Oregon*'s stacks. Surely no worm had ever sported the torn, lacy fronds—fins? a sort of gill?—that arose at intervals from the creature's body. And there was its color, viscid pink and oily blue, like a drowned man's thumb. And its head . . . if that vacuous, saw-toothed, eyeless maw could be called a head.

The worm rolled as it fell away aft, exposing a slick white belly that had been scavenged by sharks. Passengers mobbed the promenade deck, but the smell soon drove all but the hardiest of them below.

Buckley stroked his moustache. "What in the name of Heaven will we tell them?"

Tell them it's a sea monster, Davies thought. *Tell them it's a Kraken. It might even be true.* But Buckley wanted a serious answer.

Davies looked a long moment at his worried First Officer. "The less said," he suggested, "the better."

The sea was full of mysteries. That was why Davies hated it.

Oregon was the first vessel to arrive at Cork Harbor, navigating in the cold sunrise without benefit of shore lights or channel markers. Captain Davies anchored well away from Great Island, where the docks and the busy port of Queenstown were—or should have been.

And here was the unacceptable fact. There was no trace of the town. The harbor was unimproved. Where the streets of Queenstown should have been—should have teemed with exporters, cargo cranes, stevedores, emigrant Irishmen—there was only raw forest sweeping down to a rocky shore.

This was both inarguable and impossible, and even the thought of it gave Captain Davies a sensation of queasy vertigo. He wanted to believe the navigator had brought them by mistake to some wild inlet or even the wrong continent, but he could hardly deny the unmistakable outline of the island or the cloud-wracked coast of County Cork.

It was Queenstown and it was Cork Harbor and it was Ireland, except that every trace of human civilization had been obliterated and overgrown.

"But that's not possible," he told Buckley. "Not to belabor the obvious, but ships that left Queenstown only six days ago are at dock in Halifax. If there'd been an earthquake or a tidal wave—if we'd found the city in ruins—but this!"

Davies had spent the night with his First Officer on the bridge. The passengers, waking to the stillness of the engines, began to mob the rails again. They would be full of questions. But there was nothing to be done about it, no explanation or consolation Davies could offer or even imagine, not even a soothing lie. A wet wind had risen from the northeast. Cold would soon drive the curious to cover. Perhaps over dinner Davies could begin to calm them down. Somehow.

"And green," he said, unable to avoid or suppress these thoughts. "Far too green for this time of year. What sort of weed springs up in March and swallows an Irish town?"

Buckley stammered, "It's not *natural*."

The two men looked at each other. The First Mate's verdict was so obvious and so heartfelt that Davies fought an urge to laugh. He managed what he hoped was a reassuring smile. "Perhaps tomorrow we'll send a landing party to scout the shoreline. Until then I think we ought not to speculate . . . since we're not very good at it."

Buckley returned his smile weakly. "There'll be other ships arriving. . . ."

"And then we'll know we're not mad?"

"Well, yes, sir. That's one way of putting it."

"Until then let's be circumspect. Have the wireless operator be careful what he says. The world will know soon enough."

They gazed a few moments into the cold gray of the morning. A steward brought steaming mugs of coffee.

"Sir," Buckley ventured, "we aren't carrying enough coal to take us back to New York."

"Then some other port—"

"If there *is* another European port."

Davies raised his eyebrows. He hadn't considered that. He wondered if some ideas were simply too enormous to be contained by the human skull.

He squared his shoulders. "We're a White Star ship, Mr. Buckley. Even if they have to send colliers from America, we won't be abandoned."

"Yes, sir." Buckley, a young man who had once made the mistake of studying divinity, gave the captain a plaintive look. "Sir . . . is this a miracle?"

"More like a tragedy, I should say. At least for the Irish."

Rafe Buckley believed in miracles. He was the son of a Methodist minister and had been raised on Moses and the burning bush, Lazarus bidden back from the grave, the multiplication of loaves and fishes. Still, he had never expected to *see* a miracle. Miracles, like ghost stories, made him uneasy. He preferred his miracles confined between the boards of the King James Bible, a copy of which he kept (and left shamefully unconsulted) in his cabin.

To be *inside* a miracle, to have it surround him from horizon to horizon, made him feel as if the floor of the world had opened under his feet. He couldn't sleep more than a pinch. He was red-eyed and pale in the

shaving mirror the next morning, and the razor
trembled in his hand. He had to steady himself with a
mixture of black coffee and flask whiskey before he
lowered a launch from the davits, per Captain Davies'
orders, and steered a party of nervous seamen toward
the pebbly beach of what had once been Great Island.
A wind was rising, the water was choppy, and rain
clouds came raggedly from the north. Chill, nasty
weather.

Captain Davies wanted to know whether it might be
practical to bring passengers ashore if the necessity
arose. Buckley had doubted it to begin with; today he
doubted it more than ever. He helped secure the
launch above the tide, then walked a few paces up the
margin of the island, his feet wet, his topcoat, hair, and
moustache rimed with saltwater spray. Five grim
bearded White Line sailors trudged up the gravel behind him, all speechless. This might be the place
where the port of Queenstown had once stood; but
Buckley felt uncomfortably like Columbus or Pizarro,
alone on a new continent, the forest primeval looming
before him with all its immensity and lure and threat.
He called halt well before he reached the trees.

The *sort-of* trees. Buckley called them trees in the privacy of his mind. But it had been obvious even from
the bridge of the *Oregon* that they were like no trees he
had ever imagined, enormous blue or rust-red stalks
from which needles arose in dense, bushy clusters.
Some of the trees curled at the top like folded ferns, or
opened into cup-shapes or bulbous, fungal domes, like
the crowns of Turkish churches. The space between
these growths was as close and dark as a badger hole
and thick with mist. The air smelled like pine, Buckley
thought, but with an odd note, bitter and strange, like
menthol or camphor.

It was not what a forest ought to look like or smell like, and—perhaps worse—it was not what a forest should *sound* like. A forest, he thought, a decent winter forest on a windy day—the Maine forests of his childhood—ought to sound of creaking branches, the whisper of rain on leaves, or some other homely noise. But not here. These trees must be hollow, Buckley thought—the few fallen timbers at the shore had looked empty as straws—because the wind played long, low, melancholy tones on them. And the clustered needles rattled faintly. Like wooden chimes. Like bones.

The sound, more than anything, made him want to turn back. But he had orders. He steeled himself and led his expedition some yards farther up the shingle, to the verge of the alien forest, where he picked his way between yellow reeds growing knee-high from a hard black soil. He felt as if he should plant a flag . . . but whose? Not the Stars and Stripes, probably not even the Union Jack. Perhaps the star-and-circle of the White Star Line. We claim these lands in the name of God and J. Pierpont Morgan.

" 'Ware your feet, sir," the seaman behind him warned.

Buckley jerked his head down in time to see something scuttle away from his left boot. Something pale, many-legged, and nearly as long as a coal shovel. It disappeared into the reeds with a whistling screech, startling Buckley and making his heart thump.

"Jesus God!" he exclaimed. "This is far enough! It would be insane to land passengers here. I'll tell Captain Davies—"

But the seaman was still staring.

Reluctantly, Buckley looked at the ground again.

Here was another of the creatures. Like a centipede, he thought, but fat as an anaconda, and the same sickly yellow as the weeds. That would be camouflage. Common in nature. It was interesting, in a horrible sort of way. He took a half step backward, expecting the thing to bolt.

It did, but not the way he expected. It moved *toward* him, insanely fast, and coiled up his right leg in a single sudden twining motion, like the explosive release of a spring. Buckley felt a prickle of heat and pressure as the creature pierced the cloth of his trousers and then the skin above his knee with the point of its daggerlike muzzle.

It had *bit* him!

He screamed and kicked. He wanted a tool to pry the monster off himself, a stick, a knife, but there was nothing to hand except these brittle, useless weeds.

Then the creature abruptly uncoiled—as if, Buckley thought, it had tasted something unpleasant—and writhed away into the undergrowth.

Buckley regained his composure and turned to face the horrified sailors. The pain in his leg was not great. He took a series of deep, lung-filling breaths. He meant to say something reassuring, to tell the men not to be frightened. But he fainted before he could muster the words.

The seamen dragged him back to the launch and sailed for the *Oregon*. They were careful not to touch his leg, which had already begun to swell.

That afternoon five Second-Class passengers stormed the bridge demanding to be allowed to leave the ship. They were Irishmen and they recognized Cork Harbor even in this altered guise; they had families inland and meant to go searching for survivors.

Captain Davies had taken the landing party's report.

He doubted these men would get more than a few yards inland before fear and superstition, if not the wildlife, turned them back. He stared them down and persuaded them to go belowdecks, but it was a near thing and it worried him. He distributed pistols to his chief officers and asked the wireless operator how soon they might expect to see another ship.

"Not long, sir. There's a Canadian Pacific freighter less than an hour away."

"Very well. You might tell them we're waiting . . . and give them some warning what to expect."

"Yes, sir. But—"

"But what?"

"I don't know how to say it, sir. It's all so strange."

Davies put his hand on the radioman's shoulder. "No one understands it. I'll write a message myself."

Rafe Buckley was running a fever, but by dinner the swelling in his leg had gone down, he was ambulatory, and he insisted on accepting Davies' offer to join him at the captain's table for dinner.

Buckley ate sparingly, sweated profusely, and to Davies' disappointment, spoke little. Davies had wanted to hear about what the ship's officers were already calling "the New World." Buckley had not only set foot on that alien soil, he had been sampled by the wildlife.

But Buckley had not finished his roast beef before he stood uncertainly and made his way back to the infirmary, where, to the Captain's astonishment, he died abruptly at half past midnight. Damage to the liver, the ship's surgeon speculated. Perhaps a new toxin. Difficult to say, prior to the autopsy.

It was like a dream, Davies thought, a strange and

terrible dream. He cabled the ships that had begun to arrive at Queenstown, Liverpool, the French ports, with news of the death and a warning not to go ashore without, at least, hip boots and a sidearm.

White Star dispatched colliers and supply ships from Halifax and New York as the sheer enormity of what had happened began to emerge from the welter of cables and alarms. It was not just Queenstown that had gone missing; there was no Ireland, no England, no France or Germany or Italy . . . nothing but wilderness north from Cairo and east at least as far as the Russian steppes, as if the planet had been sliced apart and some foreign organism grafted into the wound.

Davies wrote a cable to Rafe Buckley's father in Maine. A terrible thing to have to do, he thought, but the mourning would be far from singular. Before long, he thought, the whole world would be mourning.

1912: AUGUST

Later—during the troubled times, when the numbers of the poor and the homeless rose so dramatically, when coal and oil grew so expensive, when there were bread riots in the Common and Guilford's mother and sister left town to stay (who could say for how long?) with an aunt in Minnesota—Guilford often accompanied his father to the print shop.

He couldn't be left at home, and his school had closed during the general strike, and his father couldn't afford a woman to look after him. So Guilford went with his father to work and learned the rudiments of platemaking and lithography, and in the long interludes between paying jobs he re-read his radio magazines and wondered whether any of the grand wireless projects the writers envisioned would ever come to pass—whether America would ever manufacture another DeForrest tube, or whether the great age of invention had ended.

Often he listened as his father talked with the shop's two remaining employees, a French-Canadian engraver named Ouillette and a dour Russian Jew called Kominski. Their talk was often hushed and usually gloomy. They spoke to oné another as if Guilford weren't present in the room.

They talked about the stock-market crash and the coal strike, the Workers' Brigades and the food crisis, the escalating price of nearly everything.

They talked about the New World, the new Europe, the raw wilderness that had displaced so much of the map.

They talked about President Taft and the revolt of Congress. They talked about Lord Kitchener, presiding over the remnant British Empire from Ottawa; they talked about the rival Papacies and the colonial wars ravaging the possessions of Spain and Germany and Portugal.

And they talked, often as not, about religion. Guilford's father was an Episcopalian by birth and a Unitarian by marriage—he held, in other words, no particular dogmatic views. Ouillette, a Catholic, called the conversion of Europe "a patent miracle." Kominski was uneasy with these debates but freely agreed that the New World must be an act of divine intervention: what else *could* it be?

Guilford was careful not to interrupt or comment. He wasn't expected to offer an opinion or even to have one. Privately, he thought all this talk of miracles was misguided. By almost any definition, of course, the conversion of Europe *was* a miracle, unanticipated, unexplained, and apparently well beyond the scope of natural law.

But was it?

This miracle, Guilford thought, had no signature. God had not announced it from the heavens. It had simply happened. It was an event, presaged by strange lights and accompanied by strange weather (tornadoes in Khartoum, he had read) and geological disturbances (damaging earthquakes in Japan, rumors of worse in Manchuria).

For a miracle, Guilford thought, it caused suspiciously many side effects . . . it wasn't as clean and peremptory as a miracle ought to be. But when his father raised some of these same objections Kominski was scornful. "The Flood," he said. "That was not a tidy act. The destruction of Sodom. Lot's wife. A pillar of salt: is that *logical?*"

Maybe not.

Guilford went to the globe his father kept on his office desk. The first tentative newspaper drawings had shown a ring or loop scrawled over the old maps. This loop bisected Iceland, enclosed the southern tip of Spain and a half-moon of northern Africa, crossed the Holy Land, spanned in an uncertain arc across the Russian steppes and through the Arctic Circle. Guilford pressed the palm of his hand over Europe, occluding the antiquated markings. *Terra incognita,* he thought. The Hearst papers, following the national religious revival, sometimes jokingly called the new continent "Darwinia," implying that the miracle had discredited natural history.

But it hadn't. Guilford believed that quite firmly, though he didn't dare say so aloud. Not a miracle, he thought, but a *mystery.* Unexplainable, but maybe not *intrinsically* unexplainable.

All that land mass, those ocean depths, mountains, frigid wastes, all changed in a night . . . Frightening, Guilford thought, and more frightening still to consider the unknown hinterlands he had covered with his hand. It made a person feel fragile.

A mystery. Like any mystery, it waited for a question. Several questions. Questions like keys, fumbled into an obstinate lock.

He closed his eyes and lifted his hand. He imagined a terrain rendered blank, the legends rewritten in an unknown language.

Mysteries beyond counting.

But how do you question a continent?

BOOK ONE

SPRING, SUMMER 1920

*"Oh ye hypocrites, ye can discern the face of the sky: but can ye
not discern the signs of the times?"*
—GOSPEL ACCORDING TO ST. MATTHEW

CHAPTER ONE

The men who crewed the surviving steamships had invented their own legends. Tall tales, all blatantly untrue, and Guilford Law had heard most of them by the time the *Odense* passed the fifteenth meridian.

A drunken deck steward had told him about the place where the two oceans meet: the Old Atlantic of the Americas and the New Atlantic of Darwinia. The division, the steward said, was plain as a squall line and twice as treacherous. One sea was more viscid than the other, like oil, and creatures attempting the passage inevitably died. Consequently the zone was littered with the bodies of animals both familiar and strange: dolphins, sharks, rorqual whales, blue whales; anguilates, sea barrels, blister fish, banner fish. They floated in place, milky eyes agape, flank against flank and nose to tail. They were unnaturally preserved by the icy water, a solemn augury to vessels unwise enough to make the passage through their close and stinking ranks.

Guilford knew perfectly well the story was a myth, a horror story to frighten the gullible. But like any myth, taken at the right time, it was easy to believe. He leaned into the tarnished rail of the *Odense* near sunset, mid-Atlantic. The wind carried whips of foam from a cresting sea, but to the west the clouds had opened and the sun raked long fingers over the water. Somewhere beyond the eastern horizon was the threat and promise of the new world, Europe transformed, the miracle continent the newspapers still called Darwinia. There might not be blister fish crowding the keel of the ship, and the same salt water lapped at every terrestrial shore, but Guilford knew he had crossed a real border, his center of gravity shifting from the familiar to the strange.

He turned away, his hands as chill as the brass of the rail. He was twenty-two years old and had never been to sea before Friday last. Too tall and gaunt to make a good sailor, Guilford disliked maneuvering himself through the shoulder-bruising labyrinths of the *Odense,* which had done yeoman duty for a Danish passenger line in the years before the Miracle. He spent most of his time in the cabin with Caroline and Lily, or, when the cold wasn't too forbidding, here on deck. The fifteenth meridian was the western extremity of the great circle that had been carved into the globe, and beyond this point he hoped he might catch a glimpse of some Darwinian sea life. Not a thousand dead anguilates "tangled like a drowned woman's hair," but maybe a barrelfish surfacing to fill its lung sacs. He was anxious for any token of the new continent, even a fish, though he knew his eagerness was naive and he took pains to conceal it from òther members of the expedition.

The atmosphere belowdecks was steamy and close. Guilford and family had been allotted a tiny cabin midships; Caroline seldom left it. She had been seasick the first day out of Boston Harbor. She was better now, she insisted, but Guilford knew she wasn't happy. Nothing about this trip had made her happy, even though she had practically willed herself aboard.

Still, walking into the room where she waited was like falling in love all over again. Caroline sat with back arched at the edge of the bed, combing her hair with a mother-of-pearl brush, the brush following the curve of her neck in slow, meditative strokes. Her large eyes were half-lidded. She looked like a princess in an opium reverie: aloof, dreamy, perpetually sad. She was, Guilford thought, quite simply beautiful. He felt, not for the first time, the urge to photograph her. He had taken a portrait of her shortly before their wedding, but the result hadn't satisfied him. Dry plates lost the nuance of expression, the luxury of her hair, seven shades of black.

He sat beside her and resisted the urge to touch her bare shoulder above her camisole. Lately she had not much welcomed his touch.

"You smell like the sea," she said.

"Where's Lily?"

"Answering a call of nature."

He moved to kiss her. She looked at him, then offered her cheek. Her cheek was cool.

"We should dress for dinner," she said.

Darkness cocooned the ship. The sparse electric lights narrowed corridors into shadow. Guilford took Caroline and Lily to the dim chamber that passed for a dining room and joined a handful of the expedition's scientists at the table of the ship's surgeon, a corpulent and alcoholic Dane.

The naturalists were discussing taxonomy. The doctor was talking about cheese.

"But if we create a whole new Linnean system—"

"Which is what the situation calls for!"

"—there's the risk of suggesting a connectivity of *descent*, the familiarity of otherwise well-defined species . . ."

"Gjedsar cheese! In those days we had Gjedsar cheese even at the breakfast table. Oranges, ham, sausage, rye bread with red caviar. Every meal a true *frokost*. Not this mean allowance. Ah!" The doctor spotted Guilford. "Our photographer. And his family. Lovely lady! The little miss!"

The diners stood and shuffled to make room. Guilford had made friends among the naturalists, particularly the botanist named Sullivan. Caroline, though she was obviously a welcome presence, had little to say at these meals. But it was Lily who had won over the table. Lily was barely four years old, but her mother had taught her the rudiments of decorum, and the scientists didn't mind her inquisitiveness . . . with the possible exception of Preston Finch, the expedition's senior naturalist, who had no knack with children. But Finch was at the opposite end of the long trestle, monopolizing a Harvard geologist. Lily sat beside her mother and opened her napkin methodically. Her shoulders barely reached the plane of the table.

The doctor beamed—a little drunkenly, Guilford thought. "Young Lilian is looking hungry. Would you like a pork chop, Lily? Yes? Meager but edible. And applesauce?"

Lily nodded, trying not to flinch.

"Good. Good. Lily, we are halfway across the big sea. Halfway to the big land of Europe. Are you happy?"

"Yes," Lily obliged. "But we're only going to England. Just Daddy's going to Europe."

Lily, like most people, had come to distinguish between England and Europe. Though England was just as much changed by the Miracle as Germany or France, it was the English who had effectively enforced their territorial claims, rebuilding London and the coastal ports and maintaining close control of their naval fleet.

Preston Finch began to pay attention. From the foot of the table, he frowned through his wire-brush moustache. "Your daughter makes a false distinction, Mr. Law."

Table talk on the *Odense* hadn't been as vigorous as Guilford anticipated. Part of the problem was Finch himself, author of *Appearance and Revelation*, the ur-text of Noachian naturalism even before the Miracle of 1912. Finch was tall, gray, humorless, and ballooned with his own reputation. His credentials were impeccable; he had spent two years along the Colorado and the Rouge Rivers collecting evidence of global flooding, and had been a major force in the Noachian Revival since the Miracle. The others all had the slightly hangdog manner of reformed sinners, to one degree or another, save for the botanist, Dr. Sullivan, who was older than Finch and felt secure enough to badger him with the occasional quote from Wallace or Darwin. Reformed evolutionists with less tenure had to be more careful. Altogether, the situation made for some tense and cautious talk.

Guilford himself mainly kept quiet. The expedition's photographer wasn't expected to render scientific opinions, and maybe that was for the best.

The ship's surgeon scowled at Finch and made a bid

for Caroline's attention. "Have you arranged lodging in London, Mrs. Law?"

"Lily and I will be with a relative," Caroline said.

"So! An English cousin! Soldier, trapper, or shop-keeper? There are only the three sorts of people in London."

"I'm sure you're right. The family keeps a hardware store."

"You're a brave woman. Life on the frontier . . ."

"It's only for a time, Doctor."

"While the men hunt snarks!" Several of the naturalists looked at him blankly. "Lewis Carroll! An Englishman! Are you all ignorant?"

Silence. Finally Finch spoke up. "European authors aren't held in high regard in America, Doctor."

"Of course. Pardon me. A person forgets. If a person is lucky." The surgeon looked at Caroline defiantly. "London was once the largest city in the world. Did you know that, Mrs. Law? Not the rough thing it is now. All shacks and privies and mud. But I wish I could show you Copenhagen. That was a city! That was a *civilized* city."

Guilford had met people like the surgeon. There was one in every waterfront bar in Boston. Castaway Europeans drinking grim toasts to London or Paris or Prague or Berlin, looking for some club to join, a Loyal Order of this or that, a room where they could hear their language spoken as if it weren't a dead or dying tongue.

Caroline ate quietly, and even Lily was subdued, the whole table subtly aware that they had passed the halfway mark, mysteries ahead looming suddenly larger than the gray certainties of Washington or New

York. Only Finch seemed unaffected, discussing the significance of gunflint chert at a fierce pitch with anyone who cared to listen.

Guilford had first laid eyes on Preston Finch in the offices of Atticus and Pierce, a Boston textbook publisher. Liam Pierce had introduced them. Guilford had been west last year with Walcott, official photographer for the Gallatin River and Deep Creek Canyon surveys. Finch was organizing an expedition to chart the hinterlands of southern Europe, and he had well-heeled backers and support from the Smithsonian Institution. There was an opening for an experienced photographer. Guilford qualified, which was probably why Pierce introduced him to Finch, though it was possible the fact that Pierce happened to be Caroline's uncle had something to do with it.

In fact, Guilford suspected Pierce just wanted him out of town for another spell. The successful publisher and his nephew-in-law didn't always get along, though both cared genuinely for Caroline. Nevertheless, Guilford was grateful for the opportunity to join Finch in the new world. The pay was good, by current standards. The work might make him a modest reputation. And he was fascinated by the continent. He had read not only the reports of the Donnegan expedition (along the skirts of the Pyrenees, Bordeaux to Perpigna, 1918) but (secretly) all the Darwinian tales in *Argosy* and *All-Story Weekly*, especially the ones by Edgar Rice Burroughs.

What Pierce had not counted on was Caroline's stubbornness. She would not be left alone with Lily a second time, even for a season, no matter the money involved or the repeated offers to hire a day maid for her. Nor did Guilford especially want to leave her, but this expedition was the hinge point of his career, maybe the difference between poverty and security.

But she would not be lenient. She threatened (though this made no sense) to leave him. Guilford answered all her objections calmly and patiently, and she yielded not an inch.

In the end she agreed to a compromise whereby Pierce would pay her way to London, where she would stay with family while Guilford continued on to the Continent. Her parents had been visiting London at the time of the Miracle and she claimed she wanted to see the place where they had died.

Of course you weren't supposed to say that people had died in the Miracle: they were "taken" or they "passed over," as if they'd been translated to glory between one breath and the next. And, Guilford thought, who knows? Maybe it really had happened that way. But, in fact, several million people had simply vanished from the face of the earth, along with their farms and cities and flora and fauna, and Caroline could not be forgiving of the Miracle; her view of it was violent and harsh.

It made him feel peculiar to be the only man aboard *Odense* with a woman and child in tow, but no one had made a hostile remark, and Lily had won over a few hearts. So he allowed himself to feel lucky.

After dinner the crowd broke up: the ship's surgeon off to keep company with a flask of Canadian rye, the scientists to play cards over tattered felt tables in the smoking room, Guilford back to his cabin to read Lily a chapter from a good American fairy tale, *The Land of Oz*. The Oz books were everywhere since Brothers Grimm and Andersen fell out of favor, carrying as they did the taint of Old Europe. Lily, bless her, didn't know books had politics. She just loved Dorothy. Guilford had grown rather fond of the Kansas girl himself.

At last Lily put her head back and closed her eyes. Watching her sleep, Guilford felt a pang of disorientation. It was odd, how life mixed things up. How had he come to be aboard a steamship bound for Europe? Maybe he hadn't done the wise thing after all.

But of course there was no going back.

He squared the blanket over Lily's cot, turned off the light and joined Caroline in bed. Caroline lay asleep with her back to him, a pure arc of human warmth. He curled against her and let the grumbling of the engines lull him to sleep.

He woke shortly after sunrise, restless; dressed and slipped out of the cabin without waking his wife or daughter.

The air on deck was raw, the morning sky blue as porcelain. Only a few high scrawls of cloud marked the eastern horizon. Guilford leaned into the wind, thinking of nothing in particular, until a young officer joined him at the rail. The sailor didn't offer name or rank, only a smile, the accidental camaraderie of two men awake in the bitter dawn.

They stared into the sky. After a time the sailor turned his head and said, "We're getting closer. You can smell it on the wind."

Guilford frowned at the prospect of another tall tale. "Smell what?"

The sailor was an American; his accent was slow Mississippi. "Little like cinnamon. Little like wintergreen. Little like something you never smelled before. Like some dusty old spice from a place no white man's ever been. You can smell it better if you close your eyes."

Guilford closed his eyes. He was conscious of the chill of the air as it ran through his nostrils. It would be a small miracle if he could smell anything at all in this wind. And yet . . .

Cloves, he wondered? Cardamom? Incense?

"What is it?"

"The new world, friend. Every tree, every river, every mountain, every valley. The whole continent, crossing the ocean on a wind. Smell it?"

Guilford believed he did.

CHAPTER TWO

Eleanor Sanders-Moss was everything Elias Vale had expected: a buxom Southern aristocrat past her prime, spine stiff, chin high, rain streaming from a silk umbrella, dignity colonizing the ruins of youth. She left a hansom standing at the curb: apparently the renaissance of the automobile had passed Mrs. Sanders-Moss by. The years had not. She suffered from crow's feet and doubt. The wrinkles were past hiding; the doubt she was transparently working to conceal.

She said, "Elias Vale?"

He smiled, matching her reserve, dueling for advantage. Every pause a weapon. He was good at this. "Mrs. Sanders-Moss," he said. "Please, come in."

She stepped inside the doorway, folded her umbrella and dropped it without ceremony into the elephant's-foot holder. She blinked as he closed the door. Vale preferred to keep the lights turned low. On gloomy days like this the eye was slow to adjust. It was a hazard to navigation, but atmosphere was paramount: he dealt, after all, in the commerce of the invisible.

And the atmosphere was working its effect on Mrs. Sanders-Moss. Vale tried to imagine the scene from her perspective, the faded splendor of this rented town house on the wrong side of the Potomac. Sideboards furnished with Victorian bronzes: Greek wrestlers, Romulus and Remus suckling at the teats of a wolf. Japanese prints obscured by shadows. And Vale himself, prematurely white-haired (an asset, really), stout, his coat trimmed in velvet, homely face redeemed by fierce and focused eyes. Green eyes. He had been born lucky: the hair and eyes made him plausible, he often thought.

He spun out silence into the room. Mrs. Sanders-Moss fidgeted and said at last, "We have an appointment . . . ?"

"Of course."

"Mrs. Fowler recommended—"

"I know. Please come into my study."

He smiled again. What they wanted, these women, was someone *outré*, unworldly . . . a monster, but *their* monster; a monster domesticated but not quite tame. He took Mrs. Sanders-Moss past velvet curtains into a smaller room lined with books. The books were old, ponderous, impressive unless you troubled to decipher the faded gilt on their threadbare spines: collections of nineteenth-century sermons, which Vale had bought for pennies at a farm auction. The *arcanum,* people assumed.

He steered Mrs. Sanders-Moss into a chair, then sat opposite her across a burnished tabletop. She mustn't know that he was nervous, too. Mrs. Sanders-Moss was no ordinary client. She was the prey he had been stalking for more than a year now. She was well-connected.

She hosted a monthly salon at her Virginia estate which was attended by many of the city's intellectual lights—and their wives.

He wanted very much to impress Mrs. Sanders-Moss.

She folded her hands in her lap and fixed him with an earnest gaze. "Mrs. Fowler recommended you quite highly, Mr. Vale."

"Doctor," he corrected.

"Dr. Vale." She was still wary. "I'm not a gullible woman. I don't consult spiritualists, as a rule. But Mrs. Fowler was very impressed by your readings."

"I don't read, Mrs. Sanders-Moss. There are no tea leaves here. I won't look at your palm. No crystal ball. No tarot cards."

"I didn't mean—"

"I'm not offended."

"Well, she spoke very highly of you. Mrs. Fowler, I mean."

"I recall the lady."

"What you told her about her husband—"

"I'm happy she was pleased. Now. Why are *you* here?"

She put her hands in her lap. Restraining, perhaps, the urge to run.

"I've lost something," she whispered.

He waited.

"A lock of hair. . . ."

"Whose hair?"

Dignity fled. Now the confession. "My daughter's. My first daughter. Emily. She died at two years. Diphtheria, you see. She was a perfect little girl. When she was ill I took a lock of her hair and kept it with a few of her things. A rattle, a christening dress . . ."

"All missing?"

"Yes! But it's the hair that seems . . . the most terrible loss. It's all I have of her, really."

"And you want my help finding these items?"

"If it's not too trivial."

He softened his voice. "It's not trivial at all."

She looked at him with a gush of relief: she had made herself vulnerable and he had done nothing to hurt her; he had understood. That was what it was all about, Vale thought, this roundelay of shame and redemption. He wondered if doctors who treated venereal diseases felt the same way.

"*Can* you help me?"

"In all honesty, I don't know. I can try. But you have to help *me*. Will you take my hand?"

Mrs. Sanders-Moss reached tentatively across the table. Her hand was small and cool and he folded it into his own larger, firmer grip.

Their eyes met.

"Try not to be startled by anything you might see or hear."

"Speaking trumpets? That sort of thing?"

"Nothing as vulgar. This isn't a tent show."

"I didn't mean—"

"Never mind. Also, remember you may have to be patient. Often it takes time, contacting the other world."

"I have nowhere to go, Mr. Vale."

So the preliminaries were over and all that remained was to focus his concentration and wait for the god to rise from his inner depths—from what the Hindu mystics called "the lower chakras." He didn't relish it. It was always a painful, humiliating experience.

There was a price to be paid for everything, Vale thought.

The god: only he could hear it speak (unless he lent it his own, merely corporeal tongue); and when it spoke, he could hear nothing else. He had heard it for the first time in August of 1914.

Before the Miracle he had made a marginal living with a traveling show. Vale and two partners had trawled the hinterlands with a mummified body they purchased through the back door of a mortuary in Racine and billed as the corpse of John Wilkes Booth. The show played best in ditch towns where the circus never came, away from the rail lines, deep in cotton country, wheat country, Kentucky hemp country. Vale did all right, delivering the pitch and priming the crowds. He had a talent for talk. But it was a dying trade even before the Miracle, and the Miracle killed it. Rural income plummeted; the rare few with spending money wouldn't part with their pennies just for a glimpse of an assassin's leathery carcass. The Civil War was another generation's apocalypse. This generation had its own. His partners abandoned Mr. Booth in an Iowa cornfield.

By the blistering August of that year Vale was on his own, peddling Bibles from a frayed sample case and traveling, often as not, by boxcar. Twice he was attacked by thieves. He had fought back: saved his Bibles but lost a supply of clean collars and partial vision in one eye, the green of the iris faintly and permanently clouded (but that played well, too).

He had walked a lot that day. A hot Ohio Valley day. The air was humid, the sky flat white, commerce listless. In the Olympia Diner (in some town, name forgotten, where the river coiled west like lazy smoke), the waitress claimed to hear thunder in the air. Vale spent his last money on a chicken-and-gravy sandwich and went off in search of a place to sleep.

Past sunset he found an empty brickworks at the edge of town. The air inside the enormous building was close and wet and stank of mildew and machine oil. Abandoned furnaces loomed like scabrous idols in the darkness. He made a sort of bed high up in the scaffolding where he imagined he would be safe, sleeping on a stained mattress he dragged in from a hillside dump. But sleep didn't come easily. A night wind guttered through the empty frames of the factory windows, but the air remained close and hot. Rain began falling, deep in the night. He listened to it trickle down a thousand crevices to pool on the muddy floor. Erosion, he thought, pricking at iron and stone.

The voice—not yet a voice but a premonitory, echoing thunder—came to him without warning, well past midnight.

It pinned him flat. Literally, he could not move. It was as if he was held in place by a tremendous weight, but the weight was electric, pulsing through him, sparking from his fingertips. He wondered if he had been struck by lightning. He thought he was about to die.

Then the voice spoke, and it spoke not words but, somehow, *meanings;* the equivalent words, when he attempted to frame them, were a lifeless approximation. *It knows my name,* Vale thought. *No, not my name, my secret* idea *of myself.*

The electricity forced open his eyelids. Unwilling and afraid, he saw the god standing above him. The god was monstrous. It was ugly, ancient, its beetle-like body a translucent green, rain falling right through it. The god reeked, an obscure smell that reminded Vale of paint thinner and creosote.

How could he sum up what he learned that night? It was ineffable, unspeakable; he could hardly bring himself to sully it with language.

Yet, forced, he might say:

I learned that I have a purpose in life.

I learned that I have a destiny.

I learned that I have been chosen.

I learned that the gods are several and that they know my name.

I learned that there is a world under the world.

I learned that I have friends among the powerful.

I learned that I need to be patient.

I learned that I will be rewarded for my patience.

And I learned—this above all—that I might not need to die.

"You have a servant," Vale said. "A Negress."

Mrs. Sanders-Moss sat erect, eyes wide, like a school-girl called on by an intimidating teacher. "Yes. Olivia . . . her name is Olivia."

He wasn't conscious of speaking. He had given him-self over to another presence. He felt the rubbery peri-stalsis of his lips and tongue as something foreign and revolting, as if a slug had crawled into his mouth.

"She's been with you a long time—this Olivia."

"Yes; a very long time."

"She was with you when your daughter was born."

"Yes."

"And she cared for the girl."

"Yes."

"Wept when the girl died."

"We all did. The household."

"But Olivia harbored deeper feelings."

"Did she?"

"She knows about the box. The lock of hair, the christening dress."

"I suppose she must. But—"

"You kept them under the bed."

"Yes!"

"Olivia dusts under the bed. She knows when you've looked at the box. She knows because the dust is disturbed. She pays attention to dust."

"That's possible, but—"

"You haven't opened the box for a long time. More than a year."

Mrs. Sanders-Moss lowered her eyes. "But I've *thought* of it. I didn't *forget*."

"Olivia treats the box as a shrine. She worships it. She opens it when you're out of the house. She's careful not to disturb the dust. She thinks of it as her own."

"Olivia . . ."

"She thinks you don't do justice to the memory of your daughter."

"That's not true!"

"But it's what she believes."

"*Olivia* took the box?"

"Not a theft, by her lights."

"Please—Dr. Vale—*where is it?* Is it safe?"

"Quite safe."

"*Where?*"

"In the maid's quarters, at the back of a closet." (For a moment Vale saw it in his mind's eye, the wooden box like a tiny coffin swathed in ancient linens; he smelled camphor and dust and cloistered grief.)

"I *trusted* her!"

"She loved the girl, too, Mrs. Sanders-Moss. Very much." Vale took a deep, shuddering breath; began to reclaim himself, felt the god leaving him, subsiding into the hidden world again. The relief was exquisite. "Take back what belongs to you. But please, don't be too hard on Olivia."

Mrs. Sanders-Moss looked at him with a very gratifying expression of awe.

* * *

She thanked him effusively. He turned down the offer of money. Both her tentative smile and her shaken demeanor were encouraging, very promising indeed. But, of course, only time would tell.

When she had taken her umbrella and gone he opened a bottle of brandy and retreated to an upstairs room where the rain rattled down a frosted window, the gaslights were turned high, and the only book in sight was a tattered pulp-paper volume entitled *His Mistress's Petticoat.*

To outward appearance, the change worked in him by the manifestation of the god was subtle. Inwardly, he felt exhausted, almost wounded. There was a rawness, not quite pain, which extended to every limb. His eyes burned. The liquor helped, but it would be another day until he was completely himself.

With luck the brandy would moderate the dreams that followed a manifestation. In the dreams he found himself inevitably in some cold wilderness, some borderless vast gray desert, and when out of a misplaced curiosity or simply mischief he lifted up a random stone he uncovered a hole from which poured countless insects of some unknown and hideous kind, many-legged, pincered, venomous, swarming up his arm and invading his skull.

He wasn't a religious man. He had never believed in spirits, table-rapping, astrology, or the Resurrected Christ. He wasn't sure he believed in any of those things now; the sum of his belief resided in this single god, the one that had touched him with such awful, irresistible intimacy.

He had the skills of a confidence man and he was

certainly not averse to a profitable larceny, but there had been no collusion in the case of, for instance, Mrs. Sanders-Moss; she was a mystery to him, and so was the servant girl Olivia and the *memento mori* in the shoe box. His own prophecies took him by surprise. The words, not his own, had fallen from his lips like ripe fruit from a tree.

The words served him well enough, mind you. But they served another purpose, too.

Larceny, by comparison, would have been infinitely more simple.

But he took another glass of brandy and consoled himself: *You don't come to immortality by the low road.*

A week passed. Nothing. He began to worry.

Then a note in the afternoon mail:

Dr. Vale,
The treasures have been recovered. You have my most boundless gratitude.

I am entertaining guests this coming Thursday at six o'clock for dinner and conversation. If you happen to be free to attend, you would be most welcome.

RSVP

Mrs. Edward Sanders-Moss

She had signed it, *Eleanor.*

CHAPTER THREE

Odense docked at the makeshift harbor in the marshy estuary of the Thames, a maze of colliers, oilers, freighters and sailing ships gathered in from the outposts of the Empire. Guilford Law, plus family, plus the body of the Finch expedition and all its compasses, alidades, dried food, and paraphernalia, transferred to a ferry bound up the Thames to London. Guilford personally supervised the loading of his photographic equipment—the carefully crated 8" x 10" glass plates, the camera, lenses, and tripod.

The ferry was a cold and noisy steamer but blessed with generous windows. Caroline comforted Lily, who disliked the hard wooden benches, while Guilford gave himself up to the scrolling shoreline.

It was his first real view of the new world. The Thames mouth and London were the single most populous territory of the continent: most known, most seen, often photographed, but still wild—smug, Guilford thought, with wildness. The distant shore was dense with alien growth, hollow flute trees and reed grasses obscure in the gathering shadows of a chill afternoon. The strangeness of it burned in Guilford like a coal. After all he had read and dreamed, here was the tangible and impossible fact itself, not an illustration in a book but a living mosaic of light and shade and wind. The river ran green with false lotus, colonies of domed pads drifting in the water: a hazard to navigation, he'd been told, especially in summer, when the blooms came down from the Cotswolds in dense congregations and choked the screws of the steamships. He caught a glimpse of John Sullivan on the glass-walled promenade deck. Sullivan had been to Europe in 1918, had made collections at the mouth of the Rhine, but that experience obviously hadn't jaded him; there was an intensity of observation in the botanist's eyes that made conversation unthinkable.

Soon enough there was human litter along the shore, rough cabins, an abandoned farm, a smoldering garbage pit; and then the outskirts of the Port of London itself, and even Caroline took an interest.

The city was a random collation on the north bank of the river. It had been carved into the wilderness by soldiers and loyalist volunteers recalled by Lord Kitchener from the colonies, and it was hardly the London of Christopher Wren: it looked to Guilford like any smoky frontier town, a congregation of sawmills, hotels, docks, and warehouses. He identified the silhouette of the city's single famous monument, a column of South African marble cut to commemorate the losses of 1912. The Miracle had not been kind to human beings. It had replaced rocks with rocks, plants with stranger plants, animals with vaguely equivalent creatures—but of the vanished human population or any sentient species, no trace had ever been found.

Taller than the memorial pillar were the great iron cranes dredging and improving the port facilities. Beyond these, most striking of all, was the skeletal framework of the new St. Paul's Cathedral, astride what must be Ludgate Hill. No bridges crossed the Thames, though there were plans to build one; a variety of ferries accommodated the traffic.

He felt Lily tug his sleeve. "Daddy," she said solemnly. "A monster."

"What's that, Lil?"

"A monster! *Look.*"

His wide-eyed daughter pointed off the port bow, upriver.

Guilford told Lily the name of the monster even as his heart began to beat faster: a *silt snake*, the settlers called it, or sometimes *river snake*. Caroline took his other arm tightly as the chatter of voices ceased. The silt snake lifted its head above the ship's prow in a motion startlingly gentle, given that its skull was a blunt wedge the size of a child's coffin attached to a twenty-foot neck. The creature was harmless, Guilford knew—placid, literally a lotus-eater—but it was frighteningly large.

Below the waterline the creature would have anchored itself in the mud. The silt snake's legs were boneless cartilaginous spurs that served to brace it against river currents. Its skin was an oily white, mottled in places with algal green. The creature appeared fascinated by the human activity ashore. It aimed its apposite eyes in turn at the harbor cranes, blinked, and opened its mouth soundlessly. Then it spotted a mass of floating lotus pads and scooped them from the water in one deft bobbing motion before submerging again into the Thames.

Caroline buried her head against Guilford's shoulder. "God help us," she whispered. "We've arrived in Hell."

Lily demanded to know if that was true. Guilford assured her that it wasn't; this was only London, new London in the new world—though it was an easy mistake to make, perhaps, with the gaudy sunset, the clanking harbor, the river monster and all.

Stevedores undertook the unloading of the ferry. Finch, Sullivan, and the rest of the expedition put up at the Imperial, London's biggest hotel. Guilford looked wistfully at the leaded windows and wrought-iron balconies of the building as he rode with Caroline and Lily away from the harbor. They had hired a London taxi, essentially a horsecart with a cloth roof and a feeble suspension; they were bound for the home of Caroline's uncle, Jered Pierce. Their luggage would follow in the morning.

A lamplighter moved through the dusky streets among boisterous crowds. There was not much left of the fabled English decorum, Guilford thought, if this mob of sailors and loud women was any sample. London was plainly a frontier town, its population culled from the rougher elements of the Royal Fleet. There might be shortages of coal and oil, but the grog shops appeared to be doing a roaring business.

Lily put her head on Guilford's lap and closed her eyes. Caroline was awake and vigilant. She reached for Guilford's hand and squeezed it. "Liam says they're good people, but I've never met them," meaning her aunt and uncle.

"They're family, Caroline. I'm sure they're fine."

The Pierce shop stood on a brightly lit market street, but like everything else in the city it gave the impression of makeshift and ramshackle. Caroline's uncle Jered bounded from the doorway and welcomed his niece with a hug, pumped Guilford's hand vigorously, picked up Lily and examined her as if she were an especially satisfactory sack of flour. Then he ushered them in from the street, up a flight of iron stairs to the rooms where the family lived above the shop. The flat was narrow and sparsely furnished, but a woodstove made it warm and Jered's wife Alice welcomed them with another round of embraces. Guilford smiled and let Caroline do most of the talking. Landbound at last, he felt weary. Jered put a hollow log on the fire, and Guilford registered that even the smell of burning wood was different in Darwinia: the smoke was sweet and pungent, like Indian hemp or attar of roses.

The Pierce family had been widely scattered when the Miracle struck. Caroline had been in Boston with Jered's brother Liam; both her parents had been in England with Caroline's dying grandfather. Jered and Alice were in Capetown, had stayed there until the troubles of 1916; in August of that year they had sailed for London with a generous loan from Liam and plans for a dry goods and hardware business. Both were hardy types, thick-bodied and strong. Guilford liked them at once.

Lily went to bed first, in a spare room barely large enough to qualify as a closet, and Guilford and Caroline down the hallway. Their bed was a brass four-poster, immensely comfortable. The Pierce family had a more generous idea of how a mattress ought to be made than the pennypinching outfitters of the *Odense*. It was almost certainly the last civilized bed he would sleep in for a while, and Guilford meant to relish it; but he was unconscious as soon as he closed his eyes, and then, too soon, it was morning.

The Finch expedition waited in London for a second shipment of supplies, including five Stone-Galloway flat-bottom boats, eighteen-footers with outboard motors, due to arrive on the next vessel from New York. Guilford spent two days in a dim customs-house conducting an inventory while Preston Finch replaced various missing or damaged items—a block and tackle, a tarpaulin, a leaf press.

After that Guilford was free to spend time with his family. He lent a hand in the shop, watched Lily work her way through egg breakfasts, sausage suppers, and far too many sugar biscuits. He admired Jered's Empire Volunteer Certificate, signed by Lord Kitchener himself, which held place of honor on the parlor wall. Every returned Englishman had one, but Jered took his Volunteer duties seriously and spoke without irony of rebuilding the Dominion.

This was all interesting but it was not the Europe Guilford longed to experience—the raw new world unmediated by human intervention. He told Jered he'd like to spend a day exploring the city.

"Not much to see, I'm afraid. Candlewick to St. Paul's is a nice walk on a sunny day, or Thames Street beyond the wharves. Up east the roads are more mud than anything else. And stay away from the clearances."

"I don't mind mud," Guilford said. "I expect I'll see a lot of it in the next few months."

Jered frowned uneasily. "I expect you're right about that."

Guilford walked past the market stalls and away from

the clanging harbor. The morning sun was radiant, the air blissfully cool. He encountered much horse and cart traffic but few automobiles, and the city's civil engineering was still a work in progress. Open sewers ran through the newer neighborhoods; a reeking honeywagon rattled down Candlewick Street, drawn by two swaybacked nags. Some of the townfolk wore white handkerchiefs tied over mouth and nose, for reasons which had been obvious to Guilford since the ferry docked: the smell of the city was at times appalling, a mixture of human and animal waste, coal smoke and the stench of the pulp mill across the river.

But it was also a lively and good-natured town, and Guilford was greeted cheerfully by other pedestrians. He stopped for lunch at a Ludgate pub and emerged refreshed into the sunlight. Beyond the new St. Paul's the town faded into tar-paper shacks, farm clearances, finally patches of raw forest. The road became a rutted dirt path; mosque trees shaded the lane with their green coronets, and the air was suddenly much fresher.

The generally accepted explanation for the Miracle was that it had been just that: an act of divine intervention on a colossal scale. Preston Finch believed so, and Finch was not an idiot. And on the face of it, the argument was unimpeachable. An event had taken place in defiance of everything commonly accepted as natural law; it had fundamentally transformed a generous portion of the Earth's surface in a single night. Its only precedents were Biblical. After the conversion of Europe, who could be skeptical of the Flood, for instance, particularly when naturalists like Finch were prepared to tease evidence for it from the geological record? Man proposes, God disposes; His motives might be obscure but His handiwork was unmistakable.

But Guilford could not stand among these gently

swaying alien growths and believe they did not have a history of their own.

Certainly Europe had been remade in 1912; just as certainly, these very trees had appeared there in a night, eight years younger than he found them now. But they did not seem new-made. They generated seed (spores, more precisely, or *germinae* in the new taxonomy), which implied heritage, history, descent, perhaps even evolution. Cut one of these trees across the bole and you would find annular growth rings numbering far more than eight. The annular rings might be large or small, depending on seasonal temperatures and sunlight . . . depending on seasons that had happened *before these plants appeared on Earth.*

So where had they come from?

He paused at the roadside where a stand of gullyflowers grew almost to shoulder height. In one cuplike bud, a threadneedle crawled among blue stamenate spikes. With each movement of the insect tiny clouds of germinal matter dusted the warm spring air. To call this "supernatural," Guilford thought, was to contradict the very idea of nature.

On the other hand, what limits applied to divine intervention? None, presumably. If the Creator of the Universe wanted to give one of his creations the false appearance of a history, He would simply do so; human logic was surely the least of His concerns. God might have made the world just yesterday, for that matter, assembled it out of stardust and divine will complete with the illusion of human memory. Who would know? Had Caesar or Cleopatra ever really lived? Then what about the people who vanished the night of the Conversion? If the Miracle had engulfed the entire planet rather than one part of it surely the answer would be *no*—no Guilford Law, no Woodrow Wilson, no Edison or Marconi; no Rome, no Greece, no Jerusalem; no Neanderthal Man. For that matter, no Adam, no Eve.

And if that's so, Guilford thought, *then we live in a madhouse.* There could be no genuine understanding of anything, ever . . . except perhaps in the Mind of God.

In which case we should simply give up. Knowledge was provisional at best and science was an impracticality. But he refused to believe it.

He was distracted from gullyflowers and philosophy by the smell of smoke. He followed the lane up a gentle hillside, to an open field where mosque and bell trees had been cut, stacked with dry brush, and set ablaze. A gang of soot-blackened workingmen stood at the verge of the road minding the fires.

A husky man in dungarees and a sailor's jersey—the crew boss, Guilford supposed—waved him over impatiently. "Burn's just on, I'm afraid. Best stay behind the beaters or turn back. One or two might get past us.

Guilford said, "One or two what?"

This drew a chorus of laughter from the men, some half-dozen of whom carried thick wooden posts blunted at one end.

The crew boss said, "You're an American?"

Guilford acknowledged it.

"New here?"

"Fairly new. What is it I'm supposed to watch out for?"

"Stump runners, for Christ's sake. Look at you, you're not even wearing knee boots! Keep off the clearances unless you're dressed for it. It's safe enough when we're cutting and stacking, but the fires always draw 'em out. Stay behind the beaters until the flush is finished and you'll be all right."

Guilford stood where the crew boss directed him,

with the workmen forming a skirmish line between the road and the cleared lot. The sun was warm, the smoke chokingly thick whenever the wind reversed. Guilford had started to wonder whether the waiting would go on all afternoon when one of the laborers shouted " 'Ware!" and faced the clearing, knees braced, his frayed wooden post at quarter-arms.

"Buggers live in the earth," the crew boss said. "Fire boils 'em out. You don't want to get in the way."

Beyond the workers he saw motion in the charred soil of the clearing. Stump runners, if Guilford remembered correctly, were burrowing hive insects about the size of a large beetle, commonly found among the roots of older mosque trees. Seldom a problem to the casual passerby, but venomous when provoked. And fiercely toxic.

There must have been a dozen flourishing nests in the clearance.

The insects came from the earth in mounds and filled the smoldering spaces between the fires like shimmering black oil. The clearing yielded several distinct swarms, which turned, collided, and wheeled in every direction.

The beaters began pounding the dirt with their posts. They pounded in unison, raising clouds of dust and ash and shouting like madmen. The crew boss took a firm grip on Guilford's arm. "Don't move!" he roared. "You're safe here. They'd attack us if they could, but their first concern is moving their egg sacks away from the flames."

The beaters in their high boots continued punishing the earth until the stump-runners paid attention. The swarms rotated around the brush fires like living cyclones, pressed together until the ground was invisible under their combined mass, then turned away from the tumult of the beaters and flowed into the shadows of the forest like so much water draining from a pond.

"A loose hive won't last long. They're prey for snakes, scuttlemice, billy hawks, anything that can tolerate their poison. We'll rake the fires for a day or two. Come back in a week, you won't recognize the place."

The work continued until the last of the creatures had disappeared. The beaters leaned panting against their posts, exhausted but relieved. The insects had left their own smell in the smoky air, a tang of mildew, Guilford thought, or ammonia. He wiped his nose with the back of his hand, realized his face was covered with soot.

"Next time you come away from town, outfit yourself for it. This isn't New York City."

Guilford smiled weakly. "I'm beginning to understand that."

"Here for long?"

"A few months. Here and on the Continent."

"The Continent! There's nothing on the Continent but wilderness and crazy Americans, excuse me for saying so."

"I'm with a scientific survey."

"Well, I hope you don't plan on doing much walking with ankle-boots like those on your feet. The livestock will kill you and whittle your pins."

"Maybe a little walking," Guilford said.

He was glad enough to find his way back to the Pierce home, to wash himself and spend an evening in the buttery light of the oil lamps. After a generous supper Caroline and Alice disappeared into the kitchen, Lily was sent to bed, and Jered took down from his shelf a leatherbound 1910 atlas of Europe, the old Europe of sovereigns and nation. How meaningless it had come to be, Guilford thought, and in just eight years, these diagrams of sovereignty imposed on the land like the whim of a mad god. Wars had been fought for these lines. Now they were so much geometry, a tile of dreams.

"It hasn't changed as much as you might think," Jered said. "Old loyalties don't die easily. You know about the Partisans."

The Partisans were bands of nationalists—rough men who had come from the colonies to reclaim territory they still thought of as German or Spanish or French. Most disappeared into the Darwinian bush, reduced to subsistence or devoured by the wildlife. Others practiced a form of banditry, preying on settlers they regarded as invaders. The Partisans were certainly a potential threat—coastal piracy, abetted by various European nations in exile, made resupply problematic. But the Partisans, like other settlers, had yet to penetrate into the roadless interior of the continent.

"That may not be true," Jered said. "They're well armed, some of them, and I've heard rumors of Partisan attacks on wildcat miners in the Saar. They're not kindly disposed toward Americans."

Guilford wasn't intimidated. The Donnegan party had not encountered more than a few ragged Partisans living like savages in the Aquitaine lowlands. The Finch expedition would land on the continent at the mouth of the Rhine, American-occupied territory, and follow the river as far as it was navigable, past the Rheinfelden to the Bodensee, if possible. Then they would scout the Alps for a navigable pass where the old Roman roads had run.

"Ambitious," Jered said evenly.

"We're equipped for it."

"Surely you can't anticipate every danger. . . ."

"That's the point. People have been crossing the Alps for centuries. It's not such a hard journey in summer. But never *these* Alps. Who knows what might have changed? That's what we mean to find out."

"Just fifteen men," Jered said.

"We'll steam as far as we can up the Rhine. Then it's flat-bottom boats and portage."

"You'll need someone who knows the Continent. What little of it anyone *does* know."

"There are trappers and bush runners at Jeffersonville on the Rhine. Men who've been there since the Miracle, nearly."

"You're the photographer, Caroline tells me."

"Yessir."

"First time out?"

"First time on the Continent, but I was with Walcott at the Gallatin River last year. I'm not inexperienced."

"Liam helped you secure this position?"

"Yes."

"No doubt he thought he was doing the right thing. But Liam is insulated by the Atlantic Ocean. And by his money. He may not understand the position he's put you in. Passions run high on the continent. Oh, I know all about the Wilson Doctrine, Europe a wilderness open for resettlement by all, and so on, and it's a noble idea in its way—though I'm glad England was able to enforce an exception. But you had to sink a few French and German gunboats before their rump governments would yield. And even so . . ." He tamped his pipe. "You're going in harm's way. I'm not sure Liam knows that."

"I'm not afraid of the continent."

"Caroline needs you. Lily needs you. There's nothing cowardly about protecting yourself and your family." He leaned closer. "You're welcome to stay here as long as necessary. I can write to Liam and explain. Think about it, Guilford." He lowered his voice. "I don't want my niece to be a widow."

Caroline came through the door from the kitchen. She looked at Guilford solemnly, her lovely hair awry, then turned up the gaslights one by one until the room was ablaze with light.

CHAPTER FOUR

Spending time at the Sanders-Moss estate was much like having his testicles removed. Among the women he was a pet; among the men, a eunuch.

Hardly flattering, Elias Vale thought, but not unexpected. He entered the house as a eunuch because no other entrance was open to him. Given time, he would own the doors. He would topple the palace, if it pleased him. The harem would be his and the princes would vie for his favor.

Tonight was a *soirée* celebrating some occasion he had already forgotten: a birthday, an anniversary. Since he wouldn't be required to offer a toast, it didn't matter. What mattered was that Mrs. Sanders-Moss had once again invited him to adorn one of her functions; that she trusted him to be acceptably eccentric, to charm but not to embarrass. That is, he wouldn't drink to excess, make passes at wives, or treat the powerful as equals.

At dinner he sat where he was directed, entertaining a congressman's daughter and a junior Smithsonian administrator with stories of table-rapping and spirit manifestations, all safely second-hand and wry. Spiritualism was a heresy in these lately pious times, but it was an American heresy, more acceptable than Catholicism, for instance, with its Latin Masses and absent European Popes. And when he had fulfilled his function as a curio he simply smiled and listened to the conversation that flowed around his unobstructing presence like a river around a rock.

The hard part, at least at first, had been maintaining his poise in the presence of so much luxury. Not that he was entirely a stranger to luxury. He had been raised in a good enough New England home—had fallen from it like a rebel angel. He knew a dinner fork from a dessert fork. But he had slept under a great many cold bridges since then, and the Sanders-Moss estate was an order of magnitude more grandiose than anything he remembered. Electric lights and servants; beef sliced thin as paper; mutton dressed with mint sauce.

Waiting table was Olivia, a pretty and timid Negress whose cap sat perpetually askew on her head. Vale had pressed Mrs. Sanders-Moss not to punish her after the christening dress was rescued, which accomplished two purposes at once, to spotlight his kindheartedness and to ingratiate himself with the help, never a bad thing. But Olivia still avoided him assiduously; she seemed to think he was an evil spirit. Which was not far from the truth, though Vale would quibble with the adjective. The universe was aligned along axes more complex than poor simple Olivia would ever know.

Olivia brought the dessert course. Table talk turned to the Finch expedition, which had reached England

and was preparing to cross the Channel. The congressman's daughter to Vale's left thought it was all very brave and interesting. The junior administrator of mollusks, or whatever he was, thought the expedition would be safer on the continent than in England.

The congressman's daughter disagreed. "It's Europe proper they should be afraid of." She frowned becomingly. "You know what they say. Everything that lives there is ugly, and most of it is deadly."

"Not as deadly as human beings." The young functionary, on the other hand, wanted to appear cynical. Probably he imagined it made him seem older.

"Don't be scandalous, Richard."

"And seldom as ugly."

"They're *brave*."

"Brave enough, but in their place I'd worry more about the Partisans. Or even the English."

"It hasn't come to that."

"Not yet. But the English are no friends of ours. Kitchener is provisioning the Partisans, you know."

"That's a rumor, and you shouldn't repeat it."

"They're endangering our European policy."

"We were talking about the Finch expedition, not the English."

"Preston Finch can run a river, certainly, but I predict they'll take more casualties from bullets than from rapids. Or monsters."

"Don't say *monsters*, Richard."

"Chastisements of God."

"Just the thought of it makes me shiver. Partisans are only *people*, after all."

"Dear girl. But I suppose Dr. Vale would be out of business if women weren't inclined to the romantic point of view. Isn't that so?"

Vale performed his best and most unctuous smile.

"Women are better able to see the infinite. Or less afraid of it."

"There!" The congressman's daughter blushed happily. "The *infinite*, Richard."

Vale wished he could show her the infinite. *It would burn her pretty eyes to cinders*, he thought. *It would peel the flesh from her skull.*

After dinner the men retired to the library with brandies and Vale was left with the women. There was considerable talk of nephews in the military and their lapses of communication, of husbands keeping late hours at the State Department. Vale felt a certain resonance in these omens but couldn't fathom their final significance. War? War with England? War with Japan? Neither seemed plausible . . . but Washington since Wilson's death was a mossbound well, dark and easily poisoned.

Pressed for wisdom, Vale confined himself to drawing-room prophecies. Lost cats and errant children; the terrors of yellow fever, polio, influenza. His visions were benign and hardly supernatural. Private questions could be handled at his business address, and, in fact, his clientele had increased considerably in the two months since his first encounter with Eleanor. He was well on his way to becoming Father Confessor to a generation of aging heiresses. He kept careful notes.

The evening dragged on and showed no signs of becoming especially productive: not much to feed his diary tonight, Vale thought. Still, this was where he needed to be. Not just to bolster his income, though that was certainly a welcome side effect. He was following a deeper instinct, perhaps not quite his own. His god wanted him here.

And one does what a god wants, because that is the nature of a god, Vale thought: *to be obeyed. That above all.*

As he was leaving, Eleanor steered a clearly quite drunken man toward him. "Dr. Vale? This is Professor Randall. You were introduced, weren't you?"

Vale shook hands with the white-haired venerable. Among Eleanor's collection of academics and civil-service nonentities, which one was this? Randall, ah, something at the Natural History Museum, a curator of . . . could it be paleontology? That orphaned science.

"See him to his automobile," Eleanor said, "won't you? Eugene go with Dr. Vale. A walk around the grounds might clear your head."

The night air smelled of blossoms and dew, at least when the professor was downwind. Vale looked at his companion more carefully, imagined he saw pale structures under the surface of Randall's body. Coral growths of age (parchment skin, arthritic knuckles) obscured the buried soul. If paleontologists possessed souls.

"Finch is mad," Randall muttered, continuing some abandoned conversation, "if he thinks . . . if he thinks he can prove . . ."

"There's nothing to prove tonight, sir."

Randall shook his head and squinted at Vale, seeing him perhaps for the first time. "You. Ah. You're the fortune-teller, yes?"

"In a way."

"See the future, do you?"

"Through a glass," Vale said. "Darkly."

"The future of the world?"

"More or less."

"We talk about Europe," Randall said. "Europe, the Sodom so corrupt it was cast into the refiner's fire. And so we pluck out the seeds of Europeanism wherever we find them, whatever that means. Gross hypocrisy, of course. A political fad. Do you want to see Europe?" He swept his hand at the white-columned Sanders-Moss estate. "Here it is! The court at Versailles. It might as well be."

The stars were vivid in the spring sky. Lately Vale had begun to perceive a kind of depth in starry skies, a layering or recession that made him think of forests and meadows, of tangled thickets in which predatory animals lurked. As above, so below.

"This Creator men like Finch drone on about," Randall said. "One wants to believe, of course. But there are no fingerprints on a fossil. Washed off, I suppose, in the Flood."

Obviously Randall shouldn't be saying any of this. The climate of opinion had shifted since the Miracle and men like Randall were themselves a kind of living fossil—wooly mammoths trapped in an ice age. Of course Randall, a collector of bones, could hardly know that Vale was a collector of indiscretions.

Who would pay to know what Randall thought of Preston Finch? And in what currency, and when?

"I'm sorry," Randall said. "This could hardly interest you."

"On the contrary," Vale said, walking with his prey into the dewy night. "It interests me a great deal."

CHAPTER FIVE

The flat-bottom riverboats arrived from New York and were transferred to a cross-channel steamer, the *Argus*. Guilford, Finch, Sullivan, and the surveyor, Chuck Hemphill, supervised the loading and annoyed the vessel's cargo master until they were banished to the tarry dock. Spring sunlight washed the wharfs and softened the tarry planks; clots of false lotus rotted against the pilings; gulls wheeled overhead. The gulls had been among the first terrestrial immigrants to Darwinia, followed in turn by human beings, wheat, barley, potatoes; wildflowers (loosestrife, bindweed); rats, cattle, sheep, lice, fleas, cockroaches—all the biological stew of the coastal settlements.

Preston Finch stood on the wharf with his huge hands clamped behind his back, face shadowed by his solar topee. Finch was a paradox, Guilford thought: a hardy man, powerful despite his age, a weathered river-runner whose judgment and courage were unques-

tionable. But his Noachian geology, fashionable
though it might have become in the nervous aftermath
of the Miracle, seemed to Guilford a stew of half-truths,
dubious reasoning, and wistful Protestantism. Implausible no matter how he dressed up the matter with theories of sedimentation and quotations from Berkeley.
Moreover, Finch refused to discuss these ideas and
didn't brook criticism from his colleagues, much less
from a mere photographer. What must it be like, Guilford wondered, to have such a baroque architecture
crammed inside one's skull? Such a strange cathedral,
so well buttressed, so well defended?

John Sullivan, the expedition's other gray emi-
nence, leaned against a wharfhouse wall, arms
crossed, smiling faintly under a broad straw hat. Two
aging men, Finch and Sullivan, but Sullivan smiled—
that was the difference.

The last of the crates descended into the *Argus*'s
hold. Finch signed a manifest for the sweating cargo
master. There was an air of finality about the act. The
Argus would sail in the morning.

Sullivan touched Guilford's shoulder. "Do you have
a few free minutes, Mr. Law? There's something you
might like to see."

Museum of Monstrosities, announced the shingle above
the door.

The building was hardly more than a shack, but it
was an old building, as buildings went in London, perhaps one of the first permanent structures erected
along the marshy banks of the Thames. It looked to
Guilford as if it had been used and abandoned many
times over.

"Here?" Guilford asked. They had come a short walk

from the wharfs, behind the brick barrelhouses, where the air was gloomy and stagnant.

"Tuppence to see the monsters," Sullivan said. His drawl was unreconstructed Arkansas, but on his lips it sounded like Oxford. Or at least what Guilford imagined an Oxford accent might have been like. "The proprietor's a drunk. But he does have one interesting item."

The "proprietor," a sullen man who reeked of gin, opened the door at Sullivan's knock, took Sullivan's money into his grimy hand, and vanished wordlessly behind a canvas curtain, leaving his guests to peer at the taxidermical trophies arrayed on crude shelves around the narrow front room. The smaller exhibits were legitimate, in the sense that they were recognizable Darwinian animals badly stuffed and mounted: a buttonhook bird, a miscellany of six-legged scavengers, a leopard snake with its hinged jaws open. Sullivan raised a window blind, but the extra light was no boon, in Guilford's opinion. Glass eyes glittered and peered in odd directions.

"This," Sullivan said.

He meant the upright skeleton languishing in a corner. Guilford approached it skeptically. At first glance it looked like the skeleton of a bear—crudely bipedal, a cage of ribs attached to a ventral spine, the fearsome skull long and multiply jointed, teeth like flint knives. Frightening. "But it's a fake," Guilford said.

"How do you arrive at that conclusion, Mr. Law?"

Surely Sullivan could see for himself? "It's all string and baling wire. Some of the bones are fresher than others. That looks like a cow's femur, there—the joints don't begin to match."

"Very good. The photographer's eye."

"It doesn't take a photographer."

"You're right, of course. The anatomy is a joke. But what interests me is the rib cage, which is correctly articulated, and in particular the skull."

Guilford looked again. The ribs and ventral spine were clearly Darwinian; it was the standard back-to-front arrangement, the spine U-shaped, with a deep chordal notch. The skull itself was long, faintly bovine, the dome high and capacious: a cunning carnivore. "You think those are authentic?"

"Authentic in the sense that they're genuine bones, not papier-mâché, and obviously not mammalian. Our host claims he bought them from a settler who dug them out of a bog somewhere up the Lea, looking for something cheaper than coal to burn."

"Then they're relatively recent."

"Relatively, though no one's seen a living animal like it or anything remotely equivalent. Large predators are scarce on the Continent. Donnegan reported a leopard-sized carnivore from the Massif Central, but nothing bigger. So what does this fellow represent, Mr. Law? That's the interesting question. A large, recently-extinct hunter?"

"I hope extinct. He looks formidable."

"Formidable and, judging by the cranium, perhaps intelligent. As animals go. If there are any of his tribe still living, we may need those pistols Finch is so fond of. And if not—"

"If not?"

"Well, what does it mean to talk about an *extinct* species, when the continent is only eight years old?"

Guilford decided to tread carefully. "You're assuming the continent has a history."

"I'm not assuming it, I'm deducing it. Oh, it's a familiar argument—I simply wondered where you stood."

"The trouble is, we have two histories. One continent, two histories. I don't know how to reconcile them."

Sullivan smiled. "That's a good first pass. Forced to guess, Mr. Law? Which is it? Elizabeth the First, or our bony friend here?"

"I've thought about it, obviously, but—"

"Don't hedge. Take your pick."

"Both," Guilford said flatly. "Somehow . . . both."

"But isn't that impossible?"

"Apparently not."

Sullivan's smile became a grin. "Good for you."

So Guilford had passed a test, though the older man's motives remained obscure. That was all right: Guilford liked Sullivan, was pleased that the botanist had chosen to treat him as an equal. Mainly, however, he was glad to step out of the taxidermist's hut and into the daylight. Though London's docklands didn't smell much better.

That night he shared his bed with Caroline for the last time.

Last time until autumn, Guilford corrected himself, but there was small comfort in the thought. Frustratingly, she was cool toward him tonight.

She was the only woman he had ever slept with. He had met her in the offices of Atticus and Pierce when he was touching up his plates for *Rocky Mountain Fossil Shales.* Guilford had felt an immediate, instinctive fondness for the aloof and frowning Pierce girl. He obtained a brief introduction from her uncle and in the following weeks began to calculate her appearances at the office: she took lunch with her uncle, a secretary told him, every Wednesday noon. Guilford intercepted her after one of these meetings and offered to walk her to the streetcar. She had accepted, looking at him from under her crown of hair like a wary princess.

Wary and wounded. Caroline hadn't recovered from the loss of her parents in the Miracle, but that was a common enough grief. Guilford found he could provoke a smile from her, at least now and then. In those days her silences had been more ally than enemy; they fostered a subtler communication. In that invisible language she had said something like: *I'm hurt but too proud to admit it—can you help?* And he had answered, *I'll make you a safe place. I'll make you a home.*

Now he lay awake with the sound of an occasional horsecart passing in the night and a valley of cotton bedsheet between himself and the woman he loved. Was it possible to break an unspoken promise? The truth was that he hadn't delivered Caroline to a safe place after all. He had traveled too far and too often: out west, and now here. Given her a fine daughter but brought them to this foreign shore, where he was about to abandon them . . . in the name of history, or science, or his own reckless dreams.

He told himself that this was what men did, that men had been doing it for centuries and that if men *didn't* do it the race would still be living in trees. But the truth was more complex, involved matters Guilford himself didn't care to think about, perhaps contained some echo of his father, whose stolid pragmatism had been the path to an early grave.

Caroline was asleep now, or nearly asleep. He put a hand on the slope of her hip, a gentle pressure that was meant to say *But I'll come back.* She responded with a sleepy curl, almost a shrug, not quite indifferent. *Perhaps.*

* * *

In the morning they were strangers to one another.

Caroline and Lily rode with him to the docks, where the *Argus* was restless with the tide. Cool mists twined around the ship's rust-pocked hull.

Guilford hugged Caroline, feeling wordless and crude; then Lily clambered up into his arms, pressed her soft cheek against his and said, "Come back soon."

Guilford promised he would.

Lily, at least, believed him.

Then he walked up the gangway, turned at the rail to wave good-bye, but his wife and daughter were already lost among the crowd that thronged the wharf. *As quick as that,* Guilford thought. *As quick as that.*

Argus made her passage across the Channel in a fog. Guilford brooded belowdecks until the sun broke through and John Sullivan demanded that he come up to see the continent by morning light.

What Guilford saw was a dense green wetland combed by a westerly wind—the saltwater marshes at the vast mouth of the Rhine. Stromatolites rose like unearthly monuments, and flute trees had colonized the delta everywhere the silt rose high enough to support their spidery roots. The steam packet followed a shallow but weed-free channel—slowly, because soundings were crude and the silt often shifted after a storm—toward a denser, greener distance. Jeffersonville was a faint plume of smoke on the flat green horizon, then a smudge, then a brown aggregation of shacks built into reed-stalk hummocks or perched on stilts where the ground was firm enough, and everywhere crude docks and small boats and the reek of salt, fish, refuse, and human waste. Caroline had thought London was primitive; Guilford was thankful she hadn't seen Jefferson-ville. The town was like a posted warning: here ends civ-ilization. Beyond this point, the anarchy of Nature.

There were plenty of fishing boats, canoes, and what looked like rafts cobbled from Darwinian timber, all clotting the net-draped wharves, but only one other vessel as large as the *Argus*, an American gunship an-chored and flying her colors. "That's our ride upriver," Sullivan said, standing alongside Guilford at the rail. "We won't be here long. Finch will make obeisance to the Navy while we hire ourselves a pathfinder."

"We?" Guilford asked.

"You and I. Then you can set up your lenses. Capture us all at the dock. *Embarkation at Jeffersonville*. Should make a stirring photograph." Sullivan clapped him on the back. "Cheer up, Mr. Law. This is the *real* new world, and you're about to set foot on it."

But there was little firm footing here in the marshes. You kept to the boardwalks or risked being swallowed up. Guilford wondered how much of Darwinia would be like this—the blue sky, the combing wind, the quiet threat.

Sullivan notified Finch that he and Guilford were going to hire a guide. Guilford was lost as soon as the wharves were out of sight, hidden by fishermen's shacks and a tall stand of mosque trees. But Sullivan seemed to know where he was going. He had been here in 1918, he said, cataloging some of the marsh-land species. "I know the town, though it's bigger now, and I met a few of the old hands."

The people they passed looked rough-hewn and dangerous. The government had begun handing out homestead grants and paid passage not long after the

Miracle, but it took a certain kind of person to volunteer for frontier life, even in those difficult days. Not a few of them had been fugitives from the law.

They lived by fishing and trapping and their wits. Judging by the visible evidence, fresh water and soap were in short supply. Men and women alike wore rough clothing and had let their hair grow long and tangled. Despite which, several of these shabby individuals looked at Sullivan and Guilford with the amused contempt of a native for a tourist.

"We're going to see a man named Tom Compton," Sullivan said. "Best tracker in Jeffersonville, assuming he isn't dead or out in the bush."

Tom Compton lived in a wooden hut away from the water. Sullivan didn't knock but barged through the half-open door—Darwinian manners, perhaps. Guilford followed cautiously. When his eyes adjusted to the dimness he found the hut sparse and clean-smelling, the plank floor dressed with a cotton rug, the walls hung with various kinds of fishing and hunting tackle. Tom Compton sat placidly in one corner of the single room, a large man with a vast, knotted beard. His skin was dark, his race obviously mixed. He wore a chain of claws around his neck. His shirt was woven of some coarse local fiber, but his trousers appeared to be conventional denim, half-hidden by high waterproof boots. He blinked at his visitors without enthusiasm and took a long-stemmed pipe from the table by his elbow.

"Bit early for that, isn't it?" Sullivan asked.

Tom Compton struck a wooden match and applied it to the bowl of the pipe. "Not when I see you."

"You know why I'm here, Tom?"

"I've heard rumors."

"We're traveling inland."

"Doesn't concern me."

"I'd like you to come with us."

"Can't do it."

"We're crossing the Alps."

"I'm not interested." He passed the pipe to Sullivan, who took it and inhaled the smoke. Not tobacco, Guilford thought. Sullivan passed the pipe to him, and Guilford looked at it with dismay. Could he politely refuse, or was this something like a Cherokee summit meeting, a smoke instead of a handshake?

Tom Compton laughed. Sullivan said, "It's the dried leaves of a river plant. Mildly intoxicating, but hardly opium."

Guilford took the gnarly briar. The smoke tasted the way a root cellar smells. He lost most of it to a coughing fit.

"New hand," Tom Compton said. "He doesn't know the country."

"He'll learn."

"They all learn," the frontiersman said. "Everybody learns. If the country doesn't kill 'em first."

Tom Compton's pipe smoke made Guilford feel lighter and simpler. Events slowed to a crawl or leaped forward without interval. By the time he found his bunk aboard the *Argus* he was able to remember only fragments of the day.

He remembered following Dr. Sullivan and Tom Compton to a wharfside tavern where brown beer was served in steins made from the boles of dried flute reeds. The steins were porous and would begin to leak if you let them sit too long. It encouraged a style of drinking not conducive to clarity of thought. There had been food, too, a Darwinian fish draped across the plate like a limp black stingray. It tasted of salt and mud; Guilford ate sparingly.

They argued about the expedition. The frontiersman was scornful, insisting the journey was only an excuse to show the flag and express American claims to the hinterland. "You said yourself, this man Finch is an idiot."

"He's a clergyman, not a scientist; he just doesn't know the difference. But he's no idiot. He rescued three men from the water at Cataract Canyon—carried a man with double pleurisy safely to Lee's Ferry. That was ten years ago, but I'm sure he'd do the same tomorrow. He planned and provisioned this expedition and I would trust him with my life."

"Follow him into the deep country, you *are* trusting him with your life."

"So I am. I couldn't ask for a better companion. I *could* ask for a better scientist—but even there, Finch has his uses. There's a certain climate of opinion in Washington that frowns on science in general: we couldn't predict and can't explain the Miracle, and in certain people's minds that's the next thing to responsibility. Idols with feet of clay fare badly in the public budget. But we can hold up Finch to Congress as a sterling example of so-called reverential science, not a threat to home or pulpit. We go to the hinterland, we learn a few things—and frankly, the more we learn, the shakier Finch's academic position becomes."

"You're being used. Like Donnegan. Sure, you collect a few samples. But the money people want to know how far the Partisans have come, whether there's coal in the Ruhr valley or iron in Lorraine. . . ."

"And if we reconnoiter the Partisans or spot some anthracite—does it matter? These things will happen whether we cross the Alps or not. At least this way we gain a little knowledge from the bargain."

Tom Compton turned to Guilford. "Sullivan thinks this continent is a riddle he can solve. That's a brave and stupid idea."

Sullivan persisted: "You've been farther inland than most trappers, Tom."

"Not as far as all that."

"You know what to expect."

"Go far enough, no one knows what to expect."

"Still, you've had experience."

"More than you."

"Your skills would be invaluable."

"I have better things to do."

They drank in silence for a while. Another round of beer gave the conversation a philosophical bent. The frontiersman confronted Guilford, his weathered brown face ferocious as a bear's muzzle. "Why are *you* here, Mr. Law?"

"I'm a photographer," Guilford said. He wished he had his camera with him; he wanted to photograph Tom Compton. This sun-wrinkled, beard-engulfed wild animal.

"I know what you do," the frontiersman said. "Why are you *here?*"

To further his career. To make a name for himself. To bring back images trapped in glass and silver, of river pools and mountain meadows no human eye had seen. "I don't know," he heard himself say. "Curiosity, I guess."

Tom Compton squinted at Guilford as if he had confessed to leprosy. "People come here to get away from something, Mr. Law, or to hunt for something. To make a little money or maybe even, like Sullivan here, to learn something. But the *I don't knows*—those are the dangerous ones."

* * *

One other memory came to Guilford as he was lulled to sleep by the rocking of *Argus* on the rising tide: Sullivan and Tom Compton talking about the back country, the frontiersman full of warnings: the new continent's rivers had cut their own beds, not always according to the old maps, the wildlife was dangerous, the forage so difficult that without provisions you might as well be crossing a desert. There were unnamed fevers, often fatal. And as for crossing the Alps: well, Tom said, some few trappers and hunters had thought of crossing by the old St. Gothard route; it wasn't a new idea. But tales came back, ghost stories, rumors—*plain nonsense,* Sullivan said scornfully—and maybe so, but enough to make a sane man reconsider . . . *which excludes you,* Sullivan said, and Tom grinned hugely and said, *you too, you old madman,* leaving Guilford to wonder what unspoken agreement had been reached between the two men and what might be waiting for them in the deep interior of this huge and chartless land.

CHAPTER SIX

England at last, Colin Watson thought: but it wasn't really England at all, was it? The Canadian cargo vessel steamed up the broad estuary of the Thames, its prow cutting into tidal waters the color of green tea: tropical, at least this time of year. Like visiting Bombay or Bihar. Certainly not like coming home.

He thought of the cargo rocking in the holds below. Coal from South Africa, India, Australia, a precious commodity in this age of rebellion and the fraying Empire. Tools and dies from Canada. And hundreds of crated Lee-Enfield rifles from the factory in Alberta, all bound for Kitchener's Folly, New London, making a safe place in the wilderness, for the day when an English king was restored to an English throne.

The rifles were Watson's responsibility. As soon as the ship was moored at the primitive docks he ordered his men—a few Sikhs and grumbling Canadians—to cinch and lift the pallets, while he went ashore to sign manifests for the Port Authority. The heat was stifling, and this crude wooden town was not by any stretch of the imagination London. And yet to be here brought home the reality of the Conversion of Europe, which for Watson had been a faraway event, as strange and as inherently implausible as a fairy tale, except that so many had indisputably died.

Certainly this wasn't the country he had sailed from a decade ago. He had graduated from public school without merit and taken training from the Officer Corps at Woolwich: exchanged one barracks for another, Latin declensions for artillery maneuvers. In his naïveté he had expected G.A. Henty, a dignified heroism, Ndebele rebels fleeing the point of his sword. He had arrived instead at a dusty barracks in Cairo overseeing a rabble of bored infantrymen, until that night when the sky lit up with coruscating fire and the quaking earth shook down the British Protectorate in Egypt, among so many other things. An aimless enough life, but there had been the consolations of friendship and strong drink or, more tenuously, of God and Country, until 1912 made it clear that God was a cipher and that if He existed at all He must surely have despised the English.

Britain's remaining military power had been concentrated on shoring up her possessions in India and South Africa. Southern Rhodesia had fallen, Salisbury burning like an autumn bonfire; Egypt and Sudan were lost to the Moslem rebels. Watson had been rescued from the hostile ruins of Cairo and placed on a hideously crowded troop transport bound for Canada. He spent months in a relocation barracks in the tall-timber country of British Columbia, was transferred at last to a prairie town where Kitchener's government-in-exile had established a small-arms factory.

He hadn't been an exceptional officer before 1912.

Had he changed, or had the Army changed around him? He excelled as a sort of Officer Corps shop steward; lived monkishly, survived bitter winters and dry, enervating summers with a surprising degree of patience. The knowledge that he might as easily have been beheaded by Mahdists enforced a certain humility. Eventually he was ordered to Ottawa, where military engineers were in demand as the reconstruction gathered momentum.

It was called "reconstruction" but it was also called Kitchener's Folly: the founding of a new London on the banks of a river that was only approximately the Thames. Building Jerusalem in a green and unpleasant land. Only a gesture, critics said, but even the gesture would have been impossible if not for the crippled but still powerful Royal Navy. The United States had put forward its arrogant claim that Europe should be "free and open to resettlement and without borders"—the so-called Wilson Doctrine, which meant in practice an American hegemony, an American New World. The German and French rump regimes, gutted by conflicting claims of legitimacy and the loss of European resources, backed down after a few shots were exchanged. Kitchener had been able to negotiate an exception for the British Isles, which provoked more protest. But the displaced remnants of Old Europe, lacking any real industrial base, could hardly face down the combined power of the Royal Navy and the White Fleet.

And so, a standoff. But not, Watson thought, a stable one. For instance: this civilian freighter and its military cargo. He had been assigned to oversee a clandestine shipment of arms from Halifax to London. He supposed the armory there was being stocked, but it hadn't been the first such shipment under Kitchener's private orders and likely wouldn't be the last. Watson couldn't guess why the New World needed so many rifles and Maxim guns and mortars . . . unless the peace wasn't as peaceful as it seemed.

The voyage had passed uneventfully. The seas were calm, the days so bright they might have been hammered in blue metal. Watson had used his ample free time to reconsider his life. Compared to some, he had emerged from the tragedy of 1912 relatively lightly. His parents were dead before the Conversion and he had no siblings, no wife or children to grieve for. Only a way of life. A baggage of fading memories. The past was cut loose and the years, absent compass or ballast, had passed terribly quickly. Perhaps it was fitting then that he had blown back to England at last: to this new England, this feverish pseudo-England. To this hot, prosaic Port Authority in a brick blockhouse gray with dust. He identified himself, was shown into a back room and introduced to a portly South African merchant who had volunteered his warehouse to shelter the munitions until the Armory was ready to receive them. Pierce, the man's name was. Jered Pierce.

Watson put out his hand. "Pleased to meet you, Mr. Pierce."

The South African closed Watson's hand in his own huge paw. "Likewise, sir, I'm sure."

Caroline was frightened of London but bored in the cramped warren of her uncle's store. She had taken over her aunt Alice's chores from time to time, and that was all right, but there was Lily to worry about.

Caroline didn't want her playing alone in the street, where the dust was thick and the gutters unspeakable, and indoors she was a constant terror, chasing the cat or holding tea parties with Alice's china figurines. So when Alice offered to watch Lily while Caroline took Jered's lunch to the docks, Caroline was grateful for the break. She felt suddenly unchained and deliciously alone.

She had promised herself she wouldn't think about Guilford this afternoon, and she tried to focus her attention elsewhere. A group of grubby English children—to think, the youngest of them might have been *born* in this nightmarish place!—ran past her. One boy dragged a bush jumper behind him on a string; the animal's six pale green legs pumped frantically and its dark eyes rolled with fear. Maybe it was good, that fear. Good that in this half-human world the terror worked both ways. These were thoughts she could never have shared with Guilford.

But Guilford was gone. *Well, there,* Caroline thought: *admit it.* Only disaster could bring him back before autumn, and probably not even that. She supposed he had already entered the back country of Darwinia, a place even stranger than this grim shadow of London.

She had stopped asking herself why. He had explained patiently a dozen times, and his answers made a superficial kind of sense. But Caroline knew he had other motives, unspoken, powerful as tides. The wilderness had called out to Guilford and Guilford had run away to it, and never mind the savage animals, the wild rivers, the fevers and the bandits. Like an unhappy little boy, he had run away from home.

And left her here. She hated this England, hated

even to call it that. She hated its noises, both the clatter of human commerce and the sounds of nature (worse!) that leaked through the window at night, sounds whose sources were wholly mysterious to her, a chattering as of insects; a keening as of some small, injured dog. She hated the stench of it, and she hated its poisonous forests and haunted rivers. London was a prison guarded by monsters.

She turned onto the river road. Trenches and sewers trickled their burden of waste into the Thames; raucous gulls raced over the water. Caroline gazed aloofly at the river traffic. Far off across the brown water a silt snake raised its head, its pebbled neck bent like a question mark. She watched the harbor cranes unload a sailing ship—the cost of coal had revived the Age of Sail, though these particular sails were furled into an intricacy of masts. Men hatless or turbaned wheeled crates on immense carts and dollies; sunlit wagons nursed at shadowed loading bays. She stepped into the shade of the Port Authority building, where the air was thick but faintly cooler.

Jered met her and took the lunch box from her hand. He thanked her in his absent-minded way and said, "Tell Alice I'll be home for supper. And to set another place." A tall man in a neat but threadbare uniform stood behind him, his eyes frankly focused on her. Jered finally noticed the stare. "Lieutenant Watson? This is Caroline Law, my niece."

The gaunt-faced Lieutenant nodded at her. "Miss," he said gravely.

"Mrs.," she corrected him.

"Mrs. Law."

"Lieutenant Watson will be boarding in the back room of the store for a while."

Caroline thought: *Oh, will he?* She gave the Lieutenant a more careful look.

"The city barracks is crowded," Jered said. "We take in boarders occasionally. King and Country and all."

Not my king, Caroline thought. *Not my country.*

CHAPTER SEVEN

"You know," Professor Randall said, "I think I preferred the old-fashioned God, the one who refrained from miracles."

"There are miracles in the Bible," Vale reminded him. When the professor was drinking, which was most of the time, he inclined toward a morose theology. Today Randall sat in Vale's study expounding his thoughts, buttons popping on his vest and his forehead dotted with perspiration.

"The miracles ought to have stayed there." Randall sipped an expensive bourbon. Vale had bought it with the professor in mind. "Let God smite the Sodomites. Smiting the Belgians seems somehow ludicrous."

"Be careful, Dr. Randall. He might smite *you*."

"Surely He would have exercised that privilege long ago if He were so inclined. Have I committed a blasphemy, Mr. Vale? Then let me blaspheme some more. I doubt the death of Europe was an act of divine intervention, no matter what the clergy would like us to think."

"That's not a popular opinion."

Randall glanced at the drawn curtains, the sheltering rows of books. "Am I in *public* here?"

"No."

"It looks to me like a natural disaster. The Miracle, I mean. Obviously a disaster of some unknown kind, but if a man had never seen or even heard of, say, a tornado, wouldn't that look like a miracle too?"

"Every natural disaster is called an act of God."

"When in fact the tornado is only weather, no more supernatural than the spring rain."

"No more and no less. But you're a skeptic."

"Everyone's a skeptic. Did God lean down and put his thumbprint on the Earth, Dr. Vale? William Jennings Bryan cared deeply about the answer to that question, but I don't."

"Don't you?"

"Not in that sense. Oh, a lot of people have made political careers out of religious piety and the fear of foreigners, but that won't last. Not enough foreigners or miracles to sustain the crisis. The real question is how much we'll suffer in the meantime. I mean political intolerance, fiscal meanness, even war."

Vale opened his eyes slightly, the only visible sign of the excitement that leapt in him like a flame. The gods had pricked up their ears. "War?"

Randall might know something about war. He was a curator at the Smithsonian, but he was also one of that institution's fund-raisers. He had spoken to congressional committees and had friends on the Hill.

Was that why Vale's god had taken an interest in Randall? One of the ironies of serving a god was that one didn't necessarily understand either means or ends. He knew only that something was at stake here, compared to which his own ambitions were trivial. The resolution of some eons-long plan required him to draw this portly cynic into his confidence, and so it would be. *I will be rewarded,* Vale thought. His god had promised him. Life eternal, perhaps. And a decent living in the meantime.

"War," Randall said, "or at least some martial exercise to keep the Britons in their place. The Finch expedition—you've heard of it?"

"Certainly."

"If the Finch expedition comes under Partisan attack, Congress will raise hell and blame the English. Sabers will be rattled. Young men will die." Randall leaned toward Vale, the wattled skin of his neck creased and fleshy. "There's no truth in it, is there? That you can talk to the dead?"

It was like a door opening. Vale only smiled. "What do you think?"

"What do I think? I think I'm looking at a confidence man who smells like soap and knows how to charm a widow. No offense."

"Then why do you ask?"

"Because . . . because things are different now. I think you know what I mean."

"I'm not sure I do."

"I don't believe in miracles, but . . ."

"But?"

"So much has changed. Politics, money, fashion— the map, obviously—but more than that. I see people, certain people, and there's something in their eyes, their faces. Something new. As if they have a secret they're keeping even from themselves. And that bothers me. I don't understand it. So you see, Mr. Vale, I begin as a skeptic and end as a mystic. Blame it on the bourbon. But let me ask you again. Do you speak to the dead?"

"Yes. I do."

"Honestly?"

"Honestly."

"And what do the dead tell you, Mr. Vale? What do the dead talk about?"

"Life. The fate of the world."

"Any particulars?"

"Often."

"Well, that's cryptic. My wife is dead, you know. Last year. Of pneumonia."

"I know."

"Can I talk to her?" He put his glass on the desk. "Is that actually possible, Mr. Vale?"

"Perhaps," Vale said. "We'll see."

CHAPTER EIGHT

The Navy had a shallow-draft steamer at Jeffersonville to carry the Finch expedition to the navigable
limits of the Rhine, but their departure was delayed
when the pilot and much of the crew came down with
Continental Fever. Guilford knew very little about the
disease. "A bog fever," Sullivan explained. "Exhausting
but seldom fatal. We won't be delayed long."

And a few sultry days later the vessel was ready to sail.
Guilford set up his cameras on the floating wooden
pier, his bulky dry-plate camera as well as the roll-film
box. Photography had not advanced much since the
Miracle; the long labor struggles of 1915 had shut
down Eastman Kodak for most of that year, and the
Hawk-Eye Works in Rochester had burned to the
ground. But, as such things went, both cameras were
modern and elegantly machined. Guilford had tinted
several of his own plates from the Montana expedition

and intended to do the same with his Darwinian work, and with that in mind he kept careful notes:

Fourteen members of expedition, pier at Jeffersonville, Europe: l-r standing Preston Finch, Charles Curtis Hemphill, Avery Keck, Tom Gillvany, Kenneth Donner, Paul Robertson, Emil Swensen; l-r kneeling Tom Compton, Christopher Tuckman, Ed Betts, Wilson W. Farr, Marion ("Diggs") Digby, Raymond Burke, John W. Sullivan.

   B/ground: Naval vessel Weston, *hull gunmetal gray; J/ville harbor turquoise water under deep blue sky; Rhine marshes in a light northerly wind, gold & green & cloudshadow, 8 a.m. We depart.*

And so the journey began (it always seemed to be beginning, Guilford thought; beginning and beginning again) under a raw blue sky, spider rushes tossing like wheat in the wetlands. Guilford organized his gear in the tiny windowless space allotted to him and went up top to see whether the view had changed. By nightfall the marshy land gave way to a drier, sandier riverbank, the saltwater grasses to dense pagoda bushes and pipe-organ stalks on which the wind played tuneless calliope notes. After a gaudy sunset the land became an immense, limitless darkness. Too large, Guilford thought, too empty, and too plain a token of the indifferent machinery of God.

He slept fitfully in his hammock and woke up feverish. When he stood he was unsteady on his feet—the deck plates danced a waltz—and the smell of the galley made him turn away from breakfast. By noon he was ill enough to summon the expedition's doctor, Wilson Farr, who diagnosed the Continental Fever.

"Will I die?" Guilford asked.

"You might knock on that door," Farr said, squinting through eyeglass lenses not much larger than cigar bands, "but I doubt you'll be admitted."

Sullivan came to see him during the evening, as the fever continued to rise and a rosy erythema covered Guilford's arms and legs. He found it difficult to bring Sullivan into focus and their talk drifted like a rudderless ship, the older man attempting to distract him with theories about Darwinian life, the physical structure of its common invertebrates. Finally Sullivan said, "I'm sure you're tired—" He was: unspeakably tired. "But I'll leave you with a last thought, Mr. Law. How is it, d'you suppose, that a purely Darwinian disease, a miraculous microbe, can live and multiply in the body of ordinary mortals like ourselves? Doesn't that seem more than coincidental?"

"Can't say," Guilford muttered, and turned his face to the wall.

At the height of his illness he dreamed he was a soldier pacing the margin of some airless, dusty battlefield: a picket among the dead, waiting for an unseen enemy, occasionally kneeling to drink from pools of tepid water in which his own reflection gazed back at him, his mirror-self unspeakably ancient and full of weary secrets.

The dream submerged into a long void punctuated by lightning-flashes of nausea, but by Monday he was on the mend, his fever broken, well enough to take solid food and chafe at his confinement belowdecks as the *Weston* moved deeper inland. Farr brought him a current edition of Finch's *Diluvian and Noachian Geognosy*, and Guilford was able to lose himself for a time in the several ages of the Earth, the Great Flood that had left its mark in cataclysmic reformations of the mantle, for example the Grand Canyon—unless, as Finch allowed, these features were "prior creations, endowed by their Author with the appearance of great age."

Creation modified by a worldwide flood, which had deposited fossil animals at various altitudes or buried them in mud and silt, as Eden itself must have been buried. Guilford had studied much of it before, though Finch buttressed his argument with a wealth of detail: the one hundred classifications of drift and deluvium; geological wheels in which extinct beasts were depicted in neat, separate categories. But that single phrase ("the appearance of age") troubled him. It made all knowledge provisional. The world was a stage set—it might have been built yesterday, freshly equipped with mountains and mastodon bones and human memories—which gave the Creator an unseemly interest in deceiving his human creations and made no useful distinction between the work of time and the work of a miracle. It seemed to Guilford unnecessarily complex—though why, come to think of it, should the world be simple? More shocking, perhaps, if one could render the universe and all its stars and planets in a single equation (as the European mathematician Einstein was said to have tried to do).

Finch would say that was why God had given humanity the Scriptures, to make sense of a bewildering world. And Guilford had to admire the weight and poetry, the convolute logic of Finch's work. He wasn't geologist enough to argue with it . . . though he did come away with the impression of a lofty cathedral erected on a few creaking two-by-fours.

And Sullivan's question nagged. How had Guilford

caught a Darwinian bug, if the new continent was truly a separate creation? For that matter, how was it that men could digest certain Darwinian plants and animals? Some were poisonous—far too many—but some were nourishing, even delectable. Didn't that imply a hidden similarity, a common, if distant, origin?

Well, a common Creator, at least. Common ancestry, Sullivan had implied. But that was impossible on the face of it. Darwinia had existed for hardly more than a decade . . . or might have existed much longer, but not in any form sensible to the Earth.

That was the paradox of the New Europe. Look for miracles, find history; look for history, run headlong into the blunt edge of a miracle.

Rain chased the expedition for a day and a half, the lowlands glittering under a fine silver mist. The Rhine undulated through wild forests, Darwinian forests of a particularly deep and mossy green, finally passed into a gentle plain carpeted with a broad-leafed plant Tom Compton called fingerwort. The fingerwort had begun to bloom, tiny golden blossoms giving the meadows the glow of a premature autumn. It was an inviting view, by Darwinian standards, but if you walked in the fingerwort, the frontiersman said, you wore boots to your knees or risked a case of hives caused by the plants' astringent yellow sap. Hovering insects called nettleflies swarmed the fields by day, but despite their thorny appearance they didn't bite human flesh and would even perch on a fingertip, their translucent bodies finely filigreed, like miniature Christmas ornaments.

The *Weston* anchored in mid-river. Guilford, newly

mended though still somewhat weak, went ashore to help Sullivan collect fingerwort and a dozen other meadow species. The voucher specimens were prepared between the frames of Sullivan's plant-press, the dried flats layered into a box wrapped in oilcloth. Sullivan showed him a particularly vivid orange flower common along the sandy shore: "For all its structure, it might be cousin to an English poppy. But these flowers are male, Mr. Law. Insects disperse pollen by literally devouring the stamens. The female flower—here's one: you see?—is hardly a flower at all in the conventional sense. More like a thread dipped in honey. One immense pistil, with a ciliate structure to carry the male pollen to the gynoecium. Insects are often trapped on it, and pollen with them. The pattern is common in Darwinia, non-existent among terrestrial plants. The physical resemblance is real but coincidental. As if the same process of evolution had acted through different channels—like this river, which approximates the Rhine in general but not in the specific. It drains roughly the same highlands to roughly the same ocean, but its elbows and meanders are entirely unpredictable."

And its whirlpools, Guilford thought, *and its rapids,* though the river had been gentle enough so far. Did the river of evolution pose similar hazards?

Sullivan, Gillvany, Finch and Robinson ruled the daylight hours—Digby, the expedition's cook, called them "Plants and Ants, Stones and Bones." Night belonged to Keck, Tuckman and Burke, surveyors and navigators, with their sextants and stars and maps by lamplight. Guilford enjoyed asking Keck exactly where the expedition was, because his answers were inevitably strange and wonderful: "We're entering the Cologne Embayment, Mr. Law, and we'd be seeing Düsseldorf before long, if the world hadn't been turned on its head."

Weston anchored in a broad, slow turn of the river T. Compton calls Cathedral Pool. Rhine flows from a gentle rift valley, mountainous Bergischland east of us, the Rhine Gorge somewhere ahead. Generously forested terrain: mosque trees (taller than English spp.), immense khaki-colored sage-pine, complex undergrowth. Fire perhaps a threat in dry weather. This was brown coal territory in the other Europe; Compton says wildcatters have been spotted here, adits & shallow mines already operating (marginally), and we have seen crude roads & a little river traffic. Finch claims to find evidence of coking coal, says this area will be an iron and steel center someday, God willing, with pig iron from the Oolitic scarps of the Cotes de Moselle, esp. if U.S. keeps continent from being "fenced with borders."

Sullivan says coal is more evidence of an ancient Darwinia, a stratigraphic sequence caused by the Tertiary uplift of the Rhine Plateau. Real question, he says, is whether Darwinian geology is identical to old European geology, changes due solely to different weathering and river meanders; or whether Darwinian geology is only approximately the same, different in its finer points—which may affect our survey of the Alps: an unexpected gorge at Mount Genevre or Brenner would send us chastened back to J'ville.

Weather fine, blue skies, the river current stronger now.

It couldn't last, Guilford knew, this leisurely river cruise, with a well-stocked galley and long days with the camera and plant-press, graveled beaches free of troublesome insects or animals, nights as rich with stars as any Guilford had seen in Montana. The *Weston* moved farther up the rift valley of the Rhine and the gorge walls grew steeper, the scarps more dramatic, until it was easy for Guilford to imagine the old Europe here, the vanished castles ("Eberbach," Keck would intone, "Marksburg, Sooneck, Kaiserpfalz . . ."), massed Teutonic warriors with spikes and tassles on their helmets.

But this was not Old Europe and the evidence was everywhere: thornfish fluttering in the shallows, the cinammon reek of sage-pine forests (neither sage nor pine but a tall tree that grew branches in a spiral terrace), the night cries of creatures yet unnamed. Human beings had been this way—Guilford saw the occasional passing raft, plus evidence of tow-ropes, trappers' huts, woodsmoke, fish weirs—but only very recently.

And there was, he found, a kind of comfort in the emptiness of the country enfolded around him, his own terrible and wonderful anonymity in it, making footprints where no footprints had been and knowing that the land would soon erase them. The land demanded nothing, gave nothing more than itself.

But the easy days couldn't last. The Rheinfelden was ahead. The *Weston* would have to turn back. *And then,* Guilford thought, *we'll see what it means, to be truly alone, in all this unknown world of rock and forest.*

The Rheinfelden Cascade, or Rhine River Falls, head of navigation. This is as far as Tom Compton has been. Some trappers, he says, claim to have portaged as far as Lake Constance. But trappers are inclined to boast.

The falls are not spectacular by comparison to, say, Niagara, but they gate the river quite effectively. Mist hangs heavy, a great pale thunderhead above the sweating rocks & forested hills. Water a fast green flow, sky darkening with rain clouds, every rock and crevice invaded by a moss-like plant with delicate white blooms.

Having observed & photographed the cascade we retreat to a point of portage: Tom Compton knows of a local fur breeder who might be willing to sell us animals for pack.

Postscriptum to Caroline & Lily: Miss you both greatly, feel as if I'm talking to you in these pages even though I am very far away—deep in the Lost (or New) Continent, strangeness on every horizon.

The fur breeder turned out to be a truculent German-American who called himself "Erasmus" and who had corralled for breeding, on a crude farm a distance from the river, an enormous herd of fur snakes.

Fur snakes, Sullivan explained, were the continent's most exploitable resource, at least for now. Herbivorous herd animals, they were common in the upland meadows and probably throughout the eastern steppes; Donnegan had encountered them in the foothills of the Pyrenees, which suggested they were widely distributed. Guilford was fascinated and spent much of the remainder of the day at Erasmus's kraal, despite the pervasive odor, which was one of the fur snakes' less attractive points.

The animals resembled, Guilford thought, not so much snakes as grubs—bloated, pale "faces" with cowlike eyes, cylindrical bodies, six legs obscured under ropes of matted hair. As a resource they were a virtual Sears-Roebuck catalog: fur for clothing, hides for tanning, fat for tallow, and a bland but edible meat. Snake furs were the Rhine's staple of commerce, and snake fur, Sullivan asserted, had even made an appearance in New York fashion circles. Guilford supposed the smell didn't survive the shearing, or who would want such a coat, even in a New York winter?

More important, the fur snakes made workable pack animals, without which the survey of the Alps would be a great deal more difficult. Preston Finch had already retired to Erasmus' hut to negotiate for the purchase of fifteen or twenty of the animals. And Erasmus must drive a hard bargain, since by the time Diggs had his mess tent set up Finch and Erasmus were still bargaining—raised voices were audible.

At last Finch stormed out of the sod hut, ignoring dinner. "Horrible man," he muttered. "Partisan sympathizer. This is hopeless."

The Navy pilot and crew remained aboard the *Weston*, preparing to sail back down the Rhine with specimens, collections, field notes, letters home. Guilford sat with Sullivan, Keck, and the frontiersman Tom Compton on a bluff above the river, enjoying plates of Digby's reconstituted corned-beef hash and watching the sun wester.

"The trouble with Preston Finch," Sullivan said, "is that he doesn't know how to yield a point."

"Nor does Erasmus," Tom Compton said. "He's not a Partisan, just a general-purpose jackass. Spent three years in Jeffersonville brokering hides, but nobody could tolerate the man's company for long. He's not made for human companionship."

"The animals are interesting," Guilford said. Like thoats, in the Burroughs novel. Martian mules.

"Well then maybe you should take a picture of 'em," Tom Compton said, and rolled his eyes.

By morning it was obvious negotiations had collapsed altogether. Finch wouldn't speak to Erasmus, though he begged the pilot of the *Weston* to hold up at least another day. Sullivan, Gillvany, and Robinson went specimen-collecting in the forests near Erasmus' grazing pastures, obviously hoping the issue would by some miracle be settled before they returned to camp. And Guilford set up his camera by the kraal.

Which brought Erasmus stomping out of his lopsided sod hut like an angry dwarf. Guilford had not had any personal introduction to the herder and he tried to refrain from flinching.

Erasmus—not much above five foot tall, his face lost in Biblical curls of beard, dressed in patched denim overalls and a snakeskin serape, stopped a careful distance from Guilford, frowning and breathing noisily. Guilford nodded politely and went about the business of adjusting his tripod. Let the Old Man of the Mountain make the first move.

It took time, but Erasmus eventually spoke. "What exactly do you think you're doing?"

"Photographing the animals, if that's all right."

"You might have asked first."

Guilford didn't respond. Erasmus breathed a few minutes more, then: "So that's a camera, is it?"

"Yes sir," Guilford said, "a Kodak plate camera."

"You take plate photos? Like in *National Geographic*?"

"Just about exactly like."

"You know that magazine—*National Geographic*?"

"I've worked for it."

"Eh? When?"

"Last year. Deep Creek Canyon. Montana."

"Those were your pictures? December 1919?"

Guilford gave the snake herder a longer look. "Are you a member of the Society, Mr., uh, Erasmus?"

"Just call me Erasmus. You?"

"Guilford Law."

"Well, Mr. Guilford Law, I'm not a member of the National Geographic Society, but the magazine comes upriver once in a while. I take it in trade. Reading material is hard to come by. I have your photographs." He hesitated. "These pictures of my stock—they'll be published?"

"Perhaps," Guilford said. "I don't make those decisions."

"I see." Erasmus pondered the possibilities. Then he drew in a great gulp of the heavy kraal air. "Would you care to come back to my cabin, Guilford Law? Now that Finch is gone, maybe we can talk."

Guilford admired the snake farmer's collection of *National Geographic* stacked on a wooden shelf—fifteen issues in all, most of them water-stained and dog-eared, some held together with binding twine, sharing space with equally tattered obscene postcards, cheap Westerns, and a recent *Argosy* Guilford hadn't seen. He praised the meager library and said nothing about the pressed-earth floor, the reek of crudely cured hides, the oven-like heat and dim light, or the filthy trestle table decorated with evidence of meals long finished.

At Erasmus' prodding Guilford reminisced for a time about Deep Creek Canyon, the Gallatin River, Walcott's tiny fossil crustaceans: crayfish from the siliceous shale, unbelievably ancient, unless you accepted Finch's caveats about the age of the Earth. The irony was that Erasmus, an old Darwinian hand who had been born in Milwaukee and lived downstream from the alien Rheinfelden, found the idea of Montana creek beds intensely exotic.

Talk drifted at last to the subject of Preston Finch.

"Don't mean to offend," Erasmus said, "but he's a pompous blowhard, and that's that. Wants twenty head of snake at ten dollars a head, if you can imagine such a thing."

"The price isn't fair?"

"Oh, the *price* is fair—more than fair, actually; that's not the problem."

"You don't want to sell twenty head?"

"Sure I do. Twenty head at that price would keep me through the winter."

"Then, if I may ask, what's the problem?"

"Finch! Finch is the problem! He comes into my home with his nose in the air and talks to me like I'm a child. Finch! I wouldn't sell Preston Finch a road apple for a fortune if I was starving."

Guilford considered the impasse. "Erasmus," he said finally, "we can do more and go farther with those animals than without. The more successful the survey, the more likely you are to see my photographs in print. Maybe even in the *Geographic*."

"My animals?"

"Your animals and you yourself, if you're willing to pose."

The snake breeder stroked his beard. "Well. Well. I *might* pose. But it makes no difference. I won't sell my animals to Finch."

"I understand. What if I asked you to sell them to me?"

Erasmus blinked and slowly smiled. "Then maybe we have the making of a bargain. But look, Guilford Law, there's more to it. The animals will carry your boats above the Falls and you can probably follow the river as far as the Bodensee, but if you want pack animals into the Alps someone will have to herd them from above the falls to the shore of the lake."

"You can do that?"

"I've done it before. Lot of herds winter there. That's where most of my stock comes from. I would be willing to do it for you, sure—for a price."

"I'm not authorized to negotiate, Erasmus."

"Bullshit. Let's talk terms. Then you can go dicker with the treasury or whatever you have to do."

"All right . . . but one more thing."

"What?"

"Are you willing to part with that *Argosy* on your shelf?"

"Eh? No. Hardly. Not unless you have something to trade for it."

Well, Guilford thought, maybe Dr. Farr wouldn't miss his copy of *Diluvian and Noachian Geognosy.*

Erasmus's farm below the Rheinfelden. His kraal, the fur snakes. Erasmus with his herd. Storm clouds rising in the NW; Tom Compton predicts rain.

Postscriptum. With the aid of our "Martian mules" we will be able to portage the folding motor-launches— clever & light constructions, white oak and Michigan pine, sixteen-footers with watertight storage and detachable skags—and travel above the cascades probably as far as Lake Constance (which Erasmus calls the Bodensee). All that we have collected and learned to date sails back to J'ville with the Weston.

Preston Finch I think resentful of my parley with Erasmus—he looks at me from under his solar topee like an irritable Jehovah—but Tom Compton seems impressed: he is at least willing to speak to me lately, not just suffer my presence on Sullivan's account. Even offered me a draw on his notorious & spittle-drenched pipe, which I politely declined, though perhaps that put us back to

Square One—he has taken to waving his oilcloth bag of dried leaf at me & laughing in a manner not altogether flattering.

We march in the morning if weather is at all reasonable. Home seems farther away than ever, & the land grows stranger by the day.

CHAPTER NINE

Caroline adjusted to the rhythms of her uncle Jered's household, strange as those rhythms were. Like London, or most of the world these days, there was something provisional about her uncle's home. He kept odd hours. Often it was left to Alice (and more often now, Caroline herself) to mind the store. She found herself learning the uses of nuts and bolts, of winches and penny nails and quicklime. And there was the mildly entertaining enigma of Colin Watson, who slept on a cot in the storeroom and crept in and out of the building like a restless spirit. Periodically he would take an evening meal at the Pierce table, where he was faultlessly polite but about as talkative as a brick. He was gaunt, not gluttonous, and he blushed easily, Caroline thought, for a soldier. Jered's table talk was sometimes coarse.

Lily had adjusted easily enough to her new environment, less easily to the absence of her father. She still asked from time to time where Daddy was. "Across the English Channel," Caroline told her, "where no one has been before."

"Is he safe?"

"Very safe. And very brave."

Lily asked about her father most often at bedtime. It was Guilford who had always read to her, a ritual that left Caroline feeling faintly and unreasonably jealous. Guilford read to Lily with a wholeheartedness Caroline couldn't match, distrustful as she was of the books Lily liked, their unwholesome preoccupation with fairies and monsters. But Caroline took up the task in his absence, mustering as much enthusiasm as she could. Lily needed the reassurance of a story before she could wholly relax, abandon vigilance, sleep.

Caroline envied the simplicity of the ritual. Too often, she carried her own burden of doubt well into the morning hours.

Still, the summer nights were warm and the air rich with a fragrance that was, though strange, not entirely unpleasant. Certain native plants, Jered said, blossomed only at night. Caroline imagined alien poppies, heavy-headed, narcotic. She learned to leave her bedroom window open and let the flowered breezes play over her face. She learned, as the summer progressed, to sleep more easily.

It was Lily's sleeplessness, as July waned, that served as notice that something had changed in Jered's house.

Lily with dark bands beneath her eyes. Lily picking dazedly at breakfast. Lily silent and grim at the dinner table, cringing away from Caroline's uncle.

Caroline found herself unwilling to ask what was wrong—wanting nothing to *be* wrong, hating the idea of yet another crisis. She summoned her courage one warm night after another chapter of "Dorothy," as Lily called these repetitious fables, when Lily was still restless.

The little girl drew her blanket above her chin. "It wakes me up when they fight."

"When *who* fight, Lily?"

"Aunt Alice and Uncle Jered."

Caroline didn't want to believe it. Lily must be hearing other voices, perhaps from the street.

But Lily's room had only a postage stamp of a window, and it looked out on the back alley, not the busy market street. Lily's room was in fact a reconstructed closet off the rear hall, a closet Jered had converted into a tiny but comfortable bedchamber for his niece. Enough space for a girl, her bear, her book, and for her mother to sit a while and read.

But the closet shared a wall with Jered and Alice's bedroom, and these walls weren't especially thick. Did Jered and Alice argue, late at night, when they thought no one could hear? They seemed happy enough to Caroline . . . a little aloof, perhaps, moving in separate spheres the way older couples often do, but fundamentally content. They couldn't have argued often before or Lily would have complained or at least showed symptoms.

The arguments must have started after Colin Watson arrived.

Caroline told Lily to ignore the sounds. Aunt Alice and Uncle Jered weren't really angry, they were only having disagreements. They really loved each other very much. Lily seemed to accept this, nodded and closed her eyes. Her demeanor improved a little over the next few days, though she was still shy of her uncle. Caroline put the matter out of her mind and didn't think of it again until the night she fell asleep halfway through a chapter of Dorothy and woke, well after midnight, cramped and uncomfortable, next to Lily.

Jered had been out. It was the sound of the door that woke her. Lieutenant Watson had been with him; Jered said a few inaudible words before the Lieutenant retired to his cellar. Then came Jered's heavy tread in the corridor, and Caroline, afraid for no reason she could define, pulled Lily's door closed.

She felt a little absurd, and more than a little claustrophobic sitting cross-legged in this lightless chamber in her nightgown. She listened to the unbroken rhythm of her daughter's breath, gentle as a sigh. Jered rumbled down the hallway on his way to bed, trailing a steam-engine reek of tobacco and beer.

Now she heard Alice's low voice greet him, almost as deep as a man's, and Jered's, all chest and belly. At first Caroline couldn't distinguish the words, and she couldn't hear more than a phrase even when they began to raise their voices. But what she did hear was chilling.

. . . *don't know how you could get involved.* . . . (Alice's voice.)

. . . *doing my Goddamned duty* . . . (Jered.)

Then Lily woke and needed comforting, and Caroline stroked her golden hair and soothed her.

. . . *you know he might be killed.* . . .

. . . *nothing of the kind!*

. . . *Caroline's husband! Lily's father!*

. . . *I don't rule the world* . . . *I didn't* . . . *wouldn't* . . .

And then quite suddenly the voices lapsed into silence. She imagined Jered and Alice dividing the big bed into territory, marking borders with shoulders and hips, as she and Guilford had sometimes done, after an argument.

They know something, she thought. *Something about Guilford, something they don't want to tell me.*

Something bad. Something frightening.

But she was too tired, too shocked to make sense of it. She kissed Lily mechanically and retreated to her own room, to her open window and lazily twining curtains and the odd perfume of the English night. She doubted she could sleep, but slept in spite of herself; she didn't want to dream but dreamed incoherently of Jered, of Alice, of the sad-eyed young Lieutenant.

CHAPTER TEN

The summer of 1920 was a chill one, at least in Washington, for which people blamed the Russian volcanoes, the fiery line of geologic disturbance which marked the eastern border of the Miracle and which had been erupting sporadically since 1912, at least according to the refugees who left Vladivostok before the Japanese troubles. Blame it on volcanoes, Elias Vale thought, on sunspots, on God, the gods—all one and the same. He was simply glad to step out of the dreary rain, even into the drearier Main Hall of the National Museum, currently under renovation—work which had been postponed in 1915 and each of the four following years, but for which Eugene Randall had finally prodded funds from the national treasury.

Randall turned out to be an administrator who took his work seriously, the worst kind of boor. And a lonely man, compounding the vice. He had insisted on bringing Vale to the museum the way mothers insist on displaying their infants: the admiration is expected and its absence would be considered an insult.

I am not your friend, Vale thought. *Don't humiliate yourself.*

"So much of this work was postponed for so long," Randall was saying. "But at last we're making headway. The problem is not what we lack but what we have— the sheer *volume* of it—like packing a trunk that's a size too small. Whale skeletons to the South Hall, second story, west wing, and that means marine invertebrates to the North Hall, which means the picture gallery has to be enlarged, the Main Hall renovated. . . ."

Vale gazed blankly at the scaffolding, the tarpaulins protecting the marbled floor. Today was Sunday. The workers had gone home. The museum was gloomy as a funeral parlor, the corpse on view being Man and All His Works. Rain curtained the leaded windows.

"Not that we're rich." Randall led him up a flight of stairs. "There was a time when we had almost enough money—the old days—bequests thick as fleas, it seems now. The permanent fund is a shadow of itself, only a few residual legacies, useless railroad bonds, a dribble of interest. Congressional appropriations are all we can count on, and Congress has been chary since the Miracle, though they're paying for the repairs, steel stacks for the library . . ."

"The Finch expedition," Vale added, moved by an impulse that might have been his god's.

"Aye, and I pray they're safe, the situation being what it is. We have six sitting congressmen on the Board of Regents, but in matters of state I doubt we rank alongside the English Question or the Japanese Question. Though I may be maligning Mr. Cabot Lodge."

For weeks Vale's god had left him more or less alone,

and that was pleasant: pleasant to focus on simple mortal concerns, his "indulgences," as he thought of his drinking and whoring. Now, it seemed, the divine attention had been once again provoked. He felt its presence in his belly. But why here? Why this building? Why Eugene Randall?

As well ask, Why a god? Why *me?* The real mysteries.

On into the labyrinth, to Randall's oak-lined office, where he had papers to pick up, a stop between the latest afternoon salon of Mrs. Sanders-Moss and an evening seance, the latter strictly private, like an appointment with an abortionist.

"I know there's tension with the English on the issue of arming the Partisans. I fervently hope no harm comes to Finch, unlikable as he may be. You know, Elias, there are religious factions who want to keep America out of the New Europe altogether, and they're not shy about writing to the Appropriations Committee. . . . Ah, here we are." A manila file extracted from his desk top. "That's all I need. Now I suppose it's on to the infinite . . . no, I can't joke about it." Shyly: "This isn't meant to insult you, Elias, but I do feel the fool."

"I assure you, Dr. Randall, you're not being foolish."

"Pardon me if I'm not convinced. Not yet. I—" He paused. "Elias, you look pale. Are you all right?"

"I need—"

"What?"

"Some air."

"Well, I—Elias?"

Vale fled the room.

He fled the room because his god was rising and it was going to be bad, that was obvious, a full *visitation*, he felt it, and the manifestation had clogged his throat and soured his stomach.

He meant to retrace his steps to the door—Randall vainly calling after him—but Vale took a wrong turn and found himself in a lightless gallery where the bones of some great alien fish, some benthic Darwinian monster, had been suspended by cords from the ceiling.

Control yourself. He managed to stand still. Randall would have no patience with operatic gestures.

But he desperately wanted to be alone, at least for a moment. In time the disorientation would pass, the god would manipulate his arms and legs, and Vale himself would become a passive, semiconscious observer in the shell of his own body. The agony would retreat and eventually be forgotten. But now it was too imminent, too violent. He was still himself—vulnerable and afraid—and yet he was *in a presence,* surrounded by a virulently dangerous other Self.

He sank to the floor begging for oblivion; but the god was slow, the god was patient.

The inevitable questions ran through his tortured mind: *Why me? Why am I elected for this duty, whatever it is?* And to Vale's surprise, this time the god offered replies: wordless certainties, to which Vale appended inadequate words.

Because you died, the phantom god responded.

This was chilling. *I'm* not *dead,* Vale protested.

Because you drowned in the Atlantic Ocean in 1917 when an American troop ship took a German torpedo.

The god's voice sounded like Vale's grandfather, the ponderous tone the old man had adopted when he harped about Bull Run. The god's voice was made of memories. His memories, Elias Vale's memories.

But the words were wrong. This was nonsense. It was insanity.

You died the day I took you.

In an empty and ruined brick building by the Ohio River. How could both those things be true? A warehouse by a river, a violent death in the Atlantic?

He whispered, "I died?"

Wrenching silence, except for Randall's timid footsteps in the dark beyond the bone-draped gallery.

"Then," Vale asked, "is this—the Afterlife?"

He received no answer but a vision: the museum in flames, and then a blackened ruin, and stinking green gods walking like insectile conquerors among the toppled bricks and heatless ashes.

"Mr. Vale? Elias?"

He looked up at Randall and managed a rictus of a grin. "I'm sorry. I—"

"Are you ill?"

"Yes. A little."

"Perhaps we should call off the, uh, meeting tonight."

"No need." Vale felt himself stand. He faced Randall. "Occupational hazard. I only need a breath of air. Couldn't find the door."

"You should have said something. Well, follow me."

Out into the cold of the early evening. Out into a rainy, empty street. Out into the Void, Elias Vale thought. Somewhere deep inside himself, he felt an urge to scream.

CHAPTER ELEVEN

Keck and Tuckman couldn't say what hazards might lie ahead. According to their instruments, the new Rheinfelden was at roughly the location of the old European cascade, but the approximation was crude, and the white-water rapids that used to run below the falls were either absent or buried under a deeper, slower Rhine. Sullivan saw this as more evidence for a Darwinian that had evolved somehow *in parallel* with the old Europe, in which the ancient tumble of a single rock might have changed the course of a river, at least within certain limits. Finch put it down to the absence of human intervention: "The old Rhine was fished, locked, navigated, and exploited for more than a thousand years. Naturally it came to follow a different course." Whereas this Europe was untouched, Edenic.

Guilford reserved his opinion. Either explanation seemed plausible (or equally implausible). He knew only that he was tired: tired of distributing supplies

among the crude saddlebags of Erasmus' snakes; tired
of manhandling the big Stone-Galloway boats, whose
much touted "lightness" turned out to be a relative
thing; tired of pacing the fur snakes and their load as
they portaged the Rheinfelden in a miserable drizzle.

They came down at last to a pebble-sharp beach from
which the boats could be safely launched. Supplies
were divided equally between the waterproof fore-and-
aft compartments of the boats and the saddlebags of
the fur snakes. Erasmus would herd the animals to their
summer pastures at the eastern extremity of Lake Constance and had agreed to meet the expedition there.

Launching the boats would have to wait for morning. There was only enough daylight left to pitch the
tents, to nurse fresh aches, to pry open ration tins, and
to watch the swollen river, green as a beetle's back and
wide as Boston Bay, as it hurried toward the falls.

Guilford did not wholly trust the boats.

Preston Finch had commissioned and named them:
the *Perspicacity*, the *Orinoco*, the *Camille* (after Finch's
late wife), and the *Ararat*. The motors were prototypes,
small but powerful, screws protected from rocks by the
skags and the engine compartments from high water
by a series of canvas shields. The boats would do well
enough, Guilford thought, if the Rhine remained relatively placid as far as Lake Constance. But they would
be worse than useless against white water. And their advantage in weight was offset by the need to pack jerri-
cans of gasoline, a stiff load to portage and a waste of
potentially useful space.

But the boats would be cached at the Bodensee and
would function more than adequately on the return
trip, stripped of motors and absent gasoline, with the

river current to carry them. And they worked satisfactorily the first day out, though the noise of the engines was deafening and the stink of exhaust obnoxious. Guilford enjoyed being close to the water rather than riding above it—to be a part of the river, resisted by its flow and rocked by its eddies, a small thing in a large land. The rain passed, the day brightened, and the gorge walls were gaudy with vine-like growths and capped with gnarled pagoda trees. *Surely we have outpaced Erasmus and his snakes,* Guilford thought, and Erasmus might be the only other human being within a hundred square miles, barring a few vagrant Partisans. *The land owns us now,* Guilford thought. *The land, the water, the air.*

Camp where a nameless creek enters the Rhine. Pool of calm water, Keck fishing for thorn and blue maddies. Miniature sage-pine among the rocks, foliage almost turquoise, dwarfed by winds & a rocky soil.

Postscriptum. The fish are abundant & will make a palatable evening meal, though Diggs proclaims his martyrdom as he cleans them. Offal goes into the river— billyflies chase it downstream. (The billyflies will bite if provoked; we sleep under mosquito netting tonight. Other insects not especially common or venomous, although a crablike creature made off with one of Keck's fish—nabbed it from a wet rock & scuttled into the water with it! "Claws like a lobster," Keck says cheerfully. "Count your toes, gentlemen!")

The next day they were forced to portage a rocky rapids, a grim task without pack animals. The boats were muscled ashore and the route surveyed; fortunately the pebbled river margin remained fairly broad and there was a ready supply of driftwood—dry, hollow flute logs that had been tumbled against the gorge wall by spring floods—to serve as makeshift rollers. But the portage exhausted everyone and wasted a day; by sundown Guilford was only just able to drag his aching bones under the mosquito netting and sleep.

In the morning he loaded and helped launch the *Perspicacity*, alongside Sullivan, Gillvany, and Tom Compton. *Perspicacity* was last in the water; by the time they reached mid-river the lead boat, Finch's *Ararat*, was already out of sight beyond the next bend. The river ran fast and shallow here and Guilford sat foremost watching for rocks, ready with an oar to steer the keel away from obstacles.

They were making steady progress against the current when the motor coughed and died.

The sudden silence startled Guilford. He was able to hear the drone of the *Camille*, a hundred yards ahead, and the lapping of water, and Sullivan swearing quietly as he pulled back the canvas shield and opened the motor compartment.

Without an engine the *Perspicacity* slowed at once, balanced between momentum and river current. The Rhine gorge was suddenly static. Only water moved. No one spoke.

Then Tom Compton said, "Loose the other oars, Mr. Gillvany. We need to turn and make for shore."

"Only a little water in the compartment," Sullivan said. "I can restart the motor. I think."

But Tom Gillvany, who did not much care for river travel, nodded uneasily and unhooked the oars.

Guilford used his own oar to bring the boat around. He took a moment to wave at *Camille*, signaling the problem, and Keck waved back acknowledgment and began to turn. But the *Camille* was already alarmingly far away. And now the shore had begun to reverse, to slip away. The Rhine had taken control of *Perspicacity*.

The pebbled beach from which they had launched swept past. "Oh, Jesus," Gillvany moaned, paddling hectically. Sullivan, white-faced, abandoned the engine and took up an oar. "Make a steady pace," Tom Compton said, his low voice not unlike the rumble of the water. "When we're close enough I'll snub the boat. Here, give me the bow line."

Guilford thought of the rapids. He supposed everyone in the boat had begun to think of the rapids. He could see them now, a line of white into which the river vanished. The shore seemed no closer.

"Steady!" the frontiersman barked. "Dammit, Gillvany, you're flapping like a fuckin' bird! *Dig* the water!"

Gillvany was a small man and chastened by the outburst. He bit his lip and pushed his oar into the river. Guilford worked in silence, arms straining. Sweat drenched his face, a tang of salt when he licked his lips. The day was no longer cool. Darwinian shore birds, like coal-black sparrows, swooped blithely overhead.

The river bottom was jagged now, shark-fin rocks trailing white wakes as *Perspicacity* neared shore. There was a quick hollow crack from the aft of the boat: "Lost a skag," Sullivan said breathlessly. "Pull!"

The next snap was the screw, Guilford guessed; it sent a grinding shudder through the boat. Gillvany gasped, but no one spoke. The roar of the water was loud.

The shore became a tumble of boulders, close but forbidding, rushing past perilously quickly. Tom Compton swore and grabbed the bow rope, stood and leaped from the boat. He landed crushingly hard on a slick flat-topped rock, rope unwinding like an angry snake beside him as Guilford paddled vainly against the current. The frontiersman righted himself hastily and snubbed the rope around a granite spur just as *Perspicacity* drew it taut. The rope sang and whipped from the water. Guilford braced himself as the boat bucked and twisted wildly toward the rocks. Sullivan fell against the motor block. Gillvany, unprepared, rolled over the starboard side into the wash.

Guilford threw a coil of rope into the water where Gillvany had disappeared, but the entomologist was gone—vanished into the quick green water and away, no wake or eddy to mark his passage.

Then *Perspicacity* struck the rocks and heeled up under the fierce pressure of the Rhine, Guilford clinging to an oarlock with all the strength that was left in him.

Above the unnamed rapids, stranded for two days now. Perspicacity under repair. Skag and screw can be replaced from spares.

Tom Gillvany cannot.

Postscriptum. I did not know Tom Gillvany well. He was a quiet, studious man. According to Dr. Sullivan, a scholar respected in his field. Lost to the river. We searched downstream but could not recover his body. I will remember his shy smile, his sobriety, and his unashamed fascination with the New Continent.

We all mourn his passing. The mood is grim.

A hollow where the Rhine gorge is rocky and steep, a sort of natural cavern, shallow but tall as a church: Cathedral Cavern, Preston Finch has named it. Cairn of stone to honor Dr. Gillvany. Driftwood marker with legend inscribed by Keck with a rock hammer, In Memory of Dr. Thomas Markland Gillvany, and the date.

Postscriptum. Silent as we are, there is not much to hear: the river, the wind (rain has closed us in once more), Diggs humming Rock of Ages *as he stokes the fire.*

We have been bloodied by this land.

Tomorrow, if all goes well, we launch again. And onward. I miss my wife and child.

Because he could not sleep, Guilford left his tent after midnight and navigated past the embers of the fire to the mouth of the cave, outlined in steely moonlight, where Sullivan sat with a small brass telescope, peering into the night sky. The rain had passed. Mare's-tail clouds laced the moon. Most of the sky above the Rhine gorge was bright with stars. Guilford cleared his throat and made a space for himself amidst the rock and sand.

The older man looked at him briefly. "Hello, Guilford. Mind the billyflies. Though they're sparse tonight. They don't like the wind."

"Are you an astronomer as well as a botanist, Dr. Sullivan?"

"Strictly an amateur stargazer. And I'm looking at a planet, actually, not a star."

Guilford asked which planet had attracted Sullivan's attention. "Mars," the botanist said.

"The red planet," Guilford said, which was just about the sum of his knowledge concerning that heavenly body, except that it possessed two moons and had been the subject of some fine writing by Burroughs and the Englishman, Wells.

"Less red than it once was," Sullivan said. "Mars has darkened since the Miracle."

"Darkened?"

"Mars has seasons, Guilford, just like Earth. The ice

caps retreat in summer, the darker areas expand. The planet appears reddish because it is probably a desert of oxidized iron. But lately the red is palliated. Lately," he said, bracing the telescope against his knee, "there are shades of blue. The shift has been measured spectrographically; the eye is a little less sensitive."

"Meaning what?"

Sullivan shrugged. "No one knows."

Guilford peered into the moon-silvered sky. The Conversion of Europe was mystery enough. Daunting to think of another planet grown similarly wild and strange. "May I use the telescope, Dr. Sullivan? I'd like to see Mars myself."

He would look the mystery in the eye: he was that brave, at least.

But Mars was only a swimming point of light, lost in the Darwinian heavens, and the wind was chill and Dr. Sullivan was not talkative, and after a time Guilford went back to his tent and slept restlessly until morning.

CHAPTER TWELVE

The end product of fear, fear not baseless but without any tangible object, was anesthesia. Each new omen seemed bleaker, until bleakness became the landscape through which Caroline must toil, eyes averted, registering nothing. Or at least as little as possible.

She told her aunt that Lily was having trouble sleeping. Alice turned and looked absently into the depths of the dry goods store, past rows of stitched white grain bags, into a latticework of sunbeams from the high rear window. She wiped her hands on her apron. "Jered comes in at odd hours. He may have disturbed her, walking down the hall. I'll speak to him."

The secret was kept, she was not privy to it, and Caroline was privately relieved. Lily slept better after that, though she had picked up nervous tics in the absence of her father: tugging her lower lip until it was sore, twining her hair around her fingers. She hated to be left alone.

Colin Watson continued to haunt the house, a smoky presence. Caroline tried to draw him into conversation but he said little about his life or work; only that the Service seemed to have forgotten him, that he had few duties to perform save rounds of guard duty at the Armory: he had been misplaced, he seemed to suggest, in Kitchener's obsessive shuffling of the British forces. He couldn't say why there were so many soldiers in London these days. "It's like a plague," Caroline said, but the Lieutenant wouldn't be provoked. He only smiled.

Soldiers and warships. Caroline hated to go down to the harbor now; most of the British Navy seemed to have anchored there in the last few weeks, battered dreadnaughts bristling with guns. The women in the market street talked about war.

War with whom, for what purpose, Caroline couldn't fathom. It might have something to do with the Partisans, the returned dregs of Europe, their ridiculous claims and threats; or the Americans or the Japanese or—she tried not to pay attention.

"I miss Daddy," Lily announced. It was Sunday. The dry-goods store was closed; Jered and Alice were taking inventory and Caroline had brought Lily to the river, to the blue river under a hot blue sky, to watch the sailing ships or see a river monster. Lily liked the silt snakes as much as Caroline hated them. Their great necks, their cold black eyes.

"Daddy will come back soon," she told her daughter, but Lily only frowned, hardened against consolation. *Faith is a virtue*, Caroline thought, *but nothing is certain. Nothing. We pretend, for the sake of children.*

How perfect Lily was, sitting splay-legged on a log bench with her doll in her lap. "Lady" was the doll's name. "Lady, Lady," Lily sang to herself, a two-note song. The doll's flesh-colored paint had been worn down to bone porcelain on her cheeks and forehead. "Lady, dance," Lily sang.

It was at that moment, an uneasy peace brief as the tolling of a bell, that Caroline saw Jered hurrying down a log-paved embankment toward her. Her heart skipped a beat. Something was wrong. She could see the trouble in his eyes, in his walk. Without thinking, she put her hands on Lily's shoulders; Lily said, "That hurts!"

Jered stood before her breathlessly. "I wanted to talk to you, Caroline," he said, "before you saw the *Times*."

He was patient and compassionate, but in the end Caroline remembered it as if she had read it in the brutal cadences of a newspaper headline:

PARTISANS ATTACK U.S. STEAMER
"Weston" Returns Damaged to Jeffersonville,

and then, more terrifying:

Fate of Finch Expedition Unknown.

But these were only naked facts. Far worse was the knowledge that Guilford was beyond her help, impossibly far away, possibly injured, possibly dead. Guilford dead in the wilderness and Caroline and Lily alone.

She asked her uncle the awful question: "Is he dead?" she whispered, while the earth twisted under her feet and Lily ran to the bench where Lady had been abandoned, eyelids drooping, with her skirt hiked over her head.

"Caroline, no one knows. But the ships were attacked well after they put the expedition ashore at the Rheinfelden. There's no reason to believe Guilford has been hurt."

They will all lie to me now, Caroline thought: *make me a widow and tell me he's fine.* She turned her face to the sky, and the sunlight through her eyelids was the color of blood.

CHAPTER THIRTEEN

For the purpose of the séance they drove to Eugene Randall's apartment, a sad widower's digs in Virginia, one wall a shrine to his deceased spouse Louisa Ellen. Stepping inside was like stepping into the archaeology of a life, decades reduced to potsherds and clay tablets. Randall kept the lights low and proceeded directly to the liquor cabinet.

"I don't want to be drunk," he explained. "I just don't want to be sober."

"I could use a shot myself," Elias Vale said.

Inevitably, Vale lost himself to his god.

He thought of it as "summoning" the god, but in fact it was Vale who was summoned, Vale who was used. He had never volunteered for this duty. He had never been given a choice. If he had resisted . . . but that didn't bear thinking about.

Randall wanted to speak to his lost Louisa Ellen, the horse-faced woman in the photographs, and Vale made a show of calling to her across the Great Barrier, eyes rolled to conceal his own agony. In fact he was retreating into himself, stepping out of the god's path, becoming passive. No longer his, the need to draw breath, the rebellious tides of bile and blood.

He was only distantly conscious of Randall's half-hearted questions, though the emotional gist of it was painfully obvious. Randall, the lifelong rationalist, wanted desperately to believe he could speak to Louisa Ellen, who had been carried off by a vicious pneumonia less than a year ago; but he couldn't easily abandon a lifetime's habit of thought. So he asked questions only she could answer, wanting proof but terrified that he might not get it.

And Vale, for the first time, felt another presence in addition to his god. This one was a tortured, partial entity—a shell of suffering that might actually once have been Louisa Ellen Randall.

Her voice choked out of Vale's larynx. His god modulated the tone.

Yes, Vale said, she remembered that summer in Maine, long before the Miracle of the New Europe, a cottage by the sea, and it had rained, hadn't it, all that cool July, but that had not made her unhappy, only grateful for beach walks whenever the clouds abated, for the fire in the hearth at night, for her collection of chalky seashells, for the patchwork quilt and the feather bed.

And so on.

And when Randall, florid with the pulse of blood through his clotted veins, asked: "Louisa, it *is* you, isn't it?"—Vale said yes. When he asked, "Are you happy?"—Vale said, "Of course." Here his voice faltered fractionally, because the Louisa Ellen Randall in his mind screamed out her suffering and her hatred for the god that had abducted her, who brought her here unwilling from—from—

But these were the Mysteries.

It was not Louisa Ellen's voice (though it still sounded like hers) when Randall's flagging skepticism began to recover and Vale's god delivered a sort of *coup de grâce*, an oracle, a prophecy: a warning to Randall that the Finch expedition was doomed and that Randall should protect himself from the political consequences. "The Partisans have already fired on the *Weston*," Vale said, and Randall blanched and stared.

It was a concise and miraculous prophecy. The wire services featured the story the following night. It ran under banner headlines in the Washington papers.

Vale neither knew nor cared about all that. His god had left him, that was the welcome fact. His aching body was his own again, and there was enough liquor in the house to keep him in a therapeutic oblivion.

CHAPTER FOURTEEN

Lake Constance. The *Bodensee*.

It was not much more, geographically speaking, than a wide place in the river. But in the morning mist it might have been a great placid ocean, gentle as silk, fresh sunlight cutting through the fog in silver sheets. The northern shore, just visible, was a rocky abeyance thick with silent forest, mosque trees and sage-pine and stands of a broad-leafed, white-boled tree for which not even Tom Compton had a name. Moth-hawks swept over the shimmering water in rotating swarms.

"More than a thousand years ago," Avery Keck said, "there was a Roman fort along these shores." Keck, who had taken Gillvany's place in the *Perspicacity*, spoke over the ragged syncopation of the boat's small motor. "In the Middle Ages it was one of the most powerful cities in Europe. A Lombard city, on the trade route between Germany and Italy. Now it might never have existed. Only water. Only rocks."

Guilford wondered aloud what had happened to the vanished Europeans. Had they simply died? Or could they have traveled to a mirror-Earth, in which Europe survived intact and the rest of the world had gone feral and strange?

Keck was a gaunt man of about forty years, with the face of a small-town undertaker. He looked at Guilford dolefully. "If so, then the Europeans have their own fresh wilderness to hack and gouge at and go to war over. Just like us, God help 'em."

Camp at Bodensee. Diggs at his fire. Sullivan, Betts, & Hemphill at their tents. Meadow green with a small leafy spreading plant like turquoise clover. High overcast, cool gusty wind.

Postscriptum. Or perhaps I should stop pretending these notes are "postscripts" & admit that they are letters to Caroline. Caroline, I hope you see them one day soon.

Journey largely uneventful since Gillvany's tragic death, though that event hangs over us like a cloud. Finch in particular has grown sullen & uncommunicative. I think he blames himself. He writes relentlessly in his notebook, says little.

We made our camp in the meadows Erasmus described. Have seen herds of wild fur snakes in great profusion, moving over the land like cloud shadows on a sunny day. Ever-resourceful, Tom Compton has even stalked and killed one, so we dine on snake meat— greasy steaks that taste like wild fowl, but a refreshing change after tinned rations. Our boats are securely stowed well up a beach, under tarps and beneath an outcropping of mossy granite, effectively hidden from all but the most exhaustive search. Though who do we suppose will find them in this empty land?

We await the arrival of Erasmus with our pack snakes

*and supplies. Tom Compton insists we could have had
any number of animals free of charge—they are (often
quite literally!) all around us—but Erasmus's beasts are
trained to pack and bridle and have already relieved us
of the need to ferry all our kit by boat.*

This assumes Erasmus will show up as promised.

*We all know each other very well by now—all our quirks
& idiosyncrasies, which are legion—and I have even had
several rewarding conversations with Tom Compton, who
has shown me more respect since the near wreck of the*
Perspicacity. *In his eyes I am still the pampered Easterner
who makes a soft living with a photo-box (as he calls it),
but I have shown enough initiative to impress him.*

*Certainly he has had a hard enough life to justify his
skepticism. Born in San Francisco an impoverished
mixed-breed, by his own account the descendant of
slaves, Indians, & failed goldminers—he managed to
teach himself to read and found employment in the Merchant Marine, eventually made his way to Jeffersonville,
a rough town with uses for his rough talents and toler-
ance for his rough manners.*

*I know you would find him crude, Caroline, but he is
a fundamentally good man & useful in a crisis. I'm
glad of his company.*

*We have waited a week already for Erasmus and will
wait at least another. Fortunately I have the copy of* Argosy *for which I traded Finch's geology tome. The magazine contains an instalment of E.R. Burroughs'* Lost
Kingdom of Darwinia, *more of his imagined "ancient
hinterland" complete with dinosaurs, noble savages,
and a colony of evil-minded Junkers to rule them. A
princess requires rescue. I know your disdain for this type
of fiction, Caroline, and I have to admit that even Burroughs' wild Darwinia pales against close contact with
the real thing: these too-solid hills and shadowy, cool*

forests. But the magazine is a delightful distraction & I am much envied by the other Expeditionaries, since I have been chary about loaning the volume.

I find myself looking forward to civilization—the tall buildings, the newsstands, and such.

Erasmus arrived with the pack animals and accepted payment in the form of a check drawn on a Jeffersonville bank. He spent an evening in camp and expressed his condolences, though not his surprise, regarding Gillvany's death.

But his arrival was overshadowed by Avery Keck's discovery. Keck and Tom Compton had gone on another snake hunt, Keck observing both the local geography and the frontiersman's tracking skills. Not that the snakes required much tracking, as Keck explained over the campfire. They had simply cut off one snake from the herd and taken it down with a single shot from Tom Compton's rifle. Dragging the carcass back to camp was the difficult part.

More interesting, Keck said, was that they had come across an insect nest and its midden.

The insects, Keck said, were ten-legged invertebrate carnivores, distantly related to the stump runners Guilford had encountered outside London. They tunneled in boggy lowland areas where the soil was loose and wet. A fur snake or any other animal wandering into the insects' territory would be repeatedly bitten by the colony's venomous drones, then swarmed and stripped of its meat. Cleaned bones were meticulously shuttled to the colony's rim—the famous midden.

"The older a colony, the bigger its midden," Keck said. "I saw one nest in the Rhinish lowlands that had grown like a fairy ring, about a hundred meters across. The one Tom and I found is about average, in my experience. A perfect circle of pitted white bones. Mainly the bones of unlucky fur snakes, but—" Keck unwrapped the oilcloth package he had carried back to camp. "We found this."

It was a long, high-domed, spike-toothed skull. It was white as polished ivory, but it glittered redly in the firelight.

"Well, shit!" Diggs exclaimed, which earned him a stiff look from Preston Finch.

Guilford turned to Sullivan, who nodded. "Similar to the skull we saw in London." He explained the Museum of Monstrosities. "Interesting. It looks to me like a large predator, and it must have been widely distributed, at least at one time."

"At one time?" Finch asked scornfully. "Do you mean 1913? Or 1915?"

Sullivan ignored him. "How old would you judge this specimen to be, Mr. Keck?"

"Couldn't venture a guess. Obviously it's neither fossilized nor weathered, so—relatively recent."

"Which means we might run into one of these beasties on the hoof," Ed Betts put in. "Keep your pistols loaded."

Tom Compton had never seen a living sample of the creature, however, in all his wilderness experience, nor had the snake trader Erasmus—"Though people *do* disappear in the bush."

"Resembles a bear," Diggs said. "California grizzly, if that's an adult specimen. Might be drawn to garbage and such. How about we police the camp a little more scientifically from now on?"

"Maybe they avoid people," Sullivan said. "Maybe we frighten them."

"Maybe," Tom said. "But that jaw could swallow a man's leg up to the knee and probably snap it at the joint. If we frighten them, it ought to be mutual."

"We'll double the night watch," Finch decided.

Even Eden had its serpent, Guilford thought.

Come morning they set out across the gently rolling meadowland, southward toward the mountains. The fur snakes made passable riding animals—they didn't mind bearing human cargo and would even respond to direction from a crude bridle—but their bodies were simply too wide to straddle comfortably (not to mention greasy and evil-smelling), and no one had yet invented a functional snake saddle. Guilford preferred to walk, even after the second day, when the march seemed infinitely more grueling, when calves and ankles and thighs made their most concerted protests.

The meadowed hills rolled steadily higher. Fresh water was harder to find now, though the snakes could sense a creek or pool from a mile's distance. And the mountains on the horizon, subject of Keck's relentless triangulation, were clearly a barrier: the end of the road, even if Finch and company found an accessible pass where Brenner or Mount Genevre had been. *Then we turn around,* Guilford thought, *and take our pressed plants and punctured bugs back to America, and people will say we helped "tame" the continent, though that's a joke: we're a very small pinprick of knowledge on the skin of this unknown country.*

But he was proud of what they had accomplished. We walked, he told the frontiersman, where no one else had walked, puzzled out at least a few of Darwinia's secrets.

"We haven't fucked the continent," Tom Compton agreed, "but I guess we've lifted her skirts."

Guilford trudged through the cool afternoon with Compton and Sullivan and their pack animals. Low clouds drifted across the sky, blindingly white at the

margins, woolly gray beneath. His boots left brief im-
prints in the spongy meadow growth. Down a western
slope of land Keck had spotted another insect midden,
a ring of bone around a deceptively peaceful patch of
green, like a troll's garden, Guilford thought. They
gave it a wide berth.

Tom Compton brooded on another matter. "There
have been campfires behind us the last couple of
nights," he said. "Five, six miles back. I don't know
what that means."

"Partisans?" Sullivan asked.

"Probably just hunters, maybe followed us up past
the Rheinfelden—followed Erasmus, more likely,
poaching on his territory. The Partisans, they're mostly
coast pirates out of the rogue settlements. They don't
come inland as a rule, unless they're hunting or
prospecting, which makes them less likely to practice
politics at gunpoint."

"Still," Sullivan said, "I liked it better when we were
alone."

"So did I," the frontiersman said.

*Hill camp by a nameless creek. Land rising visibly now.
Distant snow-capped alpine range. Stands of forest,
mostly mosque trees, & a new plant, a small bush with
hard & inedible yellow berries. (Not true berries, Sullivan says, but that's what they look like.) Stiff & cooling
wind keeps the billyflies away, or perhaps they simply
don't care for the altitude.*

*Postscriptum. Looking north at dinnertime I see what
seems like all of Darwinia: a wonderful melancholy ta-
pestry of light & shadow as the sun westers. Reminds me
of Montana—equally vast & empty, though not so
stark; cloaked in mild green, a rich and living land,
however strange.*

Caroline, I think of your patience in London without me, minding Lily, putting up with Jered's moods and Alice's uncommunicative nature. I know how much you hated my trip out West, and that was when you still had the comforts of Boston to console you. I trust it is worth the discomfort, that my work will be in greater demand when we're finally back home, that the upshot will be a better & more secure future for both my ladies.

Curious dreams lately, Caroline. I repeatedly dream I am wearing a military uniform, walking alone in some sere wasteland of a battlefield, lost in smoke & mud. So real! Almost the quality of a memory, though of course no such thing has happened to me, & the Civil War stories I heard at the family table were frankly less visceral.

Expeditionary madness, perhaps? Dr. Sullivan also reports odd dreams, & even Tom Compton grudgingly admits that his sleep is troubled.

But how could I sleep comfortably without you next to me? In any case, daylight chases away the dreams. By day our only dream is of the mountains, their blue-white peaks our new horizon.

Tom Compton was standing watch at dawn, when the Partisans attacked.

He sat at the embers of a fire with Ed Betts, a rotund man whose chin kept drifting toward his chest. Betts didn't know how to keep himself awake. Tom did. The frontiersman had stood these watches before, usually alone, wary of robbers or claim jumpers, especially when he hunted the coal country. It was a trick of the mind, to put away sleep until later. It was a skill Betts didn't have it.

Still, there was no warning when the first shots came from the dim woods to the east. There was barely enough light to turn the sky an India-ink blue. Four or five rifles barked in rough unison. "What the hell,"

Betts said, then slumped forward with a hole in his neck, dousing the fire with blood.

The frontiersman rolled into the dirt. He fired his own rifle at the margin of the woods, more to wake the camp than defend it. He couldn't see the enemy.

The fur snakes squealed their fear and then began to die in a second volley of bullets.

Guilford was asleep when the attack began—dreaming again of the Army picket, his twin in khaki, who was trying to deliver some vital but unintelligible message.

Yesterday's march had been exhausting. The expedition had followed a series of lightly wooded ridgetops and ravines, prodding the reluctant fur snakes under the arches of the mosque trees, climbing and descending. The snakes disliked the close confinement of the woods and expressed their discontent by mewling, belching, and farting. The stink was cloying in the still air and was not abated by a steady drizzle, which only added the sour-milk stench of wet fur to the mix.

Eventually the land leveled. These high alpine meadows had blossomed in the rain, the false clover opening white star petals like summer snowflakes. Pitching tents in the drizzle was a tedious chore, and dinner came out of a can. Finch kept a lantern burning in his tent after dark—scribbling his theories, Guilford supposed, reconciling the day's events with the dialectic of the New Creation—but everyone else simply collapsed into bedrolls and silence.

The eastern horizon was faintly blue when the first shots were fired. Guilford came awake to the sound of cries and percussion. He fumbled for his pistol, heart hammering. He had been carrying the pistol fully loaded since Keck recovered the monster skull, but he wasn't a marksman. He knew how to fire the pistol but had never killed anything with it.

He rolled out of his tent into chaos.

The attack had come from the tree line to the east, a black silhouette against the dawn. Keck, Sullivan, Diggs, and Tom Compton had set up a sort of skirmish line behind the heaped bodies of three dead fur snakes. They were firing into the woods sporadically, starved for targets. The remaining fur snakes shrieked and yanked at their tethers in futile panic. One of the animals fell as Guilford watched.

The rest of the expeditionaries were tumbling out of their tents in terrified confusion. Ed Betts lay dead beside the campfire, his shirt scarlet with blood. Chuck Hemphill and Ray Burke were on their hands and knees, shouting, "Get down! Keep your heads down!"

Guilford crawled through the circle of tattered canvas to join Sullivan and company. They didn't acknowledge his presence until he had ducked up and fired a pistol shot into the dark of the woods. Tom Compton put a hand on his arm. "You can't shoot what you can't see. And we're outnumbered."

"How can you tell?"

"See the muzzle flash."

A fresh volley of bullets answered Guilford's single shot. The snake carcasses shook with thudding impacts.

"Christ!" Diggs said. "What do we do?"

Guilford glanced back at the tents. Preston Finch had just emerged, hatless and bootless, adjusting his bottle-glass lenses and firing his ivoried pistol into the air.

"We run," Tom Compton said.

"Our food," Sullivan said, "the specimens, the samples—"

The close whine of a bullet interrupted him.

"Fuck all that!" Diggs said.

"Get the attention of the others," Tom said. "Follow me."

The Partisans—if they *were* Partisans—had encircled the camp, but they were sparse on the unwooded western slope of the hill and easier to shoot. Guilford counted at least two enemy dead, though Chuck Hemphill and Emil Swensen were killed and Sullivan winged, a bloody puncture in the meat of his arm. The rest followed Tom Compton into the mist of the ravine where the sunlight had not begun to penetrate. It was a slow and agonizing route, with only the frontiersman's shouted commands to keep the expeditionaries in any sort of order. Guilford could not seem to draw breath enough to satisfy his body; the air burned in his lungs. Shadows and fog made uneasy cover, and he heard, or imagined he heard, the sound of pursuit only paces behind him. And where was there to run? A glacial creek bisected this valley; the ridge wall beyond it was rocky and steep.

"This way," Tom insisted. South, parallel to the water. The soil underfoot grew marshy and perilous. Guilford could see Keck ahead of him in the swirling cloud, but nothing farther. *Keep up,* he told himself.

Then Keck stopped short, peering down at his feet. "God help us," he whispered. The texture of the ground had changed. Guilford closed in on the surveyor. Something crackled under his boots.

Twigs. Hundreds of dried twigs.

No: *bones.*

An insect midden.

Keck shouted at the frontiersman ahead of him: "You brought us here deliberately!"

"Shut up." Tom Compton was a bulky shade in the

mist, someone else beside him, maybe Sullivan. "Keep quiet. Step where I step. Everybody follow the man in front of him, single file."

Guilford felt Diggs push him from behind. "They're still coming, get a fuckin' move on!"

Never mind what might be ahead. Follow Keck, follow Tom. Diggs was right. A bullet screamed out of the fog.

More small bones crunched underfoot. Tom was following the midden-line, Guilford guessed, circling the insect nest, one step away from oblivion.

Keck had brought one of these bugs to the campfire a few days ago. Body about the size of a big man's thumb, ten long and powerful legs, mandibles like steel surgical tools. Best not think about that.

Diggs cried out as his foot slipped off an unseen skull, sending him reeling toward the soft turf of the insect nest. Guilford grabbed one flailing arm and pulled him back.

The sky was lighter when they reached the opposite side of the midden. *Not to our advantage,* Guilford thought. The Partisans might see the nest for what it was. Even then, they would be forced to follow the narrow defile of the midden-edge, either along the ravine wall as the expeditionaries had or close to the creek—either way, they might make easier targets.

"Form a line just past these trees," the frontiersman said. "Reload or hoard your ammunition. Shoot anyone who tries to circle around, but wait for a clean shot."

But the Partisans were too intent on their quarry to watch the ground. Guilford looked carefully at these men as they stepped out of the low mist and into what they must have mistaken for a rocky ledge or patch of moss. He counted seven of them, armed with military rifles but without uniforms save for high boots and slouch hats. They were grinning, sure of themselves.

And their boots protected them—at least briefly. The lead man was perhaps three-quarters of the distance across the soft open ground before he looked down and saw the insects swarming his legs. His tight smile disappeared; his eyes widened with comprehension. He turned but couldn't flee; the insects clung tenaciously to one another, making strands of faintly furry rope to bind his legs and drag him down.

He lost his balance and fell screaming. The bugs were over him instantly, a roiling shroud, and on the several men behind him, whose screams shortly drowned out his own.

"Shoot the stragglers," Tom said. "Now."

Guilford fired as often as the rest, but it was the frontiersman's rifle that found a mark most often. Three more Partisans fell; others fled the sound of screams.

The screaming didn't last long, mercifully. The lead man's body, rigid with poison, angled up like the prow of a sinking ship. A glint of bone gleamed through the black swarm. Then the whole man disappeared beneath the churning moist soil.

Guilford was transfixed. The Partisans would become part of the midden, he thought. How long until their skulls and ribs were cast up like broken coral on a beach? Hours, days? He felt ill.

"Guilford," Keck whispered urgently.

Keck was bleeding vigorously from the thigh. *Best bind that,* Guilford thought. *Staunch the blood. Where is the medical kit?*

But that wasn't what Keck wanted to say.

"Guilford!" Eyes wide, grimacing. "Your leg!"

Something crawling on it.

Maybe the insect had been thrown out of the nest by

the Partisan's thrashing. It scuttled up Guilford's boot before he could react and drove its mandibles through the cloth of Guilford's trousers.

He gasped and staggered. Keck caught him under the arms. Sullivan brushed the insect away with his pistol butt, and Keck crushed it under his heel.

"Well, damn," Guilford said calmly. Then the venom reached an artery, a dose of hypodermic flame, and he closed his eyes and fainted.

INTERLUDE

This happened near the End of Time, as the galaxy collapsed into its own singularity—a time when the stars were few and barren, a time when the galaxies themselves had grown so far apart that even distortions in the Higgs field did not propagate instantly.

Elsewhere in the universe the voices of galactic noospheres grew faint, as they resigned themselves to dissolution or furiously constructed vast epigalactic redoubts, fortresses that would withstand both the siren song of the black holes and the thermal cooling of the universe. In time, as white dwarfs and even neutron stars dissipated and died, the only coherent matter remaining would be these strongholds of sentience.

A trillion-year autumn had passed. Noospheres, huge constructs which housed the remnants of planetary civilizations, had drifted for eons among the fossil stars of the galaxy's spiral arms. They had recomplicated and segmented themselves, meeting in million-year cycles to exchange knowledge and to create hybrid offspring, metacultures embedded in infant noospheres dense as neutron stars. They vectored themselves through space along distortion lines in the Higgs field, calling out across their own event horizons, singing their names. They knew each other intimately. There had not been a war for countless ages—not since the self-immolation of the Violet Empire, the last of the Biotic Prefectures, 10^9 years ago.

But autumn was drawing to a close, and the harsh reality of universal winter loomed ahead.

Time to cleave together. Time to build, to restore, to protect, and to remember. Time to gather the summer's harvest; time to conserve warmth.

The galaxy's noospheres shared memories that ranged back to the Eclectic Age, when death was abolished, long before the Earth or its mother star had formed. Now it was time to pool those memories—to make a physical Archive that would outlast even the loss of free energy, an Archive linked isostatically with other Archives in the universe, an Archive which would harbor sentience well into the Heat Death and might even create an artificial context in which new sentiences would eventually flourish.

To that end noospheres gathered above the ecliptic of the dying galaxy, their immense new labors fed by plumes of antimatter that seethed from the pole of the central singularity. The Archive, when it was finished, would contain all that the galaxy had been since the Eclectic Age.

Age by age the Archive grew, a physical object as wide as a dozen stellar systems, braced against the tides of its own mass by systematic distortions of local space. A machine operating at stellar temperatures, it radiated a burnished amber light into an increasingly light-

less void—even this sparse radiation a residual ineffi-
ciency that would be eliminated over the next several
million years.

The Archive was a temporal telescope, a recording,
a memory—in essence, a book. It was the ultimate history book, fed and refreshed by temporal discontinu-
ities built into its matrix, a record of every known
sentient act and thought since the dawn of the Eclectic
Age. It was unalterable but infinitely accessible, aloof
and antientropic.

It was the single largest act of engineering ever attempted by galactic sentience. It pressed the noospheres to their technological limit and often, it
seemed, beyond. Its construction required ceaseless
work, by the noospheres and their sentient nodes, by
Turing constructors large and small, by virtual machines embedded in the isostatic lattices of reality itself, a labor that endured for more than ten million
years.

But it was finished at last, a holistic library of galactic
history and a fortress against the evaporation of matter.
Noospheres ringed the Archive in a joyous orbital
dance. Perhaps, beyond the still-inviolable boundaries
of the singularities, new universes were being born
from the ashes of the old. That possibility was being in-
vestigated; faint signals flashed between this and other
Archives, proposals for universe-building that daunted
all of Sentience Itself. Perhaps one day . . .

But that was speculation. For now, galactic sentience
reveled in what it had created.

Monofilaments of Higgs distortion swept the
Archive, spooling history in sequential order. Sentient
nodes and subnodes delighted in exploring the past—
one, two, three times, as the Archive was read and
reread. Knowledge became involute, knew itself; so-

phants among the noospheres debated the difference between the Knowing and the Known.

Tragedy struck without warning and without explanation some 10^3 years after the structure was finished.

The Archive, the noospheres discovered, had been quietly infiltrated and corrupted. Semisentient entities—self-propagating, evolving parasite codes hidden in the network of Higgs signals that passed between galaxies—had commandeered the Archive's structural protocols. Information was being lost, irretrievably, moment by moment.

Worse, information was being *changed*.

The Archive evolved into a new and distorted form. Subsentient virtual entities, relics of a war that had devastated a distant galaxy long before the beginning of this galaxy's Eclectic Age, were using the Archive as a platform to preserve their algorithms against thermal death. They lacked moral regard for any entity not themselves, but they were fully aware of the purpose of the Archive and of its designers. They had not simply captured the structure, they had taken it hostage.

Static memories embedded in the Archive as records became, in effect, new seed-sentiences: *new lives*, trapped in an epistructure they could never perceive and manipulated by entities beyond their conception. These new lives, though products of the Archive's corruption, could not be terminated or erased. That would stain the conscience of Sentience beyond redemption. In theory, the Archive could be emptied, cleansed, and rewritten . . . but that would be equivalent to murder on a collosal scale.

Moreover, these lives must be saved, must be *remembered*. It was the goal Sentience had pursued since its inception, to redeem itself from death. The new and strange quasi history evolving inside the Archive could not simply be abandoned.

Noospheres retreated from the Archive, fearful of contagion; Sentience conferred with itself, and a thousand years passed.

The Archive must be repaired, it was decided. The invaders must be expelled. The new seed-sentences would ultimately be lost, along with the Archive itself, if nothing was done. The viral invaders would not be satisfied until the cooling universe contained nothing but their own relentless codes. It was a task no less difficult than building the Archive, and far more problematic—because the cleansing would have to begin *within the Archive itself.* Individual sentient nodes by the billions would have to enter the Archive both physically and virtually. And they would meet a cunning opposition.

Individuals—in effect, ghosts—who had long since merged their identities into the noospheres were stripped of their eons of augmentation, rendered nearly mortal for their penetration into the corrupted Archive.

One of those billions was an ancient terrestrial node which had once been named Guilford Law. This seed-consciousness, barely complex enough to retain its own ancient memory, was launched with countless others into the Archive's fractal depths.

History's last war had begun.

Guilford Law remembered war. It was war that had killed him, after all.

BOOK TWO

WINTER, SPRING 1920–21

"Esse est percipii."
—BISHOP BERKELEY

CHAPTER FIFTEEN

FROM THE JOURNAL OF GUILFORD LAW:

I mean to recount these events while I still can.

It is a miracle I am still alive, and it will be another miracle if any of us survive the winter. We have found shelter in this unspeakably strange place—of which more later—but food is scarce, the climate frigid, and there is the ever-present possibility of another attack.

Today I am still weak. (I hold a pencil the way Lily does, and my writing looks like hers), and the daylight is already fading.

I hope someday Lily will read these words even if I can't deliver them to her myself. I think of you, Caroline, and of Lily, so often and so vividly that I can almost touch you. Though less easily now that the fever has diminished.

Of all my feverish phantasms, you are the only ones I will miss.

More tomorrow, if circumstances allow.

* * *

Three months have passed since the Partisans attacked our expedition. During much of that time I was unconscious or raving. What follows is my reconstruction of events. Avery Keck, John Sullivan, and "Diggs" Digby have filled in the gaps for me, with contributions from the other survivors.

I have to be succinct, due to limitations of strength and time. (Light comes fitfully through these high stone embrasures, filtered by oilcloth or animal skins, and I have to make a contribution to our survival even if it's a modest one—mainly helping Diggs, who has lost the use of his left arm, to cook our meager suppers. He'll need me soon. Diggs is stoking the fire now and Wilson Farr has gone for a bucket of snow.)

After we left the Bodensee, and as we approached the Alps, we were attacked by a band of armed Partisans whose only apparent motive was to murder us and plunder our supplies. We lost Ed Betts, Chuck Hemphill, and Emil Swensen in the first volleys— would have lost more if we had camped closer to the tree line. Tom Compton's quick thinking saved us. He led us around one of the region's huge insect middens, a trap into which the pursuing Partisans stumbled and were consumed. Those who did not die in the nest fled or were shot.

They weren't the only victims. One of the insects managed to inject its poison into my bloodstream. By nightfall I was at death's door, according to Dr. Farr. I was not expected to survive, and most of the rest of the expeditionaries suffered numerous major or minor wounds. Preston Finch survived with only a twisted ankle, but his spirit was crushed; he spoke in monosyllables and abandoned the leadership role to Sullivan and Tom Compton.

When the survivors had rallied sufficiently to limp

back to the ruined encampment they found the scientific equipment and samples burned, the animals slaughtered, rations and medical supplies stolen.

It pains me to think of it even now. All our work, Caroline! All Sullivan's voucher samples, his notes, his plant press, lost. Both of my cameras were destroyed and the exposed plates shattered. (Sullivan broke the news when I eventually regained consciousness.) My notebook survived only because I kept it on my person at all times. We did manage to salvage a few other notes, plus writing implements and enough scraps of paper that many of the surviving expeditionaries are keeping their own winter diaries.

I couldn't mourn the dead, Caroline, any more than I could open my eyes or do more than draw breath while the poison burned through my body.

I mourned them later.

The wounded needed rest and food. Once again, Tom Compton was our salvation. He cauterized my insect bite and treated it with the sap of a bitter weed. Dr. Farr accepted this wilderness midwifery because there was no civilized medicine left to us. Farr used his own medical skill to bind wounds and set broken bones. From the remnants of our supplies we fashioned a more defensible and less obvious camp, in case more Partisans were lurking. Few of us were well enough to travel.

The logical next step was to seek help. Lake Constance was only a few days behind us. Erasmus would have gone back to his hut and his kraal by now, but the boats were waiting—unless they too had been discovered by hostile forces—and the journey down the Rhine would be less difficult than the journey up. Figure a month to reach Jeffersonville, less than that for a rescue party to return.

Tom Compton volunteered to go, but he was needed to help shelter and treat survivors. His hunting and trapping experience meant he could forage for food even without ammunition for the rifle he carried. In fact he took to hunting fur snakes with a Bowie knife. The animals eventually learned to shy at the smell of him, but they remained so docile that he could slit a snake's throat before the dumb beast realized it was in danger.

We dispatched Chris Tuckman and Ray Burke, unhurt in the attack, to seek help. They took what remained of our tinned food (a pittance) and a tent that hadn't burned, plus pistols, a compass, and a generous portion of our hoarded ammunition.

Three months have passed.

They haven't come back.

No one has come. Of the original fifteen, nine of us remain. Myself, plus Finch, Sullivan, Compton, Donner, Robertson, Farr, and Digby.

Winter came early this year. Icy sleet, and then a granular, relentless snow.

Sullivan, Wilson Farr, and Tom Compton nursed me back to a semblance of health—fed me vegetable gruel and carried me, when we were forced to travel, on a travois rigged behind a wild snake. For obvious reasons, I lost weight—more, even, than the rest of us, and we're a hungry crowd these days.

Caroline, you should see me. That "little belly" you complained of is only a memory. I've had to make new notches in my belt. My ribs are as plain as the tines of a pitchfork, and when I shave (we have a mirror, a razor) my Adam's apple bobs like a cat under a bedsheet.

As I said, we found shelter for the winter. But the shelter we found—

Caroline, I cannot begin to describe it! Not tonight, at any rate.

(Listen: Diggs at his work again, his forked-branch crutch knocking the stone floor, water hissing as the kettle goes over the fire—he'll be needing me soon.)

Perhaps if I describe it as I first saw it . . . through a fever haze, of course, but I was not delirious, although it might sound that way.

Caroline, be patient. I fear your incredulity.

Picture us, a ragged band of men in animal furs, some walking, some limping, some dragged on harnesses, starved and freezing as we cross another snowy ridge and peer down into yet another wilderness valley. . . . Diggs with his ruined arm, Sullivan limping pitifully, me on a sledge because I still could not walk any significant distance. According to Farr I was suffering the effect of the insect venom on my liver. I was feverish and yellow and—well, I won't go into detail.

Another alpine valley, but this one was different. Tom Compton had scouted it out.

It was a broad river valley, cut from stony soil and populated with dour, spiky mosque trees. From my place on the sledge, wrapped in furs, that was all I saw at first: the slope of the valley and its dark vegetation. But the rest of the party fell quickly silent, and I raised myself up to see what had alarmed them, and it was the single thing I had least expected to see in this desolate land:

A city!

Or the ruin of a city. It was a vast mosaic through

which a river had run riot, visibly aged but obviously the work of intelligent builders. Even at this distance it was apparent the architects were long gone. Nothing walked this city's relentlessly parallel streets. The buildings still intact were iron-gray boxes hewn from stone, softened by mist and time. And the city was *large*, Caroline, large beyond believing—a ruin that could have contained all of Boston and a couple of counties more.

For all its apparent age, the city's outlying structures were more or less complete and handily available. This ruin promised everything we had despaired of finding: shelter for ourselves and our animals, a supply of fresh water, and (given the wooded hills and evidence of nearby snake herds) plentiful game. Tom Compton had scouted the city and environs and thought we could winter here. He warned us that the city was an uninhabited ruin, that we would have to work hard to keep ourselves warm in its drafty warrens, even with plentiful firewood. But since we had pictured ourselves dying in our snakeskin tents—or simply frozen to death in some Alpine pass—even this grim prospect seemed the gift of a benevolent God.

Of course the city raised countless questions. How had it come to exist, in a land void of human habitation, and what had happened to its builders? Were its builders even human, or some novel Darwinian race? But we were too exhausted to debate the ruin's provenance or meaning. Only Preston Finch hesitated before descending the slope of the valley, and I don't know what he feared; he hadn't spoken aloud for days.

The prospect of shelter buoyed our spirits. We collected mosque and sage-pine windfall along the way, and before the stars began to shine in the wintry sky we had a fire roaring, casting fitful light among the colossal stones of the Nameless City.

* * *

Dear Caroline: I have not been as faithful in keeping this journal as I would have liked. Events are pressing.

There hasn't been any new disaster—don't worry—only the ongoing disaster of our isolation and the demands of the primitive life.

We live like Red Indians, in order to live at all. My fever has passed (for good, I hope) and my poisoned leg has regained its sensation and even some strength. I can walk a fair distance with only a stick for support and I have begun to accompany Tom Compton and Avery Keck on their hunting expeditions, though I'm still confined to the broad sweep of the valley. By spring I should have no trouble keeping up with the expedition when we finally make for Lake Constance and home.

For hunting we bundle ourselves in furs and hide boots. Our clothes are stitched with bone needles, the rags of our civilized clothing salvaged for thread. We have two rifles and even some ammunition, but most of our hunting is by bow or knife. Tom made the bows and shafts from local wood and bone, and he is still our only marksman. A rifle shot, he points out, could attract unwelcome attention, and the bullets might be needed on the journey home. I doubt the Partisans are anywhere nearby. Winter must hinder them as much as it hinders us. But several of us have experienced the sense of being watched from time to time.

We have captured a few fur snakes and corralled them in a ruined foundation with a half-roof for shelter. Sullivan looks after them and makes sure they have enough forage and water. He has switched from botany to animal husbandry, at least for the duration.

I've grown closer to Sullivan, perhaps because our

parallel injuries (my leg, his hip) kept us confined together for some weeks. Often we're left alone with Diggs or Preston Finch. Finch remains nearly wordless, though he helps with the physical labor. Sullivan, by contrast, talks to me freely, and I almost as freely to him. You might be wary of his atheism, Caroline, but it's a *principled* atheism, if that makes any sense.

Last night we were assigned the late watch, a plush duty if you don't mind the hours. We kept the fire burning and swapped stories, as usual, until we heard a commotion from the stables, as we call the semi-collapsed structure where the animals are kept. So we donned our furs and limped into the frigid night to investigate.

Snow had been falling all afternoon, and Sullivan's torch cast a flickering glow across a boulevard of unsullied white. With its broken stones and fractured walls cloaked in snow the City seems only temporarily vacated. The buildings are identical, though in various stages of decay, and identically made, of huge bricks cut from raw granite and set in place without benefit of mortar. The bricks or blocks are perfectly square, about ten feet on a side. The buildings themselves are identically square and arranged in squares of four, as if by a meticulous but unimaginative child.

The doorways may once have possessed wooden doors, but if they ever existed they have long since rotted and weathered away. The openings are about twice as high as a man's head and several times wider than his girth, but this, Sullivan points out, tells us virtually nothing of the original inhabitants—the doors of cathedrals are larger than the doors of sod huts, but the men who pass through them are the same. Nevertheless, the impression lingers of some squat, gigantic race, antediluvian, pre-Adamic.

We had put up a crude mosquewood fence to keep our twelve captive snakes corralled in their ruin. Usually they're fairly quiet, barring the usual belching and mewling. Tonight the noise was nearly continuous, a collective moan, and we tracked it under the half-fallen stone eaves, where one of our herd was giving birth.

Or rather (we saw as we came closer) it was *laying eggs*. The eggs emerged from the beast's pendulous abdomen in glittering clusters, each egg about the size of a softball, until a gelatinous mass of them lay steaming in a mound of windblown snow.

I looked at Sullivan. "The eggs will freeze in this weather. If we build a fire—"

Sullivan shook his head. "Nature must have made a provision," he whispered. "If not, we're too ignorant to help. Stand back, Guilford. Give them room."

And he was right. Nature *had* made a provision, if an awkward one. When the female finished dropping her eggs a second animal, perhaps the male parent, approached the pearlescent mass and in a singular motion of its six limbs managed to scoop the eggs from the snow into pouches arrayed along its belly . . . there, presumably, to incubate until the hatchlings could survive on their own.

The moaning and barking finally relented, and the herd went back about its business.

We fled to the warmth of our own shelter. We had taken over two immense rooms in one of the less exposed buildings, partitioned and sealed them from the weather with snakeskins and made an insulating floor of dried rushes. The effect was cheerful, if only by comparison with the frigid outer dark.

Sullivan grew thoughtful, warming his hands, putting a kettle of snow at the edge of the fire for root tea. "They're born," he said, "they reproduce, they die . . . Guilford, if they *didn't* evolve, it's inevitable that they *will* evolve—selected by nature, bred by circumstance. . . ."

"The handiwork of God, Finch would say." Since Finch was perpetually silent, I felt obliged to take his part, if only to keep Sullivan interested.

"But what does that *mean*?" Sullivan stood up, nearly toppling the kettle. "How I would love to have an explanation so wonderfully complete! And I don't mean that sarcastically, Guilford; don't give me your sorrowful stare. I'm serious. To look at the color of Mars in the night sky, at six-legged fur-bearing snakes laying eggs in the snow, and see nothing but the hand of God . . . how sweetly simple!"

"Truth is simple," I said, smarting.

"Truth is *often* simple. Deceptively simple. But I won't put my ignorance on an altar and call it God. It feels like idolatry, like the worst kind of idolatry."

Which is what I mean, Caroline, by "principled atheism." Sullivan is an honest man and humble about his learning. He comes from a Quaker family and will even, when he's tired, slip into the Quaker habit of tongue: *I tell thee, Guilford* . . .

"This city," he brooded. "This thing we *call* a city, though notice, it's nothing but boxes and alleys . . . no plumbing, no provision for the storage of food; no ovens, no granaries, no temples, no playing fields . . . this city is a key."

To what? I wanted to ask.

He ignored me. "We haven't explored it closely enough. The ruin is miles wide."

"Tom scouted it."

"Briefly. And even Tom admits . . ."

Admits what? But Sullivan was sliding into introspection and it would have been useless to push him. I knew his moods too well.

For many of us Darwinia has been a test of faith. Finch believes the continent is a patent miracle, but I suspect he wishes God had left a signature less ambiguous than these wordless hills and forests. Whereas Sullivan is forced into a daily wrestle with the miraculous.

We drank our tea and shivered under our Army blankets. Tom Compton had insisted we keep a night watch ever since the Partisan attack. Two men by the midnight fire was our best effort. I often wondered what we were watching *for*, exactly, since another attack, had it come, would have overwhelmed our defenses whether or not there was time to rouse the sleeping men.

But the city has a way of provoking wariness.

"Guilford," Sullivan said after a long silence. "When you sleep, these days . . . do you dream?"

The question surprised me.

"Seldom," I said.

But that was a lie.

Dreams are trivial, Caroline, aren't they?

I don't believe in dreams. I don't believe in the Army picket who looks like me, even if I see him whenever I close my eyes. Fortunately Sullivan didn't press the matter, and we sat out what remained of our watch without speaking.

Mid-January. Unexpected bounty from the last hunting expedition: plenty of dressed meat, winter seeds, even a couple of Darwinian "birds"—moth-hawks, brainless bipedal leather-winged creatures, but they taste like lamb, of all things, juicy and succulent. Everyone ate to contentment except Paul Robertson, who is down with the flu. Even Finch smiled his approval.

Sullivan still talks of exploring the ruins—he is almost obsessed with the idea. And now, with our larders bolstered and the weather taking a mild turn, he means to put his plan into action.

For spare hand and litter bearer he has enlisted Tom Compton and me. We set out tomorrow, a two-day expedition into the heart of the city.

I hope this is wise. I dread it a little, to be honest.

CHAPTER SIXTEEN

It was an unseasonably cold London winter, more bitter than any of the Boston winters Caroline remembered. A wolf-winter, Aunt Alice called it. Supply boats
came less frequently up the ice-choked Thames,
though the harbor boiled with industry and smoke-
stacks blackened the sky. Every building in London
added a plume of coal smoke or the grayer smudge of
a peat or wood fire. Caroline had learned to take some
solace in these sullen skies, emblems of a wilderness
beaten back. She understood now what London really
was: not a "settlement"—who, after all, would want to
settle in this unproductive, vile country?—but a gesture of defiance toward an intractable nature.

Nature would win, of course, in the end. Nature always did. But Caroline learned to take a secret pleasure
in each paved road and toppled tree.

A mid-January steamer arrived with a shipment of
stock Jered had ordered last summer. There were enor-

mous spools of chain and rope, penny nails, pitch and tar, brushes and brooms. Jered hired a truck from the warehouse to the store every morning for a week, replacing sold-through inventory. Today he unloaded the last of the supplies into the stockroom and paid the teamster, whose horses snorted fog into a brisk back-alley wind, while Caroline and Alice arranged the shelves indoors. Aunt Alice worked tirelessly, dusted her hands on her apron, spoke seldom.

She avoided Caroline's eyes. She had been like this for months: cold, disapproving, brusquely polite.

They had argued at first, after the shock of the Partisan attack on the *Weston*. Alice refused to believe Guilford was dead. She was resolute on the matter.

Caroline knew quite simply and plainly that Guilford had died; she had known it from the moment Jered had told about the *Weston*, though that was proof of nothing; the expedition itself had been put ashore upriver. But even Jered acknowledged that they would have been easy prey for determined thieves. Caroline kept her feelings to herself, at least at first. But in her heart she was a widow well before the summer ended.

No one else conceded the truth. There was always hope. But September passed without word, and hopes dimmed with autumn and vanished, for all practical purposes, by winter.

Nothing had been proven, Alice said. Miracles were possible. "A wife ought to have faith," she told Caroline.

But sometimes a woman knows better.

The argument wasn't settled, couldn't be settled. They simply ceased to speak of it; but it colored every conversation, cast its shadow over the dinner table and insinuated itself between the ticking of the clock.

Caroline had taken to wearing black. Alice kept Guilford's suitcase in the hallway closet as an object lesson.

But more than that weary disagreement was bothering Alice today, Caroline thought.

She had a clue before the morning's work was finished. Alice went to the counter to serve a customer and came back to the storeroom wearing the pinched look that meant she had something unpleasant to say. She narrowed her eyes on Caroline, while Caroline tried not to flinch.

"It's bad enough to grieve," Alice said grimly, "when you don't know for a fact that he's dead. But it's worse, Caroline—far, *far* worse—to *finish* grieving."

And Caroline thought, *She knows*.

Not that it mattered.

That evening, Jered and Alice took themselves to the Crown and Reed, the local pub. When she was certain they were gone Caroline escorted Lily downstairs and briefly into the cold street, to a neighbor, a Mrs. de Koenig, who charged a Canadian dollar to look after the girl and keep quiet about it. Caroline told Lily good-bye, then buttoned her own jacket and hood against the winter chill.

Stars shivered above the frozen cobbles. Gas lamps cast a wan light across crusts of snow. Caroline hurried into the wind, fighting a surge of guilt. Contagion from her aunt, she thought, this feeling of wickedness. She was not doing anything wicked. She couldn't be. Guilford was dead. Her husband was dead. She had no husband.

Colin Watson stood waiting at the corner of Market and Thames. He embraced her briefly, then hailed a cab. He smiled as he helped her up, the smile a jejune thing half-hidden by his ridiculous moustache. Caroline supposed he was suppressing his natural melancholy for her. His hands were large and strong.

Where would he take her tonight? For a drink, she thought (though not at the Crown and Reed). A talk. That was all. He needed to talk. He was thinking of resigning his commission. He'd been offered a civilian job at the docks. He hadn't lived in Jered's storeroom since last September; he had taken a room at the Empire and was alone most nights.

That made things easier—a room of his own.

She couldn't stay with him as long as she would have liked. Jered and Alice mustn't know what she was doing. Or, if they knew, there must be at least a certain doubt, a gap of uncertainty she could defend.

But she wanted to stay. Colin was kind to her, a sort of kindness Guilford had never understood. Colin accepted her silences and didn't try to pry them open, as Guilford had. Guilford had always believed her moods reflected some failure of his own. He was solicitous—thoughtful, certainly, after his own lights—but she would have liked to weep occasionally without triggering an apology.

Lieutenant Watson, tall and sturdy but with moods of his own, allowed Caroline the privacy of her grief. Perhaps, she thought, it was how a gentleman treated a widow. The upheaval of the world had cracked the foundations of civility, but some men were still gentle. Some still asked before they touched. Colin was gentle. She liked his eyes best of all. They watched her attentively even as his hands roamed freely; they understood; ultimately, they forgave. It seemed to Caroline there was no sin in the world those quiet blue eyes couldn't redeem.

She stayed too late and drank more than she should have. They made scalding, desperate love. Her Lieutenant put her in a cab, when she insisted, an hour later than she had planned, but she made the cabbie let her off a block before Market. She didn't want to be seen climbing out of a hansom at this hour. Somehow, obscurely, it implied vice. So she walked off-balance into the teeth of the wind before reclaiming Lily from Mrs. de Koenig, who wheedled another dollar from her.

Jered and Alice were home, of course. Caroline struggled to maintain her dignity while she put away her coat and Lily's, saying nothing except to soothe her daughter. Jered closed his book and announced tonelessly that he was going to bed. He stumbled on the way out of the room. He'd been drinking, too.

But if Alice had, she didn't show it. "That little girl needs her sleep," she said flatly. "Don't you, Lily?"

"I'll put her to bed," Caroline said.

"She doesn't look like she needs much putting. Asleep on her feet, at this hour. Bed's warm and waiting, Lily! You go along, love, all right?"

Lily yawned agreeably and waddled off, leaving her mother defenseless.

"She slept late this morning," Caroline offered.

"She's not sleeping well at all. She's afraid for her father."

"I'm tired, too," Caroline said.

"But not too tired to commit adultery?"

Caroline stared, hoping she hadn't heard correctly.

"To fornicate with a man not your husband," Alice said. "Do you have another word for it?"

"This is beneath you."

"Perhaps you should find another place to sleep. I've

written Liam in Boston. He'll want you home as soon as we can book passage. I've had to apologize. On your behalf."

"You had no right to do that."

"Every right, I think."

"Guilford is dead!" It was her only counterargument, and she regretted using it so hastily. It lost its gravity, somehow, in this underheated parlor.

Alice sniffed. "You can't possibly know that."

"I feel the loss of him every day. *Of course* I know it."

"Then you have a funny way of grieving." Alice stood up, not concealing her anger. "Who told you you were special, Caroline? Was it Liam? I suppose he treated you that way, walled you up in his big Boston house, the suffering orphan. But everyone lost someone that night, some more than their parents . . . some of us lost everything we loved, every person and every place, sons, daughters, brothers, sisters, and some of us didn't have wealthy relations to dry our eyes and servants to make our comfortable beds."

"Unfair!"

"We don't get to make the rules, Caroline. Only keep them or break them."

"I won't be a widow for the rest of my life!"

"Probably not. But if you had any sense of decency at all you might think twice before conducting an affair with a man who helped murder your husband."

CHAPTER SEVENTEEN

Don't you think you've had enough?"

The voice seemed to condense out of the tavern air, smoky, liquid, and ingratiating. But it wasn't a message Vale wanted to hear. How best to sum up his response?

Be succinct, he thought. "Please fuck off."

A figure took the stool beside him. "That's not called for, is it? Really, don't mind me, Elias. I'm only here to chat."

Groaning, he turned his head. "Do I know you?"

The man was tall. He was also suave, carefully dressed, and handsome. Though perhaps not as handsome as he seemed to think, flashing those horsey white teeth like beacon lights. Vale guessed he was twenty-two, twenty-three—young, and far too confident for his age.

"No, you don't know me. Timothy Crane."

Hand like a piano player's. Long bony fingers. Vale ignored it. "Fuck off," he repeated.

"Elias, I'm sorry, but I have to talk to you whether you like it or not." The accent was New England, maddeningly aristocratic.

"Who are you, one of the Sanders-Moss nephews?"

"Sorry. No relation. But I know who you are." Crane leaned closer. Dangerously close. His breath tickled the fine hair on Vale's right ear. "You're the man who speaks to the dead."

"I'm the man who would like to convince you to fuck off."

"The man who has a god inside him. A painful and demanding god. At least if it's anything like mine."

Crane had a cab waiting at the curb. *Jesus Christ,* Vale thought, *what now?* He had the blurred sensation of events accelerating beyond his comprehension. He gave the cabbie his home address and settled in next to this grinning jackanapes.

It had been a quiet autumn, a quieter winter. The gods followed their own agenda, Vale supposed, and although the game with Eugene Randall had not played itself out—there had been two more séances, to no visible effect—the resolution seemed comfortably distant. Vale had even entertained the wistful notion that his god might be losing interest in him.

Apparently not.

The chatty Mr. Crane shut up in the presence of the driver. Vale tried to force himself sober—braced his shoulders, frowned and blinked—as the taxi crawled past electric light standards, globes of ice suspended in the frigid night. Washington winters weren't supposed to be so cruel.

They arrived eventually at Vale's town house. The street was quiet, all windows primly dark. Crane paid the cabbie, removed two immense suitcases from the vehicle, lugged them through Vale's front door, and dropped them insolently next to the umbrella stand.

"Staying a while?"

"Afraid so, old chap."

Old chap? Preserve me, Vale thought. "Do we have that much to talk about?"

"Lots. But it can wait until morning. Suppose you get a good night's sleep, Elias. You're really in no condition. We can discuss this when we're both more refreshed. Don't worry about me! I'll curl up on the sofa. No formalities between us."

And damned if he didn't stretch out on the velvet settee, still smiling.

"Look here. I'm too tired to throw you out. If you're still here in the morning—"

"We'll talk about it then. Fine idea."

Vale threw up his hands and left the room.

Morning arrived, for Elias Vale, just shy of noon.

Crane was at the breakfast table. He had showered and shaved. His hair was combed. His shirt was crisp. He poured himself a cup of coffee.

Vale was faintly aware of the stale sweat cooking out of his own clogged pores. "How long do you imagine you're staying?"

"Don't know."

"A week? A month?"

Shrug.

"Maybe you're not aware of this, Mr. Crane, but I live alone. Because I like it that way. I don't want a houseguest, even under these, uh, circumstances. And frankly, nobody asked me."

"Not their style, is it?"

The gods, he meant.

"You're saying I have no choice?"

"I wasn't offered one. Toast, Elias?"

Two of us, Vale thought. He hadn't anticipated that. Though of course it made sense. But how many more god-stricken individuals were out there walking the streets? Hundreds? Thousands?

He folded his hands. "*Why* are you here?"

"The eternal question, isn't it? I'm not sure I know. Not yet, at least. I gather you're meant to introduce me around."

"As what, my catamite?"

"Cousin, nephew, illegitimate child . . ."

"And then?"

"And then we'll do as we're told, when the time comes." Crane put down the butter knife. "Honestly, Elias, it's not my choice either. And I suspect it's temporary. No offense."

"No offense, but I hope so."

"In the meantime we'll have to find a bed for me. Unless you want my luggage cluttering up your front room. Do you entertain clients here?"

"Often. How much do you know about me, anyway?"

"A little. What do you know about me?"

"Nothing at all."

"Ah."

Vale made a desperate last try: "Isn't there a hotel in town—?"

"Not what *they* want." The smile again. "For better or worse, our fates appear to be intertwined."

The astonishing thing was that Vale did get used to Crane's occupation of his attic room, at least in the way one grows accustomed to a chronic headache. Crane was a considerate houseguest, more meticulous than Vale about cleaning up after himself, careful not to interrupt when Vale was with paying customers. He did insist on being taken to the Sanders-Moss salon and introduced as Vale's "cousin," a financier. Fortunately Crane seemed to have genuine working knowledge of banking and Wall Street, almost as if he had been raised to it. And maybe he had. He was vague about his past but hinted at family connections.

Just now, in any case, the Sanders-Moss table talk turned most often to the loss of the Finch expedition, the prospect of war. The Hearst papers had been touting a war with England, claimed to have evidence that the English were funneling weapons to the Partisans, which would make them at least indirectly responsible for the loss of American lives. An issue Vale cared nothing about, though his god apparently took an interest.

When they were together in the town house they tried to ignore one another. When they did talk—generally after Vale had taken a drink—they talked about their gods.

"It doesn't just threaten," Vale said. Another cold night, trapped indoors with Crane for company, a bitter wind rattling the casement windows. Tennessee whiskey. *Timor mortibus conturbat me.* "It promised I would live. I mean live . . . forever."

"Immortality," Crane said calmly, paring an apple with a kitchen knife.

"You too?"

"Oh, yes. Me too."

"Do you—*believe?*"

Crane peered at him quizzically. "Elias. When was the last time you cut yourself shaving?"

"Eh? I can't remember—"

"Long ago?"

"Long ago," Vale conceded. "Why?"

"Appendicitis, influenza, consumption? Broken bones, toothache, hangnail?"

"No, but—what are you saying?"

"You know the answer, Elias. You just don't have the nerve to test yourself. Haven't you ever been tempted, standing over a basin with a razor in your hand?"

"I have no idea what you mean."

Crane spread his left hand on the dining table and drove the knife smartly through it. The blade cracked through small bones and into wood. Vale recoiled and blinked.

Crane winced, briefly. Then he smiled. He tightened his grip on the shaft of the knife and pulled the blade out of his hand. A drop of blood welled out of the wound. Just one. Crane dabbed it away with a napkin.

The skin beneath was smooth, pink, seamless.

"Christ," Vale whispered.

"Apologies for damaging the table," Crane said. "But you see what I mean."

CHAPTER EIGHTEEN

FROM THE JOURNAL OF GUILFORD LAW:

Excuse my handwriting. The fire is warm but doesn't cast much useful light. Caroline, I think of you reading this and take some comfort in the thought. I hope it is warm where you are.

We are relatively warm here by the standards we've grown accustomed to—maybe too warm. Unnaturally warm. But let me explain.

We left this morning on our hobble-legged expedition to the heart of the ruins, Tom Compton, Dr. Sullivan, and I. We must have made a comical sight (Diggs certainly seemed to think so)—the three of us bundled in snake fur, white as dandelion clocks, two of us limping (on opposite legs), four days' supplies lashed to a sledge behind a grunting snake. A "snipe-hunt," Digby calls this little voyage.

In any case, we ignored the jibes, and soon enough

our beast had pulled us deeper into the ruins, into the oppressive silence of the city. I cannot communicate, Caroline, the eeriness of this haunted place, its slablike structures so uniformly arrayed and far extended. The snow, as we made our way southwest under a sunny sky, lay bright and crisp beneath the sledge. But the low angle of the winter sun meant that we traveled most often in shadow, down broad avenues cloaked in wintry melancholy.

Tom Compton led the fur snake by its rope halter. The frontiersman was in no mood to talk, so I hung back with Dr. Sullivan, hoping the sound of a human voice would dispel the gloom of these immense, repetitive alleys. But the mood had affected Sullivan, too.

"We've been assuming the city was built by intelligent beings," he said. "That may not be so."

I asked him to explain.

"Appearances are deceptive. Have you ever seen an African termite hill? It's an elaborate structure, often taller than a man. But the only architect is evolution itself. Or think of the regularity and complexity of a honeycomb."

"You're saying we might be inside some kind of insect hive?"

"What I'm saying is that although these structures are obviously artificial, the uniformity of size and presumably of function argues against a *human* builder."

"What kind of insect carves granite blocks the size of the Washington Monument?"

"I can't imagine. Worse, it's unprecedented. No one has reported anything like it. Whoever or whatever built this city, they seem to have left no progeny and had no obvious antecedents. It's almost a separate creation."

This mirrored my own thoughts too closely. For all its strangeness, Darwinia possesses its own beauty—

moss-green meadows, sage-pine glades, gentle rivers.
The ruins have none of that charm. For endless hours
we traveled the city's relentlessly regular streets, sun an-
gling low behind monoliths of cracked stone. The snow
ahead of us was trackless and blank. Neither Sullivan
nor I thought twice about that until Tom pointed out
the peculiarity of it. In the four or five days since the last
snowfall no animal had left its track here, nor any flying
things, not even moth-hawks. Moth-hawks are common
in these parts; whole flocks of them roost in the ruined
structures at the rim of the city. (Easy game, if you're desperate enough to want to eat the things. You sneak up on
a roosting flock at night, with a torch; the light dazzles
them; a man can kill six or seven with a stick before they
gather their wits and fly away.) But not here. Granted,
there's little enough forage deep in these stone-choked
warrens. Still, the absence of life seems ominous. It
heightens the nerves, Caroline, and I admit that as the
afternoon passed and the shadows lengthened we were
all three of us on our toes, apt to start at the slightest
commotion.

Not that there was any commotion. Only the crackle
of hidden ice, the soft collapse of sun-softened snow.
With dusk we made our camp, undisturbed. It speaks
to the size of this place that we have still not reached
what Sullivan calculates to be the center of the city. We
carried kindling with us, mosque-tree branches, dense
but hollow and not especially heavy; we used them to
make a fire in one of the structures with a more or less
intact roof. We couldn't hope to heat the cathedral-
sized interior, but we were out of the wind and able to
make a cozy-enough corner for ourselves.

In any case it is warmer here than at the perimeter.
Sullivan points out that the stone floor is warmer than
he can account for, almost warm enough to melt ice,

perhaps due to an underground spring or other source of natural heat. Tom Compton overcame his wary silence long enough to tell us that, one clear night when he camped in the hills after a snake hunt, he had seen a blue-green fairy glow shining deep within the city. Some kind of vulcanism, maybe, though Sullivan says the geology is wrong. We've seen no sign of it ourselves.

I should add that Tom Compton, ordinarily the staunchest of pragmatists, seems more unnerved than either Sullivan or I. He said a peculiar thing tonight as I began this entry . . . mumbled it, leaning into the fire so intently that I worried an ember would ignite his briar-patch beard:

"I dreamed of this place," he said.

He wouldn't elaborate, but I felt a chill despite the fire. Because, Caroline, I've dreamed of this place too, dreamed of it deep in the fever sleeps of autumn, when the poison was still coursing through my body and I couldn't tell day from night . . . *I dreamed of the city too*, and I don't know what that means.

. . . and dreamed again last night.

But I have more than that to tell you, Caroline, and not much time. Our supplies are limited and Sullivan insists we use each moment as economically as possible. So I will tell you in the plainest and most direct words what we found.

The city isn't just a grid of squares. It has a center, as Sullivan suspected. And at the center is not a cathedral or a marketplace but something altogether stranger.

We came upon the building this morning. It must once have been visible from a great distance, but erosion has camouflaged it. (I doubt even Finch would

deny that these ruins are terribly old.) Today the structure is surrounded by a field of its own rubble. Huge
stone blocks, some polished as if fresh from the quarry,
others worn into a grotesquery of angles, impeded our
progress. We left our sledge behind and hiked through
the maze-like passages created by chance and weather
until we found the core of the central building.

Rising from this bed of rubble is a black basaltic
dome, open on roughly a quarter of its periphery. The
vault of the dome is at least two hundred feet high at
its apex and as broad as a city block. The unbroken sec-
tions are still smooth, almost silky, worked by a technique Sullivan can't identify.

A perpetual fog cloaks the dome, which is perhaps
why none of us had seen it from the slopes of the valley. Melted snow and ice, Sullivan guessed, heated
from below. Even in the rubble field the air was no-
ticeably warm, and no snow had collected on the dome
itself. It must be well above the freezing point of water.

The three of us gazed mutely at this scene. I mourned
my lost camera. What a plate it would have made! *The
desolate Alpine ruins of the European hinterland.* Caroline,
we might have lived for a year on a photograph like that.

None of us voiced his thoughts. Maybe they seemed
too fantastic. Certainly mine did. I was reminded again
of E.R. Burroughs' adventure stories, with their volcanic
caverns and their beast-men worshiping ancient gods.

(I know you disapprove of my reading habits, Caroline, but the fantasies of Mr. Burroughs are proving to
be a fair Baedeker to this continent! All we lack is a
suitable Princess, and a sword for me to buckle on.)

We returned to the sledge, fed our snake, gathered
what supplies we could carry and hiked back to the
dome. Sullivan was as excited as I have ever seen him;
he had to be restrained from dashing madly all over

the site. He settled for a camp just beyond the rim of the dome and is obviously frustrated we haven't gone farther—but there's a lot of territory under this incline of polished stone, all strewn with rock, and it's frankly a little unnerving to have that unsupported mass of granite hanging over our heads.

The interior was nearly lightless, in any case—the sun had declined beyond a gap-toothed rank of ruins—and we were forced to build a hasty fire before we lost the light entirely.

We met the night with a mixture of excitement and apprehension, crouched over our fire like Visigoths in a Roman temple. There is nothing to see beyond our circle of firelight but its flickering reflection on the high inner circumference of the vault.

No, that's not entirely true. Sullivan has drawn our attention to another light, fainter still, the source of which must be deep inside this rubble-choked structure. A natural phenomenon, I dearly hope, though the sense of *another presence* is strong enough to raise hackles.

Not light enough to write by, though. Not without risking blindness. More tomorrow.

HERE THE JOURNAL ENDS.

"A little more rope, please, Guilford."

Sullivan's voice rose from the depths as if buoyed on its own echoes. Guilford played out another few feet of rope.

The rope had been one of the few useful items rescued from last summer's attack. These two spools of hempen fiber had saved more than one life—provided harnesses for the animals, rigging for tents, a thousand useful things. But the rope was only a precaution.

At the center of the domed ruin they had found a circular opening perhaps fifty yards in diameter, its rim cut into a spiral of stone steps each ten feet wide. The shallow stairs were intact, their contours softened by centuries of erosion. A stream of water cut the well's southern rim, fell, became mist, merged into fog-hidden deeps. Faint daylight came from above, a cool lambent glow from beneath. *The heart of the city,* Guilford thought. Warm and still faintly beating.

Sullivan wanted to explore it.

"The slope is trivial," he said. "The passage is intact and it was obviously meant to be walked. We're in no more danger here than we would be out in the cold."

Tom Compton stroked his mist-dewed beard. "You're stupider than I thought," he said, "if you mean to climb down there."

"What would *you* suggest?" Sullivan wheeled to face the frontiersman. He was as angry as Guilford had seen him, his face a thunderous brick-red. "That we walk back to our pathetic little shambles and pray for sunny weather? Creep north to the Bodensee come spring, unless cold kills us first, or the Partisans, or the Rhein-felden? *Damn* thee, Tom, this might be our only chance to *learn* something from this place!"

"What good is learning," the frontiersman asked, "if you take it to your grave?"

Sullivan turned away scornfully. "What good is friendship, then, or love, or life itself? What *don't* you take to your grave?"

"Wasn't planning on taking anything there," Tom said. "At least not yet."

He reeled the rope from his hands.

* * *

It won't be so bad in daylight, Guilford thought, and there *was* daylight here, through the breached vault of the dome, dim as it might be. In any case, the rope was reassuring. They rigged harness to link themselves together. The slope might be gentle but the stone was slick with moisture, a fall could turn into a slide, and there was no telling how far into the fog this decline might reach. Below ground level the limit of visibility was a scant few yards. A dropped stone gave back uncertain echos.

Sullivan went first, favoring his bad leg. Then Guilford, favoring his own. The frontiersman followed behind. The down-spiraling walkway was broad enough that Guilford was able to avoid looking directly into the well's smoky deeps.

He couldn't guess what this well had been made for or who might have walked this way in ages past. Nor how far down it might descend, into what lava-heated cavern or glowing underworld. Hadn't the Aztecs used wells for human sacrifice? Certainly nothing much *good* could have happened down this rabbit hole.

Sullivan called a halt when they had descended, by Guilford's estimate, a hundred feet or more. The rim of the well was as invisible now as the bottom, both hidden in lofting spirals of fog. Sullivan was winded and gasping, but his eyes were bright in the strange, dim radiance.

Guilford wondered aloud whether they hadn't come far enough. "No offense, Dr. Sullivan, but what exactly do you expect to find here?

"The answer to a hundred questions."

"It's some kind of well or cistern," Guilford said.

"Open your eyes, for God's sake! A well is what this is *not*. If anything, it was designed to keep groundwater out. Do you think these stones *grew* here? The blocks

are cut and the joints are caulked . . . I don't know what
the caulking material is, but it's remarkably well preserved. In any case, we're already below the water
table. This is not a *well*, Mr. Law."

"Then what is it?"

"Whatever its purpose—practical or ceremonial—it
must have been important. The dome is a landmark,
and I'd guess this passageway was meant to accommodate a great deal of traffic."

"Traffic?"

"The city builders."

"But they're extinct," Guilford said.

"You hope," the frontiersman muttered from behind.

But there was no end to the descent, only this spiral of
stone winding monotonously into blue-tinted fog, until
even Sullivan admitted he was too fatigued to go any
farther.

"We need," he said at length, "more men."

Guilford wondered who he had in mind. Keck?
Robertson? One-armed Digby?

Tom looked up the way they had come, now a color-
less overcast. "We shouldn't wait to turn back.
Daylight'll be gone soon—what there is of it." He cast
a critical eye at Sullivan. "When you get your breath
back—"

"Don't worry about me. Go on! Reverse order. I'll
follow behind."

He was pale and dewed with sweat.

The frontiersman shrugged and turned. Guilford
followed Tom, calling a halt whenever the line between himself and Sullivan grew taut. Which it often
did. The botanist's breathing was audible over a considerable distance now and it grew more labored as

they climbed. Before long Sullivan began to cough. Tom looked back sharply and slowed the ascent to a crawl.

The fog had begun to thicken. Guilford lost sight of the far wall, stone steps vanishing behind a twining curtain of vapor. The rope served a purpose now, as even Tom Compton's broad back grew faint in the mist.

With the loss of visible landmarks came disorientation. He couldn't guess how far they had come or how much of the climb remained. *Doesn't matter,* he told himself sternly. *Every step is one step closer.* His bad leg had began to hurt him, a vicious pain that ran like a wire from calf to knee.

Shouldn't have gone so far down, Guilford thought, but Sullivan's enthusiasm had been contagious, the sense of some immense revelation waiting, if only they could reach it. He stood a moment, closed his eyes, felt chill air flow past him like a river. He smelled the mineral smells of granite and fog. And something else. Muskier, stranger.

"Guilford!"

Tom's voice. Guilford looked up sheepishly.

"Watch where you're standing," the frontiersman said.

It was the brink of the escarpment. Another step and he might have fallen.

"Keep your left hand on the wall. You too, Sullivan."

Sullivan came into view, nodding wordlessly. He was a shade, a wraith, a gangly spirit.

Guilford was groping his way behind the frontiersman when the rope suddenly cinched at his waist. He called a halt and turned.

"Dr. Sullivan?"

No answer. The rope remained taut. When he looked back he saw only fog.

"Dr. Sullivan—are you all right?"

No answer, only this anchoring weight.

Tom Compton came scrabbling out of the mist. Guilford backed up, slacking the rope, peering into the dimness for any sign of Sullivan.

He found the botanist lying on the wide granite ledge, face down, one hand still touching the damp rock wall.

"Ah, Christ!" Tom dropped to his knees. He turned Sullivan over and searched his wrist for a pulse.

"He's breathing," the frontiersman said. "More or less."

"What's wrong with him?"

"Don't know. His skin's cold and he's ungodly pale. Sullivan! Wake up, you son of a bitch! Work to do!"

Sullivan didn't wake up. His head lolled to one side, limply. A trickle of blood escaped one nostril. *He looks shrunken,* Guilford thought dazedly. *Like someone let the air out of him.*

Tom stripped his pack and bunched it under the botanist's head. "Stubborn fucker, wouldn't slow down for love of life . . ."

"What do we do now?"

"Let me think."

Despite their best efforts, Sullivan wouldn't wake up.

Tom Compton rocked on his heels for a time, deep in thought. Then he hitched his pack over his shoulder and shrugged out of the rope harness. "Hell with it. Look, I'll bring blankets and food from the sledge for both of you. After that you stay with him; I'll go for help."

"He's wet and nearly freezing, Tom."

"He'll freeze faster in the open air. Might kill him to move him. Give me a day to reach camp, another day to get here with Keck and Farr. Farr will know what to do. You'll be all right—I don't know about Sullivan, poor bastard." He frowned fiercely. "But you stay with him, Guilford. Don't leave him alone."

He might not wake up, Guilford thought. *He might die. And then* I'll *be alone, in this godforsaken hole in the ground.*

"I'll stay."

The frontiersman nodded curtly. "If he dies, wait for me. We're close enough to the top, you ought to be able to tell night from day. You understand? Keep your fucking wits about you."

Guilford nodded.

"All right." Tom bent over the unconscious shape of Sullivan with a tenderness Guilford had never seen in him, smoothed a strand of gray hair from the botanist's dank forehead. "Hang on, you old cock-knocker! You damn stupid *explorer.*"

Guilford took the blankets Tom brought him and made a rough bed to shield Sullivan from cold air and cold stone. Compared to the atmosphere outside the temperature in the well was nearly balmy—above the freezing point; but the fog cut through clothing and chilled the skin.

When Tom vanished into the mist Guilford felt profoundly alone. No company now but his thoughts and Sullivan's slow, labored breathing. He felt both bored and near panic. He found himself wishing stupidly for something to read. The only reading matter that had survived the Partisan attack was Digby's pocket New Testament, and Diggs wouldn't allow it out of his possession. Diggs thought the onion-leafed book had saved his life: it was his lucky charm. *Argosy* was long lost.

As if a person *could* read, in this arsenic-colored dusk.

He knew night had fallen when the light above him faded entirely and the moist air turned a deeper and more poisonous shade of green. Minute particles of dust and ice wafted out of the deeps, like diatoms in an ocean current. He rearranged the blankets around Dr. Sullivan, whose breathing had grown harsh as the rasp of a saw blade in wet pine, and ignited one of the two mosquewood torches Tom Compton had brought him. Without a blanket of his own, Guilford shivered uncontrollably. He stood up whenever his feet grew numb, careful to keep one hand on the rock wall. He propped the torch in a cairn of loose rocks and warmed his hands at the low flame. Mosquewood dipped in snake tallow, it would burn for six or eight hours, though not brightly.

He was afraid to sleep.

In the silence he was able to hear subtle sounds—a distant rumbling, unless that was the pulse of his own blood, amplified in the darkness. He remembered a novel by H.G. Wells, *The Time Machine,* and its subterranean Morlocks, with their glowing eyes and terrible hungers. Not a welcome memory.

He talked to Sullivan to pass the time. Sullivan might be listening, Guilford thought, though his eyes were firmly closed and blood continued to ooze sluggishly from his nose. Periodically Guilford dipped the tail of his shirt into a trickle of meltwater and used it to wipe the blood from Sullivan's face. He talked fondly about Caroline and Lily. He talked about his father, clubbed to death during the Boston food riots when he had doggedly tried to enter his print shop, as he had done every working day of his adult life. Dumb courage. Guilford wished he had some of that.

He wished Sullivan would wake up. Tell some stories of his own. Make his case for an ancient, evolved Darwinia; hammer the miraculous with the cold steel of reason. *Hope you're right about that,* Guilford thought. *Hope this continent is not some dream or, worse, a nightmare. Hope old and dead things remain old and dead.*

He wished he had a hot meal and a bath to look forward to. And a bed, and Caroline in it, the warm contours of her body under a snowdrift of cotton sheet. He didn't like these noises from the deeps, or the way the sound rose and ebbed like an impossible tide.

"I hope you don't die, Dr. Sullivan. I know how you'd hate to give up without understanding any of this. No easy task, though, is it?"

Now Sullivan drew a deep, convulsive breath. Guilford looked down and was startled to see the botanist's eyes spring open.

Sullivan looked hard at him—or *through* him—it was hard to tell which. One of his pupils was grotesquely dilated, the white rimmed with blood.

"We don't die," Sullivan gasped.

Guilford fought a sudden urge to back away. "Hey!" he said. "Dr. Sullivan, lie still! Don't excite yourself. You'll be all right, just relax. Help's on the way."

"Didn't he tell you that? Guilford tell Guilford that Guilford won't die?"

"Don't try to talk." *Don't talk,* Guilford thought, *because you're frightening the crap out of me.*

Sullivan's lips curled into a one-sided frown, awful to behold. "You've seen them in your dreams. . . ."

"Please don't, Dr. Sullivan."

"Green as old copper. Spines on their bellies. . . . They *eat* dreams. Eat everything!"

In fact the words struck a chord, but Guilford

pushed the memory away. The important thing now was not to panic.

"Guilford!" Sullivan's left hand shot out to grasp Guilford's wrist, while his right clutched reflexively at empty air. "This is one of the places where the world ends!"

"You're not making sense, Dr. Sullivan. Please, try to sleep. Tom will be back soon."

"You died in France. Died fighting the Boche. Of all things."

"I don't like to say it, but you're scaring me, Dr. Sullivan."

"I cannot die!" Sullivan insisted.

Then he grunted, and all the breath sighed out of him at once.

After a time Guilford closed the corpse's eyes.

He sat with Dr. Sullivan for several hours more, humming tunelessly, waiting for whatever might climb out of the dark to claim him.

Shortly before dawn, exhausted, he fell asleep.

They want so badly to come out!

Guilford can feel their anger, their frustration.

He has no name for them. They don't quite exist. They are trapped between idea and creation, incomplete, half-sentient, longing for embodiment. Physically they are faint green shapes, larger than a man, armored, thorny, huge muzzles opening and closing in silent anger.

They were bound here after the battle.

The thought is not his own. Guilford turns, weightless. He is floating deep in the well, though not on water. The air it-

*self is radiant around him. Somehow, this uncreated light is
both air and rock and self.*

*The picket floats beside him. A spindly man in a U.S. Army
uniform. Light flows through him, from him. He is the soldier
from Guilford's dreams, a man who might be his twin.*

Who are you?

Yourself, *the picket answers.*

That's not possible.

Seems not. But it is.

*Even the voice is familiar. It's the voice in which Guilford
speaks to himself, the voice of his private thoughts.*

And what are these? *He means the bound creatures.*
Demons?

You may call them that. Call them monsters. They
have no ambition but to become. Ultimately, to be
everything that exists.

*Guilford can see them more clearly now. Their scales and
claws, their several arms, their snapping teeth.*

Animals?

Much more than animals. But that, too, given a
chance.

You bound them here?

I did. In part. With the help of others. But the binding is imperfect.

I don't know what that means.

See how they tremble on the verge of incarnation?
Soon, they'll assume the physical once again. Unless
we bind them forever.

Bind them? *Guilford asks. He is afraid now. So much of
this defies his comprehension. But he can sense the enormous
pressure from below, the terrible desire thwarted and stored for
eons, waiting to burst forth.*

We will bind them, *the picket says calmly.*

We?

You and I.

The words are shocking. Guilford feels the impossible weight of the task, as immense as the moon. I don't understand any of this!

Patience, little brother, *the picket says, and lifts him up, up through the eerie light, through the fog and heat of almost-incarnation, like an angel in a ragged army uniform, and as he rises his flesh melts into air.*

Tom Compton loomed over him, holding a torch.

I would get up, Guilford thought, *if I could.* If it weren't so cold here. If his body hadn't stiffened in a thousand places. If he could order his dizzying thoughts. He had some vital message to impart, a message about Dr. Sullivan.

"He died," Guilford said. That was it. Sullivan's body lay beside him, under a blanket. Sullivan's face was pale and still in the lantern light. "I'm sorry, Tom."

"I know," Tom said. "You did a good job staying with him. Can you walk?"

Guilford tried to put his feet under him but only managed to bang his hip on a ridge of stone.

"Lean on me," the frontiersman said.

Once again, he felt himself lifted.

It was hard to stay awake. His torpid body wanted him to close his eyes and rest. "We'll build a fire when we're out of his hole," the frontiersman told him. "Step lively now."

"How long has it been?"

"Three days."

"Three?"

"There was trouble."

"Who's with you?"

They had reached the rim of the well. The interior of the dome was suffused with watery daylight. A gaunt figure waited, slouched against a slab of rock, canvas hood pulled over his face. The mist obscured his features.

"Finch," Tom said. "Finch came with me."

"Finch? Why Finch? What about Keck, what about Robertson?"

"They're dead, Guilford. Keck, Robertson, Diggs, Donner, and Farr. All dead. And so will we be, if you don't keep moving."

Guilford moaned and shielded his eyes.

CHAPTER NINETEEN

Spring came early to London. The thawing marshes to the east and west gave the air an earthy scent, and Thames Street, freshly paved from the docks to Tower Hill, rattled with commerce. To the west, work had begun again on the dome of the new St. Paul's.

Caroline dodged a herd of sheep headed for market, feeling as if she were bound for slaughter herself. For weeks she had refused to see Colin Watson, refused to accept his invitations or even read his notes. She was not sure why she had agreed to see him now—to meet him at a coffee shop on Candlewick Street—except for the persistent feeling that she owed him something, if only an explanation, before she left for America.

After all, he was a soldier. He followed orders. He wasn't Kitchener; he wasn't even the Royal Navy. Just one man.

She found the place easily enough. The shop was

dressed in Tudor woodwork. Its leaded windows dripped with condensation, the interior heated by the steam from a huge silver samovar. The crowd inside was rough, working-class, largely male. She gazed across a sea of woollen caps until she spotted Colin at a table at the rear, his coat collar turned up and his long face apprehensive.

"Well," he said. "We meet again." He raised his cup in a sort of mock-toast.

But Caroline didn't want to spar with him. She sat down and came to the point. "I want you to know, I'm going home."

"You just got here."

"I mean to Boston."

"Boston! Is that why you wouldn't see me?"

"No."

"Then won't you at least tell me why you're leaving?" He lowered his voice and opened his blue eyes wide. "Caroline, please. I know I must have offended you. I don't know how, but if it's an apology you want, you can have it."

This was harder than she had expected. He was bewildered, genuinely contrite. She bit her lip.

"Your aunt Alice found out about us, is that it?"

Caroline dipped her head. "It wasn't the best-kept secret."

"Ah. I suspected as much. I doubt Jered would have put up a fuss, but Alice—well, I assume she was angry."

"Yes. But that doesn't matter."

"Then why leave?"

"They won't have me any longer."

"Stay with me, then."

"I can't!"

"Don't be shocked, Caroline. We needn't live in sin, you know."

Dear God, in a moment he'd be proposing! "You *know* why I can't do that! Colin—*she told me.*"

"Told you what?"

Two seamen at the nearest table were smirking at her. She lowered her voice to match Colin's. "That you murdered Guilford."

The Lieutenant sat back in his chair, goggling. "God almighty! *Murdered* him? She said that?" He blinked. "But, Caroline, it's absurd!"

"By sending guns across the Channel. Guns to the Partisans."

He put down his cup. He blinked again. "Guns to the—ah. I see."

"Then it's true?"

He looked at her steadily. "That I murdered Guilford? Certainly not. About the weapons?" He hesitated. "Up to a point, it may be. We aren't supposed to discuss these things even among ourselves."

"It *is* true!"

"It *may* be. Honestly, I don't know! I'm not a senior officer. I do what I'm told, and I don't ask questions."

"But guns are involved?"

"Yes, a number of weapons have passed through London."

That was nearly an admission. Caroline thought she ought to be angry. She wondered why her anger was suddenly so elusive.

Maybe anger was like grief. It took its own sweet time. It waited in ambush.

Colin was thoughtful, concerned. "I suppose Alice might have heard something through Jered . . . and he probably knows more about it than I do, come to that.

The Navy employs his warehouse and his dray teams from time to time, with his consent. He might well have done other work for the Admiralty. Fancies himself a patriot, after all."

Alice and Jered arguing in the night, keeping Lily awake: was *this* what they had been fighting about? Jered admitting that guns had gone through his warehouse on the way to the Partisans, Alice afraid that Guilford would be hurt . . .

"But even if weapons went across the Channel, you can't be sure they had anything to do with Guilford. Frankly, I can't imagine why anyone would want to interfere with the Finch party. The Partisans operate along the coast; they need coal and money far more than they need munitions. Anyone could have fired on the *Weston*—bandits, anarchists! And as for Guilford, who knows what he ran into past the bloody Rheinfelden? The continent is an unexplored wilderness; it's dangerous by nature."

She was ashamed to feel her defenses crumbling. The issue had seemed icily clear when Alice explained it. But what if Jered was as guilty as Colin?

She shouldn't be having this conversation . . . but there was nothing to stop it now, no moral or practical obstacle. This man, whatever he might have done, was being honest with her.

And she had missed him. She might as well admit it.

The seamen in their striped jerseys grinned lewdly at her.

Colin reached for her hand. "Walk with me," he said. "Somewhere away from the noise."

She let him talk all the way along Candlewick and up Fenchurch to the end of the pavement, let herself be soothed by the sound of his voice and the seductive idea of his innocence.

The mosque trees had been a dull green all winter, but sudden sun and melting snow had coaxed new blades from the tree crowns. The air was almost warm.

He was a soldier, she told herself again. Of course he did what he was told; what choice did he have?

Jered was another matter. Jered was a civilian; he didn't have to cooperate with the Admiralty. And Alice knew that. How the knowledge must have burned! Bitter, her voice had been, arguing with her husband in the dark. Of course she blamed Jered, but she couldn't leave him; she was chained to him by marriage.

So Alice hated Colin instead. Blind, displaced, unthinking hatred. Because she couldn't afford the luxury of hating her own husband.

"See me again," Colin begged. "At least once more. Before you leave."

Caroline said she would try.

"I hate to think of you at sea. There have been threats to shipping, you know. They say the American fleet is massed in the North Atlantic."

"I don't care about that."

"Perhaps you should."

Mrs. de Koenig passed her a note from Colin later that week. There was a general mobilization, he said; he might be shipped out; he wanted to see her as soon as possible.

War, Caroline thought bitterly. Everyone was talking about war. Only ten years since the world was shaken to its foundations, and now they want to fight over the scraps. Over a wilderness!

The *Times*, a six-page daily pressed on fibrous

mosque-pulp paper, had devoted most of its recent editorials to chastening the Americans: for administering the Continent as if it were an American protectorate, for "imposing boundaries" on the British Isles, for various sins of arrogance or complacency. Caroline's accent provoked raised eyebrows at the stores and market stalls. Today Lily had asked her why it was so bad to be an American.

"It isn't," Caroline told her. "That's all just talk. People are upset, but they'll calm down sooner or later."

"We're riding a ship soon," Lily said.

"Probably."

She had stopped taking meals with Alice and Jered. She would have rented a room for herself and Lily at the Empire if her stipend from home had been more generous. But even pub meals were an ordeal now, with all this talk of war. Her aunt and uncle were stiffly formal with Caroline when they couldn't avoid her altogether, though they still fawned over Lily. Caroline found this easier to bear since her talk with Colin. She found herself nearly pitying Alice—poor staunchly moral Alice, locked into a network of guilt as tight as those curls she wove into her graying hair.

"Sleep," Caroline told Lily that night, tucking her under her cotton sheets, smoothing the fabric. "Sleep well. We'll be traveling soon."

One way or another.

Lily nodded solemnly. Since Christmas, the girl had stopped asking about her father. The answers were never satisfactory.

"Away from here?" Lily asked.

"Away from here."

"Somewhere safe?"

"Somewhere safe."

* * *

A sunlit morning. There was pavement being poured on Fenchurch, the smell of tar wafting over the town, everywhere the clap of horses' hooves and the flat ring of buckles and reins.

She saw Colin waiting on Thames Street near the docks, sunlight at his back, reading the newspaper. Her sense of excitement rose. She didn't know what she would tell him. She didn't have a plan. Only a collection of hopes and fears.

She had taken a bare handful of steps toward him when sirens wailed from the city center.

The sound paralyzed her, raised gooseflesh on her shoulders.

The crowd on the quay seemed paralyzed too. Colin looked up from his paper in consternation. Caroline raised her arm; he ran to her. The sirens wailed on.

She fell into his embrace. *"What is it?"*

"I don't know."

"I want my daughter." Something bad was happening. Lily would be frightened.

"Come on, then." Colin took her hand and gently pressed it. "We'll find Lily. But we have to hurry."

The wind came from the east—a steady spring wind, smoky and fragrant. The river was placid and white with sails. South along the marshy bank of the Thames, the stacks of the gunboats had only just appeared.

CHAPTER TWENTY

It's simple, Crane had told him. We're part of something that's getting stronger. And they're part of something that's getting weaker.

Maybe it looked that way from Crane's point of view. Crane had slid into the ranks of Washington's elite—well, the semi-elite, the under-elite—like a gilded suppository. Only months in town, and now he was working for Senator Klassen in some shadowy capacity; had lately taken his own apartment (for which small mercy thank the gods); he was a fixture at the Sanders-Moss salon and had earned the right to condescend to Elias Vale in public places.

Whereas Vale's own invitations had dropped off in number and frequency, his clients were fewer and less affluent, and even Eugene Randall saw him less often.

Randall, of course, had been subpoenaed by a congressional committee investigating the loss of the Finch expedition. Perhaps even a deceased spouse takes second place to such lofty obligations. The dead, in any case, were notoriously patient.

Still and all, Vale had begun to wonder whether the gods were playing favorites.

He sought distraction where he could find it. It was one of his newer clients, an elderly Maryland abortionist, who had given Vale the amber vial of morphine and a chased-silver hypodermic syringe. Had shown him how to find a vein and raise it and prick it with the hollow needle, a process which made him think abstractly of bees and venom. *Oh sting of oblivion.* He took to the habit recklessly.

The kit—it folded into a neat silver sleeve about the size of a cigarette case—was in his jacket pocket when he arrived at the Sanders-Moss estate. He hadn't planned to use it. But the afternoon went badly. The weather was too wet for winter, too cold for spring. Eleanor welcomed him with an uneasy expression—one can only coax so much mileage out of a lost christening dress, Vale supposed—and after lunch a drunken junior congressman began to bait him about his work.

"Stock market tips, Mr. Vale? You talk to the dead, they must have a few choice observations. But I don't suppose the dead have much opportunity to invest, do they?"

"In this district, Congressman, they don't even vote."

"Touched a sore point, Mr. Vale?"

"It's Doctor Vale."

"Doctor of what would that be exactly?"

Doctor of Immortality, Vale thought. *Unlike you, you rotting slab of meat.*

"You know, Mr. Vale, I happen to have looked into your past. Did a little research, especially when Eleanor here told me how much she was paying you to read her palm."

"I don't read palms."

"No, but I bet you know how to read a balance sheet."

"This is insulting."

The congressman smiled gleefully. "Why, who told you that, Mr. Vale? John Wilkes Booth?"

Even Eleanor laughed.

"This is not the guest bathroom!" The maid Olivia tapped irritably at the door. "This the *help* bathroom!"

Vale ignored her. The hypodermic kit lay open on the green-tile floor. He slumped on the toilet. He had cranked open the pebbled window; a chill rain came in. The chain of the water closet tapped restlessly against the damp white wall.

He had taken off his jacket, rolled up his sleeve. He slapped the crotch of his left arm until a vein came up. *Fuck them all*, Vale thought primly.

The first shot was easeful, a still calm that enveloped him like a child's blanket. The bathroom looked suddenly vague, as if wrapped in glassine.

But I am immortal, Vale thought.

He remembered Crane driving the knife through the back of his hand. Crane, it turned out, had a perverse fondness for self-mutilation. Liked to pierce himself with knives, cut himself with blades, prick himself with needles.

Well, I am no stranger to needles myself. Vale preferred the morphine even to Kentucky whiskey. The oblivion was more certain, somehow more comprehensive. He wanted more of it.

"Mr. Vale! That you in there?"

"Go away, Olivia, thank you."

He reached for the syringe again. *I am, after all, im-*

mortal. I cannot die. The implications of that fact had grown somewhat unnerving.

This time his skin resisted the needle. Vale pushed harder. It was like probing cheddar cheese. He thought he had found the vein at last, but when he pushed the plunger the skin beneath began to discolor, a massive, fluid bruise.

"Shit," he said.

"You have to come out or I'll tell Mrs. Sanders-Moss, she'll have somebody break down this door!"

"Only a little longer, Olivia dear. Be nice and go away."

"This is not the guest bathroom! You been in there an hour already!"

Had he? If so, it was only because she wouldn't let him concentrate on the task at hand. He refilled the syringe.

But now the needle wouldn't pierce his skin at all.

Had he dulled the point? The tip looked as lethally sharp as ever.

He pushed harder.

He winced. There was pain, remarkably. The soft skin dimpled and cratered and reddened. But it didn't break.

He tried the flesh on his wrist. It was the same, like trying to cut leather with a spoon. He lowered his pants to his ankles and tried the inside of a thigh.

Nothing.

Finally, in angry desperation, Vale jabbed the weeping needle against his throat where he imagined an artery might be.

The tip snapped off. The syringe drooled its contents uselessly down his open collar.

"Shit!" Vale exclaimed again, frustrated almost to tears.

The door burst open. Here was Olivia, gaping at him, and the upstart junior congressman behind her, and wide-eyed Eleanor, and even Timothy Crane, frowning officiously.

"Huh!" Olivia said. "Well, *that* figures."

"A shot of morphine in the niggers' toilet? Uncouth, Elias, to say the least."

"Shut up," Vale said wearily. The initial effect of the morphine, if any, had worn off. His body felt dry as dust, his mind maddeningly lucid. He had allowed Crane to take him to his car, after Eleanor made it clear that he would not be welcome on the property again and that she would call the police if he tried to return. Her exact words had been less diplomatic.

"They're generous employers," Crane said.

"Who?"

"The gods. They don't care what you do on your own time. Morphine, cocaine, women, sodomy, murder, backgammon—it's all the same to them. But you can't stupefy yourself when they want your attention, and you certainly can't inject a lethal overdose into your arm, if that was what you were attempting to do. Stupid thing to try, Elias, if I may say so."

The car turned a corner. Dismal day was passing into dismal evening.

"This is business now, Elias."

"Where are we going?" Not that he particularly cared, though he felt the queasy presence of the god inside him, ramping up his pulse, straightening his spine.

"To visit Eugene Randall."

"I wasn't told."

"I'm telling you now."

Vale looked listlessly at the upholstery of Crane's brand-new Ford. "What's in the bag?"

"Have a look."

It was a leather doctor's bag, and it contained just three articles: a surgical knife, a bottle of methyl alcohol, and a box of safety matches.

Alcohol and matches—to sterilize the knife? The knife to—

"Oh, no," Vale said.

"Don't be priggish, Elias."

"Randall isn't important enough for . . . whatever you have in mind."

"It's not what *I* have in mind. We don't make these decisions. You know that."

Vale stared at the blithe young man. "It doesn't bother you?"

"No. Not that it matters."

"You've done this before, haven't you?"

"Elias, that's privileged information. I'm sorry if you're shocked. But really, who do you think we're working for? Not some Sunday school god, not the proverbial loving shepherd. The shoving leopard, more like."

"You mean to kill Eugene Randall?"

"Certainly."

"But why?"

"Not for me to say, is it? Most likely the problem is the testimony he plans to give the Chandler Committee. All he needs to do, and I know his dear departed Louisa Ellen already told him so, is to let the committee get on with its work. There are five so-called witnesses who will say they saw English-speaking gentlemen firing mortars and regulation Lee-Enfields at the *Weston*. Randall would save himself and the Smithsonian a great deal of trouble if he simply agreed to smile and nod, but if he insists on muddying the issue—"

"He believes Finch's people may still be alive."

"Yes, that's the problem."

"Even so—in the long run, what does it matter? If it's a war the gods want, Randall's testimony is hardly a serious impediment. Most likely the papers won't even report it."

"But they will report Randall's murder. And if we're careful, they'll blame it on British agents."

Vale closed his eyes. The wheels turn within the wheels, *ad infinitum*. For one agonizing moment he yearned for the morphine syringe.

Then a sullen determination rose in him, not precisely his own. "Will this take long?"

"Not long at all," Crane told him soothingly.

Perhaps it was the lingering effect of the morphine in his bloodstream, but Vale felt the presence of his god beside him as he walked the empty museum corridor to Randall's office. Randall was alone, working late, and probably the gods had arranged that, too.

His god was unusually tangible. When he looked to his left he could see it, or imagined he saw it, walking next to him. Its body was not pleasant or ethereal. The god was as obnoxiously physical as a full-grown steer, though more grotesque by a long reach.

The god had far too many arms and legs, and its mouth was a horror, sharp as a beak on the outside, wet and crimson within. A ridge of tumorous bumps stitched its belly to its neck, a sort of spine. He disliked the color of the god, a lifeless mineral green. Crane, walking to the right of him, saw nothing.

Smelled nothing. But the smell was tangible, too, at

least to Vale's nose. It was an astringent, chemical smell—the smell of a tannery, or a broken bottle in a doctor's office.

They surprised Eugene Randall in his office. (But how much more surprised would Randall have been if he could see the hideous god! Obviously he couldn't.) Randall looked up wearily. He had taken on the position of director since Walcott left the Institution, and the job had worn him down. Not to mention the congressional subpoena and his wife's postmortem nagging.

"Elias!" he said. "And you're Timothy Crane, aren't you? We met at one of Eleanor's salons."

There would not be any talking. That time had passed. Crane went to the window behind Randall and opened his medical bag. He brought out the knife. The knife glistened in the watery light. Randall's attention remained fixed on Vale.

"Elias, what is this? Honestly, I don't have time for—"

For what? Vale wondered as Crane stepped swiftly forward and drew the knife across Randall's throat. Randall gurgled and began to thrash, but his mouth was too full of blood for him to make much real noise.

Crane put the bloody instrument back in the bag and withdrew the brown bottle of methyl alcohol.

"I imagined you meant to sterilize the knife," Vale said. Idiotic notion.

"Don't be silly, Elias."

Crane emptied the bottle across Randall's head and shoulders and splashed the last of it over his desk. Randall dropped from his chair and began to crawl across the floor. One hand was clutched to his throat, but the wound pulsed gobbets of blood between his fingers.

Next, the matches.

* * *

Crane's left hand was alight when he emerged from Randall's burning office. Crane himself was fascinated, turning his hand before his eyes as the blue flames sighed into extinction for lack of fuel. Both flesh and cuff were unharmed.

"Exhilarating," he said.

Elias Vale, suddenly queasy, looked for his attendant god. But the god was gone. Nothing left of it but smoke and firelight and the awful stench of burning meat.

CHAPTER TWENTY-ONE

Guilford rode a fur snake, recovering his strength as Tom Compton led the animals up the slope of the valley. It wasn't an easy climb. Ice-crusted snow bit at the snakes' thick legs; the animals complained mournfully but didn't balk. Maybe they understood what lay behind them, Guilford thought. Maybe they were eager to be away from the ruined city.

After dark, in a sleeting snow, the frontiersman found a glade within the forest and built a small fire. Guilford made himself useful by collecting windfall from the nearby trees, while Preston Finch, cloaked and grim, fed kindling to the flames. The fur snakes huddled together, their winter coats glistening, breath steaming from their blunt nostrils.

Dinner was a freshly killed moth-hawk, cleaned and charred, plus strips of snake pemmican from Tom Compton's pack. The frontiersman improvised a lean-to out of sage-pine branches and loose furs. He had salvaged a number of furs, one pistol, and the three pack animals from the most recent attack. All that remained of the Finch Expedition.

Guilford ate sparingly. He wanted desperately to sleep—to sleep off chronic malnutrition, sleep off three days of hypothermia in the well, the shock of Sullivan's death, the frostbite that had turned his toes and fingertips an ominous china white. But that wasn't going to happen. And right now he needed to know exactly how bad the situation had become.

He asked the frontiersman how the others had died.

"It was all over by the time I got back," Tom said. "Judging by their tracks, the attackers came from the north. Armed men, ten or fifteen, maybe spotted Diggs's kitchen fire, maybe just got lucky. They must have come in shooting. Everybody dead but Finch, who hid out in the stables. The bandits left our snakes behind—they had snakes of their own. Left one of their own men, too, leg-shot, couldn't walk."

"Partisans?" Guilford asked.

The frontiersman shook his head. "Not the one they left behind, anyhow."

"You talked to him?"

"Had a word with him. He wasn't going anywhere. Both legs fucked up beyond repair, plus I introduced him to my knife when he got truculent."

"Jesus, Tom!"

"Yeah, well, you didn't see what they did to Diggs and Farr and Robertson and Donner. These people aren't human."

Finch looked up abruptly, hollow-eyed, startled.

Guilford said, "Go on."

"It was obvious from his accent this shitheel was no Partisan. Hell, I've drunk with Partisans. They're mostly repatriate Frenchmen or Italians who like to get tight and fly their flag and take a few shots at American colonists. The big-time Partisans are pirates, armed merchantmen, they'll bag some creaky old frigate and steal the cargo and call it import duties and spend the money in a backwater whorehouse. Travel up the Rhine, the only Partisans you meet are wildcat miners with political opinions.

"This guy was an American. Said he was recruited in Jeffersonville and that his people came into the hinterland bounty-hunting the Finch expedition. Said they were paid good money."

"Did he say who paid 'em?"

"Not before he passed out, no. And I didn't have a second chance to ask him. I had Finch to worry about, and you and Sullivan back at the well. Figured I'd sling the son of a bitch on a sledge and drag him along by daylight." The frontiersman paused. "But he escaped."

"Escaped?"

"I left him alone just long enough to harness the snakes. Well, not alone, precisely—Finch was with him, for all the difference that makes. When I got back, he was gone. Ran off."

"You said he passed out. You said his legs were shot up."

"He did, and his legs were bloody meat, a couple of bones obviously broken. Not the kind of wound you can fake. But when I came back he was gone. Left footprints. When I say he ran, I mean he *ran*. Ran like a jackrabbit, headed off into the ruins. I suppose I could have tracked him but there was too much else to do."

"On the surface of it," Guilford said carefully, "that's impossible."

"On the surface of it it's bullshit, but all I know is what I see."

"You say Finch was with him?"

Tom's frown deepened, an angle of discontent in the frost-rimed cavern of his beard. "Finch was with him, but he hasn't had a word to say on the subject."

Guilford turned to the geologist. Every indignity the expedition had suffered since Gillvany's death was written on Finch's face, plus the special humiliation of a man who has lost command—who has lost lives for which he was nominally responsible. There was nothing pompous about Finch any longer, no dignity in his fixed stare, only defeat.

"Dr. Finch?"

The geologist looked at Guilford briefly. His attention flickered like a candle.

"Dr. Finch, did you see what happened to the man Tom talked to? The injured man?"

Finch turned his head away.

"Don't bother," Tom said. "He's mute as a stick."

"Dr. Finch, it might help us if we knew what happened. Help us get home safe, I mean."

"It was a miracle," Preston Finch said.

His voice was a sandpapered croak. The frontiersman gave him an astonished stare.

Guilford persisted gently: "Dr. Finch? What is it you saw, exactly?"

"His wounds healed. The flesh knitted itself together. The bones mended themselves. He stood up. He looked at me. He laughed."

"That's it?"

"That's what I saw."

"That's a big help," Tom Compton said.

The frontiersman sat watch. Guilford crawled into the lean-to with Finch. The botanist stank of stale sweat and snake hides and hopelessness, but Guilford didn't

smell much sweeter himself. Their human effluvia
filled the narrow space, and their breath condensed to
ice in the frigid air.

Something had stirred Finch to a fresh alertness. He
stared past layered furs into the brutal night. "This isn't
the miracle I wanted," he whispered. "Do you understand that, Mr. Law?"

Guilford was cold through and through. He found it
hard to make himself concentrate. "I understand very
little of this, Dr. Finch."

"Isn't that what you thought of me, you and Sullivan? Preston Finch, the fanatic, looking for evidence
of divine intervention, like those people who claim
to have found pieces of the Ark or the One True
Cross?"

Finch sounded old as the night wind. "I'm sorry if
you got that impression."

"I'm not insulted. Maybe it's true. Call it hubris. Sin
of pride. I didn't think things through. If nature and
the divine are no longer separate then there might also
be dark miracles. That awful city. The man whose
bones unbroke themselves."

*And tunnels in the earth, and my twin in a tattered Army
uniform, and demons straining at incarnation.* No: not
that. *Let it all be illusion,* Guilford thought. *Fatigue and
malnutrition and cold and fear.*

Finch coughed into his hand, a wrenching sound.
"It's a new world," he said.

No denying it. "We need to get some sleep, Dr.
Finch."

"Dark forces and light. They're at our shoulders."
He shook his head sadly. "I never wanted that."

"I know."

A pause. "I'm sorry you lost your photographs, Mr.
Law."

"Thank you for saying so."

He closed his eyes.

They traveled each day, a little distance, not far.

They followed game trails, rocky riverbeds, snowless patches beneath the mosque and sage-pine trees, places they wouldn't leave obvious tracks. Periodically, the frontiersman left Guilford to supervise Finch while he went hunting with his Bowie knife. Often there was snake meat, and the moth-hawk roosts were a common last resort. But for many months there had been no vegetables save a few hard-scavenged roots or tough green mosque-tree spines boiled in water. Guilford's teeth had loosened, and his vision was not as acute as it once had been. Finch, who had lost his glasses in the first attack, was nearly blind.

Days passed. Spring was not far off, by the calendar, but the skies remained dark, the wind cold and piercing. Guilford grew accustomed to the aching of his joints, the constant pain at every hinge in his body.

He wondered if the Bodensee had frozen. Whether he would see it again.

He kept his tattered journal inside his furs; it had never left his possession. The remaining blank pages were few, but he recorded occasional brief notes to Caroline.

He knew his strength was failing. His bad leg had begun to pain him daily, and as for Finch—he looked like something dragged out of an insect midden.

Temperatures rose for three days, followed by a cold spring rain. The season was welcome, the mud and wind were not. Even the fur snakes had grown moody and gaunt, foraging in the muck for last year's ground cover. One of the animals had gone blind in one eye, a cataract that turned the pupil gauzy and pale.

Fresh storms came towering from the west. Tom Compton scouted out a rockfall that provided some natural shelter, a granite crawl space open on two sides. The floor was sand, littered with animal droppings. Guilford blocked up both entrances with sticks and furs and tethered the snakes outside to act as an alarm. But if the little cavern had once been occupied, its tenant showed no sign of returning.

A torrent of cold rain locked them into the sheltered space. Tom hollowed out a fire pit under the stones' natural chimney. He had taken to humming ridiculous, sentimental old Mauve Decade tunes—"Golden Slippers," "Marbl'd Halls," and such. No lyrics, just raw basso melodies. The effect was less like song and more like an aboriginal chant, mournful and strange.

The rain storm rattled on, easing periodically but never stopping. Runnels of water coursed down the stone. Guilford scratched out a trench to conduct moisture to the lower opening of the cave. They began to ration their food. *Every day we stay here,* Guilford thought, *we're a little weaker; every day the Rhine is a little more distant.* He supposed there was some neat equation, some equivalency of pain and time, not working in their favor.

He dreamed less often of the Army picket, though the picket was still a regular fixture of his nights, concerned, imploring, and unwelcome. He dreamed of his father, whose doggedness and sense of order had conducted him to an early grave.

No judgment implied, Guilford thought. *What brings a man to this desolate tag-end of the Earth, if not a ferocious single-mindedness?*

Maybe the same single-mindedness would carry him back to Caroline and Lily.

You cannot die, Sullivan had said. Perhaps not. He

had been lucky. But he could certainly force his body beyond all tolerable limits.

He turned to face Tom, who sat with his spine against the cold rock, knees drawn. His hand groped periodically for the pipe he had lost months ago. "In the city," Guilford said, "did you dream?"

The frontiersman's response was glacial. "You don't want to know."

"Maybe I do."

"Dreams are nothing. Dreams are shit."

"Even so."

"Dreamed one dream," Tom said. "Dreamed I died in some field of mud. Dreamed I was a soldier." He hesitated. "Dreamed I was my own ghost, if that makes any sense."

Too much sense, Guilford thought.

Well, not sense, exactly, but it implied . . . dear God, *what?*

He shivered and turned away.

"We need food," Tom said. "I'll hunt tomorrow if the weather allows." He gazed at Preston Finch, sleeping like a corpse, the skin of his face tattooed against his skull. "If I can't hunt, we'll have to slaughter one of the snakes."

"We'd be cutting our own throat."

"We can reach the Rhine with two snakes."

For once, he didn't sound confident.

Morning was clear but very cold. "Stoke the fire," the frontiersman told Guilford. "Don't let it go out. If I'm not back in three days, head north without me. Do what you can for Finch."

Guilford watched him amble into the raw blue light of the day, his rifle slung on his shoulder, his motion cadenced, conserving his energy. The fur snakes turned their wide black eyes on him and mewed.

"I never wanted this," Finch said.

The fire had burned low. Guilford crouched over it, feeding damp twigs into huddled flame. The moisture burned off quickly, more steam than smoke. "What's that, Dr. Finch?"

Finch stood up, stepped cautiously out of the cave and into the frigid daylight, fragile as old paper. Guilford kept an eye on him. Last night he had been raving in his sleep.

But Finch only stood against a rock, loosened his fly, and urinated at length.

He hobbled back, still talking. "Never wanted this, Mr. Law. I wanted a sane world, d'you understand that?"

Finch was hard to understand in general, when he spoke at all. Two of his front teeth had loosened; he whistled like a kettle. Guilford nodded abstractedly as he fed the fire.

"Don't patronize me. *Listen.* It made sense, Mr. Law, the Conversion of Europe, it made sense in the context of the Biblical Flood, Babel, the destruction of Sodom and Gommorah, and if it was not the act of a jealous but comprehensible God then it could only be chaos, horror."

"Maybe it only looks that way because we're ignorant," Guilford said. "Maybe we're like monkeys staring in a mirror. There's a monkey *in* the mirror, but no monkey *behind* the mirror. Does that make it a miracle, Dr. Finch?"

"You didn't see that man's body give up its wounds."

"Dr. Sullivan once said 'miracle' is a name we give our ignorance."

"Only one of the names. There are others."

"Oh?"

"Spirits. Demons."

"Superstition," Guilford said, though his hackles rose.

"Superstition," Finch said tonelessly, "is what we call the miracles we don't approve of."

Not much paper left, nor ink. I'll be brief. (Except to say I miss you, Caroline, and have not abandoned hope of seeing you again, holding you in my arms.)

Tom Compton gone now four days, one past his limit. I should move on, but it will be difficult without his help. I still hope to see his hairy shape come ambling out of the forest.

Dr. Finch is dead, Caroline. When I woke up he was not in the shelter. I stepped out into the crisp morning to discover he had hanged himself with our rope from the branch of a sage-pine tree.

Last night's rain had frozen to him, Caroline, and his body glistened like a perverse Christmas ornament in the sunlight. I shall cut him down when I feel stronger, & make this little stone cavern his monument & grave.

Poor Dr. Finch. He was tired, and sick, and I suspect he didn't want to go on living in what he came to believe is a demon-haunted world. And maybe there is some wisdom in that.

But I shall carry on. My love to you & Lily.

CHAPTER TWENTY-TWO

The plush lobby of the Empire Hotel was abandoned. The residents had gathered at the crown of the street to watch the shelling. Caroline passed by the red-velvet furniture and hurried up the stairs with Colin and Lily behind her.

Colin unlocked the door of his room. Lily was at the window instantly, craning to see the battle past the wall of a warehouse. Lily had been grateful to leave Mrs. de Koenig: she wanted to see what was happening, too.

"Fireworks," Lily said solemnly.

"Not really, darling. This is something bad."

"And *loud*," Lily reported.

"Very loud." *Are we safe here?* Caroline wondered. Was there somewhere else to go?

Artillery fire rattled the walls. American artillery, Caroline thought. What did that mean? It meant, she supposed, that she was an enemy national in a country at war. And that might be the least of her worries. The docks were ablaze, she saw as she pulled Lily away from the window—and the shipyards, the customs house, probably Jered's warehouse full of munitions. The wind was gentle but persistent, and from the east, and something was already burning at the far end of Candlewick Street.

The Lieutenant cleared his throat. She turned and found him standing uncertainly in the frame of the open door.

"I should be with my regiment," he said.

She hadn't anticipated this. The prospect terrified her. "Colin, no—don't leave us alone here."

"Duty, Caroline—"

"Duty can go to hell. I won't be left again. I won't let Lily be left, *not now.* Lily needs someone she can depend on."

And so do I, she thought. *So do I, God knows.*

Colin looked helpless and unhappy. "Caroline, for God's sake, we're at war!"

"And what are you going to do? Win the war all by yourself?"

"I'm a soldier," he said helplessly.

"For how long—ten years? More? God, aren't you *finished?* Don't you *deserve* to be finished?"

He didn't answer. Caroline turned her back to him. She joined Lily at the window. The smoke from the wharves obscured the river, but she could see the stacks of the American gunboats, downstream, and the English shipping they had already sunk, shattered dreadnaughts listing into the Thames.

The artillery fell silent. She could hear voices now, shouting in the street below. A bitter tang of smoke and burning fuel haunted the air.

The silence was protracted. Finally Colin said, "I

could resign my commission. Well, no, not in time of war. But, God knows, I've *thought* of it. . . ."

"Don't explain," Caroline said briskly.

"I don't want anything to hurt you." He hesitated. "This is probably not the best time to mention it, but I happen to be in love with you. And I care about Lily."

Caroline stiffened. *Not now,* she thought. *Not unless he means it. Not if it's an excuse for him to leave.*

"Try to understand," he begged.

"I do understand. Do you?"

No answer. Only the sound of the door quickly closing. *Well, that's that,* Caroline thought. *I've seen the last of Lieutenant Colin Watson, damn him. Just us now, Lily, and no crying, no crying.*

But when she turned he was still in the room.

The principal targets of the attack were the Armory and the several British military vessels anchored at the wharves, all destroyed in the first hour of the bombardment. The Armory and the dockside warehouses burned throughout the night. Seven British gunships were scuttled, the hulks burning sullenly in the sluggish Thames.

Initial damage to the Port of London was relatively slight, and even the wharf fires might have been brought under control if not for the stray rounds that exploded at the eastern end of Candlewick.

The first civilian casualty of the attack was a baker named Simon Emmanuel, recently arrived from Sydney. His shop had emptied of customers as soon as the American ships sailed upriver. He was at the ovens trying to salvage several dozen raisin buns when an artillery shell entered through the roof and exploded at his feet, killing him instantly. The resulting fire engulfed Emmanuel's shop and spread quickly to the stables next door, the brewery across the street.

Local citizens attempting a bucket brigade were driven off by an explosion in a newly installed gas main. Two city employees and a pregnant woman died in the detonation.

The wind from the east turned dry and gusty. It shrouded the city in smoke.

Caroline, Colin, and Lily spent the next day in the hotel room, though they knew it would be impossible to stay much longer. Colin left to buy food. Most of the shops and Market Street stalls had closed and some few of those had been looted. He came back with a loaf of bread and a jar of molasses. The Empire's own kitchen was a casualty of war, but the hotel supplied bottled water free of charge in the dining room.

Caroline spent the morning watching the city burn.

The dock fires had been contained, but the east end burned freely; there was nothing to keep the fire from engulfing the whole of the city. The fire was massive now, moving at its own pace, dashing suddenly forward or hesitating with the pulse of the wind. The air stank of ashes and worse.

Colin spread a handkerchief on a side table and put a molasses-soaked wedge of bread in front of her. Caroline took a bite, then set it aside. "Where are we going to go?" They would have to go somewhere. Soon.

"West of the city," Colin said calmly. "People are already sleeping in the high heather. There are tents. We'll bring blankets."

"And after that?"

"Well, it depends. Partly on the war, partly on us. I'll

have to keep shy of military police, you know, at least for a while. Eventually we'll buy passage."

"Passage where?"

"Anywhere, really."

"Not the continent!"

"Of course not—"

"And not America."

"No? I thought you wanted to go back to Boston."

She thought of introducing Colin to Liam Pierce. Liam had never cared for Guilford, but still, there would be questions, objections raised. At best, an old life to resume, with all its burdens. No, not Boston.

"In that case," Colin said, "I'd thought of Australia." He said it with a rehearsed modesty. Caroline suspected he'd thought of it often. "I have a cousin in Perth. He'll put us up until we're settled."

"There are kangaroos in Australia," Lily said.

The Lieutenant winked at her. "Plenty of kangaroos, my girl. Thick on the ground."

Caroline was charmed but breathless. Australia? "What would we do in Australia?"

"Live," Colin said simply.

The next morning a porter knocked at the door and told them they would have to leave at once or the hotel couldn't guarantee their safety.

"Surely not so soon," Caroline said. Colin and the porter ignored her. Probably it was true, they ought to leave. The air had grown unbearably foul overnight. Her lungs ached, and Lily had started to cough.

"Everybody east of Thames Street out," the porter insisted, "that's what the Mayor's Office says."

Strange how long it took a city to burn, even a city as small and primitive as London.

She gathered her bags together and helped Lily pack. Colin had no luggage—no possessions he seemed to care about—but he folded the hotel's bedsheets and blankets together into a bundle. "The hotel won't mind," Colin said. "Not under the circumstances."

What he meant, she thought, was that the hotel would be ashes by morning.

Caroline adjusted her hair in the bureau mirror. She couldn't see at all well. The atmosphere outside was a perpetual twilight, and the gas had been off since the attack. She combed this spectral wraith of herself, then reached for her daughter's hand. "All right," she said. "We'll go."

Colin disguised himself during their trek into the vast tent city that had sprung up west of the city. He wore an oversized rain slicker and a slouch hat, both purchased at outrageous prices from a rag vendor working the crowd of refugees. Army and Navy personnel had been detailed to emergency relief. They circulated among the makeshift shelters distributing food and medicine. Colin didn't want to be recognized.

Caroline knew he was afraid of being captured as a deserter. In the literal sense, of course, he *was* a deserter, and that must be difficult for him, though he refused to discuss it. "I was hardly more than an accounts clerk," he said. "I won't be missed."

By their third day in the tent city, food had grown scarce but optimistic rumors spread wildly: a Red Cross steamer was coming up the Thames; the Americans had been defeated at sea. Caroline listened to the rumors indifferently. She'd heard rumors before. It was enough that the fire seemed at last to be burning itself out, with the help of a frigid spring rain. People talked about rebuilding, though privately Caroline thought the word ludicrous: to reconstruct the reconstruction of a vanished world, what folly.

She spent an afternoon wandering among the smoldering campfires and fetid trench latrines, searching for her aunt and uncle. She regretted having made so few friends in London, having lived such an insular existence. She would have liked to see a familiar face, but there were no familiar faces, not until she came across Mrs. de Koenig, the woman who had looked after Lily so often. Mrs. de Koenig was glum and alone, wrapped in a streaming tarpaulin, her hair knotted and wet; at first she failed to recognize Caroline.

But when Caroline asked about Alice and Jered, the older woman shook her head miserably. "They waited too long. The fire came down Market Street like a live thing."

Caroline gasped. "They died?"

"I'm sorry."

"Are you certain?"

"Certain as rain." Her red-rimmed eyes were mournful. "I'm sorry, Miss."

Something is always stolen, Caroline thought as she trudged back through the mud and rotting plants. *Something is always taken away.* In the rain it was possible to cry, and she cried freely. She wanted to be finished crying when she had to face Lily again.

CHAPTER TWENTY-THREE

Fireworks bloomed over the Washington Monument, celebrating the victory in the Atlantic. Sudden lights colored the Reflecting Pool. The night air smelled of gunpowder; the crowd was gleeful and wild.

"You'll have to leave town," Crane said, smiling vaguely, hands in his pockets. He walked with a Brahman slouch, at once imperial and self-mocking. "I assume you know that."

When had Vale last seen a public celebration? A few halfhearted Fourth of July fêtes since the strange summer of 1912. But the victory in the Atlantic had rung across the country like the tolling of a bell. In this throng, at night, they wouldn't be recognized. It was possible to talk.

He said, "I would have liked time to pack."

Crane, unlike the gods, would tolerate a complaint.

"No time, Elias. In any case, people like us don't need worldly possessions. We're more like, ah, monks."

The celebration would go on until morning. A glorious little war: Teddy Roosevelt would have approved. The British had surrendered after devastating losses to their Atlantic fleet and their Darwinian colonies, fearing an attack on Kitchener's rump government in Canada. The terms of the victory weren't harsh: a weapons embargo, official endorsement of the Wilson Doctrine. The conflict had lasted all of a week. Not so much war, Vale thought, as Diplomacy by Other Means, and a warning to the Japanese should they choose to turn their martial attention westward.

Of course, the war had served another purpose, the gods' purpose. Vale supposed he would never know the sum of that purpose. It might be no more than the increase of enmity, violence, confusion. But the gods were generally more incisive than that.

There had been a sidebar in the *Post*: British nationals and sympathizers were being questioned in connection with the murder of Smithsonian director Eugene Randall. Vale's name hadn't been mentioned, though it would probably make the morning edition. "You ought to thank me," he told Crane, "for taking the fall."

"Colorful expression. You aren't, of course. You're too useful. Think of it this way: you're discarding a *persona*. The police will find you dead in the ashes of your town house, or at least a few suggestive bones and teeth. Case closed."

"Whose bones will they be?"

"Does it matter?"

He supposed not. Some other victim. Some impediment to the due and proper evolution of the cosmos.

Crane said, "Take this." It was an envelope containing a rail ticket and a roll of hundred-dollar bills. The destination printed on the ticket was New Orleans. Vale had never been to New Orleans. New Orleans might as well have been East Mars, as far as he was concerned.

"Your train leaves at midnight," Crane said.

"What about you?"

"I'm protected, Elias." He smiled. "Don't worry about me. Perhaps we'll meet again, in a decade or two or three."

God help us. "Do you ever wonder—is there any *end* to it?"

"Oh, yes," Crane said. "I think we'll see the end of it, Elias, don't you?"

The fireworks reached a crescendo. Stars erupted to the roar of cannonade: blue, violet, white. A good omen for the new Harding administration. Crane would flourish, Vale thought, in modern Washington. Crane would rise like a rocket.

And I will sink into obscurity, and maybe that's for the best.

New Orleans was warm, almost sultry; the spring became tropical. It was a strange town, Vale thought, barely American. It looked transported from some French Caribbean colony, all lacy ironwork and thunder and soft patois.

He took an apartment under an assumed name in a seedy but not slummy part of town. He paid his rent with a fraction of Crane's money and began scouting second-story offices where he might conduct a little spiritualist business. He felt strangely free, as if he had left his god in the city of Washington. Not true—he understood that—but he savored the feeling while it lasted.

His craving for morphine was not physical, and perhaps that was part of the package of immortality, but he remembered the intoxication fondly and spent a few evenings trolling the jazz bars in search of a connection. He was walking home through a starry, windy night when two strangers jumped him. The men were muscular, their blunt faces shadowed under navy watch caps. They dragged him into an alley behind a tattoo shop.

They must have been god-ridden, Vale decided later. Nothing else made sense. One had a bottle, one had a length of threaded steel rod. They demanded nothing, took nothing. They worked strictly on his face.

His immortal skin was slashed and gouged, his immortal skull fractured in several places. He swallowed several of his immortal teeth.

He did not, of course, die.

Swathed in bandages, sedated, he heard a doctor discuss his case with a nurse in a languid Louisiana drawl. *A miracle he survived. No one will recognize him after this, God knows.*

Not a miracle, Vale thought. *Not even a coincidence.* The gods who had closed his skin to the morphine needle in Washington could just as easily have staved off these cutting blows. He had been taken because he never would have volunteered.

No one will recognize him.

He healed quickly.

A new city, a new name, a new face. He learned to avoid mirrors. Physical ugliness was not a significant impediment to his work.

CHAPTER TWENTY-FOUR

Guilford found the Bodensee where a glacial stream entered the lake, frigid water coursing over slick black pebbles. He followed the shoreline slowly, meticulously, riding the fur snake he had named Evangeline. "Evangeline" for no reason save that the name appealed to him; the animal's gender was a mystery. Evangeline had foraged more successfully than Guilford had over the last week, and her six splined hooves covered ground more efficiently than his toothpick legs.

A gentle sun blessed the day. Guilford had rigged a rope harness to keep himself sprawled on Evangeline's broad back even when he lost consciousness, and there were times when he drifted into a nodding half sleep, head slumped against his chest. But the sunlight meant he could shed a layer of furs, and that was a relief, to feel air that was not lethally cold against his skin.

As snakes went, Evangeline had proved intelligent. She avoided insect middens even when Guilford's attention lapsed. She never strayed far from fresh water. And she was respectful of Guilford—perhaps not surprising, given that he had killed and cooked one of her compatriots and set the other free.

He was careful to keep an eye on the horizon. He was as alone as he had ever been, frighteningly alone, in a borderless land of shaded forests and rocky, abyssal gorges. But that was all right. He didn't much mind being alone. It was what happened when people were around that worried him.

He credited Evangeline with finding the arch of stone where the expedition's boats had been cached. She had nosed her way patiently along the pebbled shore, hour by hour, until at last she stopped and moaned for his attention.

Guilford recognized the stones, the shoreline, the hilly meadows just beginning to show green.

It was the right place. But the tarpaulin was gone, and so were the boats.

Dazed, Guilford let himself down from the fur snake's back and searched the beach for—well, anything: relics, evidence. He found a charred board, a rusted nail. Nothing else.

The breeze slapped small waves against the shore.

The sun was low. He would need wood for a fire, if he could muster the energy to build one.

He sighed. "End of the road, Evangeline. At least for now."

"It will be, if you don't get a decent meal into yourself."

He turned.

Erasmus.

"Tom figured you'd show up here," the snake herder said.

* * *

Erasmus fed him real food, lent him a bedroll, and promised to take him and Evangeline back to his makeshift ranch beyond the Rheinfelden, just a few days overland; then Guilford could hitch a ride downriver when Erasmus floated his winter stock to market.

"You talked to Tom Compton? He's alive?"

"He stopped by the kraal on his way to Jayville. Told me to look out for you. He ran into bandits after he left you and Finch. Too many to fight. So he came north and left decoy fires and generally took 'em on a goose chase all the way to the Bodensee. Saved your bacon, Mr. Law, though I guess not Preston Finch."

"No, not Finch," Guilford said.

They paralleled the Rhine Gorge, following the land route Erasmus had established. The snake herder called a halt at a pool of water fed by an unnamed tributary, shallow and slow. Sunlight had heated the water to a tolerable temperature, though it was not what Guilford would call warm. Still, he was able to wash himself for the first time in weeks. The water might have been lye, for all the skin and dirt he shed. He came out shivering, naked as a grub. The season's first billyflies bumped his torso and fled across the sunlit water. His hair dangled over his eyes; his beard draped his chest like a wet Army blanket.

Erasmus put up the tent and scratched out a pit for the fire while Guilford dried and dressed.

They shared canned beans, molasses-sweet and smoky. Erasmus cooked coffee in a tin pan. The coffee was thick as syrup, bitter as clay.

The snake herder had something on his mind.

"Tom told me about the city," Erasmus said, "about what happened to you there."

"You know him that well?"

"We know each other, put it that way. The connection is, we both been to the Other World."

Guilford shot him a wary glance. Erasmus gave him back a neutral expression.

"Hell," the snake herder said, "I would of sold Tom those twenty head if he'd asked. Yeah, we go back some. But Finch showed up all blood and thunder, pissed me off . . . not to speak ill of the dead."

Erasmus found a pipe in his saddlebag, filled it and tamped it and lit it with a wooden match. He smoked tobacco, not river weed. The smell was exotic, rich with memory. It smelled like leather-bound books and deep upholstery. It smelled like civilization.

"Both of us died in the Great War," Erasmus said. "In the Other World, I mean. Both of us talked to our own ghosts."

Guilford shivered. He didn't want to hear this. Anything but this: not more madness, not now.

"Basically," Erasmus said, "I'm just a small-potatoes third-generation Heinie out of Wisconsin. My father worked in a bottling company most of his life and I would of done the same if I hadn't shied off to Jeffersonville. But there's this Other World where the Kaiser got into a tangle with the Brits and the French and the Russians. A lot of Americans got drafted and shipped off to fight, 1917, 1918, a lot of 'em killed, too." He hawked and spat a brown wad into the fire. "In that Other World I'm a ghost, and in this one I'm still flesh and blood. You with me so far?"

Guilford was silent.

"But the two worlds aren't strictly separate anymore. That's what the Conversion of Europe was all about, not to mention that so-called city you wintered in. The two worlds are tangled up because there's something wants to destroy 'em both. Maybe not destroy, more like *eat*—well, it's complicated.

"Some of us died in the Other World and went on living in this one, and that makes us special. We have a job ahead of us, Guilford Law, and it's not an easy job. I don't mean to sound as if I know all the details. I don't. But it's a long and nasty job and it falls on us."

Guilford said nothing, thought nothing.

"The two worlds get a little closer all the time. Tom didn't know that when he walked into the city—though he may have had an inkling—but he knew it for sure by the time he left. He knows it now. And I think you do, too."

"People believe a lot of things," Guilford said.

"And people refuse to believe a lot of things."

"I don't know what you mean."

"I think you do. You're one of us, Guilford Law. You don't want to admit it. You have a wife and daughter and you'd just as soon not be recruited into Armageddon, and I can hardly blame you for that. But it's for their sake, too—your children, your grandchildren."

"I don't believe in ghosts," Guilford managed.

"That's too bad, because the ghosts believe in you. And some of those ghosts would like to see you dead. Good ghosts and bad ghosts, there's both kinds."

I won't entertain this fantasy, Guilford thought. Maybe he'd seen a few things in his dreams. In the well at the center of the ruined city. But that proved nothing.

(How could Erasmus have known about the picket? Sullivan's cryptic last words: *You died fighting the Boche.* . . . No, set that aside; think about it later. Yield nothing. Go home to Caroline.)

"The city," he heard himself whisper. . . .

"The city is one of *theirs*. They didn't want it found. And they're going to great lengths to keep it hidden. Go there in six months, a year, you won't find it. They're stitching up that valley like a sack of flour. They can do that. Pinch off a piece of the world from human knowledge. Oh, maybe you or I could find it, but not an ordinary man."

"I'm an ordinary man, Erasmus."

"Wishing won't make it so, my mother used to say. Anyhow." The snake herder groaned and stood. "Get some sleep, Guilford Law. We still have a distance to travel."

Erasmus didn't raise the issue again, and Guilford refused to consider it. He had other problems, more pressing.

His physical health improved at the snake farm. By the time the stock boats arrived from Jeffersonville he was able to walk a distance without limping. He thanked Erasmus for his help and offered to ship him *Argosy* on a regular basis.

"Good idea. That book of Finch's was a slow read. Maybe *National Geographic*, too?"

"Sure thing."

"*Science and Invention?*"

"Erasmus, you saved my life at the Bodensee. Anything you want."

"Well—I won't get greedy. And I doubt I saved your life. Whether you live or die is out of my hands."

Erasmus had loaded his stock into two flat-bottomed river boats piloted by a Jeffersonville broker. It was Guilford's ride back to the coast. He offered the snake herder his hand.

Guilford said, "About Evangeline—"

"Don't worry about Evangeline. She can go wild if

she likes. Once people name an animal it's too late for common sense to prevail."

"Thank you."

"We'll meet again," Erasmus said. "Think about what I said, Guilford."

"I will."

But not now.

The riverboat captain told him there had been trouble with England. A battle at sea, he said, and strictly limited news over the wireless, "though I hear we're walkin' all over 'em."

The snakeboats made good time as the Rhine broadened into the lowlands. The days were warmer now, the Rhinish marshes emerald-green under a bright spring sky.

He took Erasmus' advice and arrived in Jeffersonville anonymously. The town had grown since Guilford last saw it, more fishermen's shacks and three new permanent structures on the firm ground by the docks. More boats were anchored in the bay, but nothing military; the Navy had a base fifty miles south. Nothing commercial was sailing for London—nothing legal, anyway.

He looked for Tom Compton, but the frontiersman's cabin was vacant.

At the Jeffersonville Western Union office he arranged for a bank transfer from his personal account in Boston, hoping Caroline hadn't closed it out on the assumption he had died. The money arrived without a problem, but he couldn't get a message through to London. "From what I hear," the telegraph operator told him, "there's nobody there to receive it."

He heard about the shelling from a drunken American sailor at the waterfront dive where he was supposed to meet the man who would take him across the Channel.

Guilford wore a blue pea coat and a woollen watch cap pulled low across his brow. The tavern was crowded and dank with pipe smoke. He took a stool at the end of the bar but couldn't help overhearing the talk that flowed around him. He paid no particular attention until a fat sailor at the next table said something about London. He heard "fire" and "fucking wasteland."

He walked to the table where the seaman sat with another man, a lanky Negro. "Excuse me," Guilford said. "I don't mean to eavesdrop, but you mentioned London? I'm anxious for news—my wife and daughter are there."

"I've left a few bastards there myself," the sailor said. His smile faded when he saw Guilford's expression. "No offense . . . I only know what I heard."

"You were there?"

"Not since the shooting started. I met a stoker claims he was up the Thames with a gunboat. But he talks when he drinks, and what he says ain't all the Christian truth."

"This man is in Jeffersonville?"

"Shipped out yesterday."

"What did he tell you about London?"

"That it was shelled. That it burned to the ground. But talk is cheap. You know how people are. Christ, look at you, shaking like that. Have a fuckin' drink on me."

"Thanks," Guilford said. "I'm not thirsty."

He hired a channel pilot named Hans Kohn, who operated a scabbed but seaworthy fishing trawler and was willing to take Guilford as far as Dover, for a price.

The ship left Jeffersonville after dark, on a gentle swell under a moonless sky. Twice Kohn changed course to avoid Navy patrols, faint silhouettes on the violet horizon. There was no question of navigating the Thames, Kohn told him: "That's locked up tight. There's an overland route from Dover, a dirt-track road. Best I can do."

Guilford went ashore at a crude wooden landing along the Kentish coast. Kohn put back to sea. Guilford sat on the creaking dock for a time, listening to the cry of shore birds as the eastern sky turned a milky vermilion. The air smelled of salt and decay.

English soil at last. The end of a journey, or at least the beginning of the end. He felt the weight of the miles behind him, as deep as this ocean he had crossed. He thought about his wife and little girl.

The overland route from Dover to London consisted of a trail hacked out of the English wilderness, muddy and in places barely wide enough to accommodate a single horse and rider.

Dover was a small but thriving port town cut into the chalky coastal soil, surrounded by windswept hills and endless blue-green miles of star sorrel and a leaf-crowned reed the locals called shag. The town had not been much affected by the war; food was still relatively plentiful, and Guilford was able to buy a saddle-trained mare, not too elderly, that would carry him overland to London. He wasn't a natural rider but found the horse an immensely more comfortable mount than Evangeline had been.

For a time he was alone on the London road, but as he crossed the highland meadows he began to encounter refugees.

At first it was only a few ragged travelers, some mounted, some hauling mud-crusted carts stacked with blankets and china and tattered wooden tea chests. He spoke to these people briefly. None had encouraging news, and most of them shied at the sound of his accent. Shortly after dusk he came across a crowd of forty families camped on a hillside, their fires glittering like the lights of a mobile city.

His paramount thought was of Caroline and Lily. He questioned the refugees politely but could discover no one who had known or seen them. Discouraged and lonely, Guilford reined his horse and accepted an invitation to join a circle around one of the campfires. He shared his food freely, explained his situation, and asked what exactly had happened to London.

Answers were short and brutal.

The city had been shelled. The city had burned.

Had many died?

Many—but there was no counting, no toll of the dead.

As he approached the city Guilford began to entertain the troubling suspicion that he was being followed.

There was a face he'd seen, a familiar face, and he seemed to see it repeatedly among the increasing number of refugees, or pacing him along the forest road, or peering at him from the fretwork of mosque trees and pagoda ferns. A man's face, young but careworn. The man was dressed in khaki, a battered uniform without insignia. The man looked remarkably like the picket from Guilford's dreams. But that was impossible.

Guilford tried to approach him. Twice, on a lonely stretch of road deep in the twilight of the forest, he shouted at the man from his horse. But no one answered, and Guilford was left feeling foolish and frightened.

Probably there was no one there at all. It was a trick of the weary eye, the anxious mind.

But he rode more cautiously now.

His first sight of London was the blackened but intact dome of the new St. Paul's, brooding over a field of mist and rubble.

A makeshift rope ferry carried him to the north shore of the Thames. Drizzle fell steadily and pocked the turbulent river.

He found an encampment of refugees in the treeless fields west of town, a vast and stinking clutter of tents and trench latrines in the midst of which a few Red Cross flags drooped listlessly in the rain.

Guilford approached one of the medical tents where a nurse in a hairnet was handing out blankets. "Excuse me," he said.

Heads turned at the sound of his accent. The nurse glanced at him and barely nodded.

"I'm looking for someone," he said. "Is there a way to find out—I mean, any kind of list—?"

She shook her head curtly. "I'm sorry. We tried, but too many people simply wandered away after the fire. Have you come from New Dover?"

"By way of there."

"Then you've seen the number of refugees. Still, you might try asking at the food tent. Everyone gathers at the food tent. It's in the western meadow." She inclined her head. "That way."

He looked across several broad acres of human misery, frowning.

The nurse straightened. "I'm sorry," she said, her voice softening. "I don't mean to sound thoughtless. It's just that there are . . . *so many*."

* * *

Guilford was walking toward the mess tent when he saw the phantom again, passing like his own shadow through the mud and rent canvas and smoky fires.

"Mr. Law? Guilford Law?"

He thought at first the ghost had spoken. But he turned and saw a ragged woman gesturing to him. It took him a moment to recognize her: Mrs. de Koenig, the widow who had lived next door to Jered Pierce.

"Mr. Law—is that really you?"

"Yes, Mrs. de Koenig, it's me."

"Dear God, I thought you were dead! We all thought you'd died on the Continent!"

"I've come looking for Caroline and Lily."

"Oh," Mrs. de Koenig said. "Of course." But her toothless smile faded. "Of course you have. Tell you what. Let's have a drink, Mr. Law, you and me, and we'll talk about that."

CHAPTER TWENTY-FIVE

Dear Caroline,

Probably you will never see this letter. I write it with that expectation, and only a faint hope.

Obviously, I survived the winter in Darwinia. (Of the Finch expedition, the only survivors are myself and Tom Compton—if he is still alive.) If the news is reaching you for the first time I hope it does not come as too great a shock. I know you believed I died on the Continent. I suppose that belief explains your conduct, much of it at least, since the autumn of '20.

Maybe you think I despise you or that I'm writing to ventilate my anger. Well, the anger is real. I wish you had waited. But that question is moot. I attach no blame. I was in the wilderness and alive; you were in London and thought I had died. Let's just say we acted accordingly.

I hesitate to write this (and there's small enough chance of you reading it). But the habit of addressing my thoughts to you is hard to break. And there are matters between us we need to resolve.

And I want to beg a favor.

Since I'm enclosing my notes and letters written to you from the Continent, let me finish the story. Something extraordinary has happened, Caroline, and I need to set it down on paper even if you never see this. (And maybe it's better for you if you don't.)

I looked for you in ruined London. Shortly after I arrived I found Mrs. de Koenig, our neighbor on Market Street, who told me you'd left on a mercy ship bound for Australia. You left, she tells me, with Lily and this man (I will not say "this deserter," though from what I understand he is one), this Colin Watson.

I won't dwell on my reaction. Enough to say that the days that followed are vague in my mind. I sold my horse and spent the money on some of what had been salvaged from the High Street distilleries.

Oblivion is a dear purchase in London, Caroline. But maybe that's always the case, everywhere.

After a long time I woke to find myself lying in an open heath in the mist, brutally sober and achingly cold. My blanket was soaked through and so were my filthy clothes. Dawn was breaking, the sun just lightening the eastern sky. I was at the perimeter of the refugee camp. I looked at the few fires smoldering unattended in the gray light. When I was steadier I stood up. I felt abandoned and alone. . . .

But I wasn't.

I turned at some suggestion of a sound and saw—
Myself.

I know how strange that sounds. And it was strange, strange and disorienting. We never see our own faces,

Caroline, even in mirrors. I think we learn at an early age to pose for mirrors, to show ourselves our best angles. It's a very different experience to find one's face and body occupying the space of another person.

For a time I just stared at him. I understood without asking that this was the man who had paced me on the ride from New Dover.

It was obvious why I hadn't recognized him sooner. He was undeniably myself, but not exactly my reflection. Let me describe what I saw: a young man, tall, dressed in threadbare military gear. He wore no hat and his boots were muddy. He was stockier than I am, and he walked without limping. He was clean-shaven. His eyes were bright and observant. He smiled, not threateningly. He carried no weapon.

He looked harmless.

But he wasn't human.

At least not a living human being. For one thing, he wasn't entirely *there*. I mean, Caroline, that the image of him faded and brightened periodically, the way a star twinkles on a windy night.

I whispered, "Who are you?"

His voice was firm, not ghostly. He said, "That's a complicated question. But I think you know part of the answer already."

Mist rose up around us from the sodden ground. We stood together in the chill half-light as if a wall divided us from the rest of the world.

"You look like me," I said slowly. "Or like a ghost. I don't know what you are."

He said, "Take a walk with me, Guilford. I think better on my feet."

So we strolled across the heather on that fogbound morning. I guess I should have been terrified. I was, on some level. But his manner was disarming. The expression on his face seemed to say: *How absurd, that we have to meet like this.*

As if a ghost were to apologize for its clumsy trappings: the winding-sheet, the chains.

Maybe it sounds as if I accepted this visitation calmly. What I really felt was more like entranced astonishment. I believe he chose a time to appear when I was sufficiently vulnerable—dazed enough—to hear him over the roar of my own dread.

Or maybe he was a hallucination, provoked by exhaustion and liquor and grief. Think what you like, Caroline.

We walked in the faint light of morning. He seemed happier, or at least most solid, in the deep shadow of the mosque trees bordering the meadow. His voice was a physical voice, rich with the human noise of breath and lungs. He spoke without pretension, in colloquial English that sounded as familiar as the rumble of my own thoughts. But he was never hesitant or lost for words.

This is what he said.

He told me his name was Guilford Law and he had been born and raised in Boston.

He said he'd lived an unexceptional life until his nineteenth year, when he was drafted and sent overseas to fight a foreign war . . . a European war, a "World War."

He asked me to imagine a history in which Europe was never converted, in which that stew of kingdoms and despotisms continued to simmer until it erupted into a global conflict.

The details aren't important. The gist is that this phantom Guilford Law ended up in France, facing the German army in static, bloody trench battles made more nightmarish by poisonous gas and aerial attacks.

This Guilford Law—"the picket," as I've come to think of him—was killed in that war.

What amazed him was that, when he closed his eyes for the last time on Earth, it wasn't the end of all life or thought.

And here, Caroline, the story becomes even more peculiar, even more mad.

We sat on a fallen log in the cool of the morning, and I was struck by his easy presence, the solidity, the sheer apparent *heft* of him. His dark hair moved when the wind blew; he breathed in and out like any other living thing; the log jostled with his weight as he shifted to face me.

If what the picket told me is true then Schiaparelli and like-minded astronomers are correct: life exists among the stars and planets, life both like and unlike our own, in some cases different in the extreme.

The universe, the picket said, is immensely old. Old enough to have produced scientific civilizations long before human beings perfected the stone axe. The human race was born into a galaxy saturated with sentience. Before our sun congealed from the primal dust, the picket said, there were already wonders in the universe so large and subtle that they seem more magic than science; and greater wonders to come, enterprises literally eons in the making.

He described the galaxy—our little cluster of some several million stars, itself only one of several billion such clusters—as a kind of living thing, "waking up to itself." Lines of communication connect the stars: not telegraph or even radio communication but something that plays upon the invisible essence (the "isotropic energy," by which I gather he means the aether) of space itself; and these close-seined nets of communication have grown so intricate that they possess an intelligence of their own! The stars, he suggested, are literally *thinking among themselves,* and more than that: *remembering.*

Preston Finch used to quote Bishop Berkeley to the effect that we are all thoughts in the mind of God. But what if that's literally true?

This Guilford Law was a physical animal until the day he died, at which point he became a kind of thought . . . a *seed sentience,* he called it, in the mind of this local God, this evolving galactic Self.

It was not, he said, an especially exalted existence, at least at first. A human mind is still only a human mind even when it's translated into Mind at Large. He woke into the afterlife with the idea that he was recovering from a shrapnel wound in a French field hospital, and it required the appearance of a few of the predeceased to convince him he had actually died! His "virtual" body (he called it) resembled his own so closely that there seemed to be no difference, though that could change, he was told. The essence of life is change, he said, and the essence of eternal life is eternal change. There was much to learn, worlds to explore, new forms of life to meet—to *become,* if the spirit so moved him. His organic body had been limited by its physical needs and by the brain's ability to capture and retain memories. Those impediments were lifted.

He would change, inevitably, as he learned to inhabit the Mind that contained him, to tap its memories and wisdom. Not to abandon his human nature but to build on it, expand it.

And that, in sum, is what he did, for literally millions of centuries, until "Guilford Law," the so-called seed-sentience, became a fraction of something vaster and more complex.

What I was talking to this morning was both Guilford Law and this larger being—billions upon billions of beings, in fact, linked together and yet retaining their individuality.

You can imagine my incredulity. But under the circumstances any explanation might have seemed plausible.

Can you read this as anything other than the raving of a man driven mad by isolation and shock?

The shock is real enough, God knows. I grieve for what both of us have lost.

And I don't expect you to believe me. All I ask is your patience. And your good will, Caroline, if that stock is not exhausted.

I asked the picket how any of this could have happened. *I* was Guilford Law, after all, and I *hadn't* died in any German war, and that was as plain as the rising of the sun.

"Long story," he said.

I said I wasn't going anywhere.

The afterlife, the picket said, wasn't what he had expected. Most fundamentally, it wasn't a *supernatural* afterlife—it was a man-made (or at least intelligent-creature-made) paradise, as artificial as the Brooklyn Bridge and in its own immense way equally finite. Recovered souls from a million planets were linked together in physical structures he called "noospheres," planet-sized machines which traveled the galaxy on endless voyages of exploration. A paradise, Caroline, but not *heaven*, and not without its problems and enemies.

I asked him what enemies these gods could have.

"Two," he said.

One was Time. Sentience had conquered mortality, at least on the scale of the galaxy. Since before the advent of mankind, any arguably sentient creature that died within the effectual realm of the noospheres was taken up into paradise. (Including every human being from Neanderthal Man to President Taft and beyond. Some, he implied, had required a fair degree of "moral reawakening" before they could adjust to the afterlife. I gather we're not the most craven species in the galaxy, but we're not the most angelic by a long shot.)

But Sentience Itself was mortal, and so was the Milky Way Galaxy, and so was the universe at large! He uttered a few phrases about "particle decay" and "heat death" that I followed only vaguely. The sum of it was that *matter itself* would eventually die. With all the intelligence at their disposal, the noospheres devised a way to prolong their existence beyond that point. And they contrived to build an "Archive," a sum of all sentient history, which could be consulted not only by the noospheres themselves but by similar entities embedded in other, inconceivably distant galaxies.

So one enemy was Time, and that enemy had been, if not conquered, at least rendered toothless.

The other enemy he called *psilife*, from the Greek letter psi, for "pseudo."

Psilife was the ultimate result of attempts to mimic evolution in machines.

Machines, he said, could achieve consciousness, within certain limits. (I think he used these words—"consciousness" and "machines"—in a technical sense, but I didn't press him.) Both organic and true machine consciousness utilized something he called "quantum indeterminacy," whereas psilife was a kind of *mathematics*.

Psilife produced "system parasites," or what he called—as nearly as I can repeat it—"mindless Algol Rhythms preying on complexity, inhabiting it and then devouring it."

These Algol Rhythms did not hate sentient beings any more than the hunter wasp hates the tarantula in which it deposits its eggs. Psilife inhabited sentient "systems" and devoured sentience itself. It used communication and thought as a means of manufacturing copies of itself, which would copy themselves in turn, and so *ad infinitum*.

And psilife, though not conventionally sentient and without individuality, could emulate these qualities—could act with a kind of concentrated if antlike intelligence, a blind cunning. Imagine if you can a vast *intelligence* utterly devoid of *understanding*.

Psilife had arisen at various times and places throughout the universe. It had threatened Sentience and had been beaten back, though not to extinction. The Archive was thought to be impermeable to penetration by psilife; the decay of conventional matter would mean the end as well of these virulent Algol Rhythms.

But that wasn't the case.

The Archive was corrupted by psilife.

The Archive.

Caroline, what do you suppose would constitute the ultimate history, from a god's-eye view?

Not someone's *interpretation* of the past, however thoughtful and objective. Nor could it be the past *itself*, which is difficult to consult in any direct and simple fashion.

No, the ultimate practical history book would be history in a looking glass, the past re-created faithfully in some accessible way, to be opened like a book in all its original tongues and dialects; a faithful working model, but with all the empty spaces removed for the purpose of simplification, and accessible to Mind at Large in a fashion that wouldn't alter or disturb the book itself.

The Archive was static, because history doesn't change, but it was swept at long intervals by what the picket called a "Higgs field," which he compared to a phonograph needle following the groove of a recording. The record doesn't change, but a *dynamic* event— the music—is coaxed out of a fixed object.

In a sane world, of course, the music is identical each time the record is played. But what if you put a Mozart symphony on the phonograph and it turned into *Die Zauberflöte* halfway through?

Dazed as I was, I could see where this was headed.

The picket's World War was the Mozart symphony. The conversion of Europe was *Die Zauberflöte*.

"You're telling me we're *inside* this Archive?"

He nodded calmly.

I shivered. "Does that mean—are you telling me that *I'm* a sort of history book—or a page, at least, or a paragraph?"

"You were meant to be," he said.

* * *

This was an awful lot to absorb, of course, even in a receptive state. And, Caroline, when I think of you reading this . . . you must be certain I've gone mad.

And maybe you're right. I would almost prefer to believe it myself.

But I wonder whether this letter is really addressed to you . . . to *you*, I mean, to Caroline in Australia . . . or to that other Caroline, the Caroline whose image I carried into the wilderness, the Caroline who sustained me there.

Maybe she's not altogether extinct, that Caroline. Maybe she's reading over your shoulder.

Do you grasp the enormity of what this specter told me?

He suggested—in broad daylight and in the plainest language—that the world around me, the world you and I inhabit, is nothing more than a sustained illusion inside a machine at the end of time.

This went far beyond what I could easily accept, despite all my experience with Mssrs. Burroughs, Verne, and Wells.

"I can't make it any more plain," he said, "or ask you to do more than consider the possibility."

It gets more complicated. When we were a "history book," Caroline, every event, every action, was predetermined, a rote repetition of what had gone before—though of course there was no way we could have known that.

But psilife has injected "chaos" (his word) into the system—which is the equivalent of what the theologians call "free will"!

Which means, the picket said, that you and I and all the other sentient beings who had been "modeled" in the Archive have become independent, unpredictable moral entities—*real lives*, that is; *new* lives, which Sentience is sworn to protect!

The psilife invasion, in other words, has freed us from a machine-like existence . . . even though psilife means to hold us hostage and ultimately to exterminate us all.

(Tempting to think of these psilife entities as the Rebel Angels. They gave us status as moral creatures by bringing evil into the world—and must be fought to the death even though they freed us!)

We talked a while longer, as the last of the morning mist burned off and the day turned brighter. The picket grew more ghostly in the light of noon. He cast a shadow, but it wasn't as dark as mine.

At last I asked him the most important question: why had he come here, and what did he want from me?

His answer was lengthy and disquieting.

He asked for my help.

I refused it.

Dr. Sullivan, when he argued with Preston Finch, would often quote Berkeley back at him. The words stuck with me: "Things and actions are what they are, and the consequences of them will be what they will be; why then should we wish to be deceived?"

Sometimes we do, though, Caroline. Sometimes we do wish to be deceived.

It might surprise you to know I'm going back to the Continent, probably to one of the Mediterranean settlements: Fayetteville or Oro Delta. The weather is warm there. The prospects are fresh.

But I mentioned that I have a favor to ask.

Your life in Australia is yours to pursue, Caroline. I know you carry a burden of unhappiness I was never able to lift from your shoulders. Maybe you found a way to lay that burden down for good and all. I hope so. I won't question your decision and I won't come after Lily uninvited.

But please—I beg this one favor of you—please don't let Lily go on thinking I'm dead.

I'm sending this with a Mr. Barnes, who signed on with a Red Cross refugee transport bound for Sydney, on the understanding that he'll forward it to any living relative of Lieutenant Colin Watson. I've instructed him to do nothing that would compromise the Lieutenant's position vis-à-vis the military. Mr. Barnes seems trustworthy and discreet.

Also enclosed, my notes from the winter on the Continent. Think of them as letters I couldn't send. Maybe when Lily's older she'll want to see them.

I know I'm not the husband you hoped for. I sincerely hope time and memory will be gentle to both of us.

I doubt we'll meet again.

But please remember me to Lily. Maybe we're all only phantoms in a machine. It's an explanation Dr. Sullivan might have been interested to hear. But no matter what we are—we *are*. Lily is my daughter. I love her. That love is real, if nothing else. Please tell her so. Tell her I love her very much and always.

Always.

Always.

INTERLUDE

The seed-sentience Guilford Law dropped into the Archive on a nucleus of complex matter no larger than a grain of sand.

A steady rain of such grains fell into the Archive continuously. They were seed-sentiences drawn from every world, every species whose history was jeopardized by the psilife incursion. Each grain was in effect a weapon, stealthed against recognition and cued to interact with the Archive's hermetic substructure in ways that would divert the attention of the enemy.

Battles raged at every point within the Archive. Subsentient Turing packets roamed freely, seeking out the algorithmic signature of psilife and interrupting its reproduction. Psilife nodes, in turn, mutated or disguised their reproductive codes. Predator packets flourished for a time, then died back as the invaders targeted and stalled their attack sequences. The war became an ecology.

Guilford's role lay elsewhere. His autonomic systems tapped the functional architecture of the Archive and delivered him to the replica of the archaic Earth. He could not manifest himself as a phenomenological being—at least, not functionally, and not for long—but he could communicate directly with the replica Guilford Law.

What happened here was important. Psilife had radically altered the ontosphere that was the heart of the Archive. The scars of battle were everywhere.

The continent of Europe had been revised in a single stroke, overridden with a mutant history. Psilife had attempted to create an evolutionary sequence which would permit their entry into the ontosphere through the vehicle of subsentient insectile creatures.

The effort had met effective resistance. Their goal had been to transform the Earth entirely. They had converted only a fraction of it.

But the replica world was permanently changed. Lives which had been cut short—such as Guilford's—warped into new, autonomous, wholly sentient shapes. Many of these were permeable conduits from the substructure of the Archive into its core ontology. Roads, that is, through which spirits—such as Guilford's, or the parasitical nodes of psilife—might enter and alter the plenum of history.

The seed-consciousness which was Guilford Law felt rage at the damage already done. And fear: fear for the new seed-minds created by the psilife invasion, who might not be salvageable: who might face, in other words, the horror of utter extinction.

Entities who had been no more than reconstructions of the past had become hostages—vulnerable, perhaps doomed, if the psilife incursion into the ontosphere continued unresisted.

* * *

As a seed-sentience, isolated from his noosphere, Guilford could not hope to comprehend more than a fraction of the war. He wasn't meant to. He had come, with others, for the sole purpose of intervening in the battle for the Earth.

He understood the Earth well enough.

In Europe, the psions had been bound (but only temporarily) in their abortive access point: a well, as it appeared in this plenum, linking the hidden structures of the Archive to the ontological Earth. The psions had used huge insectile creatures as their avatars, invested their means and motives in these animals, used them to build a crude stone city to protect their access point.

That city had fallen in an earlier battle. The passageway had been effectively sealed.

For now.

New activity had drawn him. The Higgs field, sweeping the Archive to create ontological time, clocked toward a new psilife diaspora. Another Armageddon. Another battle.

All this he sensed directly: the well, and his own avatar Guilford Law, the continent some called Darwinia; even the altered Martian landscape, with its ahistorical seed-minds struggling for autonomy. Crises past and crises future.

He could not intervene, not directly. Nor could he simply capture and rule an avatar, as the psions did. He respected the moral independence of the seed-lives. He approached his avatar tentatively. He struggled to narrow himself to the avatar's mental range . . . to become the purely mortal thing he had once been.

It was strange to rediscover that core of self, the chaotic bundle of fears and needs and aspirations that was the embryo of all sentience. Among his thoughts:

This once was me. This once was all that existed of me, naked and alone and afraid, no other Self. A mote on a sea of inanimate matter.

He was suffused with pity.

He entered the avatar's perceptions as a phantom, which was all that he could manifest of himself in the Archive's ontosphere. There is a battle coming, he told his avatar. You have a role to play. I need your help.

His avatar listened through Guilford's plodding explanation. The words were clumsy, primitive, barely adequate.

And then his avatar refused him.

"I don't care what you say." The younger Guilford's voice was frank and final. "I don't know what you are or whether you're telling the truth. What you're describing, it's medieval—ghosts and demons and monsters, like some tenth-century morality play."

The infant sentience was bitter. He had been abandoned by his wife. He had seen far more than he could comprehend. He had watched his compatriots die.

The elder Guilford understood.

He remembered Belleau Wood and Bouresches. He remembered a wheat field red with poppies. He remembered Tom Compton, cut down by machine-gun fire. He remembered grief.

BOOK THREE

"For each age is a dream that is dying, or one that is coming to birth."
—A. W. E. O'SHAUGHNESSY

CHAPTER TWENTY-SIX

In the Campanian Lowlands many of the old names had been revived. The Bay of Naples still opened to the Tyrrhenian Sea, was still bounded by Cape Miseno and the Sorrento Peninsula, was still dominated by the active volcano Vesuvius (though the first settlers commonly called it "Old Smoky"). The land was arable, the climate reasonably gentle. The dry spring wind blowing from Asia Minor was still known as the *scirocco*.

Settlement on the slopes and hills took idiosyncratic names: Oro Delta, Palaepolis, Fayetteville, Dawson City. Disciples of the utopian Upton Sinclair had founded Mutualville on the island once called Capri, though commerce had moderated their strict communal regimen. The harbor had been improved to promote trade. It was common now to see freighters from Africa, refugee ships from the tumbled lands of Egypt and Arabia, American oil tankers where there had once been only fishing boats and trawlers.

Fayetteville was not the largest settlement hugging the bay. It was less an independent town these days than it was a finger of Oro Delta stretched down the coast, catering to farmers and farmworkers. The lowlands produced rich crops of corn, wheat, sugar beets, olives, nuts, and hemp. The sea provided docketfish, curry crabs, and salt lettuce. No native crops were cultivated, but the spice shops were well stocked with dingo nuts, wineseed, and ginger flax foraged from the wildlands.

Guilford approved of the town. He had watched it grow from the frontier settlement it had been in the twenties into a thriving, relatively modern community. There was electricity now in Fayetteville and all the other Neapolitan townships. Streetlights, pavement, sidewalks, churches. And mosques and temples for the Arabs and Egyptians, though they mainly congregated in Oro Delta down by the waterfront. A movie theater, big on Westerns and the preposterous Darwinian adventures churned out by Hollywood. And all the less savory amenities: bars, smokehouses, even a whorehouse out on Follette Road past the gravel pit.

There was a time when everybody in Fayetteville knew everybody else, but that time had passed. You were liable to see all kinds of strange faces on the streets nowadays.

Though the familiar ones were often more disturbing.

Guilford had seen a familiar face lately.

It paced him along the hilly roads when he went walking. All this spring he had seen the face at odd moments: gazing from a wheat field or fading into sea fog.

The figure wore a tattered and old-fashioned military uniform. The face looked like his own. It was his double: the ghost, the soldier, the picket.

* * *

Nicholas Law, who was twelve years old and keen to enjoy what remained of the summer sunlight, excused himself and bolted for the door. The screen clattered shut behind him. Through the window Guilford caught a glimpse of his son, a blur in a striped jersey heading downhill. Past him, there was only the sky and the headland and the evening blue sea.

Abby came from the kitchen, where she had taken dessert out of the refrigerator. Something with ice cream. Store-bought ice cream, still a novelty in Guilford's mind.

She stopped short when she saw the abandoned plate. "He couldn't wait for dessert?"

"Guess not." *Stickball at twilight,* Guilford thought. The broad green lawn in front of the Fayetteville school. He felt a pang of dislocated nostalgia.

"You're not hungry either?"

She was holding two desserts. "I'll take a taste," he said.

She sat across the table, her pleasant face skeptical. "You've lost weight," she said.

"A little. Not necessarily a bad thing."

"Off by yourself too often." She sampled the ice cream. Guilford noticed the fine filaments of gray at her temples. "There was a man here today."

"Oh?"

"He asked if this was Guilford Law's house, and I said it was, and he asked if you were the photographer with the shop on Spring Street. I said you were and he could probably reach you there." Her spoon hovered over the ice cream. "Was that right?"

"That was fine."

"Did he come to see you?"

"May have. What did this gentleman look like?"

"Dark. He had odd eyes."

"Odd in what way, Abby?"

"Just—odd."

He was unsettled by the story of this stranger at the door and Abby alone to greet him. "It's nothing to worry about."

"I'm not worried," Abby said carefully. "Unless you are."

He couldn't bring himself to lie. She wasn't easily fooled. He settled for a shake of his head. Plainly she wanted to know what was wrong. Plainly, he couldn't tell her.

He had never spoken of it—not to anyone. Except in that long-ago letter to Caroline.

At least the man at the door had not been Guilford's double. *You forget*, he thought, *after so many years. When a memory is so strange, so foreign to the rigor of daily life, it falls right out of your head . . . or it rattles there, half-noticed, like a pea in a whistle. Until something reminds you. Then it comes back fresh as an old dream stored in ice, unwrapped and glinting in the light of day.*

So far there had only been glimpses—harbingers, perhaps; omens; rogue memories. Maybe it meant nothing, that youthful face tracking him in a crowd and then gone, gazing like a sad derelict from evening alleyways. He wanted to think it meant nothing. He feared otherwise.

Abby finished dessert and carried away the dishes. "Mail came from New York today," she said. "I left it by your chair."

He was grateful to be released from this dark chain of thought. He moved into what Abby called "the living room," though it was only the long south end of the plain rectangular house Guilford had built, largely by hand, a decade ago. He had framed the structure and poured the foundations; a local contractor had plastered and shingled it. Houses were easier in a warm climate. It was Abby and Nicholas who had brought the house to life, with framed pictures and tablecloths and antimacassars, with rubber balls and wooden toys lurking under the furniture.

The mail amounted to several back issues of *Astounding*, plus a stack of New York papers. The newspapers looked depressing: details of the war with Japan, better reporting than the wire-service coverage in the *Fayetteville Herald* but more dated.

Guilford turned to the magazines first. His taste for fantasy had ebbed in the years after he lost Caroline and Lily, but the newer magazines had drawn him back. Vast airships, planetary travel, alien life: all these things seemed to him both more and less plausible than they used to. But the stories could be relied on to carry him away.

Except tonight. Tonight he finished whole pages without remembering what he'd read. He contented himself with staring at the gaudy and infinitely promising cover illustrations.

He was nodding in his chair when he heard the fire truck clanging its way into town from the station on Lantern Hill.

Then the telephone rang.

Telephones were relatively new to Fayetteville, and he hadn't grown accustomed to having one at home, though he'd used the one at work for more than a year. The grating ring went up his spine like a fish knife.

The voice at the other end was Tim Mackelroy, his assistant at the studio. Come quick, Tim said, Christ, it's terrible, but come quick, the shop is burning down.

CHAPTER TWENTY-SEVEN

Guilford had built his house away from town, a half mile by dirt track from the nearest paved road. He could see Fayetteville from the front door, a distant grid of streets and homes, and a plume of smoke rising from what was probably Spring Street.

He told Abby he'd sort this out. She shouldn't wait up for him. He would call as soon as he had solid information. Until then she shouldn't worry pointlessly; if worse came to worst, the business was insured with the Oro Delta Trust. They would rebuild.

Abby said nothing, only kissed him and watched from the window as he drove the battered Ford away in a rising cloud of dust.

It had been a dusty month. The sky was gaudy, the sun about to touch the rim of the western sea.

* * *

Guilford passed Nick, who was still cycling toward town. He stopped long enough to toss Nick's bike in the back and make room for the boy up front.

Nick was somber when he heard the news, but Nick was often somber. Large eyes in a small face. He frowned constantly. No smiles for Nick, only different frowns. Even when he was happiest—playing, reading, working on his models—he wore his frown of concentration, a firm compression of the lips.

"How could the studio catch on fire?" Nick asked.

Guilford said he didn't know. It was too soon to figure that out. The urgent business was to make sure Tim Mackelroy was safe and then to see what could be salvaged.

Wild hillside gave way to terraced fields. Guilford turned onto the paved High Road. Traffic was light, only a few motorcars, horsecarts from the Amish settlement up toward Palaepolis, a couple of farm trucks coming back empty from the granaries. Follette Road was Fayetteville's main street, and he saw smoke as soon as he took the corner by the feed and grain warehouse. A pumper truck blocked the intersection of Follette and Spring.

There wasn't much left of Law & Mackelroy, Photographers. A few charred timbers. A shell of blackened bricks.

"Wow," Nick breathed, the smoke reflected in his eyes.

Guilford found Tim Mackelroy standing under the marquee of the Tyrrhenian Talking Picture Theater. His face was streaked with smoke and tears.

Across the cobbled road the F.F.D. pumper played a steady stream of water over the smoldering ruins. The crowd had already begun to disperse. Guilford recognized most of the people there: a lawyer from Tunney's law office, the salesgirl from Blake's; Molly and Kate from the Lafayette Diner. When they saw him they made shy, sympathetic faces. Guilford told Nick to wait in the car while he talked to Mackelroy.

Tim had been his partner since '39, when the shop expanded. Tim ran the commercial side of the operation. Guilford stuck to photography these days and spent most of his time in the portrait studio. It was—or had been—a good business. The work was often routine, but he didn't mind that. He enjoyed the studio and the darkroom and he enjoyed bringing home enough money to pay for the house on the headland and Nick's school and a future for himself and Abby. He did some electronics repair on the side, now and then. He had arranged to import a big stock of Edicron and G.E. receiving tubes when the radio tower went in above Palaepolis—did a booming business for a while, since half the radios people had brought in from Stateside arrived with bad tubes, solder joints eroded by salt air, or parts knocked loose by the sea voyage.

Things had been rough after London, of course. Guilford had spent his first five years in Oro Delta crewing the harbor boats or taking in crops, exhausting work that left little time for thought. Nights had been especially hard. The Campanian farms were already producing bounty harvests of grain and grapes by '21, so there was no lack of local liquor and wine, and Guilford had taken some solace—more than a little solace—in the bottle.

He put the bottle down after he met Abby. She had been Abby Panzeca then, a second-generation American-Sicilian who had come to Darwinia with family stories of the Old World rattling around her head. In Guilford's experience such people were usually disappointed; often as not they drifted back to the States.

But Abby had stuck around, made a life for herself. She was waiting tables at an Oro Delta dive called Antonio's when Guilford found her. She joked with the Neapolitan longshoremen who frequented the place, but they didn't touch her. Abby commanded respect. She wore an aura of dignity that was almost blinding, like the glow around an electric light.

And she clearly liked Guilford, though she didn't pay him serious attention until he stopped coming into Antonio's with the stink of fish all over himself. He cleaned up, saved his salary, worked double shifts until he could afford to buy the gear to start his own photo studio—the only portrait studio in town, even if it wasn't much more, in those days, than a storeroom over a butcher shop.

They were married in 1930. Nick came along in '33. There had been another child, a baby girl, in '35, but she died of influenza before she could be christened.

The shop had fed his family for fifteen years.

Nothing remained of it but bricks and char.

Mackelroy stared woefully through a mask of soot. "I'm sorry," he said. "There was nothing I could do."

"You were here when it started?"

"I was in the office. Thought I'd make up some invoices before I headed home. A little after business hours. That was when they came through the windows."

"*What* came through the windows?"

"Milk bottles, it looked like, full of rags and gasoline. Smelled like gasoline. They came through the window like bricks, scared the crap out of me, then *boom*, the room's burning and I can't get through the flames to the fire extinguisher. I called the fire department from the phone in the diner, but the fire burned too fast—it was just about a done deal before the pumper got here."

Guilford thought: *Bottles?*
Gasoline?

He took Mackelroy by the shoulders. "You're telling me somebody did this *on purpose?*"

"Sure as hell wasn't an accident."

Guilford looked back toward his car.

Toward his son.

Three things, perhaps not coincidence:

The arson.

The picket.

The stranger Abby had talked to this morning.

"Fire chief wants to talk to you," Mackelroy was saying, "and I think the sheriff wants a word too."

"Tell them to call me at home."

He was already running.

"Son of a bitch!" Nick said in the car.

Guilford gave him a distracted glance. "You want to watch that kind of language, Nick."

"You said it first."

"Did I?"

"About five times in the last ten minutes. Shouldn't we slow down?"

He did. A little. Nick relaxed. Summer-brown wildlands fled past the Ford's dusty window.

"Son of a bitch," his father said.

Abby was safe, if concerned, and Guilford felt somewhat foolish for hurrying home. Both the fire chief and the sheriff had telephoned, Abby said. "All of that can wait till morning," he told her. "Let's lock up and get some sleep."

"*Can* you sleep?"

"Probably not. Not right away. Let's get Nick tucked in, at least."

Once Nick was squared away, Guilford sat at the kitchen table while Abby perked coffee. Coffee this close to midnight signified a family crisis. Abby moved around the kitchen with her usual economy. Tonight, at least, her frown resembled Nick's.

Abby had aged with supreme grace. She was stocky but not fat. Save for the gray just beginning to show at her temples, she might have been twenty-five.

She gave Guilford a long look, debating something with herself. Finally she said, "You may as well talk about it."

"What's that, Abby?"

"For the last month you've been nervous as a cat. You hardly touch an evening meal. Now this." She paused. "The fire chief told me it wasn't an accident."

His turn to hesitate. "Tim Mackelroy says a couple of homemade firebombs came through the window."

"I see." She folded her hands. "Guilford, why?"

"I don't know."

"Then what's been bothering you?"

He said nothing.

"Is it something that happened before we met?"

"I doubt it."

"Because you don't talk about those times much. That's all right—I don't have to know everything about you. But if we're in danger, if *Nick* is in danger—"

"Abby, honestly, I don't know. True, I'm worried. Somebody torched my business, and maybe it was random lunacy or maybe somebody out there is holding some kind of grudge. All I can do is lock up and talk to Sheriff Carlysle in the morning. You know I wouldn't let anything happen to you or Nick."

She gazed at him a long time. "I'll go to bed, then."

"Sleep if you can," Guilford told her. "I'll sit out here a while."

She nodded.

The arson.

The stranger at the door.

The picket.

You leave a thing behind, Guilford thought, *and time passes, ten, fifteen, twenty-five years, and that ought to be the end of it.*

He remembered it all vividly, in all the bright colors of a dream, the killing winter in the ancient city, the agony of London, the loss of Caroline and Lily. But, Christ, that had been a quarter of a century ago—what could be left of that time that would make him worth killing?

If what the picket had told him then was true—

—but he had written that off as a fever dream, a distorted memory, a half hallucination—

But if what the picket had told him was true, maybe twenty-five years was the blink of an eye. The gods had long memories.

Guilford went to the window. The bay was dark, only a few commercial vessels showing lights. A dry wind moved the lace curtains Abby had hung. Stars shivered in the sky.

Time to be honest, Guilford thought. No wishful thinking. Not when your family's at stake.

It was possible—admit it—that old debts were about to be collected.

The hard question: Could he have prevented this?

No.

Anticipated it?

Maybe. He had wondered often enough if there might not one day be a reckoning. Far as the world knew, the Finch expedition had simply vanished in the wilderness between the Bodensee and the Alps. And the world had got on well enough without him.

But what if that had changed?

Abby and Nicholas, Guilford thought.

No harm must come to them.

No matter what the gods wanted.

He followed Abby to bed a couple of hours before dawn. He didn't want to sleep, only to close his eyes. The presence of her, the soft music of her breath, eased his thoughts.

He woke to sunlight through the east window, to Abby, fully dressed, her hand on his shoulder.

He sat up.

"He's back," she said. "That man."

CHAPTER TWENTY-EIGHT

He thought of all the ways the continent had changed in the last quarter century.

New harbors, settlements, naval bases. Rail and roads to the interior. Mines and refineries. Airstrips.

The new District system, the elected Governors, the radio networks. Homesteads on the Russian steppes, this side of the volcanic zone that divided Darwinia from Old Asia. Skirmish battles with Arabs and Turks. The bombing of Jerusalem, this new war with the Japanese, the draft riots up north.

And so much land still empty. Still a vastness of forest and plain into which a man might, for all purposes, vanish.

Abby had given the stranger a seat at the breakfast table. He was working his way through a plate of Abby's flapjacks. He handled the knife and fork like a five-year-old. A dewdrop of corn syrup lingered in his thicket of beard.

Guilford gazed at the man with a torrent of emotion: shock, relief, renewed fear.

The frontiersman speared a last bite of breakfast and looked up. "Guilford," he said laconically. "Long time."

"Long time, Tom."

"Mind if I smoke?"

A fresh briar. A tattered cloth bag of river weed.

Guilford said, "Let's go outside."

Abby touched Guilford's arm questioningly. "District police and the fire chief want you to call them. We need to talk to the trust company, too."

"It's okay, Abby. Tom's an old friend. All that other business can wait a while. What's burned is burned. There's no hurry now."

Her eyes expressed grave reservation. "I suppose so."

"Keep Nick in the house today."

"Thank you kindly for the meal, Mrs. Law," Tom Compton said. "Very tasty."

The frontiersman hadn't changed in twenty-five years. His beard had been trimmed since that awful winter, and he was stockier—healthier—but nothing *fundamental* had changed. A little weathering, but no sign of age.

Just like me, Guilford thought.

"You're looking well, Tom."

"Both of us are healthy as horses, for reasons you ought to have figured out. What do you tell people, Guilford? Do you lie about your age? It was never a problem for me—I never stayed in one place long enough."

They sat together on the creaking front porch of the house. Morning air came up the slopes from the bay, fresh as cool water and scented with growing things. Tom filled his pipe but didn't light it.

Guilford said, "I don't know what you mean."

"Yeah, you do. You also know I wouldn't be here if it wasn't important. So let's not shovel too much shit, okay?"

"It's been a quarter century, Tom."

"It's not that I don't understand the urge. Took me ten years, personally speaking, before I broke down and said okay, the world's fucking up and I been tapped to help fix it. That's not an easy thing to believe. If it's true it's fucking frightening, and if it's *not* true, then we all ought to be locked up."

"We all?"

The frontiersman applied match to bowl. "There are hundreds of us. I'm surprised you don't know that."

Guilford sat silently for a time in the morning sunlight. He hadn't had much sleep. His body ached, his eyes ached. Just about twelve hours ago he had been in Fayetteville staring at the ashes of his business. He said, "I don't mean to be inhospitable, but there's a lot on my mind."

"You have to stop this." The frontiersman's voice was solemn. "Jesus, Guilford, look at you, living like a mortal man, married, for Christ's sake, and a kid in there, too. Not that I blame you for wanting it. I might have liked that kind of life myself. But we are what we are. You and Sullivan used to congratulate yourselves for being so fuckin' open-minded, not like old Finch, making history out of wishes. But here you are—Guilford Law, solid citizen, no matter how much evidence there is to the contrary, and God help anybody who doesn't play along."

"Look, Tom—"

"Look yourself. Your shop burned down. You have

enemies. The people inside this house are in danger. Because of you. *You*, Guilford. Better to face a hard truth than a dead wife and child."

"Maybe you shouldn't have come out here."

"Well pardon my hairy ass." He shook his head. "By the way. Lily's in town. She's staying at a hotel in Oro Delta. Wants to see you."

Guilford's heart did a double beat. "Lily?"

"Your daughter. If you remember that far back."

Abby didn't know what the burly backwoodsman said to her husband, but she could read the shock in Guilford's face when he stepped back through the door.

"Abby," he said, "I think maybe you and Nick ought to pack a few things and spend a week with your cousin in Palaepolis."

She came into his arms, composed herself, looked up at him. "Why?"

"Just to be on the safe side. Till we sort out what's going on."

You live with a man this long, Abby thought, *you learn to listen past the words.* There wouldn't be any debate. Guilford was afraid, deeply afraid.

The fear was contagious, but she kept it tied in a knot just under her breastbone: Nicholas mustn't see it.

She felt like an actress in a half-remembered play, struggling to recall her lines. For years now she had anticipated—well, not *this*, certainly, but something, some climax or crisis invading their lives. Because Guilford was not an ordinary man.

It wasn't only his youthful appearance, though that had become more obvious—strikingly obvious—over the last few years. Not just his past, which he seldom discussed and jealously guarded. More than that. Guilford was set apart from the ordinary run of men, and he knew it, and he didn't like it.

She'd heard stories. Folktales. People talked about the Old Men, by which they meant the venerable frontiersmen who still wandered through town now and again. (This Tom Compton being a prize example.) Stories told on the long nights between Christmas and Easter: The Old Men knew more than they said. The Old Men kept secrets.

The Old Men weren't entirely human.

She had never believed these things. She listened to the talk and she smiled.

But two winters ago Guilford had been out back chopping firewood, and his hand had slipped on the haft of the old axe, and the blade had gone deep into the meat of his left leg below the knee.

Abby had been at the frost-rimed window, watching. The pale sun hadn't set. She had seen it all quite clearly. She had seen the blade cut him—he had *wrenched* it out of himself, the way he might have wrenched it out of a slab of wet wood—and she had seen the blood on the blade and the blood on the hard ground. It had seemed as though her heart might stop beating. Guilford dropped the axe and fell, his face suddenly white.

Abby ran to the back door, but by the time she crossed the distance to him he had managed, impossibly, to stand up again. The expression on his face was strange, subdued. He looked at her with what might have been shame.

"I'm all right," he said. Abby was startled. But when he showed her the wound it was already closed—only a faint line of blood where the axe had gone in.

Not possible, Abby thought.

But he wouldn't talk about it. It was just a scratch, Guilford insisted; if she had seen anything else it must have been a trick of the afternoon light.

And in the morning, when he dressed, there wasn't even a scar where the blade had cut him.

And Abby had put it out of her mind, because Guilford wanted it that way and because she didn't understand what she'd seen—maybe he was right, maybe it wasn't what she had thought, though the blood on the ground had been real enough, and the blood on the axe.

But you don't see a thing like that, Abby thought, *and just forget it.* The memory persisted.

It persisted as a subtle knowledge that things were not what they seemed, that Guilford was perhaps more than he had allowed her to know; and that, by implication, their life could never be a wholly normal life. Some morning will come, Abby had told herself, when a reckoning is due.

Was this the morning?

She couldn't say. But the skin of illusion had been broken. This time the bleeding might not stop.

The two men sat on the grassy slope beyond the elm tree Guilford had planted ten years ago.

Abby packed a bag. Nick packed, too, happy at the prospect of a trip but aware of the change that had overtaken the household. Guilford saw the boy in the doorway, peering at his father and at the bearded apparition with him. Apprehension colored his eyes.

"I didn't want this either," Tom Compton said. "Last thing I ever wanted was to have my life fucked up by a ghost. But sooner or later you have to face facts."

" 'Things and actions are what they are, and the consequences of them will be what they will be; why then should we wish to be deceived?' "

"Wasn't that one of Sullivan's sermons?"

"Yes, it was."

"I miss that son of a bitch."

Nick brought a baseball and glove out of the house, playing catch with himself while he waited for his mother, tossing the ball high overhead and running to intercept it. His dirty blond hair fell into his eyes. *Time for a haircut*, Guilford thought, *if you want to play center field.*

"Didn't like the look of myself in that ratty army outfit," the frontiersman said. "Didn't like this ghost dogging my heels telling me things I didn't want to hear. You know what I mean." He looked at Guilford steadily. "All that about the Archive and so-and-so-million-years of this and that. You listen a little while and you're about ready to kick the fuckin' gong. But then I talked to Erasmus, you remember that old river rat, and he told me the same damn thing."

Nick's baseball traversed the blue sky, transited a pale moon. Abby's silhouette moved across an upper-story window.

"A whole lot of us died in that World War, Guilford. Not everybody got a knock on the door from a ghost. They came after us because they *know* us. They know there's at least a chance we'll take up the burden, maybe save some lives. That's all they want to do, is save lives."

"So they say."

"And these other assholes, this Enemy of theirs, and the fuckers *they* recruited, they're genuinely dangerous. Just as hard to kill as we are, and they'll kill men, women, children, without thinking twice."

"You know that for a fact?"

"Solid fact. I learned a few things—I haven't had my head in the ground these last twenty years. Who do you think burned down your business?"

"I don't know."

"They must have figured you were there. They're not real tidy people. Scattershot, that's their method. Too bad if somebody else gets in the way."

Abby came out into the sunlight to pluck laundry from a line. There was a breeze from the sea, billowing bedsheets like mainsails.

"The people we're up against, the psions took 'em for the same reason our ghosts came after us—because they're likely to cooperate. They're not real moral people. They lack some necessities in the conscience department. Some of 'em are con men, some of 'em are killers."

"Tell me what Lily's doing in Oro Delta."

The frontiersman refilled his pipe. Abby folded sheets into a wicker basket, casting glances toward Guilford.

Sorry, Abby, Guilford thought. *This isn't how I wanted it to go. Sorry, Nick.*

"She's here because of you, Guilford."

"Then she knows I'm alive."

"As of a couple years ago. She found your notes in her mother's things."

"Caroline's . . . dead, then."

"Afraid so. Lily's a strong woman. She found out her father maybe didn't die on the Finch expedition, maybe he's even alive somewhere, and he left her this weird little story about ghosts, murderers, a ruined city. . . . See, the thing is, she *believed* it. She started asking questions. Which put the bad guys onto her."

"For asking questions?"

"For asking questions too publicly. She's not just smart, she's a journalist. She wanted to publish your notes, if she could authenticate them. Came to Jeffersonville digging up these old stories."

Abby retreated to the house. Nick tired of his baseball, dropped his glove on the lawn. He scooted into the shade of the elm, looking at Tom and Guilford, curious, knowing he shouldn't approach them. Adult business, weighty and strange.

"They tried to hurt her?"

"Tried," Tom Compton said.

"You stopped them?"

"I got her out of the way. She recognized me from your description. I was like the Holy Grail—proof that it wasn't all lunacy."

"And you brought her here?"

"Fayetteville would have been her next stop anyhow. You're the one she's really looking for."

Abby carried a suitcase to the car, hefted it into the trunk, glanced at Guilford, walked back to the house. The wind carried her dark hair behind her. Her skirt danced over the contours of her legs.

"I don't like this," Guilford said. "I don't like her being involved."

"Hell, Guilford, everybody's *involved*. This isn't about you and me and a few hundred guys talking to spirits. This is about whether your kids or your kids' kids die forever, or worse, end up slaves to those fuckin' animals out of the Other World."

A cloud crossed the sun.

"You been out of the game for a while," the frontiersman said, "but the game goes on. People have been killed on both sides, even if we're harder to kill than most. Your name came up and you can't ignore that. See, they don't care if you decide to sit out the war, that doesn't matter, you're a potential danger to them and they want to cross you off the list. You can't stay in Fayetteville."

Guilford looked involuntarily down the long dirt road, scouting for enemies. Nothing to see. Only a dust devil stirring the dry air.

He said, "What choice do I have?"

"No choice, Guilford. That's the hard part: Stay here, you lose it all. Settle down somewhere else, same thing happens sooner or later. So . . . we wait."

"We?"

"All us old soldiers. We know each other now, directly or through our ghosts. The real battle's not yet. The real battle's up there some years in the future. So we keep apart from people, mostly. No fixed address, no families, anonymous jobs, maybe out in the bush, maybe in the cities, places you can keep to yourself, paying attention, you know, keeping an eye on the bad guys, but mainly . . . waiting."

"Waiting for what?"

"The big fight. The resurrection of the demons. Waiting until we're called, basically."

"How long?"

"Who knows? Ten years, twenty years, thirty years . . ."

"That's inhuman."

"That's a sober fact. Inhuman is what *we* are."

CHAPTER TWENTY-NINE

He came up the stairs of the Oro Delta hotel and into the dining room with Tom Compton. He was a tall man, plain-faced, not quite homely, by all appearances about her own age, and Lily promptly forgot everything she had planned to say.

Instead she found herself trying to call up a genuine memory of Guilford Law—a memory of her own, that is, not the stories she had heard from her mother or come across in her research. She could summon only a few shadows. A shape at her bedside. The *Oz* books, the way he used to pronounce "Dorothy" in round, slow syllables. *Do-ro-thy.*

Clearly he remembered her. He stood at her table, the frontiersman beside him, wearing an expression that combined awe and doubt and—unless she was imagining this—the strictures of an ancient regret. Her heart hammered. She said, idiotically, "Ah, you must be Guilford Law."

He croaked, "You're Lily."

"You two talk," Tom said. "I need a drink."

"Watch the door for us," Lily said.

It didn't go smoothly, not at first. He seemed to want to know everything and to explain everything: asking questions, interrupting her answers, interrupting himself, beginning reminiscences that trailed into silence. He fumbled a cup of coffee onto the floor, cursed, then blushed and apologized for his language.

She said, "I'm not fragile. And I'm not five. I think I know what you're going through. This isn't easy for me, either, but can we start fresh? Two adults?"

"Two adults. Sure thing. It's just that—"

"What?"

He drew himself up. "I'm just so pleased to see you, Lil."

She bit her lip and nodded.

This is hard, Lily thought, *because I know what he is. He sits there like an ordinary man, fiddling with his cuffs, drumming a finger on the table.* But he was no more an ordinary man than Tom Compton was: they had been touched by something so immense it beggared the imagination.

Her half-human father.

She sketched out her life for him. She wondered if he would approve of her work—odd jobs at a Sydney paper, research, some magazine articles, her own by-line. She was a thirty-year-old unmarried career girl, not a flattering description. It suggested even in Lily's mind some hollow-boned spinster, probably with bad makeup and pet cats. Was that what Guilford saw, sitting across the table from him?

He seemed more concerned with her safety. "I'm sorry you had to stumble into this, Lil."

"I'm not sorry I did. Yes, it's frightening. But it's also the answer to a lot of questions. Long before I understood any of this I was fascinated by Darwinia, by the *idea* of Darwinia, even as a child. I audited some classes at the University—geology, genesis theory, what they call 'implicit historiography,' the Darwinian fossil record and such. There's so much to know about the continent, but always a mystery at the center of it. And nobody has as much as a ghost of an answer, unless you count the theologians. When I came across your notes—and met Tom, later on—well, it meant there *was* an answer, even if it's a strange one, even if it's hard to accept."

"Maybe you were better off not knowing."

"Ignorance is not bliss."

"I'm afraid for your life, Lil."

"I'm afraid for everybody's life. I can't let that stop me."

He smiled. Lily added, "I'm not joking."

"No, of course not. It's just that for a second there you reminded me of someone."

"Oh? Who?"

"My father. Your grandfather."

She hesitated. "I'd like to hear about him."

"I'd like to tell you."

What he saw in her, truthfully, was a great deal of her mother. Save for her lighter coloring she might have *been* Caroline—she seemed as willful as Caroline, certainly, but without the hard core of anxiety and doubt. Caroline had always been inclined to turn away from the world. Lily wanted to tackle it head-on.

Tom suggested the hotel dining room was too public for Guilford's good, especially with the evening crowd heading in. But there was a pebbled beach downhill from the hotel and north of the docks, and Guilford walked there with Lily.

The evening sun made patchwork shadows among the rocks. Ribbons of seaweed clung to a fractured wooden piling. A bright blue salt worm twined its way in pursuit of the ebbing tide.

Lily plucked a wild sandberry from the scrub bushes above the tide line. "The bay is beautiful," she said.

"The bay's a mess, Lil. Everything washes up here. Pine tar, sewage, engine oil, diesel fuel. We take Nicholas swimming at the beaches up north of Fayetteville where the water's still clean."

"Tom told me about Nicholas. I'd like to meet him sometime."

"I'd like you to meet him. I just don't know if it's wise. If Tom's right, you've put yourself in a dangerous position. So I have to ask, Lil. Why are you here?"

"Maybe I wanted to see you."

"Is that it?"

"Yes."

"But that's not all."

"No. That's not all."

They sat together on a cracked concrete seawall.

"You were right, you know. My mother thought you were crazy—or she was shocked that you were still alive, which made her, I guess, an adulteress or something like that. She didn't like to talk about you, even after *he* left."

"This Colin Watson, you mean."

"Yes."

"Was he good to you?"

"He wasn't a bad man. Just not a very happy one. Maybe he lived in your shadow. Maybe we all did."

"He left her?"

"After a few years. But we got by."

"How did Caroline die?"

"The influenza, that year it was so bad. Nothing dramatic, she just . . . didn't get better."

"I'm sorry."

"You loved her, didn't you?"

"Yes."

"But you never came after us."

"I wouldn't have done either of you any good." *Just the opposite,* Guilford thought. *Look at Abby. Look at Nick.* "So what's next? You can't publish anything about all this. You must know that."

"I may be mortal, but I'm not powerless. Tom says there's work for me in the States. Nothing dangerous. Just watching. Telling people what I see."

"You'll get yourself killed."

"There's a war on," Lily said.

"I doubt Tokyo can hold out much longer."

"Not that war. You know what I mean."

The War in Heaven. Psilife, the Archive, the secret machinery of the world. He felt years of frustration boil up in him. "For your own sake, Lil, don't get involved. Ghosts and gods and demons—it's some nightmare out of the Dark Ages."

"But it's not!" She frowned earnestly at him. Her frown was a little like Nick's. "That's what John Sullivan believed, and he was right: it's *not* a nightmare. We live in a real world—maybe not what it appears to be, but a real world with a real history. What happened to Europe, it wasn't a miracle, it was an *attack.*"

"So we're ants in an anthill, and something decided to step on us."

"We're *not* ants! We're thinking beings—"

"Whatever that means."

"And we can fight back."

He stood up stiffly. "I have a family. I have a son. I want to run my business and raise my child. I don't want to live a hundred years. I don't want to be broken on a wheel."

"But you're one of the unlucky ones," Lily said softly. "You don't have a choice."

Guilford found himself wishing he could wind back the days until his life was intact again. Restore Abby and Nick and the photo shop and the house on the headland, *status quo ante*, the illusion he had so fervently loved.

He booked a room at the hotel in Oro Delta. He paid cash and used a fake name. He needed time to think.

He called to make sure Abby and Nick were all right at her cousin Antonio's outside Palaepolis. Tony picked up the phone. Tony ran a vineyard in the hills and owned a rambling brick house near the property, plenty of room for Abby and Nick even with Tony's own two kids tearing up the place. "Guilford!" Tony said. "What is it this time?"

"This time?"

"Two calls in fifteen minutes. I feel like a switchboard. I think you should explain some of this to me. I couldn't get a straight story out of Abby."

"Tony, I didn't call you earlier."

"No? I don't know who I talked to, then, but he sounded like you and he gave your name. Did you have a drink tonight, Guilford? Not that I'd blame you. If there's something wrong between you and Abby I'm sure you can patch it up—"

"Is Abby there?"

"Abby and Nick went back to the house. Just like you said. Guilford?"

He put down the phone.

CHAPTER THIRTY

The night was dark, the rural roads unlighted. The car's headlights raked wheat fields and rock walls. *They're out there in the dark,* Guilford thought: *faceless enemies, shadows out of the inexplicable past or the impossible future.*

Tom had insisted on coming along, and Lily with him, over Guilford's objections. She wouldn't be any safer in town, the frontiersman said. "We're her best protection right now."

To which Lily added, "I'm a farm girl. I can handle a rifle, if it comes to that."

Guilford took a corner and felt the rear of the car swing wide before he righted it. He gripped the steering wheel fiercely. Very little traffic on the coast road this time of night, thank God. "How many are we up against?"

"At least two. Probably more. Whoever bombed your

shop probably wasn't local or they would have had a better fix on you. But they're learning fast."

"Whoever called Tony's place used my voice."

"Yeah, they can do that."

"So they're—what do you call it? Demon-ridden?"

"That'll do."

"And unkillable?"

"Oh, you can kill 'em," Tom said. "You just have to work a little harder at it."

"Why go after Abby and Nick?"

"They're not after Abby and Nick. If they wanted to hurt Abby and Nick, they would have gone out to your cousin's and raised hell. Abby and Nick are bait. Which gives the bad guys the advantage, unless we found out about it sooner than they expected."

Guilford leaned into the gas pedal. The Ford's engine roared; the rear wheels kicked dust into the darkness.

Tom said, "I have a couple of pistols in my sea bag." Which he'd thrown into the back seat. "I'll break 'em out. Guilford, any armaments at the house?"

"A hunting rifle. No, two—there's an old Remington stored in the attic."

"Ammunition?"

"Lots. Lily, we're getting close. Best keep your head down."

She took one of the pistols from Tom. "That would spoil my aim," she said calmly.

Tony's car, an old roadster, was pulled up in front of the house, just visible in the sweep of the headlights. Tony's car: Abby would have borrowed it. How much time had passed since Abby and Nick had arrived? It couldn't have been much, given the drive from Palaepolis. Forty-five minutes, an hour?

But the house was dark.

"Stop the engine," Tom said. "Give us a little margin. Coast in—no lights."

Guilford nodded and twisted the key. The Ford floated into velvety night, no sound but the crush of gravel under tires as they drifted to a stop.

The front door of the house swung open on a flicker of light: Abby in the doorway with a candle in her hand.

Guilford leaped from the car and rushed her back into the house. Lily and the frontiersman followed.

"The lights don't work," Abby was saying. "Neither does the phone. What's going on? Why are we here?"

"Abby, I didn't call. It was some kind of trick."

"But I talked to you!"

"No," he said. "You didn't."

Abby put her hand to her mouth. Nick was behind her on the sofa, sleepy and confused.

"Draw those drapes," Tom said. "I want all the doors and windows locked."

"Guilford . . . ?" Abby said, eyes wide.

"We've got a little trouble here, Abby."

"Oh, no . . . Guilford, it *sounded* like you, it *was* your voice—"

"We'll be fine. Just have to keep our heads down for a little while. Nick, stay put."

Nicholas nodded solemnly.

"Get your rifle, Guilford," the frontiersman said. "Mrs. Law, you have any more of those candles?"

"In the kitchen," she said dazedly.

"Good. Lily, open up my bag."

Guilford glimpsed ammunition, binoculars, a hunting knife in a leather sheath.

Abby said, "Can't we just—drive away?"

"Now that we're here," the frontiersman answered, "I don't think they'd let us do that, Mrs. Law. But there's more of us than they expected, and we're better armed. So the odds aren't bad. Come morning, we'll look for a way out."

Abby stiffened. "Oh, God . . . I'm so sorry!"

"Not your fault."

Mine, Guilford thought.

Abby composed herself by devoting her attention to Nick: calming him, making a proper bed for him on the sofa, which Guilford had moved away from the door and into a corner of the room, back facing out. "A fort," Nick called it. "A fine fort," Abby told him.

She drew breath through clenched teeth and calculated the hours until morning. *People outside want to hurt us, and they've cut the power and the telephone lines. We can't leave and we can't call for help and we can't fight back. . . .*

Guilford took her aside, along with the young woman Tom Compton had brought to the house. As little as Guilford liked to talk his past, Abby knew about his daughter, the daughter he had left in London twenty-five years ago. Abby recognized her even before Guilford said, "This is Lily." Yes, obviously. She had the Law eyes, winter-morning blue, and the same fixed frown.

"I'm pleased to meet you," Abby said; then, realizing how it must sound, "I mean, I wish—under other circumstances—"

"I know what you mean," Lily said gravely. "Thank you, Mrs. Law."

And Abby thought: *What do you know about the Old Men? Who let you in on their secrets? How much does Guilford know? Who's out there in the dark wanting to kill my husband, my child?*

No time for that now. These things had become luxuries: fear, anger, bewilderment, grief.

Nicholas looked up at his father's face as Guilford straightened the blanket over him.

The candlelight made everything strange. The house itself seemed larger—emptier—as if it had expanded into the shadows. Nick knew something was very wrong, that the doors and windows were sealed against some threat. "Bad guys," he had heard Tom Compton say. Which made Nick think of the movies. Claim jumpers, snake rustlers, burly men with dark circles around their eyes. Killers.

"Sleep if you can," his father said. "We'll settle this all up in the morning."

Sleep was a long way off. Nick looked up at his father's face with a feeling of loss that stabbed like a knife.

"Good night, Nick," his father said, stroking his hair.

Nicholas heard, "Good-bye."

Lily took the kitchen watch.

The house had two doors, front and rear, living room and kitchen. The kitchen was better defended, with its single small window and narrow door. The door was locked. The window was locked, too, but Lily understood that neither door nor window would present much of an obstacle to a determined enemy.

She sat on a wooden chair with Guilford's old Remington rifle cradled in her lap. Because the room was dark, Lily had opened the blinds a crack and scooted her chair closer to the window. There was no moon tonight,

only a few bright stars, but she could see the lights of
freighters on the bay, an earthbound constellation.

The rifle was comforting. Even though she had
never shot anything larger than a rabbit.

Welcome to Fayetteville, Lily thought. *Welcome to Darwinia.*

All her life Lily had read about Darwinia, talked
about Darwinia—dreamed and daydreamed about
Darwinia—to her mother's great distress. The continent fascinated her. She had wanted since childhood
to fathom its strangeness for herself. And here she was:
alone in the dark, defending herself against demons.

Be careful, girl, what you wish for.

She knew virtually everything natural science had
learned about Darwinia—i.e., not much. Detail in
abundance, of course, and even some theory. But the
great central question, the simple aching human *why*,
remained unanswered. Interesting, though, that at least
one other planet in the solar system had been touched
by the same phenomenon. Both the Royal Observatory
at Capetown and the National Observatory at Bloem-
fontein had published photographs of Mars showing
seasonal differentiation and an indication of large bodies of water. A new world in the sky, a *planetary* Darwinia.

Her father's letters had made sense of all this,
though he hardly seemed to understand it himself.
Guilford and Tom and all the Old Men had done what
Guilford's friend Sullivan couldn't: explained the Miracle in secular terms. It was an *outlandish* explanation,
certainly, and she couldn't imagine what sort of exper-
iment might confirm it. But all this strange theography
of Archives and angels and demons could not have
arisen in so many places or agreed in so many details if
it weren't substantially true.

She had doubted it at first—dismissed Guilford's notes and letters as the hallucinatory raving of a half-starved survivor. Jeffersonville had changed her mind. Tom Compton had changed her mind. She had been taken into the confidence of the Old Men, and that had not merely changed her mind but convinced her of the futility of *writing* about any of this. She wouldn't be allowed to, and even if she succeeded she wouldn't be believed. Because, of course, there *was* no ruined city in the Alpine hills. It had never been mapped, photographed, overflown, or glimpsed from a distance, except by the vanished Finch expedition. The demons, Tom said, had sewn it up like a torn sleeve. They could do that.

But it was, at least in some intangible way, still there.

She kept herself awake by imagining that city deep in the Darwinian back country: the ancient soulless navel of the world. Axis of time. The place where the dead meet the living. She wished she could see it, though she knew the wish was absurd; even if she could find it (and she couldn't; she was only mortal) the city was a dangerous place to be, possibly the most dangerous place on the surface of the Earth. But she was drawn by the idea of its strangeness the way, as a child, she had once loved certain names on the map: Mount Kosciusko, the Great Artesian Basin, the Tasman Sea. The lure of the exotic, and bless that little Wollongong girl for wanting it. *But here I am,* Lily thought, *with this rifle on my knee.*

She would never see the city. Guilford would see it again, though. Tom had told her that. Guilford would be there, at the Battle . . . unless his dogged love of the world held him back.

"Guilford loves the world too much," Tom had told her. "He loves it like it's real."

Isn't it? she had asked. Even if the world is made of numbers and machines . . . isn't it real enough to love?

"For you," Tom had allowed. "Some of us can't let ourselves think that way."

The Hindus spoke of *detachment*, or was it the Buddhists? To abandon the world. Abandon desire. *How awful,* Lily thought. An awful thing to ask of anyone, much less of Guilford Law, who not only loved the world but knew how fragile it was.

The old rifle sat across her legs with a terrible weight. Nothing moved beyond the window but the stars above the water, distant suns sliding through the night.

Abby, weaponless, crouched in a corner of the dimly candlelit room. Sometime after midnight Guilford came and hunkered down on the floor beside her. He put a hand on her shoulder. Her skin was cool under the heat of his palm.

She said, "We'll never be safe here again."

"If we have to, Abby, we'll leave. Move up-country, take another name . . ."

"Will we? Even if we do go somewhere else, somewhere no one knows us—what then? Do you watch me grow old? Watch me die? Watch Nicholas grow old? Wait for whatever miracle it was that put you here to come and take you away again?"

He sat back, startled.

"You couldn't have hidden it much longer. You still look like you're on the shy side of thirty."

He closed his eyes. *You won't die,* his ghost had told him, and he had watched his cuts heal miraculously, watched the flu pass him by even when it took his baby daughter. Hated himself for it, often enough.

But most of the time he just pretended. And as for Abby, Abby aging, Abby dying . . .

He healed quickly, but that didn't mean he couldn't be killed. Some wounds were irrevocable, as even Tom was plainly aware. He couldn't imagine a future past Abby, even if that meant throwing himself off a cliff or taking the barrel of a shotgun in his mouth. Everybody was entitled to death. Nobody deserved a century of grief.

Abby seemed to read his thoughts. She took his hand and held it in hers. "You do what you have to, Guilford."

"I won't let them hurt you, Abby."

"You do what you have to," she said.

CHAPTER THIRTY-ONE

The first shot fractured a living-room window.

Nicholas, who had been dozing, sat upright on the sofa and began to cry. Abby ran to him, pressed his head down. "Curl up," she said. "Curl up, Nicky, and cover your head!"

"Stay with him," Guilford shouted. More bullets flashed through the window, whipping the curtains like a hurricane wind, punching holes the size of fists in the opposite wall.

"Guard this room," Tom said. "Lily, upstairs with me."

He wanted an east-facing window and some elevation. Dawn was only twenty minutes away. There would be light in the sky by now.

Guilford crouched behind the front door. He fired a couple of blind shots through the mail slot, hoping to discourage whoever was out there.

An answering volley of bullets tore through the mosquewood door above him. He ducked under a shower of splinters.

Bullets fractured wood, plaster, upholstery, curtains. One of Abby's kitchen candles winked out. The smell of charred wood was pungent and intense.

"Abby?" he called out. "Are you all right?"

The east-facing room was Nick's. His balsa-wood airplane models were lined up on a shelf with his crystal radio and his seashell collection.

Tom Compton tore the drapes away from the window and kicked the glass out of the lower pane.

The house was still ringing with the sound of breaking glass.

The frontiersman ducked under the sill, raised his head briefly and ducked back.

"I see four of 'em," he said. "Two hiding back of the cars, at least two more out by the elm. Are you a good marksman, Lil?"

"Yes." No sense being modest. Although she had never fired this Remington.

"Shoot for the tree," he said. "I'll cover the close targets."

No time for thought. He didn't hesitate, simply gripped the window frame with his left hand and began to fire his pistol in a steady, rapid rhythm.

The pearly sky cast a dim light. Lily came to the window, exposing her head as little as possible, and drew a bead on the elm, and then on the rough shape beside it. She fired.

This was not a rabbit. But she could pretend. She thought of the farm outside Wollongong, shooting rabbits with Colin Watson back when she still called him

"Daddy." In those days the rifle had seemed bigger and heavier. But she was steady with it. He taught her to anticipate the noise, the kick.

It had made her queasy when the rabbits died, spilling themselves like torn paper bags over the dry earth. But the rabbits were vermin, a plague; she learned to suppress the sympathy.

And here was another plague. She fired the rifle calmly. It kicked her shoulder. A cartridge rattled across the wooden floor of Nick's room and lodged under the bed.

Had the shadow-figure fallen? She thought so, but the light was so poor. . . .

"Don't stop," Tom said, reloading. "You can't take these people out with a single shot. They're not that easy to kill."

Guilford had lost the feeling in his left leg. When he looked down he saw a dark wetness above his knee and smelled blood and meat. The wound was healing already, but a nerve must have been severed; that would take time to repair.

He crawled toward the sofa, trailing blood.

"Abby?" he said.

More bullets pounded through the ruined door and window. Across the room Abby's cloth curtains began to smolder, oozing dark smoke. Something banged repeatedly against the kitchen door.

"Abby?"

There was no answer from the sofa.

He heard Tom and Lily's gunfire from upstairs, shouts of pain and confusion outside.

"Talk to me, Abby!"

The back of the sofa had been struck several times.

Particles of horsehair and cotton stuffing hung in the air like dirty snow.

He put his hand in a puddle of blood, not his own.

"I count four down," Tom Compton said, "but they won't stay down unless we finish 'em. And there might be more out back." But no second-story window faced that direction.

He hurried down the stairs. Lily followed close behind him. Her hands were shaking now. The house stank of cordite and smoke and male sweat and worse things.

Down to the living room, where the frontiersman stopped short in the arched doorway and said, "Oh, Christ!"

Someone had come in through the back door.

A fat man in a gray Territory Police uniform.

"Sheriff Carlyle," Guilford said.

Guilford was obviously wounded and dazed, but he had managed to stand up. One hand clasped his bloody thigh. He held out the other imploringly. He had dropped his pistol by the sofa—

By the blood-drenched sofa.

"They're hurt," Guilford said plaintively. "You have to help me take them to town. The hospital."

But the sheriff only smiled and raised his own pistol.

Sheriff Carlyle: one of the bad guys.

Lily struggled to aim her rifle. Her heart pumped, but her blood had turned into a cold sludge.

The sheriff fired twice before Tom got off a shot that sent him twisting against the wall.

The frontiersman stepped close to the fallen Sheriff Carlyle. He pounded three bullets into the sheriff at close range until the sheriff's head was as red and shapeless as one of Colin Watson's rabbits.

Guilford lay on the floor, fountaining blood from a chest wound.

Abby and Nicholas were behind the useless fortress of the sofa, unspeakably dead.

INTERLUDE

Guilford woke in the shade of the elm, in the tall grass, in a patch of false anemones blue as glacial ice. A gentle breeze cooled his skin. Diffuse daylight held each object suspended in its even glow, as if his perception had been washed clean of every defect.

But the sky was black and full of stars. That was odd.

He turned his head and saw the picket standing a few paces away. His shadow-self. His ghost.

Probably he should have been afraid. Mysteriously, he wasn't.

"You," he managed to say.

The picket—still young, still dressed in his tattered uniform—smiled sympathetically. "Hello, Guilford."

"Hello yourself."

He sat up. At the back of his mind was the nagging sensation that something was wrong, terribly wrong, tragically wrong. But the memory wouldn't yield itself up. "I think," he said slowly, "I'm *shot*. . . ."

"Yes. But don't worry about that right now."

That sky, the sky full of stars crisp as electricity and close as the end of his arm, that bothered him, too. "Why am I here?"

"To talk."

"Maybe I don't want to talk. Do I have a choice?"

"Of course you have a choice. You can cover your ears and whistle 'Dixie,' if you want. Wouldn't you rather hear what I have to say?"

"You're not exactly a font of good news."

"Take a walk with me, Guilford."

"You walk too much."

"I think better on my feet," the picket said.

Just as in burned London a quarter century ago, there was a forced calm inside him. He ought to be terrified: *Everything* was wrong . . . worse than wrong, some surge of memory suggested. He wondered if the picket was able to impose an emotional amnesia on him, to smother his panic.

Panic would be easy, maybe even appropriate.

"This way," the picket said.

Guilford walked with the picket up the trail beyond the house, among the brush and wind-twisted trees. He looked back at his house, small and alone on its grassy headland, and saw the ocean beyond it, glass-flat and mirroring the stars.

"Am I dead?"

"Yes and no," the picket said.

"That could be a little clearer."

"It could go either way."

Despite the unearthly calm Guilford felt a feather touch of dread. "Depending on what?"

"Luck. Resolve. You."

"Is this a riddle?"

"No. Just hard to explain."

They climbed the trails steadily. Ordinarily Guilford would have been winded by the hike, but his lungs worked more efficiently here, or the air was thicker, or he was as invulnerable as a dream. Before long they reached the high summit of the hill. The picket said, "Let's sit a while."

They found a mosque tree and put their backs against it, the way Guilford sometimes sat with Nick on a summer night, looking at the stars. Stars in the ocean, stars in the sky. More stars than he had imagined there could be. The stars were visibly rotating—not around the northern axis but around a point directly overhead.

"Those stars," he said, "are they real?"

" 'Real' is a word that means more than you think, Guilford."

"But this isn't really the hill back of my house."

"No. Just a place to rest."

This is his ground, Guilford thought. *Ghost territory.* "How does it feel, being a god?"

"That's not what I am."

"The difference is subtle."

"If you turn on an electric light, does that make you a god? Your own ancestors might have said so."

Guilford blinked at the vault of the sky. "Hell of a light bulb."

"We're inside the Archive," the picket said. "Specifically, we're enclosed in a nodular logic packet attached to the procedural protocols of the Terrestrial ontosphere."

"Well, that explains it," Guilford said.

"I'm sorry. What I mean to say is, we're still inside in

the Archive—we can't leave it, at least not yet—but we're not exactly on Earth."

"I'll take your word for it."

"I can't take you out of the Archive, but I can show you what the Archive looks like from the outside."

Guilford wasn't sure what he was being offered—and the buried sense of *urgency* still pricked at him—but since he had no real choice, he nodded. "Show me," he said.

As suddenly as that, the sky began to shift. It ceased to spin. The stars moved in a new direction, south to north, the southern horizon dropping at a dizzying speed. Guilford gasped and wanted to cling to the ground even though there was no sensation of motion. The breeze persisted, warm and gentle from the sea.

"What am I looking at?"

"Just watch," the picket said.

More stars scrolled up from the horizon, countless stars, and then retreated at a shocking speed, became blurs and bands of light . . . the arms, the disk of a galaxy. The starlight stabilized, became a vast and luminous wheel in the sky.

"The Archive's ontosphere," the picket said quietly. "It's *isness*."

Guilford couldn't frame a response. He felt awe like a band across his chest, tightening.

Now the galaxy itself began to blur together, to form an undifferentiated sphere of light.

"The ontosphere in four dimensions."

And that faded as suddenly. Now the sky was an immensity of rainbow-colored lines on velvet black, iridescent, parallel, stretching in every direction to infinity until he couldn't bear to look, until looking threatened his sanity—

"The Higgs structure of the Archive," the picket said, "visualized and simplified."

Simplified! Guilford thought.

That faded, too.

For a moment the sky was utterly dark.

"If you were outside the Archive," the picket said, "this is what you would see."

The Archive: a seamless, sealed sphere of sullen orange light that filled the western horizon and was reflected in the still water of the bay.

"It contains all that the galaxy once was," the picket said softly. "It did, at least, until the psions corrupted it. That smudge of red light over the hills, Guilford, is all that remains of the *original* galaxy, with all its stars and civilizations and voices and possibilities—an immense black hole devouring a few lifeless cinders."

"Black hole?" Guilford managed to ask.

"A singularity, matter so compacted that nothing can escape from it, not even light. What you see is secondary radiation."

Guilford said nothing. He felt a great fear battering at this envelope of calm which contained him. If what the picket had told him was true then this mass in the sky contained both his past and his future; time all fragile, tentative, vulnerable to attack. That smoldering cinder was a slate on which the gods had written worlds. Misplace an atom and planets collide.

And on that slate they had written Lily and Caroline and Abby and Nicholas . . . and Guilford. He had been extracted from it, temporarily, a number fluctuating between zero and one.

Souls like chalk dust, Guilford thought. He looked at the picket. "What do you want from me?"

"We talked about this once before."

"You want me to fight your battle. To be a soldier."

"Strange as it may seem, there are things you can do in the ontosphere that I can't. I'm asking for your help."

"My help!" He stared at the dully radiant image of the Archive. "I'm not a god! Even if I do what you want, what difference can it possibly make?"

"None, if you were the only one. But there are millions of others, on millions of other worlds, and millions more to come."

"Why waste time on me, then?"

"You're no more or less important than any of the rest. You matter, Guilford, because *every* life matters."

"Then take me home and let me look after Abby and Nick."

They were all right, weren't they? He struggled with vague, disquieting shards of memory. Memory like broken glass . . .

"I can't do that," the picket said. "I'm not omnipotent. Don't make the mistake of thinking so."

"What kind of a god are you, then?"

"Not a god. I was born of mortal parents, Guilford, just like you."

"A million years ago."

"Far more than that. But I can't manipulate the ontosphere the way you suggest. I can't rewrite the past . . . and only you can influence the future." He stood up. The picket carried himself with a dignity Guilford didn't recognize as his own. For a moment Guilford seemed to see past him . . . not *through* him, but beyond the humble appearance into something as hot and immense as the sun.

This isn't a human being, Guilford thought. Maybe it used to be a human being; maybe it even used to be

Guilford Law. But it was some other kind of creature now. *It walks between stars,* Guilford thought; *the way I might walk into Fayetteville on a sunny day.*

"Consider the stakes. If this battle is lost, your daughter will be enslaved and your grandchildren will be used as incubators for something utterly soulless. In a very real sense, Guilford, they will be eaten. It's a form of death from which there is no resurrection."

Nick, Guilford thought. *Something about Nick. Nick hiding behind the big living room sofa . . .*

"And if all the battles are lost," the picket said, "then all of this, all past, all future, everything you loved or might have loved, will be food for locusts."

"Tell me something," Guilford said. "Just one thing. Please explain why all this depends on *me.* I'm nothing special—you *know* that, if you're what you say you are. Why don't you go find somebody else? Somebody smarter? Somebody with the strength to watch his kids grow old and die? All I ever wanted—Christ!—is a life, the kind of life people have, fall in love, make babies, have a family that cares enough to give me a decent burial. . . ."

"You have a foot in two worlds. Part of you is identical to part of me, the Guilford Law who died in France. And part of you is unique: the Guilford Law who witnessed the Miracle. That's what makes this conversation possible."

Guilford put his head down. "We were alike for what, nineteen or twenty years out of a hundred million? That's hardly a significant fraction."

"I'm immensely older than you are. But I haven't forgotten what it's like to carry a gun into a muddy trench. And fear for my life, and doubt the sanity of the enterprise, and feel the bullet, feel the pain, feel the dying. I don't like asking you to walk into an even uglier war. But the choice is forced on us both." He bowed his head. "I didn't make the Enemy."

Nick behind the sofa. Abby curled over him, protecting him. Horsehair and stitched cotton and the smell of gunpowder and—and—

Blood.

"I have nothing to offer you," the picket said grimly, "but more pain. I'm sorry. If you go back, you take me with you. My memories. Bouresches, the trenches, the fear."

"I want something," Guilford said. He felt grief rising in him like a hot balloon. "If I do what you say—"

"I have nothing to offer."

"I want to die. Not live forever. Grow old and die like a human being. Is that so much to ask?"

The picket was silent for a time.

Turing packets worked tirelessly to shore up the crumbling substructures of the Archive. Psilife advanced, retreated, advanced again on a thousand fronts.

A second wave of viral codes was launched into the Archive, targeted against the psions' heavily armored clock sequences.

The noospheres hoped to disrupt the psions' timing, to sever them from the ontosphere's own Higgs clock. It was a daring plan, if dangerous; the same strategy might be turned against themselves.

Sentience waited: deeply patient, if deeply afraid.

BOOK FOUR

AUTUMN, 1965

*"Who sees the variety and not the unity,
wanders on from death to death."*
—KATHA UPANISHAD

CHAPTER THIRTY-TWO

There were hundreds of men like him working the trans-Alpine rail line.

They held Railworkers Union cards. They carved mountains with TNT, they bridged gorges, they spiked track. Or they were engineers, porters, oilers, machinists, stevedores.

When work was thin, they vanished into the wilderness for months at a time. Or they vanished, almost as easily, into the smoky urban slums of Tilson and New Pittsburgh along the Rhine.

They were solitary, silent. They had no friends, no family. They didn't look especially old (their age was hard to place), but age surrounded them like an aura. Their carriage suggested an economy of motion, a terrible and sullen patience.

Karen Wilder knew the type. She'd seen plenty of them. Just lately, she'd seen more than ever.

* * *

Karen tended bar at the Schaffhausen Grill in the town of Randall, New Inland Territories. She'd been here five years now, wandered in from a mine town in the Pyrenees, broke and looking for work. She was good at her job and had a no-nonsense arrangement with the owner. The cook kept his hands off her and she didn't have to go upstairs with the customers. (Though that was less of a problem since she turned forty last year. The offers hadn't stopped, but they had slowed down some.)

Randall was a whistlestop on the Rhine-Ruhr line. The big freight cars came through every day, heavy with coal for Tilson, Carver, and New Dresden. Below the falls, the Inland Highway crossed the tracks. The railhead had grown enormously in the last few years. Respectable families had moved in. But Randall was still a frontier town, the Homestead and Emigration Laws still funneling in a steady stream of drifters from the cities. The new hands were troublesome, Karen had found; argumentative, quick with their fists. She preferred the company of longtimers, even (or especially) the nontalkative ones, like Guilford Law.

She had known him the day he first walked in—not his name, but his *kind*.

He was a longtimer of the purest ray serene. Lean, almost skinny. Big hands. Ancient eyes. Karen found herself tempted to ask what those eyes had seen.

But he wasn't much of a talker. He'd been a regular for a year, year and a half now. He came in evenings, ate sparingly, drank a little. Karen thought maybe he liked her—he always offered a word or two about the weather or the news. When he talked to her he inclined his body toward her like a shade plant leaning toward the sun.

But he always went upstairs with the whores.

* * *

Tonight was a little different.

Mid-September, the Schaffhausen tended to attract strictly locals. The summer crowd, loggers and snake-herders, low-rent tourists riding the rails, found warmer places to go. The owner had hired a Tilson-based jazz band in an effort to attract customers, but the musicians were expensive and hard on the female talent, and the trumpeter liked to play drunken scales in the town square at dawn. So that hadn't lasted. Come September the Schaffhausen was restored to its usual calm.

Then the longtimers had begun showing up. (The Old Men, some people called them.) It didn't seem unusual at first. People like that drifted through Randall all the time, renting some dusty old room for a while, moving on. They paid their bills, no questions asked, no questions answered. They were a fact of life, like the wild snakes that roamed the southern hills.

But lately some of these men had stayed longer than usual, and more had arrived, and they sat in clusters in the Schaffhausen arguing about god-knows-what in hushed tones, and Karen's curiosity was aroused despite her best intentions.

So when Guilford Law sat at the bar and ordered a drink she put it in front of him and said, "Is there a convention in town or what?"

He thanked her politely. Then he said, "I don't know what you mean."

"The hell you don't."

He gave her a long look. "Karen, isn't it?"

"Uh-huh." *Yes, Mr. Been-here-every-night-for-a-year, that's my name.*

"Karen, it's an awkward question."

"None of my business, in other words. But something's up."

"Is it?"

"Only if you have eyes. Every rail-rat and wood-louse in the Territories must be here tonight. You folks have a look about you, you know."

Like something starved and beaten that refuses to die. But she wouldn't tell him that.

For a split second she thought he was going to confide in her. The look that crossed his face was of such purified human loneliness that Karen felt her lower lip begin to tremble.

What he said was, "You're a very pretty girl."

"That's the first time in fifteen years anybody's called me a *girl*, Mr. Law."

"It's going to be a hard autumn."

"Is it?"

"You might not see me for a while. Tell you what. If I'm back by spring, I might look you up. If that's all right, I mean."

"Okay with me, I suppose. Spring's a long time off."

"And if I don't make it back—"

Back from where? She waited for him to finish.

But he swallowed his drink and shook his head.

Pretty girl, he had said.

She got a dozen spurious compliments a day from men who were drunk or indifferently particular. Compliments meant nothing. But what Guilford Law had said stayed with her through the evening. *So simple,* she thought. *And sad, and curious.*

Maybe he would look her up . . . and maybe that would be all right with her.

But tonight he finished his drink and went home alone, moving like a wounded animal. She challenged him with her eyes. He looked away.

CHAPTER THIRTY-THREE

Lily left work at four-thirty and rode a bus to the National Museum.

The day was cool, clear, brisk. The bus was crowded with grim wage earners, middle-aged men in worsted suits and crumpled hats. None of them understood the imminence of celestial war. What they wanted, in her experience, was a cocktail, dinner, an after-dinner cocktail, the kids asleep, television tuned to one of the two national networks, and maybe a nightcap before bed.

She envied them.

There was a theme exhibit at the Museum, advertised on immense banners like baronial flags suspended above the doors:

THE TRANSFORMATION OF EUROPE
Understanding a Miracle

"Miracle," she supposed, to appease the religious lob-
bies. She still preferred to think of the continent as Darwinia, the old Hearst nickname. The irony was lost now;
most people acknowledged that Europe had a fossil history of its own, whatever that might mean, and she could
well imagine the young Charles Darwin collecting bee-
tles in the Rhine marshes, puzzling out the continent's
mystery. Though perhaps not its *central* mystery.

Off the bus, through cool air into the fluorescent
inner chambers of the museum.

The exhibit was immense. Lily ignored the majority
of it and walked directly to the glass case devoted to the
Finch Expedition of 1920 and the brief Anglo-
American Conflict. Here were examples of old-time
compasses, plant-presses, theodolites, a crude memorial retrieved years after the event from the Rhinelands
below the Bodensee: *In Memory of Dr. Thomas Markland
Gillvany.* Photographs of the members of the expedition: Preston Finch, ridiculously stiff in a solar topee;
gaunt Avery Keck; luckless Gillvany; poor martyred
John Watts Sullivan. . . . Diggs, the cook, wasn't repre-
sented, nor was Tom Compton, but here was her father,
Guilford Law, with a day's beard and a flannel shirt,
from his earlier Gallatin River expedition, a frowning
young man with a box camera and dirty fingernails.

She touched the glass case with the tip of a finger.
She hadn't seen her father for twenty years, not since
that dreadful morning in Fayetteville, the sun rising, it
had seemed to her, on an ocean of blood.

He hadn't died. Grave as his wounds were, they
healed rapidly. He had been held in the Oro Delta
County Hospital under surveillance: the Territorial Po-
lice wanted him to explain the gunshot deaths of Abby,
Nicholas, three anonymous out-of-towners, and Sheriff
Carlyle. But he was ambulatory long before the doctors

anticipated; he left the hospital during the midnight shift after overpowering a guard. A warrant was issued, but that was hardly more than a gesture. The continent swallowed fugitives whole.

He was still out there.

She knew he was. The Old Men contacted her from time to time. Periodically, she told them what she learned from her secretarial job in the office of Matthew Crane—a demon-ridden Department of Defense functionary—and they reassured her that her father was still alive.

Still out there, unmaking the Apocalypse.

The time, they insisted, was close at hand.

Lily paused before an illuminated diorama.

Here was a Darwinian fossil biped—she couldn't remember or pronounce its Latin name—a two-legged and four-armed monster that had hunted the European plains as recently as the Ice Age, and a formidable beast it was. The skeleton in the diorama stood eight feet tall, with a massive ventral spine to which dense bands of muscle had once been attached, a domed skull, a jaw full of flint-sharp teeth. And here beside it a reconstruction, complete with chitinous skin, glass eyes, serrated claws long as kitchen knives, tearing the throat of a fur snake.

A museum exhibit, like the photograph of Guilford Law; but Lily knew neither her father nor the Beast was truly extinct.

"We're closing down shortly, Ma'am."

It was the night guard, a short man with a slack paunch, nasal voice, and eyes far more ancient than his face. She didn't know his name, though they had met often before, always like this. He was her contact.

As before, she pressed a book into his hand. She had bought the book yesterday at a chain store in Arlington.

It was a popular science book, *The Martian Canals Reconsidered*, with the latest photographs from Palomar, but Lily had only glanced at it. Interleaved between its pages were documents she had photocopied from work.

"Someone must have left this," she said.

The guard accepted the book into his beefy hands. "I'll see it gets to the Lost and Found."

He had exchanged this pleasantry with her often enough that she had begun to think of it as another name for the Old Men, the Veterans, the Immortals: *the Lost and Found.*

"Thank you." She was brave enough to smile before she walked away.

Growing old, Matthew Crane thought, is like justice. It must not only happen, it must be seen to happen.

He had devised a number of techniques to ensure that he didn't appear conspicuously young.

Once a year—every autumn—he retired to the privacy of his marbled bathroom, showered, toweled himself dry, and sat before the mirror with a pair of tweezers, plucking hairs from his head to create the effect of a receding hairline. The gods were not kind enough to anesthetize him during this procedure, but he had grown accustomed to the pain.

When that was finished, he etched a few new lines into his face with the edge of a straight razor.

The technique was delicate. It was a question of cutting deeply (but not too deeply) and often. This area at the corner of the eye, for instance. He took care not to slice the eye itself, drawing the blade firmly outward along the cheek. Blood welled up, briefly. Dab and repeat. After the third or fourth cut, the stubbornly immortal flesh yielded a permanent scar.

Artistry.

He knew, of course, how all this would look to an un-tutored individual, i.e., quite ghastly. Slice, daub, slice again, like a doctor practicing cranial surgery on a corpse, and beware the nerves that ran beneath the skin. He had once given himself a droopy lip that lasted three days and prompted one of his aides to inquire whether he might have had a stroke. It was delicate work that required patience and a steady hand.

He kept the gear in a leather bag in the medicine cabinet, the Immortal's Makeup Kit: fresh razors, a whetting stone, cotton balls, tweezers.

To approximate the roughness of aged skin, he found sandpaper handy.

He preferred a number ten grit, applied until the pores grew bloody.

Obviously, the illusion couldn't be maintained indefinitely. But it wouldn't have to be. Soon the war would take another, different turn; disguises would be shed; in six months, a year . . . well, everything would be different. He had been promised as much.

He finished with the razor, cleaned it, rinsed droplets of blood from the sink, flushed bloody wads of cotton down the toilet. He was satisfied with his work and about to leave the bathroom when he noticed something peculiar about himself. The nail of his left index finger was missing. The space where it should have been was blank—a moist, pink indentation.

That was odd. He didn't remember losing the nail. There had been no pain.

He held both hands in front of him and inspected them with a deep uneasiness.

He discovered two more loose nails, right thumb and right pinky. Experimentally, he teased the thumb-nail up. It parted from the flesh with a gluey, nauseating smack and dropped into the basin of the sink, where it glistened like a beetle's wing on the steamy porcelain.

Well, he thought. *This is new.*

Some kind of skin disease? But surely it would pass. The nails would grow back. That was how things worked, after all. He was immortal.

But the gods were silent on the subject.

CHAPTER THIRTY-FOUR

Elias Vale's last client was a Caribbean woman dying of cancer.

Her name was Felicity, and she had come through the autumn rain on her stick-legs to Vale's shabby suite in the Coaltown district of New Dresden. She wore a flower-print shift that hung on her hollow body like a collapsed tent. The tumors—as his god perceived them—had already invaded her lungs and bowel.

He closed the shutters on a view of wet streets, dark faces, industrial stacks, sour air. Felicity, seventy years old, sighed at the dimming of the light. She had been shocked, at first, by the broken contours of Vale's face. That was all right, Vale thought. Fear and awe were comfortable neighbors.

Felicity asked, in a faint voice still ripe with Spanish Town inflections, "Will I die?"

She didn't need a psychic for that diagnosis. Any honest layman would know at once she was dying. The wonder was that she had been able to climb the flight of stairs to Vale's consulting room. But of course she hadn't come to hear the truth.

He sat across from her at a small wooden table, its short leg propped on a book of astrological charts. Felicity's yellow eyes glistened in the watery light. Vale offered his hand. His hand was soft, plump. Hers was gaunt, parchment skin framing a pale palm. "Your hand is warm," he said.

"Yours is cold."

"Warm hands are a good sign. That's life, Felicity. Feel it. That's all the days you lived, all running through your body like electricity. Spanish Town, Kingston, the boat to Darwinia . . . your husband, your babies, they're there, all your days together under the skin."

She said sternly, "How many more?"

Vale's god had no interest in this woman. She was important only for the fifteen-dollar consultation fee. She existed to top off his purse before he hopped a train to Armageddon.

Ready or not.

But he felt sorry for her.

"Do you feel that river, Felicity? That river of blood? River of iron and air running from high mountain heart down to the delta of fingers and toes?"

She closed her eyes, wincing slightly at the pressure of his hand on her wrist. "Yes," she whispered.

"That's a strong old river, Felicity. That's a river as wide as the Rhine."

"Where does it go to—in the end?"

"The sea," Vale said, gently. "Every river runs into the sea."

"But . . . not yet?"

"No, not yet. That river hasn't run dry."

"I feel very poorly. Some mornings I hardly can drag myself from bed."

"You're not a young woman, Felicity. Think of the children you raised. Michael, building bridges in the mountains, and Constance, with her own young ones almost grown."

"And Carlotta," Felicity murmured, her sad eyes closed.

"And little Carlotta, round and beautiful as the day she died. She's waiting for you, Felicity, but she's patient. She knows the time is not yet."

"How long?"

"All the time in the world," Vale said. Which wasn't much.

"How long?"

The urgency in her voice was chastening. There was still a strong woman in this sack of bone and rotten tissue.

"Two years," he said. "Maybe three. Long enough to see Constance's little ones out on their own. Long enough to do the things you have to do."

She sighed, a long exhalation of relief and gratitude. Her breath smelled like the butcher shop on Hoover Lane, the one with goat carcasses strung in the window like Christmas decorations. "Thank you. Thank you, Doctor."

She would be dead by the end of the month.

He folded the money into his pocket and helped her down the stairs.

New Dresden's rail yard was a vast, sooty wasteland illuminated by harsh industrial lights on steel poles. The city's towers rose up behind the longhouses like tombstones, steamy with rain.

Vale wore dark clothing. He carried a cloth bag with a few possessions in it. His money was on a belt cinched around his waist. He carried a pistol in the folds of his trousers.

He crawled under a torn section of chain-link fence, drenching his knees on the muddy ground. The soil of compressed dirt and cinders and coal fragments harbored pools of rainwater on which oil floated in rainbow slicks. He had been shivering for most of an hour, waiting while an inland train was shunted onto the nearest track. Now the diesel engine began to speed up, its headlight beaming through the rain-streaked darkness.

Go, Vale thought. *Run.*

He felt his god's sense of urgency coursing through him, and it wasn't about catching this particular train. Human history was spiraling down to the zero point, perhaps even faster than the gods had anticipated. Vale had work to do. He had come to this desolate place for a reason.

He tossed his bag through the open door of a flatcar and hurled himself after it. He landed rolling, bending back the fingers of his left hand. "Shit," he whispered. He sat up against the wooden slats of the far wall. The car was dark and stank of ancient cargo: moldy hay, snakes and cattle bound for slaughter. Rail-yard lights strobed past the open door.

He was not alone. There was another man huddled in the far corner of the car, visible in flashes. Vale's hand went instinctively to his pistol. But he saw in a flicker of hard light that the man was old, shabby, hollow-eyed, and probably drunk on aftershave or antiseptic. A nuisance, perhaps, but not a threat.

"Hey, stranger," the old man said.

"Leave me alone," Vale said crisply.

He felt the burden of his days. He had passed many anonymous years since Washington, had led a marginal life in the marginal districts of too many towns: New Orleans, Miami, Jeffersonville, New Pittsburgh, New Dresden. He had learned a few things useful to the gods and he had never lacked for food or accommodation, though he was sometimes poor. He had been, he suspected, held in reserve, waiting for the final summons, the last trumpet, the ascension of the gods over mankind.

And always there had been the fear: What if that battle never came? What if he was condemned to an endless round of cheap rooms, the confessions of impotent men and dying women and grieving husbands, the shallow consolations of discount liquor and Turkish heroin?

Soon, his god whispered. Or perhaps it was his own secret voice. Lately, the distinction escaped him.

Soon. Soon.

The train rattled deep into the countryside, past dripping mosque trees and sage-pine forests, across steel bridges slick with autumn mist, toward the wild East, toward Armageddon.

He woke in a wash of sunlight with the hobo looming over him. He scooted away from the evil-smelling old man and reached for his pistol.

The hobo backed off, holding up his grimy hands in an appeasing gesture. "No harm done! No harm done!"

The train clacked through daylight forest. Beyond the open door, a ridge declined toward a mossy river.

"Just keep the fuck away from me," Vale said.

"You hurt your hand, my friend," the hobo said.

"That's my problem."

"Looks bad."

"It'll heal." He had twisted it coming into the train last night. It didn't hurt. But it did look a little odd.

Four of the five nails were missing. The flesh beneath was pale and strange.

CHAPTER THIRTY-FIVE

They came from the coast and the hinterland, from Tilson and Jeffersonville and New Pittsburgh and a hundred smaller towns; from the Alps, the Pyrenees, the compass points of the Territories. They came together, a secret army, where roads met rail lines, in a dozen villages and nameless crossroad inns. They carried their own weapons: pistols, rifles, shotguns. Ammunition arrived in crates at the railhead towns of Randall and Perseverance, where it was unloaded into trucks and wagons and distributed to tent armories deep in the forest. Artillerymen arrived disguised as farmers, field artillery packed under hay bales.

Guilford Law had spent the last year as an advance scout. He knew these hills and valleys intimately. He followed his own path toward the City of Demons, watching the forest for signs of the enemy.

The weather was clear, cool, stable. The mosque trees didn't shed their angular foliage, only turned gray as the season passed. The forest floor, a mulch of plant tissue dotted with varicolored mold, disguised his tracks. He moved through cinnamon-scented shadow, among slim fingers of sunlight. His knee-length jacket was of cured wormhide, and underneath it he carried an automatic rifle.

The City of Demons wasn't marked on any map. Public roads came nowhere near. Topological maps and aerial surveys ignored it, and neither the land nor the climate tempted homesteaders or loggers. Private aircraft, especially the little Winchester float planes popular in the Territories, occasionally passed overhead, but the pilots saw nothing unusual. The wooded valley had been edited out of human perception in the years since it was nearly exposed by the Finch expedition. It was invisible to human eyes.

But not to Guilford's.

Go carefully now, he told himself. The land rose in a series of semi-wooded ridges. It would be too easy to make himself conspicuous, crossing these spines of ancient rock.

He approached the City, perhaps not coincidentally, from the same hillside where he had first seen it almost fifty years ago.

But no: he had seen it before that . . . he had seen it in its prime, more than ten thousand years earlier, its granite blocks freshly carved from the meat of the mountain, its avenues crowded with powerful armored bipeds, avatars of the psions. They were the product of an evolution in which invertebrates had taken a longer path toward the invention of the spine, a history that would have obliterated the old earth entirely if not for the intervention of galactic Mind. *Battles half lost,* Guilford thought, *battles half won.* In the midst of this new Europe the psions had

left a hole in the mantle of the planet, a Well, a machine that communicated directly with the enabling
codes of the Archive itself and from which, in due
time—soon—the psions would re-emerge, to inhabit
the earth even as they devoured it.

Here, and on a million Archival planets.

Now, and in the past, and in the future.

The memories were Guilford's, in a sense, but vague,
transient, incomplete. He was aware of his own limitations. He was a frail vessel. He wondered if he could
contain what the god-Guilford was preparing to pour
into him.

He lay prone at the top of the ridge and saw the City
through a screen of nettle grass. He heard wind gust-
ing among the stalks, felt billyflies settle among the
hairs of his arms. He listened to the sound of his own
breathing.

The City of Demons was being renewed.

The psions had not yet emerged from their Well, but
the streets were inhabited once more, this time by
demon-ridden men. More old war buddies, Guilford
thought. Like the Old Men gathering in the forest,
these men had died at Ypres or the Marne or at sea—
died in one world, lived in another. They were conduits
for the transit between the Archive and its ontosphere.
Lacking conscience, they were perfect vehicles for the
psions. They were the Defenders of the City of Demons
and they carried their own weapons. They had been arriving singly or in pairs for many months.

Guilford counted their tents and tried to spot their
entrenchments and artillery positions. Clear, delicate
sunlight cast cloud-shadows over the City. The Dome of
the Well had been cleared of extraneous rubble. It
stood distinctly visible now, a plume of moist air rising
from its broken shell into the autumn afternoon.

Guilford sketched the entrenchments in a pocket notebook, marking points of vulnerability, possible avenues of attack from the wooded hillside. Their clock is running fast, he reminded himself. The Turing packets had done their work. They're not as prepared as they should be.

But the defenders had dug in solidly, in concentric layers of entrenchments and barbed wire ranging from the City's crumbled perimeter to the Dome of the Well.

It wouldn't be an easy fight.

He watched the City as the afternoon waned but saw nothing more . . . only those sundial streets, counting hours against the earth.

He returned as cautiously as he had come. Shadows pooled like water among the trees. He found himself thinking of Karen, the barmaid at the Schaffhausen Grill back in Randall. What could she possibly see in him? *I am as old as leather,* Guilford thought. *Dear God, I'm barely human anymore.*

Still, it attracted him, the familiar fantasy of human warmth . . . it attracted him; but it reeked of nostalgia and pain.

Daylight had faded by the time he arrived at camp. Dinner was tinned rations, probably misappropriated from some freighter bound for the China Sea. Ancient men milled among the dark trees: Ghost Soldiers, some of them called themselves. This was an infantry unit, and the unit commander was Tom Compton, who sat pipe in hand by the bank of a stony creek contemplating the last blue of the evening sky.

Guilford could not look at Tom without a sensation of double exposure, of layered memory, because Tom had been with him at Belleau Wood, their battalion marching slow cadence into enemy fire, two fresh American soldiers determined to rout the Boche the way their grandfathers had routed Jeff Davis's armies, not quite believing in the bullets even as the bullets decimated their lines like the blade of an invisible scythe.

Other memories, other enemies: Tom and Lily and Abby and Nick. . . .

No innocence left between us, Guilford thought, *only the stink of blood.*

He reported what he had seen at the City.

"The weather should hold fair," the frontiersman said, "at least for another day. I doubt that favors us."

"We move out tonight?"

"Caissons are already rolling. Don't count on getting much sleep."

CHAPTER THIRTY-SIX

In her fifteen years at the Department of Defense, Lily thought she had taken the measure of Matthew Crane.

He was a civilian "consultant" who spent most of his time lunching with congressional overseers and signing his name to duplicate copies of appropriations paperwork. He was tall, gaunt, personable, and well-connected. His staff of three secretaries and a half dozen aides was not overtaxed. His salary was generous.

He was, of course, demon-ridden, and for the last fifteen years Lily's real work had consisted of observing Mr. Matthew Crane and occasionally passing her observations to the Old Men. She didn't know how useful or important any of this was. Possibly she would never know. Her most private fear was that she had wasted years performing trivial espionage in aid of a final Battle that might not happen in her lifetime and would probably not be resolved for ages—eons.

She was fifty years old, and she had never married, seldom even come close. She had learned to live with her solitude. It had its consolations.

The irony, perhaps, was that she had come to feel a kind of fondness for Matthew Crane. He was polite, reserved, and punctual. He wore tailored suits and was meticulous, even vain, about his clothing. She detected a vestige of human uncertainty buried under that glaze of absolute emotional control.

He was also, at least in part, a creature calculating, ruthless, and not at all human.

This morning he came into the office disheveled, clutching his left arm against his body, and brushed past the secretarial staff wordlessly. Lily exchanged a concerned look with Barb and Carol, the younger secretaries, but said nothing.

She tried never to ask herself the ultimate question: *What if he finds out who I am?* It was an old, abiding fear. Crane could be a charming man. But she knew he would never be merciful.

Alone in his office, Matthew Crane took off his jacket, stretched his arm across the lacquered desk top, and rolled up the sleeve of his shirt. He put a blotter under his elbow to soak up the blood that continued to flow.

He had stumbled against the water fountain in the lobby and somehow lacerated the skin of his left forearm. The arm was bleeding. That was an unwelcome novelty. It had been a long time since Crane had seen more than a dram of his own blood.

If this *was* his own blood. It seemed not quite right. It was the wrong shade of red, for one thing. A muddy brick red, almost brown. Something in it sparkled like flecks of mica. And the blood was viscous, like honey;

and it smelled faintly (perhaps more than faintly) of ammonia.

Blood, Matthew Crane thought feverishly, *should not do these things.*

The wound itself was minor, more an abrasion than a cut, quite superficial, really, except that it didn't rush to heal itself, and the underflesh revealed by the wound was peculiarly structured, not like honest human meat, more like the hemorrhaging honeycomb of a wasp's nest.

He buzzed Lily on the interoffice line and asked her to have some cotton and a bandage sent up from the infirmary. "And please don't make a crisis of it—I've only scratched myself."

A moment's silence. "Yes, sir," she said.

Crane replaced the phone. A drop of blood dribbled onto his pants. The smell was stronger now. Like something the janitor might use to clean a toilet.

He took several calming breaths and examined his hands. His fingers looked like an infant's fingers, pink and unformed. The last of the nails had come off during the night. He had searched for them, childishly, petulantly, but hadn't been able to find them among the pink-stained bedclothes.

He still had his toenails, however. They were trapped in his shoes. He could feel them, loose and tangled in the webbing of his Argyll socks.

Lily arrived a few moments later with cotton pads and a bottle of disinfectant. He had neglected to cover his arm, and she gaped at the wound. *She would be hysterical,* Crane thought, *if she got a closer look.* He thanked her and told her to get out.

He poured iodine over the cut and mopped up the excess with a copy of the *Congressional Proceedings.* Then he tied loose cotton around his arm with a shoelace and rolled his tattered and blood-brown sleeve down over the mess.

He would need a new jacket, but what was he supposed to do? Send Lily out to a men's shop?

Something had gone wrong, and it was more than the loss of his nails, more than the wound, more than the unnerving silence of his indwelling god. Crane felt the wrongness in his bones, literally. He ached all over. He imagined he could feel an upheaval in the mantle of the Earth, a clashing of the gears that operated the material world.

Battle is at hand, he thought, the moment of ascendancy, the dawning of a new age; the gods would erupt from their hidden valley in Europe, would build their palaces with the bones of the truculent masses, and Crane would live forever, would rule forever his barony of the conquered Earth. . . .

His god had told him so.

What had gone wrong?

Maybe nothing. But he was falling apart.

He held up his nailless fingers, ten pudgy pink sausages.

He saw from the litter on the desk that his hair had begun to fall out, too.

Matthew Crane didn't leave his office during the morning, and he canceled the day's appointments. For all Lily knew he might have died of exsanguination, except that he rang periodically with demands for more bandages, a mop and bucket, a bag of surgical cotton. ("Quickly," on this last request. "And for Christ's sake be discreet.")

Hard to be discreet, Lily thought, *when you're begging bottles of Pine-Sol from the building's janitor.*

Crane accepted these offerings through a door barely ajar; Lily was forbidden to come in.

But even through this chary aperture she could smell the bitter tang of ammonia, bleach, and something more pungent, sharp as nail polish remover. Barb and Carol wrinkled their noses, stared at their typewriters, said nothing.

They left promptly at four-thirty. The interoffice line buzzed just as Lily was tidying her own desk. She was alone in the spacious outer office, echoes muted by carpeting, the tiled ceiling, the banks of recessed lighting. Outside the office's single window, daylight was already waning. Her ficus, she observed, had begun to wilt.

Don't pick up the phone, Lily thought. *Just take your purse and leave.*

But the person she had so painstakingly created, this dutiful secretarial drone, the unloved middle-aged woman married to her work—that person wouldn't ignore the summons.

She thought briefly of what Guilford had told her about her grandfather during their brief time in Fayetteville. Her grandfather had been a Boston printer so firmly attached to his sense of duty that he had been killed while attempting to reach his print shop—which hadn't seen a paying customer for a month—in the midst of that city's food riots.

Hey, grandfather, Lily thought. *Is this what it felt like, fighting the crowd?*

The receiver was already in her hand. "Yes?"

"Please come in," Matthew Crane said.

His voice was hoarse and inarticulate. Lily looked with deep foreboding at the closed inner door.

CHAPTER THIRTY-SEVEN

Elias Vale approached the sacred city, leaving bloody tracks in the loam beneath the sage-pine trees.

He wasn't accustomed to this raw Darwinian wilderness. His god guided his steps, had steered him from the train yard at Perseverance past primitive mine heads, down dirt and gravel roads, at last into the unfenced forest. His god warned him away from the white-bone coral of the insect middens, found him fresh water to drink, sheltered him from the chill of the clear autumn nights. And it was his god, Vale supposed, who infused in him this sense of purpose, of wholeness, of clarity.

His god, to date, had not explained the rapid loss of his hair and nails, nor the way his immortal skin lacerated and sloughed away after any minor injury. His arms were a patchwork of weeping sores; his shoulders throbbed with pain; his face—which he had last seen reflected in a pool of icy water—seemed to be coming

apart along its fractured seams. His clothes were stiff
with dried fluids. He stank, a piercing chemical reek.

Vale climbed a wooden ridge, leaving his pink worm-
trail in the dry soil, his excitement flaring to a
crescendo: *Close now,* his god whispered, and as he
crested the hill he saw the city of redemption, the sacred city glittering darkly in its hidden valley, vast and
imperial and ancient, long uninhabited but alive now
with god-ridden men. The city's heart, the Well of Creation, still beat beneath a fractured dome. Even at this
distance Vale could smell the city, a mineral fragrance
of steam and sunlight on cold granite, and he wanted
to weep with gratitude, humility, exaltation. *I am home,*
he thought, *home after too many years in too many lightless
slums and dark alleys, home at last.*

He ran gladly down the wooded slope, breathless
but agile, until he reached the barbed-wire perimeter
where men like himself, half gods seeping pink-stained
plasma, greeted him wordlessly.

Wordlessly because there was no need to speak, and
because some of these men might not have been able
to speak even if they had wanted to, considering the
way their skin drooled from the faces like rotten
papier-mâché. But they were his brothers and Vale was
immensely pleased to see them.

They gave him an automatic rifle and a box of ammunition, showed him how to sling these things over
his blistered shoulder and how to arm and fire the
rifle, and when the sun began to set they took him to a
ruin where a dormitory had been installed. There was
a thin mattress for Vale to sleep on, deep in the stony
darkness, wrapped in the organic stench of dying flesh
and acetone and ammonia and the subtler odor of the
city itself. Somewhere, water dripped from stone to
stone. The music of erosion.

Sleep was elusive, and, when he did sleep, he dreamed. The dreams were nightmares of powerlessness, of being trapped and slowly suffocated in his own body, smothered and submerged in the effluvia of his flesh. In his dreams Vale longed for a different home, not the sacred city but some abandoned home that had slipped from his grasp long ago.

He woke to find his body covered in delicate green pustules, like pebbled leather.

He spent a day on a makeshift firing range with those among his mute companions who could still hold and operate a rifle.

Those who could not—whose hands had become ragged claws, whose bodies were racked with convulsions, who had budded new appendages from their enlarged spines—made their war plans elsewhere.

And Vale understood, by way of his god's silent communication, some of the truth, of the situation. These changes were natural but had come too soon, had been provoked by sabotage in the realm of the gods.

His gods were powerful, but not all-powerful; knowing, but not all-knowing.

That was why they needed his help.

And it was a pleasure to serve, even if some fraction of himself cried out against his captivity, even if he felt, from time to time, a painful nostalgia for the part of him that was merely human.

No one spoke in the sacred city, though a few men still cried out in their sleep. It was as if they had left language in the forests behind the barbed-wire barricades. All of these men were god-ridden and all of the gods were ultimately one god, so what need was there for conversation?

But the part of Elias Vale that longed for his lost humanity similarly longed for the sound of human speech. The stutter of gunfire and the slap of footsteps echoed down these stone avenues into melancholy silence, and even the soundless voice of his own thoughts began to grow faint and incoherent.

He woke, a day later, with a new skin, green as the forest and bright as shellac, though it still leaked a pale whitish fluid at the joints.

He discarded the last of his reeking clothes. There was no need for modesty in the sacred city.

Hunger, too, became a thing of the past.

He would need to eat, eventually to eat a great deal, to compensate for the lean times. But not right away.

He did need to drink copious amounts of water. Pipe had been laid from the river, and a steady flow emerged from the crude pipe end at the perimeter of the sacred city, to trickle away down the broken streets into the alpine soil. This water was cold and tasted of stone and copper. Vale drank buckets of it, and so did the other men.

If he should call them men. They were becoming, quite obviously, something else. Their bodies were changing radically. Some of them had grown a second set of arms, stubby nodules emerging from the altered musculature of their ribs, with tiny fingers that grasped blindly at the air.

He drank but didn't feel the need to urinate. His new body used liquid more efficiently, which was just as well; he had lost his penis sometime during the night. It lay on his mattress like a gangrenous thumb.

But Vale preferred not to think too hard about that. It interfered with his euphoria.

The autumn air was fine and cool.

Elias Vale had foreseen many futures, true and false. He had looked into human souls as if through sparkling glass and seen the things that swim and hover there. The gods had found that capacity quite useful. But the future he could not foresee was his own.

Did that matter?

Once his god had promised him riches, eternal life, the dominion of the Earth. All that seemed terribly intangible to him now, blandishments offered to a child.

We serve because we serve, Vale thought, a logic both circular and true.

He felt the Well of Creation beating like a heart at the heart of the sacred city.

The skin of his face had peeled away like the rind of an orange. Vale could only guess what he looked like now. There were no mirrors here.

His god took him deeper into the city, made him a part of the trusted circle of guardians arrayed around the dome of the well.

Elias Vale was honored to assume the duty.

He slept in the chill shadow of the dome that night, his head cradled on a pillow of stone. He woke to the sound of mortar fire.

CHAPTER THIRTY-EIGHT

Guilford Law moved up the ridge under the concussion of artillery.

The sound reminded him of tunnel-blasting on the Alpine railway line. All it lacked was the concussion of falling rock. Unlike tunnel-blasting, it didn't stop. It went on with a maddening irregularity, like the pulse of a panicked heart.

It reminded him of Belleau Wood and the German cannon.

"They must have known we were coming."

"They did," Tom Compton said. The two men crouched behind a rockfall. "Just not how many of us." He buttoned the collar of his ragged brown overcoat. "The devil's an optimist."

"They might bring in reinforcements."

"Doubt it. We have people at every rail station and airstrip east of Tilson."

"How much time does that buy us?"

The frontiersman shrugged.

Did it matter? No, of course it didn't matter. Everything was in motion now; nothing could be stopped or withheld.

A muted daylight touched the ridge tops. Cresting the hill, Guilford beheld chaos. The valley was still in shadow, the streets white with trails of fog. A body of men including the venerable Erasmus had managed to set up trench emplacements within artillery range of at least the nearest buildings, and a predawn bombardment from their motley collection of heavy guns, howitzers and mortars had taken the demon encampment by surprise.

Now, however, the enemy had rallied; the western flank was taking vicious punishment.

Simultaneously, Guilford and a couple of hundred other longtimers began to move downslope from the north. There was pathetically little cover among the clinging reed grass and tumbled rock of the steep valley wall. Their sole advantage was that this terrain had also made difficult the emplacement of fortifications and barbed wire.

Still hopelessly far away was the real objective: the Dome of the Well, where Sentience had imprisoned thousands of half-incarnate demons, and Guilford remembered that war, too. . . .

Because I'm with you, the picket reminded him.

Guilford carried his ghost inside him now. If he could carry that ghost as far as the Well—if any of the old men fighting with him could—the demons might be bound again.

But he had hardly framed the thought when a hidden sniper opened fire from the scrubby mosque trees clinging to the steep decline. Automatic rifle rounds tore into the men on each side of him. . . .

Into *him.*

He felt the bullets pierce him. He felt their momentum throw him into the dirt. He scrambled for cover behind a wedge of stunted trees.

The advance stalled while a mortarman tried to take out the sniper. Guilford found himself staring at Tom Compton's wounds. The frontiersman's right shoulder was notched in a flaring V, and there was a gaping hole directly under his lowest left rib.

What occupied these damaged spaces was not ruined flesh but something more vaporous and grotesque, a luminous outline, the frontiersman's own body configured as petrified flame.

Lose flesh, Guilford thought, *and your ghost shows through.*

He looked reluctantly at his own wounds. Took the inventory.

He had been hit hard. Chest and belly flayed, clothing charred. His torso glimmered like a mad party lantern. He ought to be dead. Was dead, perhaps. He seemed to possess no blood, no viscera, no meat, only this hot and pulsing light.

Deep numbers, he found himself thinking. *Strange, deep numbers.*

He didn't bleed, but he could feel his heart hammering madly in his damaged chest. Or was that an illusion too? Maybe he had been dead for twenty years . . . it had felt that way, often enough. Breathe in, breathe out, lift a hammer or twist a wrench; shun love, shun friendship, endure. . . .

Bullets rattled into pebbled soil inches from his ear.

You knew this day would come. Too long postponed.

"They're killing us," he murmured.

"No," Tom said. "Maybe that's what that sniper thinks. You know better. They're not killing us, Guilford. They can only kill what's mortal." He winced as he turned. "They're hatching the gods out of us."

"It hurts," Guilford said.

"That it does."

He remembered too much, too vividly, all that long morning.

He rolled over a brambled hedge of barbed wire, caught his foot in a snakeroot runner, fell another several yards and landed with his rifle sprawled at arm's length. Raw stone abraded his cheek. He had reached the outskirts of the City.

It was me, he thought, *at Belleau Wood; I* do *remember. Ah, Christ: the wheat field overgrown with poppies and the men falling on every side, leaving the wounded behind for the medics, if the medics weren't cut down, too, and men calling out over the roar of gunfire and sour smoke in rolling waves. . . . Look at us,* Guilford thought. Nearly two hundred half-human old men followed behind him, in snakeskin longcoats, dungarees, slouch hats for helmets, wearing holes the size of apples where the bullets had passed them through. Yet not immortal after all. The vessel of the body could bear only a certain degree of pain and magic. Some wounds could kill; some men had been left lifeless on the ridge, dead as the men at Belleau Wood.

Stripped of much of his flesh, loping now between eroded columns of stone, Guilford remembered.

He's ridden me like a horse all these years.

But we're the same.

But we're not.

Memory boiled out of the City of Demons like steam.

Once these structures had stood white and blank as marble, filled with provender and home to a blindly virulent and immensely powerful species groomed as instruments for the penetration of psilife into Archival time. They had lived like insects, brainless builders. Immersed at adulthood into the Well of Creation, they emerged as mortal gods.

It was one pathway into the ontosphere of the Archive. There were, of course, thousands of such points of entry. Psilife was both relentless and ingenious.

I have seen them before, and they frightened me: Lord, what frightens a man who walks between stars?

I remember Caroline, he thought grimly. *I remember Lily. I remember Abby and Nicholas.*

I remember the way blood looks when it mixes with rain and earth.

I remember blue skies under a sun that died a billion years ago.

I remember too many skies.

Too many worlds.

He remembered, unwillingly, the thousand Byzantiums of the ancient galaxy.

He moved deeper into these rubbled alleys, places where the noon sun couldn't reach, where shadows rivered into oceans of darkness.

He thought, *Am I dying?*

What did dying mean, when the world was made of numbers?

Tom Compton joined him, the two men walking side by side for several paces. "Look sharp," the frontiersman said. "They're close."

Guilford closed his eyes on stars, opened them on carved and eroded stone.

The smell, he thought. Acrid. Like solvent. Like something gone terribly bad. Ahead of him, where the mist lifted, he saw the bright body and razor claws of the enemy.

"Don't show yourself," Tom Compton whispered. "We're too close to the dome to risk a fight."

Ten thousand years ago, as the ontosphere measured time, the demons had been bound in their Well.

Their earthly avatars were animals. Psilife had written dangerous code into their DNA, but they posed no direct threat to the Archive unless they were god-ridden. Guilford had fought them as a god, invisible and powerful as the wind.

They would emerge from the well wearing the same powerful bodies, and the demon-ridden men defending the well were subject to the same monistic logic, their human bodies surrendering to alien genetic programs.

Sooner than the demons had expected. Fresh Turing packets had disrupted their timing. The enemy was hindered by its own clumsy metamorphosis.

But it would all be for nothing unless one of these seed-sentiences carried his ancient ghost into the deeps of the well.

Guilford Law felt the mortal Guilford's fear—after all, it was his own. He pitied this small replica of himself, this unwitting axis on which the world turned.

Courage, little brother.

The thought echoed between Guilford and Guilford like a beam of light between flawed mirrors.

The demon-ridden men—even those so utterly transformed that they could no longer handle a rifle—were still lethally dangerous. Even now, hurt as he was, Guilford felt the enormous energy that was being expended to keep him alive.

The sound of artillery had faded to the west. *Running out of ammunition*, Guilford thought. *More hand-to-hand fighting now.*

The city had been different in winter, with Tom and Sullivan trudging beside him, the sound of human voices and the mournful baying of the fur snakes and the softening curvature of the snow, back when we were ignorant enough to believe in a sane and ordered world.

He thought unhappily of Sullivan struggling to make sense of the miracle of Darwinia . . . which was, after all, not a miracle, only a technology so monstrously advanced that no single human being could make sense of it or recognize its signature. *But Sullivan wouldn't have liked this haunted world*, Guilford thought, *any more than Preston Finch did; this world wasn't kind to skeptics or zealots.*

Small-arms fire rattled nearby. Up ahead, Tom Compton waved Guilford forward along a dark stone wall scabbed with moss. The morning's clear skies had given way to tumbled, leaden cloud and fits of rain. The frontiersman's ravaged body glowed faintly—about a candle's worth—in the shadows. Tough for night-fighting. *Might as well hang out a sign*, Guilford thought. *Kill me quick, I'm only half-dead.*

But the enemy were easy to see, too.

A dozen of them moved along the silent avenue a few yards away. He crouched behind tumbled stone and watched them after they passed, their knobby backs shining like hammered metal and their long heads swiveling querulously. They were grotesquely bipedal, almost a deliberate parody of the human beings they had recently been. Some of them wore tattered remnants of clothing over their bony hips and shoulders.

The mortal fraction of Guilford Law was frightened to the point of panic.

But the mortal fraction of Guilford Law swallowed his fear.

He moved among fractured stone walls toward the center of the City, the way he had come that dreadful winter almost half a century ago, toward the Dome of the Well, the absolute edge of the phenomenal world.

CHAPTER THIRTY-NINE

Matthew Crane had turned off his overhead light. He sat in a darkened corner of the office. He had left his desk light on.

The desk itself had been cleared. In the illuminated circle of the lamp resided a single object: a pistol, an old-fashioned revolver, polished and clean.

Lily stared at it.

"It's loaded," Matthew Crane said.

His voice was gelatinous and imprecise. He gurgled when he spoke. Lily found herself calculating the distance to the desk. Could she beat him to it? Was the risk worth taking? What did he want from her?

"Don't worry, Little Flea," Crane said.

Lily said, "Little Flea?"

"Thinking of the poem. *Big fleas have little fleas upon their backs to bite 'em, and little fleas have littler fleas, and so ad infinitum.* Because you were my Little Flea, weren't you, Lily?"

She groped for the light switch. Crane said sharply, "Don't."

Lily lowered her hand. "I don't know what you're talking about."

"Too late. Too late for both of us, I'm afraid. I have my spies too, you know. Little Flea had a Littler Flea on her back when she visited the museum yesterday."

I could run, Lily thought. *But then, would he shoot me?* Hard to think. The chemical stench was making her dizzy.

"We know what we are," Crane said. "That makes this easier."

"Makes *what* easier?"

"Think of us," Crane said wetly. He coughed, bent double for a moment, straightened before Lily could take advantage of his weakness. "Think of us together all these years, Big Flea and Little Flea, and to what end? What have I accomplished, Lily? Diverted a few weapons shipments, shared state secrets, did my small part to keep the civilian government preoccupied with wars or doctrinal disputes, and now the battle is being waged. . . ." He made a gesture that might, in the darkness, have been a shrug. "Far from here. My god, why hast thou forsaken me?"

"That's not funny."

"I agree. I'm changing, Little Flea, and I don't know why."

He stood up and came a little closer to the lamp—to the pistol.

He let his long overcoat fall away. The stench intensified. Lily was able to see the pebbled skin beneath the tattered shirt, the pustulant eruptions, the skin of his face separating like torn tissue paper. His skull had begun to take on a new outline, the jaw thrusting forward, the braincase writhing beneath islands of blood and hair and thick yellow plasm.

Lily gasped.

"As bad as that, Little Flea? I don't have a mirror. But yes, I suppose it is that bad."

Her hand groped for the door.

"Run," he said, "and I'll shoot you. I really will. Point of honor. So let's make it a game instead."

She was as frightened as she had ever been—as frightened as she had been that dreadful night in Fayetteville. Then, the enemy had at least appeared human. Crane didn't, not anymore, not even in this dim light.

She breathed, "A game?"

"Forget how I look, Little Flea. That wasn't supposed to happen, I think, at least not yet. I have no control over it. Oddly, neither does my god."

"What god?"

"My absent god. Absent. That's the problem. That still, small voice falls silent. Busy elsewhere, I suspect. Unscheduled emergencies. Your people's work. But this . . . *process* . . ." He held out his blistered hands. "It *hurts*, Little Flea. And as much as I pray for a little relief . . . those prayers aren't answered."

He paused to cough, a long liquid spasm. Drops of something pink and watery landed on the desk, the carpet, her blouse.

Now, Lily thought, but her legs felt paralyzed.

"Before long," Crane said, "I won't be myself anymore. I should have known. The gods, whatever else they may be, are hungry. Above all else. They don't want Matthew Crane to survive any more than they want *you* to live, Little Flea. So you see the position I'm in."

He took another shambling step forward. His legs bent in the wrong places. Flesh cracked with each step; yellow bile leaked out of his cuffs.

"A contest. The pistol is loaded and ready to fire. Ugly as these fingers of mine are, they can still pull a trigger. And so can yours, of course. I'm not as agile as I might have been, but you're not young, either, Little Flea. I reckon you've entered the support-hose and orthopedic-shoe stage of a woman's life, correct? Maybe you're even a little arthritic on damp nights. You don't care to run for a bus these days."

All true.

"A game. Called 'grab the pistol.' I think the odds are more or less fair. Just don't wait for me to say *go*."

She didn't. Lily moved at once, one furious step after another, but it was like running in a dream; her limbs were dead weight; she was under water.

She saw the pistol in its circle of light, gloss black on buffed mahogany, lamplight catching the notches and angles of the weapon in bright constellations.

The stench of Crane's transformation was thick in the air. He made a sound Lily barely heard, a shrill animal screech.

Her right hand touched the grip of the pistol. It slid away from her a precious inch. She felt Crane's proximity now, a sulphurous heat.

But suddenly the pistol was hers. She closed her fingers on the grip.

She took a step backward from the desk, tripped on a heel, found herself sitting on the blood-stained carpet with the pistol in both shaking hands, holding it in front of her like a dime-store crucifix.

Matthew Crane—the thing that had once been Matthew Crane—reared up before her. The desk lamp fell sideways, raking harsh light across his blistered face. His eyes were cherry red, the pupils narrow black slits. *"Little Flea!"* he cried. *"Good work!"*

She fired the pistol. Her aim was low. The bullet clipped a rib, spraying a gout of bloody substance against the far wall. Crane reeled backward, supporting himself on a rack of congressional reports. He looked down at his wound, then back at Lily.

She stood up cautiously.

He smiled—if that was meant to be a smile—past the stumps of his teeth.

"Don't stop now, Little Flea," he whispered. "For god's sake don't stop now."

She didn't. She didn't stop until the pistol was empty, not until what remained of Matthew Crane was motionless on the floor.

CHAPTER FORTY

A spasm of mortar fire collapsed what remained of the Dome of the Well. Vast intact slabs of shaped rock fell and shattered, lofting pillars of dust into the autumn air. Guilford advanced through the rubble, rifle in hand. His wounds were grave and his breathing was ragged and painful. But all his limbs worked and his mind was as clear as could be expected under the circumstances.

A reef of cloud had drifted in from the mountains, turning the day cold and wet. Drizzle chilled the City and painted the ruins a drab, slick black. Guilford darkened his face with a handful of mud and imagined himself blending into these tortured angles of broken stone. The enemy had abandoned order and were stalking the human intruders almost at random—an effective strategy, since there was no guessing which corner might conceal a demon. Only their stench betrayed them.

Guilford put his head around an intact foundation stone and saw one of the monsters less than a dozen yards away.

This one had left its human origins far behind. The transformation was nearly complete: it stood over seven feet tall, its rounded skull and razor jaws similar to the specimen Sullivan had shown him in the Museum of Monstrosities. It was systematically dismembering a man who had stumbled into its clutches—no one Guilford knew personally, small consolation though that was. It razored the body apart, inspecting and discarding the pieces methodically while Guilford choked back nausea and took careful aim. When the monster reared back with some fresh nugget of human flesh, he fired.

A clean shot to the pale and vulnerable belly. The monster staggered and fell—wounded, not dead, but it didn't seem able to do more than lie on its back and flex its claws in the air. Guilford sprinted across a field of granite dust toward the collapsed Dome, anxious to find fresh cover before the sound attracted more of the creatures.

He discovered Tom Compton crouched behind a half wall, hand clutched to his throat.

"Bastards almost took my head off," the frontiersman said. He spat a red globule into the dust.

So we can still bleed, Guilford thought. *Bleed the way we did at Belleau Wood. Bleed the way we did when we were human.*

He took Tom's arm. "Can you walk?"

"I hope so. Too fuckin' soon to give up the ghost."

Guilford helped him up. The throat wound was vicious, and the frontiersman's other injuries were just as grave. Faint light flickered from his ruined body. Fragile magic.

"Quiet now," Tom warned.

They topped a hill of rubble, all that remained of the Dome that had stood for ten thousand years in the silence of this empty continent. Rifle fire popped frantically to the north and west.

"Head down," Tom cautioned. They inched forward, breathing dust until their mouths were sandpaper and their throats rusted pipes. *I remember you,* Guilford thought: Tom Compton, the First Sergeant who had dragged him through the wheat field toward Château-Thierry, pointlessly, because he was dying. . . . Over these knives of granite until they saw the Well itself, brighter than Guilford remembered it, radiant with light, its crumbling perimeter guarded by a pair of vigilant monsters, their eyes swiveling with a fierce intelligence.

Elias Vale was still able to hold and fire an automatic rifle, though his fingers had grown clumsy and strange. He was changing in ways he preferred not to think about, changing like the men around him, some of whom were no longer even remotely human. But that was all right. He was close to the Well of the Ascension, doing sacred and urgent work. He felt the close proximity of the gods.

His eyesight had been subtly altered. He found he could detect faint motion in dim light. His other senses, too. He could smell the salt-pork smell of the attackers. The rain falling on his pebbled skin was both cold and pleasing. The sound of rifle fire was acutely loud, even the rattle of pebbles a symphony of discrete tones.

More acute, too, was the sense that had attracted the gods to him in the first place, his ability to peer at least a small distance into a human soul. The beings attacking the Sacred City were only partly human—partly something much older and larger—but he felt the shape of their lives, every poignancy and tension and secret vulnerability. That skill might still be useful.

His rifle was not his only weapon.

He huddled behind a granite block while two of the more thoroughly transformed men patrolled the rim of the Well. He felt—but it was indescribable!—the immense living energy of this place, the gods imprisoned in the nonspace deep in the earth, straining at physical incarnation.

An army of them.

And he felt the presence of two half-mortal men approaching from the north.

He picked their names from the glowing air: Tom Compton. Guilford Law.

Ancient souls.

Vale clutched his rifle to his pustulant chest and smiled emptily.

Tom said, "I'll circle left, draw them off with a couple of shots. You do what you can."

Guilford nodded, watching his wounded friend scrabble away.

The Well was a pocket of algorithms embedded in the ontosphere, a pinprick opening into the deeper architecture of the Archive. The god-Guilford's only way in was through physical incarnation: he had needed Guilford to carry him here, but the battle inside the Well, the Binding, that was gods' work. *But I'm tired,* Guilford thought. *I hurt.* And with the pain and the fatigue came a crippling nostalgia; he found himself thinking of Caroline, her long black hair and wounded eyes; of Lily, five years old, spellbound under the influence of Dorothy Gale and Tik-Tok; of Abby's patience and strength; of Nicholas gazing at him with a trust he hadn't earned or deserved, a trust soon breached . . . he wanted to bring it back, bring it all back, and he wondered if that was why the gods had built their Archive in the first place: this mortal unwillingness to surrender the past, lose love to crumbling atoms.

He closed his eyes and rested his cheek on a jut of wet stone. The light inside him flickered. Blood welled up from his wounds.

The sound of Tom's rifle roused him.

At the eroded rim of the Well the two monsters swiveled their heads toward the sound of the gun. Tom fired again and one of the beasts screamed, a shriek nearly human in its pain and rage. Bile-green fluid spurted from the monster's ruptured gut.

Guilford took advantage of the distraction to move another several yards closer to the Well, dodging between man-high columns of granite.

Now both creatures were moving, approaching the source of the gunshots at an oblique angle, offering their dorsal armor against the rifle fire. They were extraordinarily large, maybe specially-appointed guardians. Their walk—bipedal, fluidly balanced—was slow, but Guilford had learned to respect their speed. Claws and forearm mandibles were exposed, bone-white, glistening with rain. Their smaller lower arms, less arms than auxiliary knives, clattered restlessly.

The rain deepened from drizzle to downpour, sheets of it streaming off ancient stone, raising plumes of vapor from the Well.

The monsters weren't affected by the rain. They paused and rocked their heads, a querulous birdlike gesture. The water gave their skins or shells a polished gleam, raising hidden colors, a rainbow iridescence that made Guilford think of his childhood, of washing pebbles in a brook to see their lustre emerge from the dross of dust and air.

Closer now. He felt the heat of the Well, the burned-insulation reek of it.

Tom stepped into the open and fired another shot, maybe the last of his hoarded ammunition. Guilford used the opportunity the frontiersman created and ran for the rim of the Well, glancing backward. *Get away while you can,* he wanted to shout, but he saw Tom's left leg buckle under him. The frontiersman dropped to one knee, managed to raise his rifle, but the nearest creature, the one he had wounded, was suddenly on him.

Guilford moaned involuntarily as the monster deftly nipped Tom's head from his body.

The sheeting rain concealed all else. The air smelled of ozone and lightning.

He shouldn't have stopped. The second monster had spotted him and was moving now at terrifying speed toward the Well, long legs pumping as efficiently as a leopard's. Running, it made no sound audible over the hiss of the rain; but when it stopped it released a cloud of stinging solvent vapors, waste products of some unimaginable body chemistry. Its eyes, expressionless and strange, focused tightly on him.

He lifted his rifle and fired two rapid shots at the creature.

The bullets chipped its gleaming armor, perhaps cracked an exposed rib, caused it to stumble back a step. Guilford fired again, fired until his clip was empty and the monster lay motionless on the ground.

Tom, he thought.

But the frontiersman was beyond repair.

Guilford turned back to the Well.

The rim was close. The spiral of stone steps was intact, though perilously littered with fresh debris. That didn't matter. He wasn't planning to take the stairs. Jump and let gravity carry him: There was no bottom to this rabbit hole, only the end of the world. He began to run.

He stopped when a human figure stood up not ten paces in front of him.

No, he realized, not human, only some poor soul less advanced in its destruction. The face in particular looked as if it had been broken long ago, bones shifting along the fault lines like volcanic plates.

This creature struggled to raise its own rifle, its arms shaking with the palsy of transformation.

Guilford took another clip of ammunition from his belt.

"You don't want to shoot me," the monster said.

The words cut through the rush of the rain and the distant crack of artillery.

Ignore him, the god-Guilford said.

"There's someone with me, Guilford. Someone you know."

He ejected the spent clip. "Who would that be?" Watching the monster struggle with its own rifle. Bad case of the shakes. Keep him talking.

No, the picket insisted.

The monster closed its eyes and said, *"Dad?"*

Guilford froze.

No.

"Is that you? I can't see—"

Guilford froze, though he felt the picket's urgent pleading.

"Dad, it's me! It's Nick!"

No, it isn't Nick, because Nick—

"Nick?"

"Dad, don't shoot! I'm inside here! I don't want to die, not again!"

The monster still struggling against its own convulsions to raise the rifle. He saw it but couldn't make sense of it. He remembered the bright, awful roses of his son's blood.

The picket was suddenly beside him, faint as mist.

Time slowed to a crawl. He felt his hammering heart beat at half speed, slow timpani notes.

The monster flailed its gun with a glacial imprecision.

The picket said, "Listen to me. Quickly, now. That isn't Nick."

"What happens to the dead? Do the demons get them?"

"Not always. And that isn't Nick."

"How do I know?"

"Guilford. Do you think I would let them take him?"

"Didn't you?"

"No. I didn't. Nick is with me, Guilford. He's with *us.*"

The picket held out his hands in a cradling motion, and for a moment—a sweet and terrible moment—Nick was there, eyes closed, asleep, twelve years old and at peace.

"That's what this is all about," the picket said. "These lives."

Guilford said, "I'm so tired. . . . Nick?"

But Nick had vanished again.

"Fire your gun," the picket said sternly.

He did.

So did the monster.

Guilford felt the bullets pierce him. The pain, this time, was brutal. But that didn't matter. Close now. He fired and fired again, until the man with the broken face lay shattered on the ground.

Guilford dragged his own broken body to the rim of the Well.

He closed his eyes and fell. Pain ebbed into mist. Free as a raindrop now. *Hey, Nick, look at me.* And he felt Nick's somnolent presence. The picket had been telling the truth. Nick was wrapped in timelessness, sleeping until the end of the ontosphere, falling into the luminous waters of the Archive, numbers deeper than any ocean, warm as summer air.

He blinked and saw the god burst out of him. This luminous thing had once been Guilford Law, dead on a battlefield in France, nurtured by Sentience, equipotent with the gods and one of them, inseparable from them, a being Guilford could not begin to comprehend, all fierce light and color and vengeful as an angry angel, binding the demons who howled their frustration across the far and fading borders of the world.

INTERLUDE

They stood a while on the high ground above the ruined City of Demons. The day was uniformly bright, but the sky was full of stars.

"What now?" Guilford asked.

"We wait," the picket said, infinitely patient.

Guilford saw more men climbing the hillside. The City was silent now, empty once more. Guilford recognized the Old Men, Tom and Erasmus among them, whole and smiling. He was surprised he could see their faces so clearly across this distance.

"Wait for what?"

"The end of all battles," the picket said.

Guilford shook his head sternly. "No."

"No?"

"No. That's not what I want. I want what I wasn't allowed to have." He looked hard at the picket. "I want a life."

"All the life you want—eventually."

"I mean a human life. I want to walk like a whole man, grow old before I die. Just . . . human life."

The picket was silent for a long stretch.

I surprised a god, Guilford thought.

Finally the picket said, "It may be within my power. Are you certain this is what you want?"

"It's all I ever wanted."

The ancient Guilford nodded. He understood—the oldest part of him, at least, understood. He said, "But the pain—"

"Yes," Guilford said flatly. "The pain. That, too."

EPILOGUE

Karen, back from her morning walk, told Guilford a huge sea wheel had washed up on the beach. After lunch (sandwiches on the veranda, though he couldn't eat more than a bite) he went to have a look at this nautical prodigy.

He took his time, hoarding his energy. He followed a path from the house through dense ferns, through bell trees dripping August nectar. His legs ached almost at once, and he was breathless by the time he saw the ocean. The Oro Delta coast possessed as benign a climate as Darwinia could boast, but summer was often crippling humid and always hot. Clouds stacked over the windless Mediterranean like great marbled palaces, like the cathedrals of vanished Europe.

Last night's storm had stranded the sea wheel high on the pebbled margin of the beach. Guilford approached the object tentatively. It was immense, at least six feet in diameter, not a perfect circle but a bro-

ken ellipse, mottled white; otherwise it looked remarkably like a wagon wheel, the flotsam of some undersea
caravan.

In fact it was a sort of vegetable, a deep-water plant,
typically Darwinian in its hollow symmetry.

Odd that it had washed up here, to grace the beach
behind his house. He wondered what force, what tide
or motion of the water, had detached the sea wheel
from its bed. Or perhaps it was more evidence of the
ongoing struggle between Darwinian and terrestrial
ecologies, even in the benthic privacy of the ocean.

On land, in Guilford's lifetime, the flowering plants
had begun to conquer their slower Darwinian analogues.
At the verge of the road from Tilson he had lately discovered a wild stand of morning glories, blue as summer.
But some of the Darwinian species were returning the
favor; skeleton lace and false anemones were said to be
increasingly common south of the Mason-Dixon Line.

The sea wheel, a fragile thing, would be black and rotted by tomorrow noon. Guilford turned to walk home,
but the pain beneath his ribs took him and he chose to
rest a moment. He wetted a handkerchief in a tide pool
and mopped his face, tasting the salt tang on his lips. His
breath came hard, but that was to be expected. Last week
the doctor at the Tilson Rural Clinic had shown him his
X-rays, the too-easy-to-interpret shadows on his liver and
lungs. Guilford had declined an offer of surgery and last-
gasp radiation therapy. This horse was too old to beat.

Forced to sit a while, he admired the strangeness of
the sea wheel, its heady incongruity. *A strange thing
washed up on a strange shore: well, I know how that feels.*

Last night's storm had cleared the air. He watched
the glossy sea give back the sky its blue. He whistled
tunes between his teeth until he felt fit enough to start
the journey back.

Karen would be waiting. He hadn't told her what the doctor had said, at least not the full story, though she obviously suspected something. She would be all right about it, but he dreaded the phone calls from friends, perhaps especially the inevitable call from Lily and all the attendant consequences: a last visit, old sins and old grief hovering in the air like voiceless birds. Not that he wouldn't like to see her again, but Lily herself was frail these days. At least he wouldn't outlive her. *Small mercies,* Guilford thought.

Given these dark musings, he was not especially surprised, when he stood up and turned away from the stranded sea wheel, to find the picket waiting for him some yards down the rocky beach.

Guilford approached the phantom amiably. Skinny and boyish, the picket looked. This wasn't his double, not anymore. This was someone else. Younger. Older.

He assayed the faintly flickering apparition. "Tell me," Guilford said, "don't you get tired of wearing those old Army rags?"

"They were my last human clothes. It wouldn't seem right to wear something else. And too conspicuous if I don't wear anything at all."

"Been a while," Guilford said.

"Thirty years," the god said, "give or take."

"So is this like one of those movies? You show up to unroll the heavenly red carpet? Out of my deathbed into the clouds and violin music?"

"No. But I'll walk you back to the house, if that's all right."

"You don't have any particular purpose, being here? Out slumming? Not that it isn't nice to see you. . . ."

"There's a question I want to ask. But not just yet. Shall we walk? I always did think better on my feet."

* * *

They talked haphazardly as they followed the path through the woods. Guilford wasn't afraid of the picket, but he did feel a certain nervous excitement. He found himself rambling about Darwinia, how the continent had changed, how the cities and railways and airplanes had civilized it, though there was still plenty of back country for those who like to get lost . . . as if the picket didn't know these things.

"You prefer the coast," the phantom said.

He did. It suited him. Maybe he liked it because it was a place where opposite elements met and meshed: the old and new worlds; the sea and the land. Past and future.

The picket listened patiently, and Guilford was lulled for a while. Then it struck him. "This is the first one, isn't it?"

"First what?" the picket asked.

"First sympathy visit. Drop in on the old bastard before he buys the farm."

"This isn't a sympathy visit."

"Then why—?"

"Think back," the picket said. "Thirty years ago, Guilford, I offered you a life like mine."

"After the Binding," Guilford agreed. "When both of us were dead."

"And do you remember what you answered?"

"Vaguely." A lie. He remembered every word.

"You said, 'I want what I wasn't allowed to have. I want to grow old before I die.' "

"Uh-huh."

"It wasn't easy. Bones from dust. Flesh from air. An aging, mortal, human body."

"It's true, I've been resurrected from the dead more than most people I know."

"I came to ask whether it was worth it."

"That's your question? That's the purpose of this little visit?"

They were nearing the house. The picket hung back in the shadow of the trees, as if he didn't want Karen to see him. In the deep shade he was almost invisible, a true phantom, barely more tangible than a breeze.

"I was born a human being," the picket said, "but I haven't been *simply* human since the stars were young. And you've done something I never did. You grew old. You *chose* to grow old. So tell me. Was it worth it?"

Guilford wondered what to say. He hated the idea of eulogizing himself. Some tasks are best left to others, surely including obituaries. But he thought of his life since the Binding, both its general shape and its isolated events—getting to know his daughter Lily; marrying Karen and making a home for her; watching the general ebb and flow of babies born, lives lost, people inventing themselves in the sad, desperate way people do. *I was born in 1898,* Guilford thought: *more than a century ago.*

That might not mean much to a god, but it impressed Guilford a great deal.

Simple question, simple answer.

"Of course it was worth it."

He turned to look for the picket, but the picket was gone, as if there had never been anything among the trees more substantial than the sunlight and the shade.

Karen wept when he told her what the doctor had said, but in the evening he wiped her tears and she firmed up. After all, she said, he wasn't dead yet. She made death sound like a promissory note from a card shark: a debt not certain to be collected.

He loved this hardness in her, like the tart crispness of a fresh apple. She broke out the special-occasion bottle of Territory whiskey—the wedding and funeral bottle, she usually called it, though not tonight—and drank a fair portion of it before wheeling off to bed. He loved her intensely. He decided he had never loved her more.

But he couldn't sleep.

He sat alone on the porch and looked at the sky.

Was that dot on the horizon Mars? He had never been good about celestial matters. Astronomy, that was one of Dr. Sullivan's hobbies. Dr. Sullivan could have pointed him at Mars without blinking.

Mars would be trouble soon. The photographic probe last winter had only hinted at the problem. On Mars, the psions had broken out of their Wells and were enslaving the natives—a gentle, almost human people, Guilford knew, though he couldn't say how or why he knew this. They would need help. More Bindings to come before the end of the world, and it was still anyone's guess how the world would end. Not even the gods knew for sure.

The Martians needed help, but Guilford couldn't supply it. That battle would have to go on without him.

Unless this was a clarion call, he thought, this burgeoning pain in his chest, a sort of trumpet note. If he died, perhaps he would find Nick, find Caroline and Abby (if they were speaking to each other), find Tom Compton for that matter . . . walk that long road from Belleau Wood to the stars. Become a god, and the gods would be called to battle, which meant. . . .

He sighed and listened to the bugs humming in the night. Billyflies probed the porch light, lives briefer than a day, generation after generation aimed like arrows into the dark. Ecclesiastes: *All the rivers run into the sea, but the sea is not full* . . .

The sea, Guilford thought, *is full of life.*

And no time for grief, and too much to do. And only a moment to rest, to close his eyes, to sleep.